THE GIRL FROM THE CORNER SHOP

Alrene Hughes

HEAD
of ZEUS

First published in the UK in 2019 by Head of Zeus Ltd

Copyright © Alrene Hughes, 2019

The moral right of Alrene Hughes to be identified as the author
of this work has been asserted in accordance with the
Copyright, Designs and Patents Act of 1988.

9 7 5 3 1 2 4 6 8

A catalogue record for this book is available from
the British Library.

ISBN (HB): 9781788543996
ISBN (E): 9781788543989

Typeset by Silicon Chips

Printed and bound in Great Britain by
CPI Group (UK) Ltd, Croydon CR0 4YY

Head of Zeus Ltd
First Floor East
5–8 Hardwick Street
London EC1R 4RG

WWW.HEADOFZEUS.COM

For Heather

Chapter 1

Helen pulled back the curtains and looked out over the roofs and chimney pots etched against a rare cloudless sky over Manchester. Jim would be two hours into his shift at the fire station by now and, because there had been no air raids overnight, there was a good chance he would be home in time for his tea and they would have all of Sunday evening together. There was so much to talk about. On New Year's Day they would be moving out of the corner shop and away from her mother into a home of their own. Then there was the five pounds Jim had won in the Christmas raffle at the working men's club, enough to buy some second-hand furniture. But best of all, she wanted to carry on the conversation they had started last night about having a baby.

As she did every Sunday, she made her mother's breakfast and took it up to her, then she set about cleaning the house and shop. And as she worked, she thought about her mother insisting that she would still have to work in the shop when she moved. She was desperate for a clean break, but Jim had told her that they needed to get a bit of money behind them and why didn't she ask for an increase in her wages for agreeing to stay on? He didn't understand that she had been under her mother's thumb all her life and she would put up with any hardship to be free of her.

She had just finished donkey-stoning the step at the front of the shop when Mrs Lowe appeared at her side, clearly agitated. 'Helen, can you help me out? I've nothin' for the kids to eat today. Could you let me have a loaf and a pint of milk on tick? Albert only got three days' work this week and I've tried to eke it out…'

'Come inside, I'll see what I can do.' Helen put the loaf and milk on the counter then added a couple of eggs and a tin of soup. 'That'll see you through.'

'You're a life saver. I'll pay you back next Sunday – when you're on your own.'

'That'll be fine, Mrs Lowe.'

The woman gathered up her groceries and at the door she stopped. 'When you move out, you'll still be working in the shop, won't you?'

'I will for the time being.'

'God help us if you go. I know she's your mother, an' all, but Elsie Slater wouldn't give you the dirt under her fingernails, let alone tick to feed hungry kids.'

When she had gone, Helen recalled her mother's words. 'Cash on the nail. You get nowt for nowt.' She had grown up with that refrain and seen poverty every day in the shop. It was the women she felt sorry for, trying to keep body and soul together, but beyond giving them a few groceries on tick, there was nothing she could do for them.

It was afternoon before her mother made an appearance. Helen was sitting by the fire working on Jim's Christmas present, a cricket sweater. She had been knitting it since the summer and had only to finish the V neck but, with the double stripe and getting the tension right so it didn't pucker, she had already undone it twice.

'Have you not finished that yet?' asked her mother. 'You'll be lucky if he has it by the start of the season the way you're going. You'd have been better saving up and buying him one.'

'I couldn't afford it, they're far too dear.'

'I've told you before, you're a married woman now and your husband should be giving you an allowance.'

Helen felt the anger rising inside her and this time she wasn't going to bite her tongue. 'No, Mam, it's you who should be giving me a decent wage. You've been paying me ten shillings a week since I left school at fourteen and I'm twenty-two now!'

'You're forgetting board and lodgings, aren't you?'

'No, I'm not. You've been charging Jim for the two of us living here.'

'I charge you the going rate, what's wrong with that?'

Helen shook her head in frustration. 'I'm telling you this, when I move out, I want you to pay me the same as any other woman working in a shop.'

'Who do you think I am, Woolworth's?'

'If you don't, I'll just get another job. I've heard they want women in the factories to replace the men called up and the money's very good.'

Her mother pretended to laugh. 'You wouldn't last two minutes in a factory. You've had it easy for too long.'

'You know what, Mam, I think I'd like to go out to work. I'd get to meet different people and maybe learn to—'

'Don't be daft, you're not cut out for factory work and you wouldn't want to be mixing with the rough and ready types you'd meet there.'

'What are you saying that for? They're ordinary people like us.'

'Ah, that's where you're wrong. We own a business and that puts us on a higher rung up the ladder. You'll be a businesswoman too when I'm gone.'

'There's no talking to you, is there? You think you're right about everything and I'm fed up with you treating me like a child. I'm a married woman, for goodness' sake.'

'Oh yes, I know that all right and I suppose it was your husband who put you up to asking for more money.'

Helen felt the tears prick her eyes. 'No, he didn't. I just want what's fair, Mam, otherwise...' Her voice wavered.

'Otherwise, what?'

Helen jammed the knitting needles into the ball of wool and stood up to face her mother. 'Otherwise, I won't just be moving out at New Year, I'll be leaving a job that pays me a pittance as well!' and she fled the room, slamming the door behind her.

She wrapped up warm and left the house to walk off her anger. She hadn't meant to say all those things, especially not about leaving her job at the shop. But that was the trouble with her mother, you couldn't reason with her. Normally, Helen would just let her win, but she had no right to speak about Jim the way she did.

She turned the corner on to the main road just as a Salvation Army band outside the Co-op struck up 'O, Come All Ye Faithful', and the small crowd gathered around them began to sing along. Her steps slowed, she joined in and, in the time it took to sing a few carols, her anger had gone. She popped a thrupenny bit into the collection box and crossed the road to the croft opposite where a man was selling Christmas trees.

Her mother looked up from peeling vegetables when she came in and she rolled her eyes at the little tree, but said nothing. Helen didn't care; this would be their first Christmas together as man and wife and she was determined to make the dreary living room behind the shop a bit festive. She put the little tree in a bucket of ash and fetched the decorations from the cellar for her and Jim to decorate it after their tea. Then she set about the cricket sweater again – with three days to go before Christmas, she was determined to finish it.

The table was set, the potatoes and vegetables were boiled and the brisket, small as it was, rested on the carving dish. The clock ticked on towards half past six; Jim would be on his bike by now. She wanted to see his face when he saw the tree, wanted to tell him how she'd stood up to her mother, wanted to share her excitement about starting a family…

The sound of the air-raid siren went from a low whine to an incessant scream in seconds – impossible to ignore. 'For Heaven's sake,' said Helen. 'That's all we need.'

'Never mind standing there complaining,' her mother shouted. 'Shape yourself and get the trays! We'll have to eat in the cellar.' There was plenty to carry down the steep stairs and they had to make several trips with the hot pots and pans. 'For God's sake, what's the point of bombing people when they're about to sit down to their tea,' she complained. 'Honestly, how long is it since we've seen a piece of brisket? Months, I'm sure, and now we have to eat it in the cellar in an air raid. It had better not be another false alarm.'

Helen was hard on her heels with the warm plates. 'We've no gravy made,' she said.

Her mother threw her hands in the air. 'There you are, a good meal ruined.'

'No, it isn't,' said Helen. 'I'll go and make some; there'll be time before the siren stops and the bombs start dropping.' She ran back upstairs calling over her shoulder, 'Don't forget to put Jim's dinner on a plate. He'll have it warmed-up when he gets home.'

Helen poured some of the juices from the meat into a pan, added water and gravy browning and stood stirring it over the gas thinking about Jim. He would normally be home around now, but she could guess what had happened. He'd have been on his bike on his way back home and at the first sound of the air-raid siren he would have turned around and raced back to the fire station to put in another shift. Only then did she remember Jim's words the previous evening. 'Liverpool's burning and they've sent so many Manchester firemen and equipment to help.' She hadn't realised the implications. That grim look on his face was because he was worried that the Luftwaffe might turn their sights on Manchester and, with only half the brigade, the city would burn.

The siren wound down, the gravy came to the boil, and the world fell eerily silent.

Helen knew the duties of a fireman during a raid. Jim had made sure she understood how they dealt with the fires and bombs and the rescues. 'It's all about good training and knowing your limits,' he had explained.

'Don't worry about me. It's my job and I'm good at it.' She had smiled at him then and told him she was proud of him, but nothing he had said stopped her being anxious every time he went on duty and terrified when there were raids.

They sat at the little card table in the cellar eating their tea in silence and, halfway through the meal, the anti-aircraft guns, just up the road in Boggart Hole Clough, exploded into action as the first wave of enemy planes droned overhead. Helen picked at her food and thought about the steady build-up of raids since October, mostly in the industrial areas, but there had been times when Jim's crew, based in the city centre, were sent as reinforcements. She pushed her plate away and, not for the first time, she wished he had chosen a less dangerous way to earn a living.

'Are you not going to finish that?' Helen shook her head and her mother reached across the table and scraped what was left on Helen's plate on to her own. 'Can't let good food go to waste.'

Later, they cleared the plates and sat at the table playing Rummy, gambling with matchsticks, listening to the sound of planes overhead and the pounding of the anti-aircraft guns. Helen pictured the incendiaries descending in their thousands, setting buildings alight across the city. They'd be landing and spitting like fireworks, before bursting into flames; harmless on roads but devastating on the roofs if they weren't extinguished quickly. Some buildings had firewatchers who, with their stirrup pumps and buckets of sand, smothered the fires. Firemen with their hoses would be tackling the worst of them to stop them spreading, knowing that blazing buildings were a beacon for the next wave of bombers carrying the heavy explosives.

Only once did an explosion sound nearby and Helen shuddered as the reverberations came up through the cellar floor and passed through her body.

'They're after the aircraft factory,' her mother remarked and picked up Helen's discarded queen to win the hand.

Around ten o'clock there was a lull in the bombing. 'I think I'll go upstairs and have a look,' said Helen. She kept her voice calm, but inside she was desperate to see any signs that the fires had taken hold in the city.

She came up out of the cellar and already she felt a rise in temperature. On the way up to her bedroom she became aware of a low sound like a wind getting up, but it wasn't until she opened her bedroom door that she realised it was the distant roar of flames devouring the city. She caught her breath at the sight of the fiery sky and stood mesmerised. It's all gone, she thought, and her blood ran cold at the thought of Jim in the middle of such an inferno. She glanced down at the street below and in the cast of orange light she could pick out the cobbles on the road and a child's hopscotch chalked on the pavement below. Then her ear caught the distant droning sound, closer and closer it came. Overhead, the searchlights flashed and arced across the sky... searching, searching.

For a moment the house seemed to tremble then a deafening roar filled her ears and she let out a scream at the sight of the huge black shapes rushing over, one after the other, flying so low that she could see the markings on their fuselages.

She shouldn't have left the cellar. Jim would be furious when he found out that she had been watching the bombing, but she was rooted to the spot. She pictured him in his uniform organising his crew, doing everything to reduce the risks to keep them safe while they tried to save whatever they could. His words came back to her again: 'You have to respect the fire, read the fire, and always remember that life comes before property.' God, how she hoped his words would protect him and his men. She jumped at the noise of a heavy explosion so close that it almost stopped her heart, and debris flew across the street, smashing windows and filling the air with the smell of burning and cordite. She turned and ran.

'It's terrible out there. The whole city's going up in flames,' she shouted as she came down the cellar steps. 'Jim'll be in the middle of it all. I know he will!'

'Helen, get a grip. He's doing his job, standing on a street with a hose in his hand; it's not as if he's fighting hand to hand in the desert, like Mrs Connor's boy.'

On and on throughout the night the waves of bombers pounded the city and Helen lay on her camp bed in the cellar, listening to it all and praying for Jim. If anyone could come through such a night it was him. It was past five in the morning before she fell asleep exhausted and, at half past six, a full twelve hours since the raid began, the all-clear finally sounded.

It should have been dark at that time, but when they came out of the cellar and opened the blackout curtains, the yard was lit by an unnatural ochre-coloured dawn.

'I don't know about you, but I'm going to bed,' said her mother. 'I hardly slept with all that racket going on.'

Helen knew she wouldn't be able to sleep with the fires still raging, so she got washed and dressed and opened up the shop just as the milkman arrived on his horse and cart. 'Bad in the city centre, I've heard. Good job I get my milk from Oldham. One crate as usual, love?' She nodded, not trusting herself to speak, so worried was she about Jim. Where was he? How long would it be before he came off duty?

The bread man brought news that Piccadilly was ablaze. 'Whole area is cordoned off. It's desperate. They say it's spreading.' She knew then where he would be, right in the heart of his patch alongside his men, and she was certain he wouldn't come home until the embers had turned to ash. Throughout the morning the customers came and went. Some brought news of the devastation: the Victoria Hotel on Deansgate razed to the ground; the cathedral, still standing but damaged; the town hall and the Midland Hotel unscathed.

Her mother eventually reappeared through the chenille curtain into the shop about eleven o'clock. 'I'm glad you're here,' said Helen, taking off her overall. 'I want to go into town to take Jim something to eat.'

'But what about the shop? You know it gets busy coming up to dinnertime.'

'Look, Mam, he's been on duty for over twenty-four hours, twelve of them fighting fires. I can't sit here any longer.'

'What's the point of going out looking for him? You'll not find him in all the chaos.'

'I don't care. I'll make him something to eat and a flask of tea and take them to the fire station. If he's there I'll see him, if not, maybe I'll get news of him at least. Anyroad, I'm opening a tin of corned beef – you can take it out of my ration.'

Chapter 2

There were roof tiles strewn over the road and glass crunched under her feet. Brian Jenkins, the landlord at the Bird i'th' Hand, was already trying to board up a window with an old door. 'Bloody Germans,' he shouted. 'What kind of people would bomb you at Christmas?'

She walked as far as Rochdale Road, where there was no serious damage to the buildings, but here and there people were sweeping up or dousing smouldering fires caused by stray incendiaries. She hadn't gone far when she heard a familiar sound behind her and turned in amazement to see a bus coming towards her. The nearest stop was a hundred yards away, but she stuck out her hand and the bus pulled up alongside her.

'You all right, love?' the conductor shouted as she jumped on the platform.

'I am now I've seen you, didn't think there'd be buses running today.'

'Limited service only. I've heard it's bad in the centre so we'll just see how far we get.'

She handed him her fare, but he shook his head and laughed. 'Nah, keep your money, love, there'll be no inspectors checkin' tickets today.'

She was surprised to see a dozen or so people sitting downstairs all looking like they were going to work. She sat next to a woman who told her she was a nurse at Ancoats Hospital. 'They'll have had a busy night – we're so close to the centre of the bombing – but everybody'll make it in today.'

The nearer they came to the city centre the more damage there was; buildings she'd known all her life were gone, others were unscathed. They were almost at Smithfield Market when the bus slowed to a stop. She could see the roof had all but gone and thick smoke was spiralling upwards. A policeman walked over to the driver's window. 'No access here, mate,' he shouted, 'too many unsafe buildings and fires everywhere. Best go back.'

Suddenly an ear-splitting scream filled the bus. A woman across the aisle had jumped on to her seat and was shaking and yelling. Helen followed her horrified gaze – the road on the other side of the junction seemed to be rippling like a moving carpet – she blinked, looked again and her stomach turned. Rats! Thousands of them, escaping from a burning building on Shudehill. They were rushing straight at the bus, but at the last minute they veered into Miller Street and headed for the river.

Meanwhile, the conductor had spoken to the driver. 'Listen,' he shouted to the passengers. 'I think this is the end of the line. It's not safe in the centre. If you want to go back, we'll be leaving in five minutes. If you want to get off here, be very careful.'

Helen had no intention of going back home; she hadn't come this close to walk away. Maybe if she used the side streets she could zigzag her way towards Piccadilly and on to the fire station – provided she didn't come across any more rats.

The streets were narrower here and in places there was rubble in the road – more than once she had to clamber over it. Shop windows had been blown out and the stock with them. A rail of dresses stood upright in the middle of one street and for one awful moment she thought there were people lying dead on the ground, only to realise that they were mannequins. She walked around them and went on up the eerily silent street until an ARP warden appeared from nowhere and yelled, 'Get out of here! There's a burst gas main!' She turned and ran down a side street, stopped to get her bearings, caught sight of Affleck and Brown's department store and was amazed to see that it was open. Oldham Street was blocked off because of a parachute bomb strewn over the tram lines, but she knew another way. Now she was walking through a pall of smoke and the choking smell of burning, following the snaking hosepipes as though they would lead her to Jim.

She felt the heat of the fires before she saw them and there was that roaring sound again, a hundred times worse than she had heard in the night. She turned the corner and the shocking sight made her cry out. Across the ornamental gardens in Piccadilly, a row of warehouses several storeys high was a mass of flames giving off thick black smoke that blotted out the sky. Her eyes scanned the road for any sign of the fire brigade and she caught her breath at the sight of the red tenders, tin helmets, thick oilskin coats. Firemen! And then she was running across the gardens towards them, jumping over flowerbeds, dodging benches, oblivious to the rising heat coming from the fierce fires.

She didn't hear the shouts. Didn't sense someone running behind her. Her only thought was for Jim. He was there, she was sure of it. If she could see him for just a moment and give him the sandwiches. He must be starving. She swerved round someone trying to catch hold of her, jumped over a bed of pruned rose stems and all the time her eyes were streaming and her throat hoarse with calling his name.

Someone caught her arm, but still she tried to reach him. Next moment there were arms around her like a vice and she was lifted off her feet. 'Let me go! Let me go!' she screamed.

'Whoa there! You can't go near the fire.' The police-man set her down. 'It's too dangerous. Go back, please.'

'I'm looking for my husband.' She shrugged him off and set off running again, but she didn't get more than a few yards before he ran in front of her and blocked her way, his arms outstretched. 'Now, listen here, you'll go no further. Your husband won't be anywhere near there. We've cleared the area. Can you not see those buildings could collapse any minute?'

She pushed him away. 'He's a fireman and this is his division. I'm sure he's here. I've brought him something to eat and drink.' She opened her bag to show him the package of sandwiches and the flask, as if that would be enough for him to let her through.

'I'm sorry, I can't let you go, it's too dangerous. I'd be failing in my duty to keep people safe.' He gripped her arm again to drag her away, but she dug her heels in.

'I'll have to arrest you if you don't leave right now,' he said sharply.

'Please, please,' she sobbed. 'I have to see him just for a—'

Her pleas were interrupted by frantic shouts followed by a blaring klaxon coming from the direction of the burning buildings, and she watched in horror as the burnt-out gable end of one warehouse began to crumble.

Only then did she realise the danger, but she couldn't move.

'Run! Run!' the policeman shouted.

'But what if Jim—'

The policeman dragged her away and raced with her across the gardens. Within seconds there was a deep rumbling sound, followed by the crash of masonry, and they were enveloped by a thick cloud of dust. They didn't stop running until they reached the far side. Her heart was bursting in her chest from running and breathing in the smoke and dust.

'You could have been killed!' the policeman shouted in her face.

Helen burst into tears. 'I only want—'

'Never mind what you want, just listen to me,' he said. 'My advice is that you go straight home. You've seen how dangerous it is and, if you were my wife, I wouldn't want you anywhere near here.'

The fright of the building collapsing brought her to her senses. Jim would be furious if he found out that she'd gone looking for him. She wiped the tears from her stinging eyes. 'I'm sorry. I just got it into my head that I had to see him. I've been worrying about him all night.'

For the first time since the constable had spoken to her, he didn't look angry. 'It's understandable, of course you're worried.' He almost smiled. 'But please go home now and wait for him there.'

She looked up at him, noticed the coating of ash on his uniform, the number on his collar, and she smiled back. 'Am I as dusty as you, Constable A333?'

'Oh, you're much worse, your hair is grey and I don't know whether it's dust or fright. Even your husband wouldn't recognise you.'

'I'm sorry for being such a pain. I'm just so worried about him.'

'You said your husband's a fireman. Well, he knows what he's doing, been well-trained, he tackles fires every day.'

'Yes, but—'

'Go home, missus, let him get on with his job.'

'All right, I'll go home and wait. Thanks for... you know... looking after me.'

He touched his helmet. 'You're welcome.'

Helen set off intending to go home, but she hadn't walked for more than a few minutes before a thought occurred to her. When she had left the house determined to see Jim her intention was to go to the fire station, but the sight of blazing warehouses and collapsing walls had sent her into a panic. But what if Jim was back at the fire station? She knew from previous bombings that fire crews worked a rota tackling big fires; a few hours on and a few hours' rest. The station house was only a short walk away. What was the harm in calling in to ask when Jim would be off duty? He might even be there and she could give him the sandwiches.

The fire station was a huge, five-storey, red brick building with three blocks in the shape of a triangle. Jim had pointed it out to her once when they were courting and he had explained that it wasn't just a fire house, there were police and ambulance stations there too, and a courtroom. A lot of the firemen even lived there.

From the outside everything seemed calm, given the scenes of destruction just down the road. She'd expected engines and firemen and urgent comings and goings. Maybe it would be all right to ask about Jim. She looked up at the elaborately carved sign above the main entrance – 'Fire Brigade Head Quarters'. She hesitated again. What should she say? Don't be daft, she told herself, just ask if Jim Harrison is in the station. She took a deep breath and pushed open the heavy mahogany door and the wall of noise hit her. Everywhere was chaos. She had imagined some sort of counter where she could state her business, instead the entrance hall was filled with noise and crowded with people, like an indoor market on a busy Saturday.

Most of them were in a state: clothes and hair dusty like hers; some with bandages seeping blood as though they had been given first aid in a rush. There was all manner of stuff littered in the fine entrance hall, probably what these poor people had managed to salvage from their homes.

There seemed to be no one in authority to ask about Jim. She'd been stupid to come looking for him; he had a job to do and if he saw her now, he'd give her a right telling-off. Just then a fireman pushed past her and one look at his grimy face and slumped shoulders told her he'd been up all night fighting fires. Without another thought, she followed in his wake, breathing in the smoky smell of him. They went through a door into an outside courtyard area – the triangle between the three blocks – and the sight that met her brought tears to her eyes. A hundred or more firemen were lying on the ground or sitting with their backs against the walls, faces blackened by smoke, their oilskin capes grey with ash. She stood a moment scanning the faces of the men nearest to her, hoping that one of them would be Jim. Each face was etched with exhaustion and despair, but she didn't recognise any of them. Slowly, she moved round the courtyard and some of the men managed a grim smile at the sight of a girl in their station, the rest were hardly aware of her. She had walked the length of one block when there was a shout. 'Hey, you're not allowed here!' An older man came towards her in a smart uniform; clearly, he had not been fighting fires. 'You need to leave,' he said. 'Civilians are not allowed in here.'

'I'm looking for my husband, he's a fireman.' She was close to tears. 'I haven't seen him for over twenty-four hours.'

'And you might not see him for another twenty-four,' he snapped. 'We're dealing with major life-threatening incidents and no fireman will go home until every fire is extinguished.'

He was right, the policeman was right, and the state of the firemen made her worries so trivial. 'I'm sorry, I meant no harm,' and without another word she walked away.

Then someone called her name. 'Wait, wait, Helen,' and she turned to see Frank, Jim's second in command and best friend, coming towards her.

The officer intervened. 'Is this your wife, Roberts?' he demanded.

'No, sir, she's Leading-Fireman Harrison's wife.'

Helen watched the man's face change at the mention of Jim's name. Something was wrong. She turned to Frank. One look was enough; she felt the shock like a blow to her stomach, her knees gave way and she sank to the floor. She couldn't speak... couldn't breathe... arms were lifting her up, half carrying her past the exhausted firemen and their averted eyes.

They took her to an office and sat her in a chair. The man in the smart uniform was speaking. 'Mrs Harrison, I'm the station officer. Now, I need you to listen very carefully.' She heard the words as though they came from far away and she tried to make sense of them, but her heart was beating wildly and she kept taking great gulps of air. Then Frank was kneeling beside her. 'Helen, please, you need to listen so I can tell you what happened.'

Her breathing slowed and she looked from Frank to the station officer and back again, struggling to form the words screaming in her head. 'Jim's dead, isn't he?'

Frank held her hand. 'We think so. Our crew was at Piccadilly trying to contain the fires in the warehouses, but they were spreading to nearby buildings. We were going to set up explosions to form a gap, a firewall, but Jim thought we could get the extending ladder between the two buildings and maybe dampen down the worst of the fire. I volunteered, but Jim said no, he would do it. He was at the very top of the ladder. I watched him the whole time, high above me, a dark outline against the red sky. It looked like the flames had died back and he gave me a wave. I turned to give the thumbs up to the crew to cut the water and, when I looked back, the ladder was empty and Jim was gone.'

She couldn't take it all in – Jim up a ladder putting out a fire she understood, but... 'Gone, Frank? What do you mean he was gone?'

'We don't know exactly. The wall collapsed so he might've been knocked off the ladder, or he missed his footing.'

'But where is he? Can I see him?' she asked.

The station officer cleared his throat. 'Mrs Harrison, the warehouses are still ablaze and the structures are unsafe. I hope you understand that I cannot order a search for your husband until such time as I deem it safe for my men to enter the ruined premises. Now, if you'll excuse me, I'll leave you to compose yourself before you go.'

'So, you've just left him in a collapsed building?' Helen was on her feet and her voice was strong. 'How do you know he's dead, he could be buried under the rubble!'

'Mrs Harrison, he fell from a great height into a burning building. I'm sorry, but he won't have survived.'

She felt the strength leave her and she covered her face and sobbed as the shock swept over her. There wasn't a coherent thought in her head, just snatches of anguish and images of Jim. She had no idea how long she sat there, only that Frank stayed with her holding her hand and, every now and again when she cried out, he would say, 'Sssh now, Helen, sssh.'

She found a handkerchief in her pocket, wiped her eyes and blew her nose. The shock had passed and been replaced with a sadness so deep that she wished she were dead. 'I'll go home now, Frank,' she said, and for the first time she saw the clean tracks of his tears on the sooty blackness of his face.

'I'd take you home, Helen, but I have to go on duty again. You understand, don't you?'

She nodded. 'Jim would want you to stay and finish the job.'

It was raining when she came out of the station house. She turned up her collar and, with her head down, she set off walking. She had only gone a few steps when she collided with someone coming the other way.

'Whoa there, you need to look where you're going.'

'I'm sorry,' and without looking up she walked on.

'You didn't go straight home, then? Did you find your husband?'

She turned to see Police Constable A333 smiling at her, but almost immediately his face was full of concern. 'What's the matter? Has something happened?'

She couldn't bear to explain.

'Come back into the station a moment,' he said.

She stared at him, uncertain.

'I'm just going off duty. The police station's in here too. Come on, step out of the rain a minute.'

And she let herself be led back inside.

'Have you had news?' he said and she nodded. 'About your husband?'

'He's gone, dead.'

The constable shook his head. 'I'm so sorry. Is there anything I can do to help you?'

'No.'

'Where are you going, home?'

She nodded.

'You shouldn't be on your own now.' He bit his lip. 'Look, I just have to sign off duty. It'll take me about ten minutes. I want you to wait right here until I come back then I'll get you home. I won't be long. Don't go anywhere.'

Helen stood a moment in the entrance hall not knowing what to do. She didn't want someone to take her home. She wanted to be alone and maybe walking in the rain would calm the awful thoughts of Jim plummeting to his death. She slipped out the door and walked quickly away.

She remembered scarcely anything of the walk home. A bus raced past her and was gone before she realised. There were people about but she kept her head down, concentrating on putting one foot in front of the other, a steady rhythm matched by the words drumming in her head. 'Oh, Jim. Oh, Jim.'

She pushed open the shop door, walked past the few people waiting to be served, and headed for the back room. Her mother looked up from wrapping a piece of cheese and shouted, 'Where have you been? I was run off my feet at dinner time.' Helen ignored her.

'Did you find him?' her mother called after her, but she was already climbing the stairs. In her bedroom she took off her damp clothes, put on her nightdress and climbed into bed. She breathed in the smell of Jim on the pillow and wept. It was growing dark by the time her mother came into the room and closed the curtains before putting on the light.

'What's to do?' she said, then she saw Helen's face. 'What's the matter?'

Helen blinked at the light and wiped her tears. 'It's Jim, they think he's dead.'

'Oh, dear God!' Her mother's voice cracked. 'What do you mean "they think"?'

'A wall collapsed and he fell off a ladder into a

building. They say he's probably dead, but they can't get him out, it's too dangerous.'

'That's terrible. Oh, Helen. Maybe they'll find him.'

Helen shook her head. 'I saw the fires in Piccadilly. You wouldn't believe what it's like in the town. I'm praying that he's all right, just trapped under the rubble, and they'll get him out when they can, but I have this awful feeling that he's gone and I'll never see him again,' and she dissolved into floods of tears.

Her mother sat on the bed and held her until she was calmer. 'Come on now, Helen, you have to hope for the best. That's all we can do. Now, I'm going to make you some tea.'

'I don't want anything. Just leave me alone.'

'But what can I do for you?'

'Nothing.'

'I'll sit with you for a while.'

'Just leave me, Mam.'

Chapter 3

Dark clouds threatened snow as Jim Harrison's coffin was carried on the back of a fire engine past the hundred firemen who lined the driveway of St Stephen's church. Helen was barely aware of them, with her eyes fixed on the flag and the helmet on top of the coffin. Her mother walked beside her holding her arm and behind them were Jim's sister and her husband, Bill, closely followed by Aunt Pearl, her godmother and her mother's cousin. The minister was waiting for her at the door, but she could make no sense of his words. He preceded her up the aisle, but still she stared straight ahead and, once she was seated, she bowed her head and closed her eyes.

Nine days she had been without him and every day her pain had grown worse. The night after she had been to the fire station, the city was bombed again. She refused to take shelter in the cellar and screamed at her mother that she wanted to die, but the Luftwaffe didn't oblige. She didn't want to see anyone who called to pay their condolences, except her and Jim's closest friends: Frank and his girlfriend Gwen Jones. Christmas came and went. She ate very little, hardly slept, didn't open her presents, just stayed in her room and focused intently on the unfinished cricket sweater then wore it every day... until today. From somewhere her mother had borrowed a black dress and coat, as well as a ridiculous little hat with a veil. She had threatened not to wear any of it, but on the day she was so frightened about the funeral that she had put up no resistance.

The church was so cold. She couldn't stop shivering and the smell of chrysanthemums sickened her. There were hymns when she had to stand up and prayers when she had to kneel and none of it had anything to do with Jim. Whatever was in the coffin wasn't Jim, that's why they wouldn't let her see him, nor was he some ghostly presence at her shoulder. She understood absolutely that he was gone and she was alone.

At the graveside she watched the little flurries of snow fall on the coffin while the minister droned on and her feet turned to ice. Then Frank was handing her Jim's helmet as if it was some sort of gift. She shuddered and stepped back... but her mother reached out and took it. 'It'll soon be over, Helen,' she whispered. 'Then we'll go home. I've invited a few people to come back to the house for some sandwiches and a cup of tea. I see our Pearl's showed up. I suppose I'll have to ask her back, even though she's not been near us since the last family funeral.'

The snow came thicker and faster on the half-mile walk back and soon their coats were flecked with white. As they turned into her street, there was some sort of commotion going on outside the shop. A few neighbours stood around, some arguing with a man in a brown overall unloading his cart while his horse stood by snorting its steaming breath.

'You can't leave it here!' Mrs Lowe from two doors down shouted. 'Can you not see all the curtains in the street are closed? They've had a death in the family.'

'Take it away and come back tomorrow,' Douglas Finney, another neighbour, called out. 'Now's not the time.'

Helen, who had barely noticed anything on the walk home and hadn't spoken all the way from the cemetery, took one look at the scene and started running. 'No! No!' she screamed at the sight of a brass bedhead propped up against the shop door, a tick mattress on the pavement and the metal bed frame in bits lying on the back of the cart. 'It can't be, it can't be,' she shouted at the man.

He tried to explain. 'Now look here, I were told to deliver this today wi'out fail. Most particular, the fella were, said he were movin' house tomorrow. I told him

I had a house clearance to do and I'd have to deliver it today.'

'What the hell?' Her mother turned on her. 'Did you know about this?'

'Oh, Mam.' She could hardly get her words out through the sobbing. 'Jim said he might buy a double bed, but that was a while ago. He didn't tell me he'd actually bought one!'

'Well, the fella bought it a couple of weeks ago,' said the man, 'and I'm sorry if you don't want it, but I can't give you the money back.'

'Now, listen here,' said Elsie. 'You weren't to know that the lad who bought it was killed in the bombings at Christmas and this girl here is his widow. She's just buried him.'

The man shrugged his shoulders. 'But it were bought and paid for and I've delivered it for free.' Elsie gave him a fierce look, but he went on. 'Anyroad, I've spent the money he gave me – it were Christmas and I've seven children, you know.'

'I don't care about that.' Elsie was getting into her stride. 'My daughter's been left a widow, so she has no need of a bloody double bed, does she? She needs the money her husband spent on it.'

'It's not my property any more – it's yours,' said the man. 'You could easily sell it.'

The argument would have continued if Frank hadn't stepped in. 'We can't stand out here arguing the toss.

Here, Bill, give us a hand to carry the bed inside, we can't leave it out in the snow.'

Elsie wasn't for giving up. 'But what about—'

'Leave it, Mam,' Helen cried. 'I just want to get in off the street.'

'Come on,' said Pearl as she linked Helen and Elsie's arms. 'I'm starved with the cold, let's get the kettle on.'

By the time the bits of the bed were stacked in the shop, the dozen mourners in the back room were helping themselves to sandwiches and a cup of tea. Helen had wanted to go straight to her room, but Elsie was having none of it. 'They've come out on a cold day to show their respects and to support you, so the least we can do is give them a cup of tea.'

Helen was grateful that they seemed to be chatting among themselves and only occasionally looked over at her to give a sympathetic look and after a while she slipped into the shop. The bits of the bed were leaning against a row of shelves, the mattress was on the floor. She ran her finger over the brass bedhead and couldn't help thinking it could do with a good polish. She sat on the mattress and thought of Jim. He had wanted it to be a surprise for her. It turned out he had arranged to borrow Douglas's handcart to transport their few belongings to the new house and no doubt the bed would have been loaded on the cart as well. Tomorrow night they would have slept in this bed in their new home and, in time, their child would have been conceived there. She smoothed the mattress. 'Oh, Jim...' she whispered, her eyes filled with tears and she ran her hands over her belly.

'Thought I'd find you out here.' It was Pearl. 'A hard day for you to get through, Helen,' and she nodded at the bed. 'What will you do with it?'

Helen shrugged. 'I don't know.'

Pearl walked slowly round the shop looking at the stock as if she was a customer deciding what to buy. Helen watched her: the heavy make-up, thin pencilled eyebrows; a navy dress, slim and elegant with her high heels. Mam's cousin, but there was no love lost between them. Mam called her a 'flighty piece' to her face and Pearl didn't shy away from calling her cousin 'a miserable bugger'.

She sat on the mattress next to Helen and stretched her legs out in front of her. 'It'll be hard for you, I know, but you're so young and you won't be the sad widow for ever. You've got your whole life in front of you.'

'There's nothing in front of me but working in this poky shop, slicing bacon and weighing cheese till I'm as crabby as Mam.'

'It doesn't have to be that way.'

'But it does.' She bowed her head as though she didn't have the strength to hold it up.

'If you don't want to be stuck here, you could get another job. It would do you good to get away from these four walls and mix with different people.'

Helen said nothing.

'You know I lost somebody too?' said Pearl.

Helen nodded. 'Your fiancé died in the war.'

'Hmm... Battle of the Somme, 1916.' She bent her knees and wrapped her arms around them. 'I'd just turned twenty-one when Sidney proposed to me on the night before he went away for basic training. Six months later he was dead and I thought my life was over.' She paused. 'And I suppose it was really... for a few years. I'd known Sidney from our first day at school but we never, you know, got together until we were older. He was always with his mates. Anyway, they all joined up together and went over the top together. Most of them didn't come home. The number of times you'd see a telegram delivered and one by one the women in the street would go to the door of the mother or the wife and sit with her. Nursing their cups of tea and, God knows, some of the time there was weeping but, more often than not, they comforted each other with silence, knowing that nothing could ease their pain.'

'But you're all right now, aren't you?'

Pearl gave a rueful smile. 'You never get over it, but you can't live with that sort of grief forever and the pain will ease, I promise.'

'But what about right now? I can't bear it. Jim was the best thing that ever happened to me. He made me feel I was worth something and, now he's gone, I don't think I can go on.' She began to cry again.

Pearl squeezed her hand. 'I know it's hard, but you need to keep going one day at a time.'

Helen felt the panic rise inside her. 'I can't do it, I can't!'

Pearl took her by the shoulders. 'Listen to me. Don't you ever say that again, Helen, you're far stronger than you think. The only trouble is that, with Jim gone, your mother'll keep you under her thumb because you're all she's got. But at some point, you need to get away from her, you know that, don't you?'

Helen nodded. 'I should've found a proper job with a decent wage long ago.' She wiped the tears from her cheeks. 'The last thing Jim said to me was that I should stand up to her more.'

'And he was right. I know Elsie's not easy to live with... Maybe I shouldn't say this, but your father was the only one to bring out the best in her and when he went...'

'I know he died when I was three, but I don't remember him at all,' said Helen. 'Mam never spoke about him.'

Pearl sighed. 'Oh, I wish I could do something more to help you.' She paused. 'Look, if you need a shoulder to cry on, or somebody to talk to, just let me know. Send me a letter or come to my work, I don't mind, and we'll meet up. Promise me, Helen, if you're not coping, you'll let me help you.'

The curtain to the back room was pulled back and

Elsie stood in the doorway. She glared at Pearl. 'Well, this is a cosy little chat, isn't it? Giving our kid the benefit of your experience, are you?'

Pearl got to her feet. 'I was only saying, if she wanted someone to talk to, she could get in touch with me.'

'And why would she do that when she's got her mother to sort her out?'

'I'm only trying to help, Elsie.'

'Well, maybe we don't need your help.' She turned to Helen. 'You'd better get back to the visitors, they're going home now and you need to thank them for coming.'

'Thanks for the advice, Pearl,' said Helen.

Pearl called after her, 'You can do it, Helen. I know you can.'

When everyone had gone, Helen washed the pots then told her mother she was going to her room.

'Hold on a minute, what are we doing about the bed?'

'I don't know – I haven't decided.'

'What do you mean "you haven't decided"? It's cluttering up the shop; we need to shift it somewhere till we can get rid of it.'

'Not now, Mam. I'm too tired,' and she left the room without another word.

The bedroom was freezing and she felt like going to bed in her clothes, but she couldn't bear to wear the awful black funeral dress for a moment longer.

She threw it on the floor and dressed quickly in her winceyette pyjamas, bedsocks and dressing gown and still she shivered. On cold nights, she would always snuggle up to Jim and he'd accuse her of stealing his warmth and within minutes they'd be like toast. She loved the closeness of him through the night; his body shaped to hers, adjusting to her sleepy movements. 'Oh, Jim, are you here, love?' she whispered. 'I miss you so much.'

She thought back to the moment when the station officer had come to the shop – with his grave expression and unblinking eyes she knew at once that they had found Jim's body and her worst nightmare had become a reality. She remembered very little of the days that followed, except for the thought of the funeral, looming over her, filling her with dread. 'A fireman's funeral,' they said, 'with a fire tender and a guard of honour,' when all she had wanted was to bury her husband quietly with no strangers gawping at her.

And now it was over, she was alone and already she sensed a different sort of grief, far worse than standing at a graveside. Jim was gone. She would never see him or hear his voice again and the emptiness grew inside her.

So, too, did the regrets. Of course, he knew that she loved him, she could say the simple words, but a shyness had always stopped her from telling him how much he meant to her. She should have said she loved the way he teased her, made her laugh, and how tender, gentle and passionate he was.

She slept right through the night and when she awoke there was a split second when she had forgotten he was dead, then the weight of her loss overwhelmed her. What would Jim say… you're stronger than you think? Well, she wasn't strong, she was weak. It could have been so different. It was New Year's Day and they should have been moving into the little house in Newton Heath. She had been so excited about it – a new start, Jim had said.

She opened up the shop as usual to serve the early morning customers on their way to work and, by the time her mother appeared, she had made up her mind.

'I'm going out,' she said. 'I'll walk over to Newton Heath to get the money back that we paid in advance for the rent.' She didn't give a fig about the rent, but it was a good excuse to get out in the fresh air, away from the shop and her mother.

It was one of those crisp, cold days with a clear blue sky, when even the two-up two-down terraced houses sparkled in the sunshine. It was a fair walk and with every step she felt her head begin to clear.

The house was one of a row of mill workers' cottages next to a park. When she went to see it with Jim it had been raining and she didn't really take in the surroundings. Once inside they had a quick look around: a parlour at the front; kitchen at the back; a yard with an outside toilet and, upstairs, a bedroom either side of the steep staircase. Standing outside it now she was struck by how tiny it looked, like a little doll's house. How she wished it could have been theirs.

They had been told to collect the key from the woman next door when they arrived with their furniture, and it seemed logical to ask her where the landlord could be found so she could cancel the tenancy.

It was a while before the door opened, and when the woman eventually appeared looking hot and bothered, hands dripping soapy water, her first words were, 'You've come for your key then?' and, before Helen could explain, she was gone. She returned a minute later and thrust the key into Helen's hand.

'No, you don't understand. I need to speak to the landlord,' said Helen. At that moment there was the piercing scream of a child.

'I have to go,' shouted the woman. 'I've a child in the sink. Come back later!' and she closed the door.

Helen looked at the key in her hand. What was she to do?

The front door stuck a little and she had to put her shoulder to it. Inside, the empty house was bitterly cold and she stood a while in the middle of the front room, hardly worth the title of parlour, seeing it again with fresh eyes. Worn lino and faded sprays of roses on the wallpaper; the fireplace still full of ash. She went past the stairs into the kitchen where there was an ancient gas cooker and next to it a Belfast sink with only one tap. An old Victorian armchair with the seat ripped open exposing the horsehair stuffing was next to the fireplace. The floor was flagged and the chill of it went straight through the soles of her shoes. Anyone wanting to live here would need a few rag rugs underfoot.

Upstairs, the bedrooms had bare floorboards. In the front bedroom there was the smell of damp and black mould over the window lintel. The back room was smaller and had no smell but plenty of cobwebs. It also had one redeeming feature – it looked out on to the park. She stood at the window a while watching a family walking by, the mother pushing an empty pram and the father holding his little girl's hand. She had been standing in the same spot a few weeks before when Jim had turned to her, a smile on his face, and said, 'Well, what do you think, Helen? Would you be happy here?' And she had reached for his hand and smiled right back. 'Yes, I think I would.'

She returned to the kitchen, sat on the fireside chair and thought about what her life might have been if Jim hadn't died. This would have been her domain, standing at the cooker making their meals. Washing the clothes in the sink and pegging them out to blow in the yard or on a rainy day draping them over the fireguard to dry. She'd have turned this little house into a palace; everything would have been shining and cosy and warm. And the children, two or three at least... She curled her legs under her, leaned back and closed her eyes. If only I could stay here forever, she thought. It felt good to be alone and for the first time since Jim's death she allowed her thoughts to focus on the future. She knew that adjusting to life without him would be hard. In the short time they had together he had brightened her days with his love and the promise of a better life. She had never been so happy. Even the dreary days spent in the shop with her mother's endless carping couldn't spoil the joy she felt when Jim came home from work. Now he was gone and it felt like her life was over too. She'd be buried in that miserable shop, stacking tins in pyramids till she dropped, and there'd be no way out.

An hour slipped by and she knew she had to leave, but still she couldn't stir herself. She shifted her position and found a soft bit of the chair to lay her head. I'll stay a bit longer, she thought, what's the harm? She brought to mind Jim's face with his broad smile and those blue eyes that could melt her heart.

Her eyes closed and within minutes she was asleep and dreaming that she was in a park pushing a pram. It was summer and the flower beds were full of busy Lizzies and the humming of bees. At the sound of a soft cry, she pulled back the baby's blanket and her heart stopped. The pram was empty. She awoke in a panic and it

ALRENE HUGHES

was a moment before she remembered where she was. This wasn't the first time, since Jim died, that she had dreamt about a baby and her thoughts returned again to that last night they had been together. Might there be a chance that she could be pregnant even now? The thought filled her with joy.

She sat up and rubbed the crick in her neck and, with a final look round the little kitchen, she went out through the front door and locked it. It was just a few steps to the neighbour's house to return the key and tell her that she wouldn't be moving in, but for some reason she couldn't explain, she held it tight in her pocket and walked on by.

42

Chapter 4

When Helen arrived back at the shop, she noticed that the brass bed wasn't there. Her mother was busy packing a woman's bag so she went through to the living room and there it was, leaning against the sideboard. She put the kettle on, made a pot of tea and brought two cups into the shop.

'You moved the bed,' said Helen, as she handed her mother the brew.

'Course I did, near give myself a hernia in the process. Anyway, it won't be here long. I put a card in the window and I've already had a couple of enquiries. We should get a good price for it.'

'You've done what?' Helen couldn't keep the anger out of her voice.

'We have to get rid of it. It's no use to you, is it?'

'You've no right to sell my property. What if I want to keep it?'

'Don't be ridiculous, Helen. You need all the money you can get, now that you haven't Jim's wages coming in. Speaking of which, did you get the two weeks' rent you paid to the landlord in advance?'

'No, I didn't. He wasn't—'

'You didn't get it? My God, Helen, I can't believe you could be so stupid. It's a good job I'm here. You wouldn't last two minutes on your own.'

'Stop it, Mam, don't speak to me like that. I'm not a child.'

But her mother wasn't listening. 'Have you been out like that?'

'What do you mean?'

'Your clothes – look at you. Your husband only buried yesterday and you haven't the decency to wear those black clothes I got for you. What will the neighbours think?'

'I can't wear those clothes, they smell of somebody else.' Helen was close to tears. 'And why are you being so nasty when you know I'm heartbroken about Jim?'

'Yes, and I'm heartbroken that you've walked away from two weeks' rent and don't want to sell that bloody big bed that's no use you.'

Helen put her hands over her ears to fend off the hurtful words. 'Stop it! Stop it! I can't take any more of this.'

'For God's sake get a grip, girl. There's many a woman has lost her man and, the longer this war lasts, the more widows there'll be. But you'll be better off than most of them. You've a decent home here and a business. You'll not go without and count your blessings too that you haven't a child to bring up.'

Helen's anger and frustration had reached boiling point. She could hardly breathe, let alone speak. She clenched her fists and stood tall, towering over her mother. It was a moment before she found her voice. 'How do you know there won't be a child?'

Her mother stepped back, her face filled with uncertainty. 'What do you mean? You're not...'

'Why would I tell you if I was? I've had enough of the way you order me around. You've always made me feel small and useless, but this is the day it stops. I'm going to get my things together, then I'll leave and I won't be back so don't try to find me!' She started up the stairs, but her mother caught her arm.

'Don't be stupid, where would you go? And what about the shop? How will I manage without you?'

Helen shook her head. 'That's all you care about, isn't it? This bloody shop. Well, I'm getting out of here, Mam, I've had enough. I'll not spend another night under this roof,' and she pulled her arm away and ran up the stairs.

She sat on the bed and stared at her shaking hands. She couldn't believe what she'd said. It was as though something had snapped inside her, but she didn't regret it for one moment. She went down to the cellar and brought up some cardboard boxes and filled them with her possessions, Then she pulled an old grip bag from under the bed, blew the dust off it and began pulling her clothes out of the wardrobe. Then, out of the corner of her eye, she caught sight of something that stopped her in her tracks and she let out a cry. There was Jim's suit swinging on a hanger – the empty jacket the saddest thing she had ever seen. She wrapped her arms around it, breathing in the familiar smell of him. Then held it away from her, picturing him the last time he wore it at the working men's club the night before he died. She smiled and reached out to brush a sprinkling of her face powder on the shoulder where she had rested her head as they danced that night. It was then that she remembered the five pound note he had won in the raffle. Hadn't he put it away safe in his inside pocket? She felt for it – nothing there. Nothing in the other pockets either. Where could it be? Then she vaguely remembered her mother coming into the bedroom during one of those times after Jim's death when she could barely lift her head off the pillow. Didn't her mother go to the wardrobe? She remembered the door creaking. Could her mother have taken it? Why would she do that? But it must have been her; there was no one else. She shoved the suit into the bag, along with the cricket sweater that he would never wear, and went to face her.

'Where is it, Mam? Where's the fiver Jim won at the club?'

Elsie was in the middle of serving a customer. 'I'll be with you in a minute, Helen.'

'You took it, didn't you?'

'Helen, I don't know what you're talking about. Now, let me finish Mrs Morrison's order, please.'

She ran back up to her room and came down with her bag; by that time Mrs Morrison had left and her mother had turned the shop sign to 'Closed'.

'That five pounds he won, it was in his suit pocket. I didn't take it, so it must have been you.'

'This is nonsense. I don't know what you're talking about. The only thing I did was hang up the black dress and coat. You're confused, Helen, look at the state of you. And you think you can go off on your own? You won't last a week before you come crawling back here.'

'You're wrong!' she screamed. 'I know you took Jim's money and I'll never come back here. I'd rather die!'

She ran out of the shop and straight across the road to her neighbour, Douglas Finney. He was a rag and bone man and he owned a handcart.

He looked up as she came in and gave her a lopsided smile, keeping his cigarette firmly in the opposite corner of his mouth. 'Are you all right, lass?' Then he noticed her tears. 'What's the matter?'

'Oh, Douglas, can I ask you a favour?'

'Course you can, love.'

'I know that Jim asked to borrow your handcart to wheel our belongings over to our new house in Newton

47

Heath and I was wondering if you would still help me to move them.'

'But I thought you were staying on at your mam's?'

'No, Douglas, I'm moving out.'

He took the dimp out of the corner of his mouth and ground it underfoot. 'Well, I won't ask you why, but are you sure you'll be all right on your own so soon after… you know?'

'I'll be fine,' she insisted. 'I just need some help.'

'Well, I'm your man. Have you got your things ready?' Helen nodded. 'Right then, I'll wheel my cart over to the shop. Will you be taking that big bed with you?'

'Oh yes,' she said. 'It's the only piece of furniture I've got.'

By the time the cart was loaded, word had got round and a few neighbours had come out to say goodbye. So shocked were they when they saw how little she had to call her own, they nipped back into their homes and came out with a few things they could spare: a tablecloth, a few bits of crockery, a frying pan, even an old patchwork quilt from Mrs Lowe.

At no point did her mother come out and it didn't go unnoticed by the neighbours. Their eyes flitted to the shop window and back and they whispered and tutted.

'Have you everything now?' said Douglas.

'No, there's just one more thing,' and she ran into the shop, straight past her mother serving a customer, and into the living room. On the sideboard sat Jim's helmet.

It had unsettled her from the day of his funeral when they wanted to present it to her, but she couldn't leave it behind, Jim would never forgive her.

It was time to go. Douglas picked up the shafts of the handcart and set it moving while she walked beside him, her arms wrapped around the dented helmet.

It was growing dark when they arrived at the house and started to unload the cart. Helen had just carried in a couple of rag rugs she'd taken from her bedroom at home, when the woman from next door wandered into the kitchen with the child on her hip.

'That were a fine bed your husband just carried in,' she said.

'Oh, he's not my husband, he's just a friend – a neighbour from where I used to live.'

'Is that right?' The woman's eyes flitted round the room. 'Is the rest of your furniture coming tomorrow?'

'Maybe… I'm not sure. I need to buy a few more things.' Helen was uneasy; not wanting to discuss her situation.

'Have you brought blackout curtains?' The woman had wandered over to the window, jiggling the whinging child. 'You know this is the only room in the house that has them, don't you? You'll need to sort the other rooms or you'll be fined for breaching the blackout regulations.'

Helen's heart sank. Now she'd have to make curtains, and how much would that cost for the material?

'Anyroad, my name's Ada Clark, what's yours?'

'Helen Harrison.'

Ada acknowledged her with a nod. 'So, where've you come from?' she said.

'Over Moston way.' That was vague enough, thought Helen, but she'd not give anything more away.

'I could make you a brew if you want.'

'No, no,' said Helen. 'That's kind of you, but I'll need to get on, sorting things out, you know?'

'Well, I'm only next door if you need anything,' and with a last look around the bare kitchen she left.

When Ada had gone Helen went to see how Douglas was getting on bolting the bed together. She came into the room and her eyes opened wide at the sight of it.

'You'll be comfortable on that,' said Douglas. 'Probably came out of one of those big Edwardian terraces on Queen's Road.'

'It almost fills the room,' said Helen. 'Good job I've got double sheets to fit it and a Witney blanket too – wedding presents we never used. And with Mrs Lowe's quilt on the top, I'll be as snug as a bug.'

Downstairs, Helen got her purse and offered Douglas a half crown for his trouble.

'Nay, lass, keep your money. I'm happy to have helped you and if you need anything else doing let me know.'

When Douglas had gone, she went upstairs and, with

the light fading fast, she made up the bed. At least she had a bed to sleep in, but when could she ever afford a dressing table or wardrobe? Back in the kitchen she drew the blackout curtains and switched on the light. The first thing she unpacked was an old kettle so she could have some tea. Then she emptied her shopping bag: bread, milk, a half pot of jam, tea, two eggs, a bit of butter and a couple of bacon rashers, all taken from the kitchen at home. It wasn't stealing, she told herself, these were her rations.

She delved into one of the cardboard boxes and took out some ornaments that she had kept in her 'bottom drawer', presents from friends when she got engaged, and saved for when she and Jim would have their own place. She set each one on the mantelpiece and stood back to admire them. It felt good to have her own pot figures; one a girl like Little Bo Peep, the other a boy carrying a piglet under his arm.

The kettle whistled, she made a brew and jam butties and sat in the old armchair to plan her next step. With the rent already paid and her savings of thirty shillings in her purse for food and coal, she had two weeks to find work before she'd be out on the street or, worse, back home with her tail between her legs. She pushed away the rising panic. What if nobody would give her a job? Don't be silly, she told herself, you'll get something.

First thing in the morning she would try the AVRO aircraft factory. She could walk there in half an hour and, if she didn't get taken on, she would walk on into town and ask at the shops. As she sat there, the room seemed to grow colder and colder and without a fire she'd be better off in bed. She undressed and climbed into the huge bed and lay there in the pitch black listening to the sounds of the house. It was comfortable, but she couldn't sleep with the turmoil in her head. What madness had led her in the space of a day to leave her home, her job, her mother... to end up alone in a strange house that she couldn't afford? What if her mother was right and she was no good on her own? If only Jim hadn't died. He'd be lying beside her now and she imagined him making love to her as he did on their last night together. Her thoughts turned again to the baby they had so wanted. She had deliberately shocked her mother by saying there might be a child, but the truth was that since Jim's death her thoughts had turned more and more to the possibility that she could be pregnant. It wasn't likely, of course, and anyway, how could she support herself and bring up a child?

The week went on and the January weather became treacherous: icy pavements that thawed and iced again overnight; then snow deep enough to cover her shoes. She walked everywhere to save money. She wanted war work, but they didn't want her. The mills were looking for experienced workers. The shops told her it was a quiet period after Christmas and to come back in a month. She returned home each day chilled to the bone and stuffed her sodden shoes with newspaper and set them next to the fire to dry out. The money went on coal, the gas meter and basic food like potatoes and porridge to fill her up and she lived in just two rooms – the kitchen and her bedroom. As well as looking for work, she was determined to clean the house from top to bottom. She had found a galvanised bucket in the coal shed, bought carbolic soap and soon everywhere smelled fresh and clean. She also bought some blackout material and made a curtain for her bedroom. The other windows would have to wait.

She had just arrived home after a day looking for work when there was a knock on the door. It was Ada, clearly expecting to be invited in. 'Just thought I'd pop round to see if you've settled in all right.'

'I'm fine, thanks,' said Helen, careful not to open the door too wide to stop Ada seeing the still unfurnished parlour.

'I haven't seen your husband at all.'

If Ada hadn't been so nosy, she might have confided that she was a widow, but Helen didn't trust her not to spread her business around strangers. 'He's not here.'

'Oh, is he away in the forces?'

'No,' said Helen.

Ada gave her an odd look. 'Only, the landlord said you were a young married couple.'

'I have to go,' said Helen. 'I've milk on the boil.'

'Well, I'll get back to the child, she'll be waking up

from her nap. You know where I am.'

Helen managed a nod and closed the door. Maybe she should have said she was a widow, but then she would have had to explain about his death and she wasn't up to discussing her grief with strangers. She should have lied and said her husband was in the army but now, by saying nothing, Ada was suspicious and no doubt she'd keep asking more awkward questions.

She had just got the fire going when there was another knock at the door. It had better not be Ada again, she thought, but she needn't have worried. There on the doorstep was her friend Gwen grinning at her. 'Well, you're a sight for sore eyes! I thought I'd never find you. I knew the house was on Droylsden Road but I didn't know the number. Then I remembered you said it was between a pub and a park.'

Helen hugged her. 'Oh, Gwen, thank goodness you've come,' and she tried not to cry.

Gwen linked her arm. 'Hey, come on now, let's get inside.'

In the kitchen they drank tea, Gwen sitting in the old chair and Helen on the rag rug in front of the fire.

'Why didn't you say you were going to move into the house? Me and Frank could have helped you.'

'I didn't plan to; I couldn't stay another moment with Mam. I had to get away.'

'So, what are you doing now? Have you got a job?'

Helen shook her head. 'I've been out every day

looking for work, but there's nothing to be had. I don't know what to do – the money I'd saved is running out. The rent's been paid for another week, but after that… I really don't want to go back home.'

Gwen looked uneasy.

'What is it?' Helen asked.

'I've just come from the shop. Your mother had a girl helping her, she couldn't have been more than fourteen.'

'She's got somebody to do my job? But I've only been away a week.'

'That's not all,' said Gwen. 'She asked me if I knew anyone who was looking for lodgings.'

'Oh God, what will I do? I've nowhere else to go!'

'Don't panic, you'll get a job. I'm sure of it,' and she knelt on the rug and put her arm round Helen. 'Now, listen, I might have some good news. I came to find you because Frank thinks you might get something from the fire service – a bit of a pension. They won't have sorted anything yet, because they're at sixes and sevens since the bombings, but things are getting back to normal and Frank says he'll speak to the station officer about you this week.'

'I don't want a pension.'

'But you're a widow, you're entitled to it.'

Helen felt the tears well in her eyes. 'I don't want to be a widow with a pension. I just want Jim,' she sobbed. 'And anyway, after next week I won't have any money for the rent, never mind anything to eat.'

'I could lend you a few shillings if that would help.'

'That's kind of you, Gwen, but I know money's tight for you as well.'

'Is there anyone else you could ask for help? What about Jim's sister and her husband? I spoke to her at the funeral, she seemed really nice.'

'She is, but I've only met her a few times. They live in Rochdale. Jim took me to see them when we got engaged, and they were at our wedding. Anyway, they've four children so they wouldn't have money to spare.'

'Then, what about that woman who was there, your mam's cousin, wasn't she?'

'Pearl, you mean? She's my godmother, but I hardly ever see her. Mam doesn't like her and, to be honest, we're not that close.'

'She looked very nice, well dressed. She might lend you a bit to tide you over.'

'She was kind to me at the funeral. She said if I needed a shoulder to cry on, or somebody to talk to, I should let her know.'

'There you are then, it's worth a try.'

Helen frowned. 'I don't know. It doesn't seem right, asking her to lend me money. What will she think of me?'

'I don't think you've any alternative if you want to keep this roof over your head.'

'She did say if I needed help...'

'Look at it this way, she can only say no.'

Chapter 5

Pearl Spencer was always the first to arrive for work at Fenner's Fashion Agency in Stevenson Square in the middle of Manchester. She unlocked the door and went down to the basement to switch on the lights. This was the heart of the business with racks and racks of beautiful coats, dresses and separates lining the walls. In the middle of the room there were large tables for folding and packing the garments to be sent to retailers all over the north of England. Back upstairs, she pushed open the heavy mahogany and brass doors and switched on the main showroom lights. They flickered for a moment before flooding the space with light. The Winton carpet was turquoise, there were upholstered gold damask sofas, gilded chairs and full-length cheval mirrors and, most importantly, the best of the new season's fashions, displayed on mannequins at intervals around the room.

On the left was a door to the dressing room and straight ahead were the offices. One for Mr Fenner, the other for her, as the office manager, and the two clerks, Dorothy the shorthand typist and Rita the office junior.

She hung up her camel-hair coat and Hermès scarf then checked her make-up and hair in the mirror behind her. It was an important week, the start of the spring season, when buyers from major retailers would visit the fashion agents in Manchester to select their new ranges. Pearl's role in all of this was to see that everything went without a hitch, and that included making sure Mr Fenner didn't lose his temper.

Dorothy arrived in a fluster and Pearl's heart sank. 'Please, don't tell me that Rita's not coming in.'

Dorothy shook her head. 'I'm sorry, Miss Spencer, I went to see her on Sunday; she's in a bad way. Turns out, her arm's broken and she can't hear a thing because of the explosion. Not only that, but I'd say her nerves have gone. The house next to hers took a direct hit – three killed and half the roof ended up in Rita's bedroom. A few feet closer and she'd have been killed too.'

'Aw, poor kid,' said Pearl. 'So, it's down to you and me to make sure this week goes well. Right then, you'll be in the dressing room as usual with the two models. I know I can trust you to make sure they get into, and out of, the right clothes at the right time.'

'But Rita's not here to help you take the orders.'

'Never mind that, I'll do it on my own. It might take a bit longer but it can't be helped.'

'Mr Fenner won't like that.'

But before Pearl could say anything there was a shout from the doorway. 'And what exactly won't Mr Fenner like?'

Pearl's heart missed a beat. There was her boss glaring at her and he shouted again, 'Don't tell me something's gone wrong, not today of all days!'

'It's nothing to worry about, Mr Fenner, everything's under control. Rita still isn't able to come back to work, but we'll manage.'

'You realise, Miss Spencer, that this business could take a beating if, as I suspect, the government decide to bring in clothes rationing? That's why we need big orders this week and if anything goes wrong, I'll hold you responsible.'

'Yes, sir, I understand.'

'Well, get on with it. I'll be in my office. Call me when the first clients arrive.' He hadn't taken half a dozen steps before he turned round. 'And the models had better not look like they've come from the nightshift on Oxford Road, if you get my drift.'

'Why does he speak to you like that?' said Dorothy. 'He wouldn't be in business two minutes if it wasn't for you sorting everything out.'

'That's enough, Dorothy, don't forget he pays our wages. Anyway, he doesn't mean it. His bark's worse than his bite. Now, get me the running order for the catwalk, please, and an order pad, while I have a final check in the dressing room.'

She went through the clothes to be shown on the catwalk, making sure they hadn't creased or been misplaced in the running order since she checked them the previous day. She stopped here and there to pick off a thread, straighten a collar or run her hand over a beautiful cocktail dress. Behind her, the door opened and she called over her shoulder, 'Just leave them there, Dorothy, and send in the models when they arrive.'

'It's not Dorothy.'

'What's that?' and she turned, a puzzled look on her face. 'Helen? My goodness, what are you doing here?'

She saw at once that Helen was upset, and was at her side in seconds to try and calm her.

'I'm sorry, Pearl, I didn't mean to cry, but...' and now she was sobbing.

Best to keep her in here where Mr Fenner wouldn't see her, thought Pearl, and she helped her to a chair. 'There, take your time and tell me what's happened.'

Helen took a deep breath and began to explain. She told her about the row with her mother. Pearl nodded; she could well imagine the sort of things Elsie would have said to her. When Helen explained she had gone to live in the house she and Jim would have moved into, Pearl raised an eyebrow and wondered whether Helen had more courage than she gave her credit for.

Helen wiped her eyes and went on. 'You said if I needed someone to talk to…' Heavens, thought Pearl, the child could hardly have picked a worse moment to share her problems, but that was unkind.

'I've tried to get work,' said Helen, 'but there isn't anything and I was going to ask you—'

'Miss Spencer,' Dorothy came bustling through the door followed by a young woman with glossy dark hair and the loveliest of smiles, clearly a model, 'they've only sent one girl from the agency, the other one has let them down.'

'Oh no!' Pearl shook her head in disbelief. 'But we booked them months ago.'

'That's the problem,' said the model. 'She's in the family way; she'd never get into the clothes.'

'And nobody thought to tell us?' Pearl closed her eyes. For a brief second, she thought of doing it herself – she would certainly fit into the clothes – but the buyers liked to ogle the young models. Besides, she was needed to introduce the collection, give a running commentary and, in the absence of Rita, she'd be taking the orders as well. Mr Fenner would be livid and she was already imagining the aftermath of that. She opened her eyes and looked at the three women in front of her.

'Helen, stand up. Take your coat off and your headscarf.'

'But—'

'Just do it, please.'

Helen did as she was asked and Pearl stepped back to examine her. 'Turn around for me. Now walk the length of the room. No, stand up straight, head held high, shoulders back. Imagine you're full of confidence. Turn and come back to me. Look straight ahead.'

Helen looked bewildered. 'I shouldn't have come here, I'm sorry.'

'Never mind all that. Did you come here to see if I could help you?'

'Yes,' said Helen.

'Well, I think I can. How would you like a week's work?'

Helen was uncertain. 'What kind of work?'

'Exactly what you've just been doing: walking up and down. You see, I need two young women to model some lovely clothes for our clients, but I've only got one.'

'Pearl, I can't be a model – look at the state of me.'

It was true that Helen looked pale and there were dark circles under her eyes. Her hair was dull and lank. She checked her watch – half an hour before the clients arrived – it wasn't long enough, but it would have to do.

She turned to the model. 'You, what's your name?'

'Anna Maguire,' she said.

'Right, Anna, I need you to help us. You've got twenty minutes to transform Helen, here, into a passable model – hair, make-up, the works.'

Anna seemed unfazed and got to work, while Pearl sat next to Helen and explained what was happening.

'All week, buyers from the big department stores will be coming here to see our clothes for the new season. If they like them, they'll buy them to sell in their shops. To show the clothes at their best we have two models, that'll be you and Anna.' She pointed to the racks of clothes. 'Dorothy will give you each garment in turn, you put it on then walk out and model it. Do you understand?'

'I'm not sure about this, Pearl. I wouldn't know how to model clothes.'

'Don't worry, when Anna's finished with you, we'll have a bit of a practice. It's really just walking the length of the room and stopping halfway in front of the clients so they can get a good look at the garments.'

The buyers were arriving and Mr Fenner was chatting and laughing, welcoming them as old friends. Pearl checked again the running order and the notes she had made on each garment emphasising their best points, but her thoughts kept returning to what was happening in the dressing room. In truth, she wouldn't be surprised if Helen came out in her dowdy coat and headed straight for the door. What was she thinking of... dragooning a girl, clearly upset, into doing something solely to get herself out of an awkward situation? She shook her head. This could be a disaster, but yet... she marvelled again at the transformation in Helen's appearance. Her blonde hair in little rolls framing her beautiful face, the Leichner foundation, the Bourjois rouge, the red lipstick... and her height... she was already tall, but with her shoulders back and her head held high, she was every inch a model.

'Gentlemen, gentlemen, if you would like to take your seats.' Mr Fenner called the buyers to order and nodded at Pearl. When they were settled, she welcomed them then gave the signal to Dorothy. Anna was first out.

'This fern-patterned tea dress is in rayon with a neat revere collar. Please note the matching fabric belt, very popular this coming season...'

Anna disappeared into the dressing room and Pearl held her breath. Come on, Helen, where are you? The dressing room door opened and Helen stepped into the showroom. Her eyes widened at the sight of the men staring at her and she was rooted to the spot. Oh, God, thought Pearl, and she turned towards her and smiled her encouragement. 'This is Helen and she's wearing a dress of finest Lancashire cotton with a full skirt.' At the sound of her voice, Helen seemed to shake herself and walked as far as the men, stopped and turned full circle to show off the dress. Pearl breathed again. 'The dress comes in three colours: mauve, lemon and pink.' Helen walked to the end of the room and back again and with a final twirl went back to the dressing room.

The fashion show went on and with every garment Helen appeared more confident. By the time the evening gowns were modelled, Pearl could not have been prouder of her beautiful goddaughter.

There was so much excitement in the dressing room afterwards with shrieks of laughter mixed with tears. 'I was so nervous and I'm still shaking.' Helen's eyes glistened. 'I can't believe what I've done.'

'But did you enjoy it?' Pearl asked.

'It was wonderful.' She threw her arms round Pearl. 'Thank you so much.' Her tears brimmed over.

'Oh, careful, don't spoil your make-up,' Pearl gave her a handkerchief. 'So, are you ready to do it all over again this afternoon?'

Helen clapped her hands. 'I can't wait.'

Pearl leaned her head against the bus window and closed her eyes. She would normally walk home, it wasn't that far to Ardwick, but it had been a long day. She thanked God that it went well. It would have been a complete disaster, if Helen hadn't arrived. Mr Fenner was pleased too. He told her afterwards that the buyers were very impressed with the new stock and that was a huge relief. She'd get the fire going when she got home and have a warm bath in her Yardley bath salts then slip into her negligee. There might even be time to read a story from *The People's Friend*.

Shortly after nine, she heard the key in the lock. She stood and fluffed up her hair in the mirror. The door opened and there he was. She held out her arms and said coyly, 'Now then, I hope you're in a good mood and you'll be kind to your Pearl tonight.'

He went to her. 'Oh yes, and I've got something here for you.' He pulled her close.

Pearl giggled. 'Oh, Harold Fenner, you're such a naughty boy!'

Chapter 6

Helen collapsed, exhausted, into the armchair and closed her eyes to ease the throbbing in her head. She had been on her feet all day and the concentration and anxiety had taken its toll. She hadn't eaten either but, by now, she was beyond hunger. The images of the day were swirling round in her mind: the beautiful clothes; the glimpse of herself in the mirrors; the surprise that she could manage a smile.

The knock on the door interrupted her thoughts and fearing it might be Ada she called out, 'Who's there?'

'It's Frank, I've brought you something.'

She was so glad to see him, even though the sight of his uniform brought a lump to her throat. 'Gwen told me you'd moved here. I'd have come sooner, but we're putting in such long shifts.' He came into the kitchen and she offered him the chair but he shook his head and leaned against the fireplace. He seemed to study her for a moment. 'You look different, Helen.'

'Do I? Oh, it's my hair.'

'Yes… your hair, but there's something else.'

Helen smiled. 'That'll be the make-up. It's different to what I would usually wear.' For some reason she thought it best not to mention she had been modelling clothes. 'You said you had something for me.'

He took a paper bag, stained with grease, from his pocket and handed it to her. She looked inside and her eyes widened. 'What…?'

'The lads had a bit of a whip-round when they got their wages.'

'I can't take this.'

'Yes, you can. The men looked up to Jim; he was a good fireman and a friend to us all. They wanted to do something.'

Helen thought of all those exhausted firemen she had seen in the station house on the day Jim died. It would have been a blow for them to lose Jim too. She nodded. 'Will you thank them for me and tell them that they were like brothers to him.'

'I will,' said Frank and he looked pleased at her words. 'But that's not all I've brought you.' He pulled a large brown envelope from inside his tunic and removed a sheaf of papers and handed them to her. Her heart sank as she read the stark black words 'Firemen Widows – Death in Service Benefits'.

'You have to fill it in and send it to the address on the top and they'll decide if you're entitled to any money.'

She couldn't hold back her tears, the very words – Widows, Death – ripped her heart.

'Helen, please don't cry. I can't bear to see you upset. I thought you'd want to get the widows' pension.'

'I don't want a pension.' Her voice cracked with emotion. 'I want Jim.'

'I don't know what to say.' He looked round the bare room. 'I just thought you could do with the money. Maybe I'd better go.'

'Oh, I'm sorry, Frank, stay for a bit, please.' She stood up. 'I'll make you a brew.'

'No, Helen, you sit down and I'll make it.' He put the kettle on. 'Have you had your tea?' he asked.

She shook her head.

'I'll make you something,' he said.

'There's only bread and cheese on the shelf.'

'Ah, that's my speciality. The lads down the station love my cheese on toast, especially with mustard. Don't suppose you've got any of that? No? Never mind.'

While she ate, he talked about the incendiary raid a few days before. 'It's the worst sort of attack for us: dropping incendiaries; setting buildings on fire. We've been run off our feet. Did you get many around here?'

'Just a bit of damage, the ARPs are really good at dousing them.'

'Is there a shelter near here?'

'There's one on Church Street, but I didn't go. I just hid under the bed.'

'Helen! You have to go in a shelter, you know that. What would Jim say?'

She didn't answer him, instead she pointed at the brown envelope. 'There's something else in there for me, isn't there?'

Frank looked uncomfortable. 'Eh… yes…'

'What is it?'

'Just a couple of things from Jim's locker at the station. I thought you'd want to have them.'

She held out her hand, but he didn't give it to her. 'What's the matter?' she said.

'You should look at them on your own. I'll leave you to it.'

She was immediately wary. 'Is it something awful? Will I be upset?'

'It's not awful, but…'

She eyed the envelope, wanting desperately to know what was in it, but frightened that its contents might send her back to that dark place she inhabited in the days after Jim's death. 'Frank, stay while I look at what's inside, please.'

There was a little blue leather box, probably from a jeweller. She opened it and there was a lovely necklace, a drop pearl on a silver chain.

'I think it was his Christmas present to you. He bought it the week before, said he'd leave it in his locker, in case you might find it at home.'

'It's beautiful,' she said.

Then she pulled out a photograph – Southport, on the sands, their honeymoon. It was blowing a gale, whipping up her skirt, and her hair in her eyes. It was just after that that Jim pulled her close and kissed her and she could feel his touch on her lips even now. She held back her tears as she smiled at the two of them together. They thought they had their whole lives in front of them. She set it aside and the sadness settled on her. She stared at her hands, twisted her wedding ring, forgot where she was, forgot about Frank.

When he eventually spoke, she looked startled.

'Helen, do you not think Jim would be shocked to see you living like this, on your own in an empty house with no food?'

Helen covered her face, suddenly ashamed. He must think she was stupid, hiding herself away in this run-down house.

'Are you going to stay here?' he asked.

She couldn't answer that, not yet. Her life was at a crossroads. If she got a steady job, she would stay in the house. If she didn't, she would have to go back home to her mam. And then, there was one other frightening and wonderful possibility: if she was carrying Jim's baby she would go back to her mother and devote her life to bringing up the child.

'Helen, are you all right?' Frank was looking anxious. 'Look, if you want to stay here you could buy a few bits of furniture with the money from the lads, but don't go on your own, they might try to overcharge a woman. Just let me know and I'll go with you.'

'Would you do that for me?'

'Of course, Jim was my mate and I'd do anything for his missus.'

'Thanks, Frank.'

'And will you promise me to fill in the pension forms?'

She knew he was right. 'I promise.' She reached again for the envelope. 'Is there anything else?'

'There is, but I'll go before you read it.'

'No, wait.' It was a piece of folded writing paper. She opened it and caught her breath, it was Jim's handwriting. Before she could stop herself, she had read the opening. *My Darling Helen*. She closed her eyes. 'What is this, Frank?'

He looked embarrassed. Had he read it?

'Some of the men have written a letter to their wives or sweethearts in case... in case they are killed doing their duty. It was something the lads who had fought in the Great War did and when this lot started... they wanted to leave some words of comfort.'

'Did you do one?'

'No, I... well, I'm not married, am I?'

Helen's hands shook as she folded the letter and put it back in the envelope. 'I think I'll just put it away for now and look at it later when... you know?'

She went with him to the door and they stood in the dark. 'I'm glad you came to see me, Frank, and thanks for bringing me the things from Jim's locker. And thank the lads for me, tell them I'm grateful.'

She sensed him move towards her, felt his hand fleetingly touch her arm. 'If you need me, leave a message at my lodgings, you know where I am.' And then he was gone, leaving behind that familiar smell that reminded her of Jim – the smell of smoke from smouldering fires.

She fastened the pearl drop around her neck and looked again at the honeymoon snap. Jim had made love to her for the first time the previous night and there she was, laughing in delight, a woman at last, satisfied beyond pleasure. Finally, she came to Jim's letter.

My Darling Helen

If you are reading this, I know I'm no longer there to look after you and you are alone. I loved you from the moment we met at the dance and, when we married, I was the happiest man in the world. I want to tell you that you are beautiful and clever and strong and don't ever let anyone say otherwise. Follow your instincts and make a life for yourself without me. I would love to say I'm somewhere close looking after you, but you know I'm not much for angels and religion. Maybe all the love I had for you will stay around you, and in the quiet moments, you'll feel that love again.

Your loving husband

Jim x

Chapter 7

The week Helen spent at Fenner's Fashion Agency was just what she needed. She never dreamt that work could be so enjoyable. She had got to know Pearl not as an absent godmother, but as a friend. Then there was Anna who had not only taught her the tricks of the modelling trade, but her happy nature had lifted her spirits every moment she was in her company.

Late on Friday afternoon, when Helen and Anna were tidying the dressing room, carefully rehanging and covering each individual garment, Pearl came in with their pay packets. 'Mr Fenner was really pleased with our hard work this week,' she told them, 'and he'd like to take us out for our tea.'

Helen and Anna looked at each other in surprise. 'He likes to reward people,' Pearl explained. 'So, can you come?'

The girls were all smiles. 'Yes, please.'

'That's great. Now, Helen, will you go to Mr Fenner's

office, he wants to have a word with you.' Helen's smile disappeared. 'Oh, don't worry, there's nothing wrong.'

She knocked on the door and his bellowing 'Come in!' made her jump. He was behind a huge desk, leaning back on his chair, a gold chain across his waistcoat, thumbs tucked into the pockets.

'Now then, lass, you've done well this week, stepping in like you did. And Pearl tells me you're out of work.'

'Yes, sir.'

'Well, I like helping young people when I can, so I'm offering you a temporary job. You'll know our office girl is likely to be off work for a few weeks and Pearl tells me you're bright enough to pick up on what needs to be done. So, what do you say?'

Helen couldn't believe it. 'Yes, sir, I'd love to come and work here.'

'Good, good. Now sometimes there's a chance of overtime.' He hesitated. 'In the evenings... entertaining clients. Would that be all right?'

Helen nodded. 'I could do that.'

'Splendid, splendid! Now, are you coming out for tea with us?'

'Oh yes, thank you for inviting me.'

'When she returned to the dressing room, Pearl was waiting. 'Well, did you take the job?'

'Of course, thanks, Pearl, it's a godsend.'

'No, you're doing us a favour, stepping in. Now let's go for our tea.'

Mr Fenner drove them down to Albert Square where he parked the car.

'Have you been in a Lyons' before?' asked Pearl. Anna had, but Helen admitted that she hadn't and didn't add that she had never been out for her tea anywhere, never mind the very grand-looking Lyons' Corner House. The place was packed, but they were able to wait inside for a table. The noise of a hundred people, at least, filled the room with constant chatter. Then there were the waitresses in their black and white uniforms rushing here and there taking orders or carrying large trays full of plates. 'They call them Nippies, because they're so fast,' said Pearl, 'but they're always very attentive to their customers, especially the ones who come in regularly, like Mr Fenner.'

Once they were seated, they were given menus to choose from. Helen was already feeling anxious, but Pearl came to her rescue. 'The fish and chips is always very good with tea and bread and butter. Why don't you have that?'

They ordered and the conversation got going and she was glad that the others had plenty to say. Pearl would draw her out a little by asking her a question or her opinion and she managed to say something, but most of the time she was content to listen. The meal tasted lovely and Mr Fenner insisted they all had jam roly-poly for pudding because, he said, 'It's nearly as sweet as you girls.'

By the time they came out of the restaurant, a full

moon hung over the town hall roof and Mr Fenner offered to give them a lift home. Anna said she was only a ten-minute walk away and she thanked him for her tea and said goodbye.

'I'll be off as well,' said Helen. 'There's plenty of moonlight to see my way home.'

Pearl wouldn't hear of it. 'No, no, we'll take you home. Besides, I want to see where you're living now.'

Helen was about to protest, but she didn't want to seem ungrateful. She only hoped that Pearl wouldn't want to come in. She needn't have worried; the car pulled up outside the house, she thanked them for everything and went to get out. Only she couldn't find the door handle, so Mr Fenner went to open it from the outside, and he took her arm to help her out. As she waved goodbye, she saw a movement in the upstairs window next door and there, caught in the light of the moon, was Ada watching her.

It had been an exhausting week at Fenner's, living on her nerves, frightened to make a mistake in front of the clients. Throughout the meal she had felt the beginning of a headache and all she wanted now was a hot water bottle and her bed. As soon as she lay down, she felt the tiredness sapping her strength. She winced a little at a cramp and moved the hot water bottle against her side. Her head was mussy and the dull ache that had nagged inside her all day grew stronger. She wiped away the tears on her cheeks then lay on her side with her knees drawn up to ease the cramps. When she awoke in the early morning she knew at once that any hope she might be pregnant had gone. 'I'm so sorry, Jim, so sorry.'

After two weeks in the office at Fenner's Fashions, Helen had learned the duties of the junior clerk: filing, addressing envelopes, making tea, tidying the showroom and generally helping Pearl. She soon realised that Pearl did most of the work while Mr Fenner spent the mornings in his office talking on the telephone and the afternoon in some hotel bar with his cronies. She liked wearing the neat, navy blue dress and matching shoes she had to wear. 'Mr Fenner insists on us having a uniform,' Pearl told her, and Helen was glad of it because she didn't have any clothes that were smart enough for the job.

At home, too, she was more settled. Frank had gone with her to the second-hand furniture shop in Collyhurst and she chose a small table with four chairs and a dressing table and wardrobe. They'd seen better days, but Frank haggled a bit and she got them for a good price. He even came round when they were delivered and helped the man carry them inside.

'I'll put up a few more shelves in the kitchen for you, next time I get a Sunday off,' he told her. 'I've a mate who'll let me have some wood.'

Somehow, she was managing when people were

around, but coming into an empty house and spending the evening alone was hard. The anguish of losing Jim and knowing there would be no baby intensified her loneliness. She tried to keep busy at the weekends, wandering around Newton Heath market and buying some remnants to make cushions or curtains. Soon the little house was cosy and welcoming and all hers.

It was a Thursday afternoon in early February and only Helen and Pearl were in the office, Dorothy having gone home early because she was worried about her mother. Helen was making a list of unpaid invoices when she looked up and saw Pearl staring at her.

'Is everything all right?' Helen asked.

'Do you like working here?' said Pearl.

'Yes, I do. I'm really grateful that you gave me the job. Are you going to tell me Rita's coming back to work?'

'No, she's still not right. You'll be here a bit longer.' She smiled. 'Do you remember, Mr Fenner told you that there'd be some overtime?'

'Yes, something to do with entertaining clients?'

'Hmm, that's it. Well, he has something arranged for tomorrow night. Would you be able to help out?'

'Yes... I could. Is it here in the showroom?'

Pearl laughed. 'No, it's in a hotel. Mr Fenner organises supper evenings for gentlemen.'

'So, what would I be doing?'

'Mostly waitressing – handing out drinks and serving the buffet. Could you manage that?'

'I think so – as long as I can leave to catch the last bus home.'

'Oh, we'll see you get home safe, don't worry. Well, that's settled then. Now, you'll need to look your best, let's go and see if we can find a nice dress for you to wear. There'll be something on the returns rail in the packing room. The retailers often send garments back if they have a flaw, like a seam undone or a missing button, but we can sort that.'

They went downstairs to the basement room and Pearl went straight to the rail and pulled out a striking, cerise cocktail dress and held it up. 'I love this,' she said. 'It's absolutely perfect for your colouring. The hem's come down at the back, but that's easily fixed. What do you think?'

Helen thought it was beautiful, she could imagine the sort of woman who would wear it, someone with poise and plenty of money. 'It's lovely, but I don't think I could wear it, it's not a dress for a waitress, is it?'

'Maybe not, but Mr Fenner likes to show off his stock. Who knows, one of the clients might be taken with it and put in an order. Come on, let's see what it looks like on.'

In the dressing room, Helen stepped into the dress and Pearl edged the garment up over her hips and on to her shoulders – it was a close fit. When the zip was pulled up Helen turned to the mirror. It clung to her curves and the structured bodice gave her a cleavage she didn't know she had.

'Oh, my goodness.' She turned to Pearl. 'I can't wear this.'

'Course you can. You wore similar dresses when you modelled for us.'

'I know, but this is different. I'm going out in it, like it's my dress and... and what will people think?'

Pearl laughed. 'Helen, there are women who go out dressed like this every evening in the city. You'll see them at the theatre, in restaurants and dinner dances. This is how wealthy women dress and you're getting a chance to experience that.'

'Well, I suppose no one on the bus will see it under my coat.'

Pearl shook her head and smiled.

Helen had never been in a hotel before. She had no idea what to expect, or how to behave. The doorman tipped his hat and called out, 'Good evening, ladies,' as they came through the doors of the Grosvenor Hotel on Deansgate. How grand it seemed with a sweeping, red-carpeted staircase, huge vases of fresh flowers, glittering lights. There were members of staff smartly dressed in maroon uniforms with silver buttons; some behind the long desk helping guests, others carrying luggage in and out. A woman rushed past her in what was surely a mink coat. A group of army officers were laughing and talking loudly. She could hardly take it in.

Pearl took her arm. 'Come on, we're going up to the Connaught Suite.'

'What's that?'

'It's a private function room,' but Helen didn't understand that either.

The suite was empty except for half a dozen girls lounging on sofas. There was an excited scream as she came in and Helen was amazed to see Anna rushing towards her. 'I can't believe it's you. I didn't know you did this sort of thing.'

'I don't and I'm a bit worried. I've never been a waitress before,' said Helen. 'You'll have to keep an eye on me in case I get something wrong.'

Anna looked puzzled for a moment then said, 'All right, I'll do that.'

Pearl clapped her hands. 'Now listen, girls, the gentlemen will have finished dinner in the dining room and they'll be here shortly. Remember to keep glasses topped up and later, when supper arrives, take the sandwiches round the room. If a gentleman asks you to sit with him at the card tables or on the sofas, that's allowed, and so is dancing later in the evening. I'll give you your wages now so you are free to leave any time after ten o'clock.'

Helen was surprised when Pearl gave her two pounds.

'Why have you given me all this money?'

'Mr Fenner likes these evenings to go well and he likes to see the girls happy. No long faces allowed.'

'Pearl, I'm not sure about this. What was all that about sitting with the men? That's not waitressing.'

'Don't worry, Helen, you don't have to sit with them if you don't want to. Just tell them you're busy taking round the drinks, and give them a nice smile when you say it. Now go and hang up your coat and put on a bit more lipstick.'

Mr Fenner arrived shortly afterwards with the rest of the guests, fifteen in total, all in dinner suits and dickie bows. Helen felt nervous and uncomfortable in the low-cut cerise dress carrying a tray of drinks. She thought of leaving, but she didn't want to let Pearl down. Then there was the two pounds she'd accepted. No, she'd have to stick it out until ten o'clock. Some men went straight to the card tables, including Mr Fenner, and she was surprised to see Pearl at his side, her hand resting on his shoulder. Others stood about talking business. She began to relax a little and remembered to smile. An older man asked her if there was any single malt whisky. She had no idea and said she would ask one of the other girls but, as she walked away, he followed her and put his hand round her waist. She was surprised but didn't say anything. She was also surprised that the girl at the drinks table was sipping a glass of champagne. 'This gentleman would like a single malt whisky, can you help?' asked Helen, and without another word she slipped out of his arm and walked away.

As the evening went on, the men became raucous and she noticed that a few of the girls were relaxing with them on the sofas. Pearl mingled with the guests and every now and again Helen heard her deep-throated laugh. The supper arrived and Pearl asked Helen to take the plates of roast beef sandwiches to the men and then serve coffee. Someone had put on a record, a slow song, 'Blue Moon', and now the girls were dancing with the men.

Helen tried not to look any of them in the eye in case they wanted her to dance or join them on a sofa. She busied herself collecting plates and empty glasses for a while then stood near the door watching couples smooching to the music and wondering what the time was.

'You look as fed up as I am.'

Helen turned to see a man smiling at her; she recognised him as one of the card players, younger and slimmer than the other men. 'I'm weighing up whether anyone would miss me if I sneaked out,' she said.

'You don't want to dance or drink champagne?'

'No, I don't think so. Anyway, I'm just a waitress.'

'A very well-dressed waitress, I must say.'

Helen blushed. 'It's the uniform they gave me. Anyway, why aren't you enjoying yourself, all the other men are?'

'I thought it would be a serious card game, but they're more interested in the girls. To be honest, I'm trying to sneak out too. What do you think? Should we just go and leave them to it?'

'What time is it?' asked Helen.

'Almost ten.'

'Right, I'm going.' She grabbed her coat from the rail and was out the door in seconds.

'Hey! Wait for me.' He came running after her, putting on his overcoat. 'Where are you going?'

'Home, of course.'

He went with her down the stairs and as they crossed the foyer, he touched her arm. 'Would you like to have a nightcap in the bar?'

'No, I need to catch the last bus.'

He looked disappointed. 'I'll take you home, my car's just outside.'

'I'm not getting in a car with you, I don't even know you.'

'All right then, I'll walk you to your stop,' and he fell into step beside her.

'You don't need to. I'll be fine.'

'No, please, I'd like to see you safe on the bus.'

'I'll be safe enough, don't worry.'

'Even so, I would feel better if you'd just let me walk with you.'

Helen shrugged her shoulders.

They crossed Deansgate and he talked about the

bomb damage to the cathedral as they walked. Then he asked, 'Do you go to the supper club often?'

'No, it's the first time I've been. Mr Fenner's my boss and he offered me some overtime, but I...'

He finished her sentence. '...won't be going again?'

'Probably not, even though I could do with the money. What about you?'

'No, I'm all right for money, thanks.'

'That wasn't what I meant.'

'I know.' She could hear the smile in his voice. 'An acquaintance invited me to play cards, but like I said, they were all half-hearted about it. I'm not in the rag trade either, so I didn't have anything in common with most of the people there.'

'And what about the girls?' As soon as the words left her mouth, she was embarrassed.

But he only laughed. 'Didn't have anything in common with them either. Maybe I shouldn't say this, but I don't think you belonged there. I watched you observing everything that went on, like an outsider. Oh, sometimes you smiled, but I could see your heart wasn't in it and the sadness would return to your face.'

She sensed the concern in his voice. Did he think she would explain why she was sad? Her grief was locked up inside her and she would never dream of sharing it with a stranger.

'And what do you do at Fenner's?' he asked.

'I work in the office, but I probably won't be there

much longer,' and she explained about Rita being caught up in the bombing and unable to work.

'Such a terrible business that was at Christmas, and there's no end to it. The Luftwaffe will be back again soon.'

They came into Stevenson's Square where her bus was waiting. 'I didn't ask you your name,' he said.

'Why would you want to know my name? You've spent less than twenty minutes in my company and you won't be seeing me again.'

'Well, who knows?' He held out his hand. 'My name's Laurence Fitzpatrick.'

She shook his hand. 'Nice to meet you.'

The engine revved up and the conductor shouted, 'Are you gettin' on or not?'

She hopped on the platform. Laurence tipped his hat as the bus pulled away and, for no reason she could think of, she called out, 'My name's Helen,' but by that time, he had been swallowed up by the darkness.

When she arrived in the office the following morning, Pearl was already at her desk. She looked up and smiled. 'You left early last night.'

'I left at ten o'clock; you said we could.'

'Yes, nothing wrong with that.' She raised an eyebrow. 'I just wondered if you had anything else to tell me.'

'What do you mean?'

'Well, I thought maybe you left with that good-looking young man. What was his name, Laurence somebody?'

Helen didn't like the knowing look on Pearl's face. 'What are you saying?'

'Only that you might've, you know, had a drink with him in the bar or maybe he gave you a lift home.'

Helen felt the flush cover her face as though she'd been caught out. But nothing had happened. She'd only walked to the bus and it was him who insisted on accompanying her.

She had been uneasy the whole evening, seeing the men so overfamiliar with the girls. How could she have been so naive: the dancing; the stray hands; the amount of champagne? Is that what was happening? And those girls with the men would... No, she wouldn't think about it, but the anger was bubbling up inside her. 'You thought I would go off with some man, not six weeks since my husband was killed!'

Pearl went to her as if she would hug her, but Helen stepped back. 'Oh, Helen, I'm sorry. I didn't mean that... I just thought...'

'Well, you thought wrong. He insisted on walking me to the bus stop, that's all. But those girls, is that what they do... go off with men?'

'I won't lie to you, Helen, some of them do, but that's up to them. As far as I'm concerned, they're waitresses. Just like you were a waitress and when your shift was finished you went home.'

Helen weighed up Pearl's words. It was true that she had left when she wanted to and she wasn't asked to sit with the men or dance with them. 'That's all very well,' she said, 'but how could you think I would be interested in another man?'

'Oh, Helen, I didn't really. It's just that sometimes women on their own get lonely and there's nothing wrong with having an innocent conversation with a man. Can't you see that?'

Maybe that was true, but Helen had learned her lesson: people could easily get hold of the wrong end of the stick.

Chapter 8

Dorothy covered her hair with her paisley headscarf and tied it under her chin. 'I hope we get a good view,' she said. 'I promised Mam I'd tell her all about it when I get home.'

Pearl pulled on a leather glove and carefully smoothed down each finger, then repeated the action on the other hand. 'They say she has a beautiful complexion. I wonder what she'll be wearing? It's a pity she can't pop over to Fenner's Fashions, we'd have her looking far more glamorous than anything Norman Hartnell put on her back. Now, are you sure you don't want to come, Helen? It's not every day you get the chance to see a king and queen.'

'No, I'll stay here and hold the fort, maybe catch up on the filing.'

'Well, you're not entirely on your own, Mr Fenner is in his office. Right then, ladies, off we go and remember, if she speaks to you, don't forget to curtsy.'

When they'd gone, Helen brewed up and took a cup of tea to Mr Fenner, but he was putting on his overcoat. 'Haven't time for that now,' he said, 'going to see a man about a dog.' More likely seeing a man about a stiff drink, she thought.

It felt odd to be the only person in the building, except for a couple of the men, packers, in the basement. She went back to the office, pushed her chair back, put her feet up on the desk and drank her tea. She would have liked to have seen the King and Queen, but she couldn't bear to go anywhere near the devastation in Piccadilly. The very thought of seeing those blackened skeletons of buildings with their gaping windows, and knowing that's where Jim had lost his life, made her feel sick.

A sound in the showroom made her sit up. There was someone out there. She went to the office door and there was a well-dressed woman with a fox fur across her shoulders, studying the mannequins. 'Hello, can I help you?' asked Helen.

The woman seemed startled, as though she hadn't expected to see anyone, and when she spoke it was in a rough Oldham accent. 'I were lookin' fer t'manager. I'm interested in seein' yer best stock.'

Helen wondered if she had just wandered in, thinking it was a shop. 'We're agents only,' she explained. 'We don't deal with the public.'

'I know that,' she snapped. 'I 'appen to be a shop

owner, high class modes only, and I'm interested in buying.' She cast her eyes round the showroom. 'Have you more stock I could see?'

Helen wasn't sure what to do. She had never dealt with retailers but, if this woman wanted to buy, then Mr Fenner would expect her to try and sell. 'Of course, would you like to come into the dressing room where we keep the samples?'

Helen began by showing her each item and explaining the cut and fabric, but the woman quickly tired of this and having glanced at maybe ten garments she cut Helen short. 'Yes, yes, these are all fine. Now, what if I wanted to buy these in bulk? Do you have them in stock or do you order them in?'

'No, we carry our own stock. We have a large basement for storage.'

'Is that so? Well, I think I'll be puttin' in a reet big order.'

'Do you want to do that now?' asked Helen.

'No, I'll be back in a few days with my business partner to discuss our requirements.' She sounded as though the words had been rehearsed. 'Anyroad, thanks fer your help,' and she walked away.

Helen called after her, 'Would you like to leave your name so I can tell Mr Fenner to expect you?' But the woman was already at the door.

She turned. 'Em… no, I don't think so,' and with a cheery, 'Ta-rah then,' she was gone.

*

Two days later Helen arrived at work to find the place in uproar. Mr Fenner was pacing about the showroom, his hands in the air. 'How in hell's name did they get in?'

Pearl spoke calmly, explaining what she knew. 'They came in through the basement. They used a hacksaw to cut through the metal grille and then crowbarred the door.'

He stopped and glared at her. 'How did they know the stock was in the basement? Nobody goes in there except people who work here.'

'Well, maybe they didn't know. They probably assumed that's where we stored everything.'

'Did they come in here?'

'No, the door was locked when I arrived.'

His eyes narrowed. 'They knew exactly where the stock was!'

Helen watched the scene play out between Pearl and Mr Fenner with ever-increasing panic. It was clear that there had been a robbery, but the sudden realisation that she might have inadvertently given away the fact that hundreds of pounds' worth of clothes were stored in the basement made her blood run cold.

Just then Pearl caught sight of Helen. 'Oh, thank goodness you're here, Helen. Will you run across to Newton Street police station and explain there's been a robbery and ask them to come over right away? Then see if you can find a locksmith and carpenter who'll come and make the basement secure.'

Mr Fenner was red in the face and bellowing, 'Talk about shutting the stable door when the horse has bolted. Don't you see, I'm ruined!' and he marched off to his office shouting, 'The whole bloody lot gone down the Swannee!'

Pearl watched him go and, after a moment's hesitation, she followed him.

Helen was glad to get out of the building and away from Mr Fenner, but how long would it take him to realise what she'd done? At the station she reported the theft and the constable gave her directions to the locksmith. On her way back she could feel the panic rising inside her; the police might even arrest her. No, she told herself, she simply had to tell the truth. Back at her desk she frantically tried to remember everything that had passed between her and the woman from Oldham. How odd it was that she happened to arrive when the building was almost deserted with everyone out watching the visit of the King and Queen. Her lack of interest in the clothes seemed strange too, given that she owned a dress shop, and why would she ask if the clothes would have to be ordered from elsewhere?

Worst of all, her own words kept coming back to her: 'No, we carry our own stock. We have a large basement for storage.'

It was all her fault. She'd told the woman exactly where to find the stock. She felt like running away and never coming back, but that would be dishonest…

'Helen, what's the matter?' Pearl was standing in the doorway.

'Oh, I'm so sorry,' she cried. 'I didn't mean to…'

'What are you saying, Helen, tell me?'

She could hardly get the words out.

'Is it about the robbery?'

Helen nodded.

'Then calm down, don't be afraid, just tell me what you know.'

Helen felt better for having explained what happened, especially as Pearl was adamant that she would have done the same thing under the circumstances. 'The woman was a customer and you did what was expected of you. You showed her the samples and answered her question about the stock. Like you, I would have assumed that she wanted to know whether we actually had the garments in stock or whether there would be a delay if they had to be ordered from the manufacturers.'

'But what will Mr Fenner say?'

'Oh, you just leave Mr Fenner to me.'

There was a knock on the office door and a tall man in a mackintosh came in. 'Hello, I'm Detective Constable Ken Kershaw. Someone reported a robbery.'

'Yes, yes,' said Pearl. 'Thanks for coming. Please sit down.'

He glanced at Helen and took a notebook from his inside pocket then turned his attention to Pearl. 'Would you be able to give me the details of what was stolen and the value, then I'll take a look at the basement. I understand that's how they got in.'

Pearl provided the information and he gave a low whistle when he heard the value. 'All that money for frocks?' he said.

She bristled. 'Not any old frocks. We only sell high class merchandise.'

'Have you any idea who might have been involved?' he asked.

'I don't, but my colleague here,' she indicated Helen, 'might be able to throw some light on who was responsible.'

He looked again at Helen and frowned. 'I know you, don't I?'

She had recognised him as soon as he came in – the deep voice, the half-smile. It was Police Constable A333, in civvies. 'You helped me—'

'Yes, I remember. How are you?'

'All right, I suppose.' She didn't want to get involved in a conversation about that terrible day in Piccadilly Gardens.

'Well, it's nice to see you again,' he said and there was kindness in his voice.

'Look, why don't I leave you two here,' said Pearl, 'and Helen can explain what happened in the showroom two days ago. In the meantime, I'll tell Mr Fenner, the owner, that you're here. I'm sure he'll want to speak to you.'

When Pearl had gone, Helen said, 'You're not in uniform now.'

'No, I transferred to CID a week after that day we met in Piccadilly. I'm based in Newton Street now.'

'That's good,' she said and stared at her hands clasped in her lap.

He shifted in his seat. 'I worried about you for weeks after that day.'

She was going to say that he shouldn't have bothered, but that seemed ungrateful and, in a way, she was glad he had thought of her. 'Thank you,' she said. 'I'm sorry I didn't wait for you that day. I just wanted to get away from the fire station.'

The silence stretched between them: a door slammed somewhere; a telephone rang…

He cleared his throat and when he spoke he was a policeman again. 'Now, in your own time, tell me what happened two days ago.'

While she spoke, he jotted down notes. 'There was only me in the showroom and a few packers in the basement; everyone else had gone out to see the King and Queen. A woman came into the showroom, said she was interested in placing an order…'

He didn't interrupt her but, when she came to the point where the woman asked about the stock, Helen's voice wavered. 'I told her… it was in the basement… so it's my fault really and now Mr Fenner says he's ruined.'

'Helen, you can't blame yourself for that. You

couldn't have known she wasn't a genuine customer.'

'But that's just it,' said Helen. 'I thought there was something odd about her.'

'In what way?'

'I'm not sure.'

'Can you describe her?'

'Oh yes,' said Helen and she gave a detailed description of her clothes, her hair and make-up. 'She had a beauty spot, here.' She touched her cheekbone. 'And she was from Oldham.'

'How do you know that?'

'I grew up next door to a woman from Oldham and she sounded just like her.'

'Well, that's certainly something to go on. If she's got form, I mean, if she's been in trouble with the police before, we might be able to find her. I'll contact Oldham police – maybe you could have a look at their photographic records. Would you do that?'

'I'd do anything to get the garments back.'

He looked pleased. 'Good, you've been very helpful, Helen. I'll be in touch if I need you.' He shook her hand. 'Now, I'd better speak to the owner before I take a look at—'

At that moment the office door flew open and in came Mr Fenner, followed by Pearl. 'This is all your fault!' He poked a finger at Helen. 'Letting a thief in here and showing them everything worth stealing.'

'Excuse me, sir. This young woman has actually

given us information that might help track down the thieves.'

'Who the hell are you?'

'Detective Constable Kershaw, I'm here to investigate the robbery.' He pointed to the door. 'Perhaps we could go to your office. I have a few questions to ask you.'

Mr Fenner glared at Helen and marched back to his office. DC Kershaw followed him, but not before he gave Helen a wink.

Chapter 9

The Ford Prefect pulled up outside the entrance of a grimy stone building and DC Kershaw turned off the engine. 'Well, this is it, Oldham police station. Are you still all right to do this?'

Helen felt a rush of nerves, but she was determined to help catch the thieves. 'Yes, I can do it, DC Kershaw.'

'Why don't you call me Ken, it's less of a mouthful.'

They signed in at the desk and waited for a detective to come and collect them. Helen studied a colourful poster showing fields and cows with a farmer telling a Land Girl, 'We could do with thousands more like you.' It looked like a good way to get through a war; out in the fresh air and away from the bombings.

The detective arrived, an older man in a tweed suit with a pipe clamped between his teeth; behind him was a policewoman. 'I'm DC Bert Holt,' he said, 'and this is Police Woman Parker.' He looked Helen in the eye and said sharply, 'Did you get a good look at the woman?'

'Yes, sir, I think I would recognise her again.'

He nodded. 'Right, you go along with Parker. She'll stay with you while you look at the photographs.' He turned to DC Kershaw. 'I've a few wanted posters upstairs of black-market villains that we think are rustling sheep up on the moors and selling the meat in Manchester. Do you want to take a look at them?'

The policewoman led Helen down a badly lit corridor and into a small windowless room where there were two chairs and a table with what looked like ledgers stacked on it. She gave Helen a piece of paper and a pencil and said, 'Take your time and study each photograph. They're all numbered so you can jot down the ones you think might be the woman, then you can go back and look at them again before you decide.'

An hour passed and Helen had looked through four ledgers, but there was no one who looked anything like the woman who came into the showroom. She had such high hopes that she'd find her, but now it seemed like looking for a needle in a haystack. She rubbed her eyes and reached for another ledger. 'I'm beginning to think we won't find her,' she said.

WPC Parker smiled. 'I know it's not easy. What would you say to a brew and a break – come back to it fresh?'

They drank their tea and Helen asked Parker how she came to be a policewoman. 'My dad was in the police, my granddad too. It was all I ever wanted to do, but it was really hard to get into. There aren't many of us even now and, with the war on, there's been so much more for us to do.'

'Is it dangerous?' Helen asked.

Parker shrugged her shoulders. 'It can be. I've been kicked and thumped a few times and being sworn at is par for the course, but policewomen mostly deal with women and children.'

'Why, are lots of women and children criminals?'

'Some are, like the woman you're looking for, but more often than not they're the victims of crime or neglect and at the mercy of drunken or violent men. Then there's the people who've been bombed out of their homes with nothing more than what they stood up in. Evacuees coming and going, maybe falling in with a bad crowd, and then there are the women on the streets…' She smiled. 'I'm sorry, you probably don't want to know all that.'

'It sounds terrible,' said Helen. 'I had no idea things like that went on. Do you not get upset by it all?'

'Yes, sometimes, but you just have to deal with it and there are good moments as well. It's just a pity that more women don't join. Then there's the Women's Auxiliary Police Corps. Have you heard of them?'

Helen shook her head.

'It was set up at the start of the war to support the service. They don't have the powers that policewomen have so they do a lot of non-criminal work in the force, especially helping women and their families. I was out on patrol with a WAPC, that's what we call them, on Saturday night when we found a girl not much more than eight or nine years old, standing outside a public house. Turns out the father's inside and he's got her begging for the money to buy his drink.'

'What did you do?'

'We went into the pub and told him we were taking the girl home. He wasn't best pleased, but I warned him if he did that again he'd be charged with neglect. Anything could have happened to her. The mother was at home with three little ones. They looked half-starved and it was freezing in the house. I warned her too, but I doubt she could do anything about the husband. I went to the local church, the vicar's very good, and he said he'd visit with some home comforts and he'd keep an eye on them.'

Helen had seen children begging before and sometimes she'd toss them a penny or two, but she had never given much thought about the child's life beyond the corner or doorway where they begged. Growing up, she'd always had enough to eat, clean clothes, a cosy fire, and she felt very uncomfortable thinking about that little girl outside the pub.

Into the fifth ledger and she hadn't got far when she stopped, leaned forward, and looked closely at the photograph. And there she was, the woman she had spoken to in the showroom, right down to the beauty spot on her cheek. 'I've found her!' she shouted.

Everything happened quickly after that. The woman's name was Thelma Evans and DC Holt had had dealings with her and her brothers before. 'Petty thieves mostly,' he said. 'I would've thought stealing posh clothes would be out of their league.' He turned to Helen. 'Now, miss, that's the easy bit over. Our next step would be to organise an identity parade and bring her in to see if you're quite so certain it's her when you come face to face with her.'

'An identity parade?'

Ken explained. 'We'll line up similar-looking women and she'll be there too, of course. If you're sure you see her in the line, just touch her shoulder.'

'And that's it? You'll arrest her?'

'It depends whether we find other evidence linking her to the clothes. If we do, you might be needed to give evidence if there's a trial.'

Helen didn't hesitate. 'I'll do anything to get the clothes back.'

'Right,' said DC Holt. 'Let's bring her in and get her in the line. Parker, you round up the women to stand alongside her.'

'Yes, sir, I'll nip over to the town hall and ask for volunteers.'

While the Oldham constabulary went about their business, Ken suggested to Helen that they should go and have something to eat. He'd noticed a UCP shop just down the street from the station. 'If I'm not mistaken there'll be a café in there.'

Helen had oxtail soup with a slice of bread while Ken tucked into a plate of tripe with vinegar and onions. 'Nearly as good as my missus makes.'

'Do you think there's any chance they'll get the stock back?'

'Well, you seeing the woman in the showroom was a good lead and we acted quickly. Now we know who she is and where she lives, her house will be searched when they pick her up and maybe the stolen goods might be there.'

'I'll be sacked if we don't get them back.'

'Maybe not. When I spoke to Mr Fenner in his office, I told him that you are a credible witness and the best chance he's got to get his stock back.'

'I doubt Mr Fenner will think that.'

'It's not your fault, Helen. It's the thieves who are to blame, so don't worry about that now, just focus on the identity parade. Are you worried about it?'

'I'm a bit nervous. What if she says something to me or denies being anywhere near the showroom?'

'Ignore her. There'll be police officers in the room to deal with her, so don't worry.' He smiled. 'Tell you what, do you fancy some rice pudding before you face the thief?'

Back at the station DC Holt explained that a box full of new clothes, bearing the Fenner labels, had been found in the loft of the woman's house. 'Nowhere near what was stolen. She said someone left them on her doorstep, but we think she kept them back for herself. So now we need to find her brothers to get the rest of their haul, before they pass it on to some black-market spiv. In the meantime, if you can identify her that'll be enough to charge her.'

Helen was so disappointed. The stock could be anywhere by now, leaving Mr Fenner ruined and everyone out of a job. Ken touched her arm. 'Are you up to this?'

Of course she was. She wouldn't let them get away with it. 'Yes, I am, let's do it.'

Helen followed DC Holt into the room to stand in front of the women lined up and WPC Parker joined them. She was pleased to see that Ken had slipped into the room to stand at the back. Her heart skipped a beat at the sight of the women lined up – she had already spotted the thief.

DC Holt explained the procedure then asked her to walk the length of the line to see if there was anyone she recognised. 'Take your time,' he said.

She walked slowly, looking into each face. The woman was towards the end of the line and Helen felt herself shaking as she approached her. She stopped and looked her straight in the face: the pencilled eyebrows; upturned nose; high cheekbones; the beauty spot. The woman stared right back, a look of contempt on her face. On to the end of the line, and Helen turned around, walked straight to the woman and stood in front of her again. There was no doubt. She touched the woman's shoulder.

What happened next was a blur – a scream in her face, a smack on the side of her head then someone hurrying her away, but not before she caught sight of the woman on the floor pinned down by Ken.

Parker had taken her into a room across the way. 'Are you hurt, Helen?' she asked.

'No, I'm fine, don't worry. She just caught me off guard.'

'Caught us all off guard. I've not seen a woman do that before. But now she's on a common assault charge as well.'

Ken rushed in. 'Are you all right, Helen? I'm sorry that happened.'

'Don't make a fuss,' she told him. 'We've got her now – let's hope the brothers are next.'

It was almost four o'clock when Helen had finished her full statement and signed the declaration that she had recognised Thelma Evans as the woman who had come to Fenner's showroom prior to the theft. She and Ken said goodbye to DC Holt and WPC Parker and were about to leave for Manchester when two rough-looking characters were brought into the station under arrest.

'Well, if it isn't Bill and Alfie Evans,' said DC Holt. 'Come to join your sister, have you?' He turned to one of the constables. 'Where did you find them?'

'In a lock-up behind Tommyfield Market; one of the traders tipped us off, and that's not all. There wasn't just these two, there was someone else – a dead ringer for one of those spivs on your wanted posters. He was sitting in a van, engine running, while the Evans brothers were loading it up. He ran off as soon as he saw us. We'll go back to the market with the poster, see if we can't track him down.'

'And the stolen goods?'

'Can't be sure it's all of it, but there's a lot of boxes.'

Helen gasped. 'You've got our stock back? I can't believe it!' She turned to Ken. 'Can we take them with us? Mr Fenner will be so pleased.'

'That might be difficult, right now,' said Ken. 'There's paperwork to be done and they'll have to establish who they belong to.'

'But they've got Fenner's labels on them.'

'I know that, but there are procedures. You will get them back, Helen, but not today.'

On the journey back to Manchester they talked about the events of the day. 'It was really good how they had all those photos of criminals,' said Helen, 'and when I recognised the woman, all they had to do was go to her house.'

'Whoa!' said Ken. 'We got lucky today – normally it takes much longer and sometimes we never catch them at all.'

'But isn't it great when you find the person who

committed the crime? You've stopped them in their tracks and ordinary people are safer and less likely to have their property stolen.'

Ken looked at her and smiled. 'Yes, when you put it like that, it is great.'

Helen smiled back. 'Thanks for everything you've done.'

'It's just my job,' he said.

'But it's a hard job, isn't it? You must be very brave.'

'I wouldn't say that. Most of the time you can avoid getting into difficult situations.'

'But you didn't hesitate when that woman attacked me.'

'No, I didn't. It's my job to protect people. Anyway, what about you? You didn't panic when she lashed out at you.'

'I didn't have the time to panic before Parker grabbed me and got me out.' She thought for a moment. 'Can I ask you something?'

'Fire away.'

'What made you join the police?'

He laughed. 'I needed a job and I'm very tall.'

'No really, tell me.'

He took a deep breath and released it. 'I think it began with wanting to be part of something important. Maybe "important" isn't the right word. I wanted to make a difference. I served my time as a motor mechanic, but every day was the same. I'd go to work, fiddle about with engines, get covered in grease and go to the pub. I wanted...' He shook his head. 'I don't know, maybe I needed every day to be different and challenging.'

'And you wanted to help people?'

'It might sound strange, but that came later. There was so much to take in at first, but after a while I began to see how important the job was; it felt good to lock up villains and to be a part of keeping the streets safe.'

'I was talking to WPC Parker and she was telling me about the Women's Auxiliary Police Corps. Do you know about it?'

'I do. There are a few knocking about, mostly in Bootle Street at Headquarters.'

'I was thinking I might like to do something like that.'

Ken gave her a sideways look. 'But you've got a job in the showroom.'

'I'm only filling in, covering for a girl who was injured in the bombing at Christmas. She'll be back soon. I've been thinking about my Jim too. I asked him once about being a fireman and he said, "At the end of every day you can hold your head up – it might have been a terrible day, but you know you've tried to help people and that's the best feeling in the world."'

'He was right. The emergency services deal with difficult problems, but sometimes we get to solve them.'

'I just wonder if I would be strong enough or brave enough.'

'I'll not lie to you, Helen, dealing with tragedy and

violence isn't easy and I have to say that, before today, I would have described you as a gentle character. But today I saw a different side to you. You hardly flinched when the woman attacked you. You held your nerve and that takes some courage. Is that enough? I'm not sure. Why don't you call into Bootle Street nick; they'll tell you more about it.'

'I might just do that.'

Ken dropped her off outside Fenner's showroom. She raced up the stairs and burst through the door. 'They've caught the thieves!' she shouted, but there was Mr Fenner with a face like thunder standing over Pearl who hastily wiped her eyes with a handkerchief.

He whipped round. 'What did you say?'

'I identified the woman and the police arrested her and her two brothers.'

'Have they indeed? So, the stock has been recovered?' He looked over her shoulder as if he expected it to be sitting in the showroom.

'No, Mr Fenner, it's in Oldham police station. They have to keep it as evidence until—'

He threw his hands in the air. 'God save me from idiots!'

Pearl spoke up. 'Please don't shout at Helen, Mr Fenner; after all, she was the one who gave the description of the woman to the police. If it wasn't for her, the stock would be long gone.'

'Are you forgetting it's her fault the thieves knew

exactly where to find it in the first place? In fact, it makes me wonder if this whole affair isn't an inside job.'

Pearl opened her mouth to protest, but Helen beat her to it. She looked him in the eye and spoke calmly. 'That's not fair. I was the only person left in the showroom that afternoon and, when a client came in, I did exactly what Pearl or yourself would have done; I showed her the garments and answered her questions. I had no way of knowing what she was up to and you wouldn't have either.' For a moment she thought he was going to explode, but she didn't blink. He turned to Pearl and stabbed a finger at her. 'I want that stock back by the end of the week or heads will roll!' and without another glance at Helen he marched out of the office.

It was almost dark by the time Helen got off the bus at All Saint's church, but luckily the Co-op was still open for her to pick up some milk and bread. She had just let herself into the house and drawn the blackout curtains in the kitchen, when there was a knock on the front door. It was Ada. 'I've a message for you,' she said. 'Can I come in?' Helen hesitated. She didn't trust Ada one bit, but she could hardly say no to her.

'All right, come through to the kitchen.'

Ada looked so smug that Helen felt like smacking

her, but instead she asked, 'So, what's the message then?'

Instead of answering, Ada cast her eyes round the kitchen. 'I see you've tried to make it a bit more cosy in here.'

Helen wasn't in the mood for Ada's slights. 'What's the message?'

'Well... a man was knocking at your door this afternoon – a good-lookin' fella. It was lucky I was just coming out to go to the shop and I told him you were at work. Least, I think that's where you were.'

'Ada, just tell me what the message is.'

'He said his name was Frank and he was a friend of yours.' She put the emphasis on the word 'friend'. 'He asked me to tell you that he'd call round later tonight after his shift.'

'Thanks for that. Now, I really need to make something to eat. I've had a long day.' But Ada didn't move.

'He told me that you're a widow... That weren't what you told me when you moved in.'

'Oh, for goodness' sake!' Helen couldn't keep her anger out of her voice. 'Yes, I am a widow, but I can't see what that has to do with you.'

'Maybe it's not my place to say this,' and Helen saw that smug look on her face again as though she'd got something over on her. 'I've noticed him before round your house.'

'So? He helps me.' Helen waved her hand at the

shelves and the table and chairs. 'He was my husband's friend.'

'Oh, that's all it is then?'

'I don't like what you're suggesting. I think you'd better go.'

Ada didn't move. 'And then, there's the gentleman who dropped you off in his car, very late at night that was.'

Helen shook her head in disbelief. Ada had been watching that night when Mr Fenner left her home after their tea at the Lyons' Corner House, but Pearl was also in the car. She was about to explain that he was her boss, but why should she and anyway it would make no difference to Ada.

'How dare you make insinuations like that.'

'Like what? I'm only sayin' what I saw and what some people might think.'

Helen took her by the arm and pushed her towards the door. 'You'd better get out of my house, right now.'

Ada shrugged her off. 'Don't be getting on your high horse. I know what I saw and, if you ask me, you're no better than you should be.'

Helen drew herself up to her full height, towering over her. 'Get out of my house!' Ada opened her mouth as if to argue, but one look at the anger in Helen's face and she backed off.

'Hmm, well don't expect me to take any more messages from your fancy men!'

As soon as Ada was over the threshold Helen slammed the door behind her. Back in the kitchen she slumped in the chair and wept. God, what a day, she thought. I don't know... attacked at the identity parade, then Mr Fenner's anger, followed by Ada's nasty accusations. But you got through this awful day, she told herself, and wiped away the tears. She had stood up to those people because they were wrong and she was right. What did Ken say? 'You kept your nerve, didn't flinch.' Well, she didn't know about that, but she did know that she wouldn't be a soft touch any longer.

She sat a while with her eyes closed, still in her coat because the room was bitterly cold. She should really light the fire and make something to eat, but she was exhausted. She must have dozed off and awoke with a start at a knock on the door.

'Who is it?' she shouted.

'A friend,' came the answer, and there was no mistaking the laugh that followed.

She opened the door. 'What the heck?'

'A present,' said Frank and he carried a large cardboard box into the kitchen and set it on the floor.

'What is it?' asked Helen.

'Hold on to the box while I lift it out.'

Helen gasped. 'Is that a—'

'A paraffin heater, yes, an old one. One of the lads was selling it. I cleaned it up, gave it a new wick and filled it with paraffin. It'll give off a lot of heat. What do you think?'

She reached for her handbag. 'It's great. How much did you pay for it?'

'I'll not take any money, Helen. This house is freezing; you can't live like this.'

'I know, it's just that sometimes I don't light a fire when I get home from work. I just go to bed.'

He shook his head. 'Well, now you can come home and light the heater. Have you had your tea?' Helen shook her head.

'I thought that might be the case,' and he reached inside his coat and took out something wrapped in newspaper. 'I brought these for us.'

She smiled. 'I thought I could smell chips and vinegar when you came in. Here, give it to me and I'll put them in the oven while I make a brew.'

Frank knelt down and got to work on lighting the heater and it wasn't long before the blue flame could be seen flickering in the window of the heater's chimney and, by the time the tea was brewed, the room was already warming up.

They ate the fish and chips out of the paper and Helen thought about mentioning Ada, but decided against it. She didn't want to repeat what she had said, it was too embarrassing. Instead, she told him about the identity parade.

'For God's sake, Helen, you could've been injured. I

don't think they should've asked you to face the woman and, not only that, she knows you're the one reported her.'

'Don't worry about me, it was fine.' She wondered about mentioning that she was thinking about joining the police. 'There was a policewoman who looked after me and she was telling me all about the Women's Auxiliary Police Corps. They're looking for women to join up.'

His eyes narrowed. 'It's a tough job, the police. Walking the streets, dealing with all sorts of characters. You're not thinking of joining them, are you?'

'I don't know... I'd like to do something worthwhile, helping people, you know?'

'It's no job for a woman, Helen, and Jim would tell you the same thing. You've no experience of the way people live, scum of the earth some of them.'

'But she said it was mostly helping women and children and the people bombed out of their homes.'

'Yes, but think it through – dead bodies, some of them unrecognisable, neglected children, abused women. You've got to understand that police work, like the fire service, is a miserable business. Take my word for it.'

'But you do it and Jim did it and he always said he never felt more alive than when the fire station bell rang and he was on his way to put out a fire.'

'You're right there, but I know one thing, he'd not be happy about you joining the police.'

Chapter 10

'Hello, ladies,' DC Kershaw greeted them with a beaming smile. 'Guess what I've got for you?'

Helen jumped out of her chair. 'Have you got the clothes back?'

'Indeed, I have.'

Now Pearl and Dorothy were on their feet too. 'Where are they?'

'At the bottom of the stairs. I've a couple of constables taking them into the basement right now.'

'Mr Fenner will be so pleased,' said Pearl.

'He should be. We've recovered nearly all the stock and arrested the other man – trying to flog them on the market.'

'That's great news,' said Pearl. 'I'll go and tell him, and Dorothy you go down to the basement and do a quick inventory of the stolen goods.'

When they'd gone Helen thanked him. 'Ken, if it

hadn't been for you getting in touch with the Oldham police, this business could have gone to the wall and all these people would be out of work. Now, you've got our stock back, things will be easier, and I won't be the whipping boy any longer.'

'Has the boss been giving you a hard time?'

'Well, let's say I'm not his favourite employee. He only keeps me on because he doesn't want to be short-staffed. Anyway, Rita's coming back next week so I'll be getting my cards.'

'Then what are you going to do?'

'I'm not sure.'

'I thought you were going to find out about the WAPC.'

Helen pulled a face. 'I was, but everybody seems to think it's a bad idea. Like I wouldn't be up to it.'

'And you believed them?'

Helen looked away, embarrassed.

'Look at me, Helen.' She turned her head, saw the concern in his face. 'They haven't seen your strength of character, like I have. You're a curious mix. Yes, you're sympathetic and caring, but there's something steely about you. I saw it in your eyes when that woman attacked you. You're stronger than you think. Why don't you go to Bootle Street – there could be a job waiting for you, if you've the courage to take it?'

'I'll need to think about it a bit more.'

Ken smiled. 'I hope that—'

'Well, you two,' Pearl stood in the doorway. 'You've put a smile on Mr Fenner's face – for a while anyway. He says thank you and he's asked me to send a letter to the chief constable.' She held out her hand and Ken shook it.

'Well, you know where to find me, if you're in need of a bobby,' he said and with a nod to Helen he left.

When he'd gone, Pearl explained that Mr Fenner had decided, with Rita fit to come back to work, she would have to leave on Friday. 'I'm so sorry, Helen, I've been trying to convince him to keep you on. You've far more nous than Rita will ever have and then there's your modelling. We'd have our own model on the premises, but he wouldn't have it.'

'I'm not surprised. He never liked me.'

'It's not you, he's a miserable bugger. He's like that with everybody. But I've got a bit of good news. There's a supper club on Friday night and he wants you to come.'

'What? Pearl, I told you I didn't want to go there again.'

'I know, I know, but I was thinking you'd need the money to tide you over till you get a new job.'

'I'm not doing it, Pearl.'

'But Mr Fenner asked for you specially.'

Helen raised an eyebrow.

'He did. He even said he'd double your money as a bit of a bonus for all you've done.'

Helen hesitated. The extra money would buy her a bit of time while she decided what to do next.

'Go on, Helen, say you'll do it, please.'

And Helen saw again the same look in Pearl's eyes that day when Fenner had ranted at her about the theft of the stock. How on earth could she put up with him?

She sighed. 'All right, I'll do it this last time – for you – but I'm leaving at ten o'clock.'

Helen had never expected to be wearing the cerise cocktail dress again and, truth be told, she felt no more at ease in it than last time. At least now she knew what to expect and the four pounds made it worthwhile. The Grosvenor Hotel was still luxurious, but she wasn't overawed this time. The men still looked wealthy, well-fed and well-dressed, but that didn't make them decent people. Pearl delivered the same instructions to the girls, but this time she knew that some of them, at least, would be much more than waitresses. She didn't blame them – they had to make a living.

When the men arrived in the Connaught Suite, she was kept busy handing out drinks and avoiding their advances. There seemed to be more than last time and the card tables were busier. She looked for Laurence, but he wasn't there.

An hour or so later, the buffet arrived and Pearl asked Helen to take a tray to room sixteen, just along the corridor where a meeting was being held. Balancing the heavy tray with one hand, she managed to knock on the door. A man's voice shouted, 'Come in.' She had to put down the tray to open the door and by the time she had done so, the man was there in the doorway. He was tall and his dark hair was slicked back with brilliantine. She held out the tray expecting him to take it, but he had already turned his back. 'Come in,' he called over his shoulder. 'Just put it on the coffee table.'

Helen was surprised to find herself in a large room with two armchairs either side of an ornate fireplace. Across the room was a huge bed. Stranger still was that there was only the man on his own. Wasn't there supposed to be a meeting? She set the tray down and turned to go.

'Just a minute, you're Helen, aren't you?' He was standing with his back to the fireplace.

'Yes, sir.'

He was smiling, his teeth straight and white. 'I'm Charles Brownlow. You don't recognise me, do you?'

Helen was still wondering why she had been sent to this room. Had there been a mistake? She had no idea who he was.

But the man was still smiling and talking. 'Don't look so worried. Why should you recognise me? Will you sit down?'

'I can't, I'm needed at the supper club. Mr Fenner—'

'Oh, don't worry about Harold, he's an old friend of mine. You won't get into trouble. Please, sit down and I'll explain everything.'

He looked respectable but, more than that, he seemed important. There was something about the way he spoke that made her do as he asked.

'I saw you a few weeks ago,' he said, 'when you were modelling at Fenner's. I told Harold then that I thought you could go far. He didn't agree, but he knows nothing about that side of the business.' He paused and stared at her. 'Hmm… to be honest, Helen, I've thought about you a lot since then.'

She lowered her eyes. What did this man want with her? How could she interrupt him and tell him she had to go?

'The thing is, Helen, there's something about you: a vulnerability that draws the eye, a naivety. As a model you give the clothes an extra dimension on the catwalk.'

Helen heard the words, but she had no idea what they meant. Was he saying she was good at modelling? Is that why she was sent to this room? She stood up. 'I'm sorry, sir, I don't know why I'm here. I'd better get back.'

'Wait. There's a chance I could get you plenty of modelling work and who knows what that could lead to?'

She hesitated. Was he offering her a job?

He pressed on. 'Will you do something for me? Walk to the window and back again.'

She did what he asked. Then he told her to face away from him. 'Your shoulders need to come back a bit. Permit me to show you.'

And Helen gasped as he pressed a cold hand between her shoulder blades and another just below her throat and she felt her posture change. 'Now you're even taller, you see what I mean?' He withdrew his hands and placed them on either side of her neck. 'Your neck is one of your best features, but you must elongate it. Raise your chin, please, straighten your neck. Do you feel the difference?'

She couldn't nod, his hands were round her neck, but she whispered, 'Yes, I see. Please let me go.'

'In a moment, there's one last thing,' and he slid his hands from her neck down over her shoulders and on to the top of her arms. 'No, you mustn't tense up. Now, slowly lower your shoulders and breathe out.' Her eyes felt heavy, she sensed his head bowing towards her, felt his lips against her skin.

She pulled away from him, but his hands caught her round her waist and he turned her into his arms. 'I want to help you, Helen, wouldn't you like that?'

'Let me go, please.'

'But I'm offering you the chance to be a model and… so much more.'

He went to kiss her and she tried to push him away.

'But I thought…' He sounded confused. 'Harold said…'

She stopped. 'What did Mr Fenner say?'

'Only that you were a widow and you've lost your job…' The look of shock on Helen's face was enough for him to let go of her. 'I'm sorry, but I was led to believe that you and I might come to some arrangement.'

'Arrangement? What kind of arrangement?'

'I'll get you work as a model and...' He looked abashed. 'I could set you up in a house, where I would visit you. You'll want for nothing, I promise you. Just like Harold and Pearl.'

She could hardly take it in. Did such things go on? Bad enough that a complete stranger would proposition her, but even more unbelievable that Pearl and Mr Fenner... She shuddered at the thought. 'Get out of my way,' she shouted, but he didn't move.

'Helen, please, I'm terribly sorry. I was just so taken with you, I couldn't get you out of my mind these past weeks. My behaviour just now was unforgivable, I know, but please could we start again? You could get to know me and—'

'Oh, for goodness' sake!' She pushed past him and rushed out the door and down the corridor.

The nerve of the man. How dare he! But her real anger was directed at Fenner and Pearl. They'd deliberately sent her to that bedroom so he could... She stopped outside the supper club door – what did he say? 'I was led to believe that you and I might come to some arrangement.' It was Fenner and Pearl who had arranged the whole thing, giving her away like a side of beef. She'd get her coat and bag and leave right now – never mind staying to ten o'clock. The clothes rack was just inside the door and it took no more than a few seconds to collect her things. But when she turned around, Fenner was standing in front of her.

'Why aren't you in room sixteen?' he demanded.

She couldn't believe what he was saying. 'I'm not there because I'm not a prostitute even if you want to turn me into one.'

'Don't you get uppity with me, like butter wouldn't melt in your mouth.'

Helen was aware that the noise of conversation in the room had fallen away like a wireless when the volume was lowered. People were looking at her and there was Pearl coming towards her looking concerned.

She took Helen's arm. 'What is it? What's going on?' Her voice was low.

'You know what's going on. You and Mr Fenner sent me to room sixteen so that one of your supper club friends could take advantage of me.' The anger was rising in Helen's voice.

But those watching looked at her and smiled, some laughed and a man called out, 'Did you not fancy him, love? I've a room down the corridor too, I'd give you something to smile about.'

Helen cried out in frustration and pushed her way out the door.

Pearl caught up with her at the top of the stairs. 'Helen, listen, please.'

'Go away, I never want to see you again!'

Pearl ran in front of her and held up her hands. 'Wait, please, I need you to listen.'

'Oh, and what are you going to tell me? That I should forget about Jim and be somebody's mistress? I trusted you and now I know why you wanted to get me into this whole supper club thing. Dressing me up like some kind of doll and giving me to a man for his plaything.' She felt the tears ready to fall.

'I promise you, Helen, I had no idea that this would happen. I'm not a part of that. I wouldn't do that to you.'

'You sent me there!'

'I thought I was sending you with some sandwiches for a meeting, I swear it. It must have been Harold; he's thick as thieves with Charles.'

'I don't believe you. He wanted me to be his mistress. "Like Pearl," he said. Are you going to deny that too?'

She bowed her head. 'No, I'm not. I've been his mistress for twenty years.'

'And I suppose you think there's nothing wrong with that?'

Pearl looked her in the face. 'He's kept me from poverty. It's my decision and, believe me, I've had to take the rough with the smooth.'

Helen shook her head and walked away.

'Helen, please,' Pearl called after her. 'Don't hold this against me. It's not my fault.'

But Helen was already running down the stairs.

Chapter 11

Pearl was upset on the way back home from the supper club. As if the blackout wasn't bad enough, she had to endure both Harold's erratic driving, mounting the pavement several times, and his ranting.

'What kind of a girl is she, turning down one of this city's most successful businessmen? Not to mention she's made a bloody fool out of me. I wanted to get in with Charlie Brownlow; he's well connected, you know, and that piece of skirt has scuppered all that.'

Pearl said nothing. She knew it was a one-sided conversation. Better to let him vent his anger. He'd assume she agreed with him anyway.

Once inside her house he sprawled on the sofa: waistcoat unbuttoned, fat belly hanging over his flies while she undid his boots and set them to the side. 'Give that fire a poke and get me a stiff drink.' He lit his cigar, puffing and puffing until it glowed red and he began again. 'Who does she think she is anyway? I gave her a job and let her come to the supper club. She could have had any of those men there. Oh, I saw the way they looked at her, but I set her up for Charlie.' He blew several smoke rings towards the ceiling. 'Bitch!'

Again, Pearl held her tongue, but he wasn't having it. 'You're her bloody godmother. Why didn't you take her back to Charlie?' It was clear he wanted an answer this time.

'Because you can't make a woman—' She stopped. That was the trouble, women could be made to do what men told them, given that the alternative was worse. 'Harold, she only buried her husband a few months ago. She'd have been shocked at the man's advances. She didn't want to be his mistress.'

'It did you no harm.'

Before she could stop herself, a half-hearted laugh escaped her lips.

'What the hell are you laughing at?' He pushed himself out of the chair and lunged towards her. The fist caught her across her eyebrow.

'Don't, Harold, please. I'm sorry, I didn't mean anything by it.' She flinched as he lifted his hand again, but he thought better of it.

'Get out of my sight,' he yelled.

She didn't need to be told twice. She ran upstairs, her heart still thumping as she undressed, and slipped between the cold sheets. She was getting too old for this.

It hadn't always been so bad. He had been handsome once, a caring lover, and generous to a fault. She hadn't been working at Fenner's Fashions for very long when he began to take an interest in her. A few weeks after that, she was promoted out of the basement, where she packed the orders, into the office as a junior clerk. Soon after that, she was sleeping with him in various hotels around the city, when he could get away from his wife and family. He couldn't get enough of her then, so he bought the house and set her up as his mistress. He could come and go as he wanted. In those early years, they'd even nip out of work at lunchtime and drive to the house. He thought nobody knew, but she'd seen the look in their eyes and the sniggering when they came back. She brazened it out for a roof over her head and a comfortable life.

But there were regrets even then… the babies, two of them. He paid, of course, and she pretended to be grateful. It was a trade-off – he didn't want the little bastards, he said, and she didn't want to be out on the street. Even now she couldn't think of them without a tear – she wiped it away.

These last few years he'd grown tired of her. She'd seen the way he sniffed round some of the younger women at the supper club and she had no doubt that he'd bedded them in the same hotels where he'd courted her. Then there were the beatings. He'd hit her a couple of times over the years, but it was more frequent this past year. The trouble was they were locked together and the key was lost. She wanted to leave him, but she'd lose the house and her job. He wanted to be free of her, but he needed her to run the business.

Her mother's words came back to her: 'You've made your bed, now you'll have to lie in it.'

As if on cue, she heard his footsteps on the stairs and turned her back to the door as he came in. He fumbled about taking off his clothes and she felt the heavy weight of him on the mattress. The smell of whisky and stale smoke wafted over her as he turned her on her back. His hands were clumsy, but as usual he was impatient and climbed on top of her. She guided him, then let him spend himself. It was nothing to her.

Afterwards, he sat up in bed and complained about indigestion. She went to the kitchen for the Milk of Magnesia and gave him a dose.

'I've been thinking about that goddaughter of yours,' he said. 'Maybe Charlie was too eager. What I want you to do is to go and see her this weekend and talk her into going out with him, you know, to get to know him. Tell her he's a nice man – very wealthy – she could land on her feet there. All right?' he said.

'All right,' Pearl answered.

Satisfied, he turned on his side and was snoring within minutes. Pearl lay there seething. Who did he think he was, sending her to persuade Helen to become a kept woman? Anyway, it was clear that she wasn't as naive as people might have thought. She had guts too and could stand her ground. No, she wouldn't go to her house; Helen would still be angry at her. Instead, she'd write a letter explaining again that she'd had no idea about the plan for Charlie to proposition her and she would never have allowed it to happen if she'd known. She might even add that becoming a mistress was the worst decision of her life.

Chapter 12

Helen had no reason to get up early, now that she had no work to go to. Besides, she had hardly slept for the last few nights, what with the worry of finding a new job and her anger at Pearl thinking she would ever contemplate becoming some man's mistress. She was shocked, too, at learning Pearl was Fenner's mistress, although she had been suspicious about their relationship. She had thought Pearl was so kind when she got her the job at Fenner's, but looking back she could see the web of deception surrounding the sleazy supper club and how she'd been drawn in. She had been completely mistaken in thinking that Pearl was an ally and her mind was made up, she would have nothing more to do with her.

The thought of having to search again for work was daunting, but come Monday morning she woke up determined to have a job by the end of the week.

After all, this time she had some experience as a clerk. Men were being called up every day, surely there would be vacancies. She had also thought about joining the police, but then she recalled Frank's words. 'It's no job for a woman… and Jim would tell you the same thing.' He was probably right.

After breakfast she nipped out to the paper shop and bought the early edition of the *Manchester Evening News*. On her way back, Ada was outside her door gossiping to a neighbour and both women gave her a cold stare. Helen walked quickly by and up her path then stopped. There on her doorstep was a large bouquet of flowers.

Ada shouted over to her. 'A man left them, not five minutes ago. He were in a car.'

Helen ignored her and fumbled for her key. Ada persisted. 'I've been thinkin'. You're supposed to be a widow, but you had a man with you when you came to look at the house. Next thing you moved in – on your own – and since then you've not been short on fancy men, have you?'

'How dare you speak to me like that!'

'Listen, love, I'm a God-fearin' woman, with a child to bring up. I don't want to live next door to a—' She stopped herself, thought better of it. 'Anyroad, if it's a man, or men, payin' your rent, you'll be out on your ear when the landlord finds out.'

'I'll have you know I pay my own rent,' Helen

shouted and she picked up the flowers, opened the door and went quickly inside. She threw the flowers on the table and screamed in frustration. Her heart was racing at the accusations of that horrible woman. She'd really got it in for her and no doubt she'd been spreading the gossip. Come to think of it, the woman in the paper shop had given her a funny look. She sank into the chair and closed her eyes. 'Oh, Jim, help me please. I can't do this anymore,' and she let the tears slip down her face. She could have stopped them, wiped her eyes, told herself not to be silly, but instead she let the silent tears turn into sobs, then howls, and she wept until she was drained and her eyes closed.

The bouquet, all cellophane and red ribbons, full of its own importance, was still on the table when she woke up. It wasn't hard to guess who they were from, but she read the card anyway. *My dear Helen, forgive me, I'm a fool. Please let me make it up to you. Charles Brownlow.*

The nerve of the man! She went out the back door and threw them in the bin then paused. Ada had seen the man leaving flowers on her doorstep, but had she been nosy enough to read the card? Helen shrugged. She can think what she likes. This is my home, she told herself, and I'm not going to be pushed out of it by a spiteful gossip. She filled the kettle and had just struck a match to light the gas when the realisation hit her. Brownlow wanting to see her again was bad enough but – she let out a scream as the match burned her fingers – he knew where she lived.

She spent the next three hours writing letters applying for half a dozen jobs advertised in the paper. Then in the afternoon, she went into town to deliver them to the newspaper office where they would be sorted into the PO boxes to be collected later by the advertisers. It was a beautiful spring day and she wandered over to Albert Square to sit in the sunshine. True, there were sandbags piled high in front of the town hall, but the tubs of daffodils lifted her spirits.

She sat on a bench next to a young woman, not much older than herself, an empty pram beside her. It was a moment before she realised that, inside her coat, the woman was holding a baby to her breast. Helen looked quickly away, shocked to see such a thing in public.

'I'm so sorry,' the young woman said, pulling the coat closer to hide the child's head. 'I don't like to do this, but I've nowhere else to go and he's so hungry.'

'That's all right,' said Helen and she tried not to look at the suckling child.

'I come every day to the housing people in the town hall to see if they've got a house for me,' she explained. 'We were bombed out at Christmas. My husband's in the army and I was living with my granny. We lost everything and ever since then we've been staying with my parents and sister. It's only a back to back and we're so overcrowded. I was in a rest centre for a while, but it was no good with a baby. He was waking people up and he kept getting sick. I feel sorry for those people still living there.'

Helen had given very little thought about the people who had been bombed out of their homes. She had read about the rest centres in the paper, but she never imagined that people would still be there four months later. She felt really sorry for the mother and might even have taken her in, except that her front bedroom was damp and she didn't have a spare bed.

'They say I'll get a house soon, but till then I'll come every day to mither them. I won't give in.' She took the baby from her breast and handed him to Helen, while she buttoned her blouse and coat.

'He's lovely,' said Helen.

'Yes, he's my pride and joy.' She laid him in the pram and covered him with a blanket. 'The men are fighting this war for the kiddies like him, but if you ask me, the women are fighting it too and, God willing, we'll come out the other side, stronger than before.' And she smiled. 'Ta-rah then, love.'

Helen sat a while longer and thought about the mother and her child. It was true what she had said about the women – she had seen poverty and hardship every day when she served in the corner shop as women tried to eke out an existence. She'd had a sheltered upbringing; she knew that now. Jim's death had knocked her sideways but, somehow, she had just about coped. The chances were, she would get a junior clerk position and that would be it. She would settle into the life of a widow with only herself to think about. But how selfish and boring would that be?

Somewhere in the distance a bell was clanging.

She wanted to do something worthwhile. Why shouldn't she join the police? Hadn't Ken said the WAPC worked with women and children?

The bell grew louder.

She knew it would be hard seeing people in distress, but to be able to help them... There was a screech of brakes and she turned to see a fire engine racing across the square and, in the time it took for the sound of the bell to fade she had made up her mind.

Bootle Street was just around the corner and she stood in front of its impressive façade with the nerves tightening in her stomach. How can you join the police, when you haven't the nerve to go into the building? She chided herself and almost walked away, but in a sudden rush of bravado, she ran up the steps two at a time and pushed open the door. Inside, a desk and behind it a surprisingly old-looking policeman. She explained that she wanted to join the WAPC.

'Is that so?' he said, looking her up and down, then he told her to wait while he got someone to speak to her. The entrance hall was very grand with a marble floor and elegant wall lights, nothing like the other police stations she'd been in. She waited and waited, her courage seeping away. *What am I thinking of? I couldn't be part of this, I wouldn't know what to do.* Just then, a lad in a black uniform rushed in and almost collided with her. 'Sorry, missus.'

'Hold on a minute, it's Tommy, isn't it?'

His face lit up. 'Helen? I didn't think I'd ever see you again. They said you'd run away from your mam and the shop.'

'I just moved out, that's all, I've got my own house now. And what about you, in uniform?'

He stood tall. 'I'm workin' for the police – I'm an auxiliary messenger.'

'I didn't think you'd be old enough.'

'I were fourteen last month, joined up on my birthday. You have to have your own bike, you know. I've been all over deliverin' important messages: ARP posts; police stations; hospitals... Anyroad, what are you doin' here?'

'I'm thinking about joining the police, came in to ask if they're taking people on.'

'Oh, you should do it, Helen. It's smashing.'

There was a shout from behind them. The policeman had returned. 'Hey you, young whipper-snapper, you know you're not supposed to come through the main door. Away with you.'

Tommy bolted for the door. 'Sorry, sarge!' and Helen

called after him, 'Don't tell my mam you've seen me.'

'Are you the one wanting to join the WAPC?' Helen's heart skipped a beat and she turned to face a policewoman – middle aged, grey hair, stocky.

'Ah, yes, I heard about it and I was just wondering if… if you're taking people on?'

The woman seemed to scrutinise her. 'Sure, why would you want to join the police?' She sounded Irish.

The question threw her. Was it enough to say she wanted to help people? She took a deep breath and tried to explain. 'I know the war has been hard on women and their children. I've seen their bombed homes and their struggle to put food on the table.'

'We're not do-gooders doling out tea and butties, love.' The woman looked so severe. 'You'd be better off in the WRVS, they've a nicer uniform too.'

Helen felt like she'd been slapped in the face, but somehow that spurred her on. Why shouldn't she join the police? She wouldn't be put off that easily. 'A police-woman told me she found a child outside a pub. Her father was inside while she was begging for his beer money. She warned the man and took the child home. The mother was at her wits' end living hand to mouth, but the policewoman managed to get the local church involved and the vicar helped the family.'

The Irish woman didn't react to Helen's words and she could feel the anger rising inside her. She took a deep breath and calmed herself. 'I know there are women who get into trouble with the police, and I'm sure there are times...' Had she already said too much?

'Go on.'

'I'm sure some of those women must be frightened and having another woman there could calm them or speak to them with... you know, with some understanding.'

'What's your name?'

'Helen Harrison.'

She nodded. 'Wait here.'

Minutes later the woman returned. 'Here, take this – it's an application form for the WAPC. Talk to your family and think long and hard about whether you want to spend your working days with unsavoury characters and desperate people. We're having interviews on Wednesday, for police constables, but if you want to apply, fill in the form and be here at ten o'clock. We'll squeeze you in before they arrive. Ask for Sergeant Duffy, that's me.'

When she arrived home, there was a letter on the mat. She recognised Pearl's handwriting immediately. No doubt it was about Charles Brownlow and how she should count herself lucky that a wealthy man was interested in her. She'd been taken in with her kindness, all right, offering an office job but, in the end, she wanted to push her into becoming some man's mistress, just like herself. She put the letter unopened on the mantelpiece.

She boiled some potatoes and heated up the mince left over from yesterday and, when she had eaten and cleared the table, she took the WAPC application form from her bag.

The first page was for basic information: name, date of birth, address, previous employment and skills, then the medical questions. Overleaf, it asked for the name and address of someone who would give a reference. That might be a bit tricky, she thought. The rest of the page was blank, except for one sentence. 'Please explain why you think you would be suited to a role in the Women's Auxiliary Police Corps.' She sighed and pushed the form away from her. Why was she suited to the role? She had no idea.

Instead of worrying, she picked up the cushion cover she had been embroidering for the past two weeks. The woman in a crinoline dress, her face hidden by a bonnet, was already completed, and Helen was looking forward to starting on the cottage garden full of flowers. She had just completed a row of daisies, when there was a knock at the door. It was Gwen.

'I used to have a friend called Helen who lived here, but she seems to have disappeared off the face of the earth.'

Helen threw her arms around her. 'Come in, come in. Thanks for coming round and I'm sorry I haven't been in touch. The girl who was injured in the bombing came back to Fenner's and I've been really busy getting things up to date before I left. Now I'm looking for a new job.'

'Any luck?'

'I've applied for a few out of the paper. Now I'll have to see if I get any replies.'

'That's funny, I was thinking of changing jobs myself. I'm fed up at Mather and Platt.' She sighed. 'Fed up with everything really.'

'Why's that? You and Frank are all right, aren't you?'

Gwen shrugged her shoulders. 'Not really, I hardly see him. He does a lot of overtime now he's been promoted.'

'Promoted?'

Gwen didn't meet her eye. 'I'm sorry, Helen, I shouldn't have said anything. He's a leading fireman now.'

Helen turned away from her and busied herself making tea. It was Jim's job, of course, and it would have been logical to promote Frank, but it hurt so much to hear that everything at the station had moved on and soon Jim would be forgotten. Worse still, Frank had never thought to tell her that he had taken her husband's place.

Gwen was still talking. 'It's not just that I don't see him, it's that he doesn't seem interested in me anymore. To tell you the truth, he's not been the same since Jim died. I've asked him to tell me what's the matter. He says it's nothing and I should stop going on about it. But I think I'm losing him.'

'He's bound to be sad, they were good pals.'

'I know, but I think there's something more to it.'

'Like what?'

'I don't know. Maybe he's found somebody else.'

'Frank wouldn't do that; he's straight as a die.'

'I know, but he'd better buck up his ideas or I might be the one who goes looking. Anyway, let's not talk about him. Tell me, what sort of job are you after?'

'I was thinking of a clerk, but then I thought I might join the police.'

'The police, really? I would've thought that would be the last thing you'd do.'

Helen was taken aback. 'What do you mean?'

'Well, Helen, I've never seen a policewoman who looked like you with your blonde hair and your lovely figure. Most of them look like the back end of a bus.'

'It shouldn't be what you look like, it's whether or not you can do the job. I went to the headquarters in Bootle Street and spoke to the woman sergeant. She certainly weighed me up, but she gave me an application form and said to bring it back on Wednesday because they were having interviews.' Helen pushed the form across the table.

Gwen quickly read it. 'What will you say about why you're suitable?'

'I don't know, but I'll try and think of something.'

'And you'd be all right dealing with criminals?'

'I don't think I'll be doing that. This is for the

Women's Auxiliary Police Corps, they assist the police doing all sorts of jobs like telephone operator, driver, clerk, but there might be a chance to work with women and children as well. That's what I'd really like to do.'

'Well, I'll go to the foot of our stairs, Helen Harrison. I never would have thought you'd want to do that.'

'Why not?'

'Well, you've not exactly mixed with the rough and ready types you'd find in a police station, have you? The only crime you've seen is snotty-nosed kids stealing farthing chews.'

Helen was determined not to be put off. 'Gwen, since Jim died, I've learned a lot about women fending for themselves. How hard it is, especially when they have children to feed and clothe.'

'I'm sorry, Helen, I wasn't criticising. You've showed guts leaving home and striking out on your own like you did. And if you want to join the police, well good luck to you.'

When Gwen had gone, Helen went back to the application and worked on it until midnight. It wasn't perfect, but she hoped it was sincere and sensible. She was about to go to bed when she remembered Pearl's letter. She took it from the mantelpiece and ripped it open. It was almost a repetition of what she had said at the Grosvenor: she knew nothing about Fenner's scheme to pair Helen up with one of his cronies; yes, she was Fenner's mistress, and she was ashamed of that. She hoped they wouldn't fall out, when they had become such close friends working together. The letter finished, 'I've been a mistress. It was the worst decision I ever made and I wouldn't want you to make the same mistake. I care about you, Helen, and if you need anything at all, I'll always help you.'

There was no point in being angry, she had already moved on. Now she had a chance to make her own way in the world, to be independent and to do something worthwhile. She just had to prove to those who might doubt her, that she could join the police.

Chapter 13

Helen arrived at Manchester Police headquarters ten minutes early for the interview and was shown into a bright, airy waiting room with lots of framed government posters on the walls.

Another lady came in, older than her, and she, too, wanted to join the WAPC. She said her name was Sissy Riley. 'I've been looking after my mother,' she explained. 'But she died last month and I got to thinking I should do something for the war effort.' She gave a shy smile. 'Don't know if I'm too old, but I'd love to be a telephone operator.'

'I'm sure you're not. My name's Helen. Hope we both get taken on.'

At ten o'clock, Sergeant Duffy came in. 'Mrs Harrison, come through please.'

Helen sat across the desk in front of three people

and Sergeant Duffy introduced herself, the deputy chief superintendent and a detective inspector.

The deputy chief superintendent began, 'Thank you for coming, Miss Harrison.'

Helen was taken aback that he had addressed her as 'Miss'. She didn't correct him; he'd already moved on. 'I'm looking first at whether you've any particular skills that would be useful in the WAPC. I see you've worked in a corner shop, not sure that's any use to us. Ah, you have office experience – filing, invoicing – that might be relevant, lots of paperwork in the police. Hmm, you're twenty-two and it strikes me a good-looking girl like yourself must have other...' he searched for the words, 'shall we say, ambitions such as marrying and having children. I wouldn't want to spend money training you, if that was the case.'

Sergeant Duffy leaned across to him and jabbed her finger at the application form. The deputy chief superintendent gave a splutter. 'Ah, I see, a widow, eh? Was your husband in the forces, my dear?'

'No, sir. He was a fireman. He was killed in the bombing at Christmas.'

'Well, you'll understand the sacrifices made in the public services better than most, I venture.'

Helen lowered her eyes and nodded.

The detective inspector cleared his throat and Helen was glad to see it was his turn to ask questions. 'Mrs

Harrison, you've given DC Kershaw as your referee. Could you tell me how you came to know him?'

At last, Helen felt she was able to talk about why she wanted to join the police. 'The first time I met him was on the day my husband died. I'd gone to look for him and PC Kershaw, as he was then, could see I was distressed. He calmed me down and advised me to go home and wait for news. I didn't see him again until there was a robbery at the business where I worked. I had spoken to the woman involved in the robbery the day before and was able to describe her in detail to DC Kershaw. He took me to Oldham police station where I picked her out in an identification parade.'

'Is it also true that you were attacked by this woman during the parade?'

'Yes, sir, but it was over in seconds.'

'And that didn't put you off wanting to join the police?'

Helen had to smile. 'Not at all, I was impressed by the policewoman who was there and she told me about the WAPC.'

'Just one more question from me, Mrs Harrison. You've spent some time in the waiting room this morning. Do you recall any of the posters on the wall?'

Helen was puzzled. 'Yes, sir. Clockwise round the room there's "Digging for Victory", "Walls have Ears"...' and she named all eight posters.

'Did you notice anything else?'

'Well, one of the light bulbs has gone and the wastepaper bin hasn't been emptied for a while.' She caught the smile he had tried to suppress as he thanked her and invited Sergeant Duffy to ask her questions.

'There are lots of jobs in the WAPC, most of them based in our offices such as clerical work, operating the switchboard... then there are drivers and mechanics. What sort of work do you think you would be suited to?'

Helen had hoped they would ask her just that question and she had her answer ready. 'I want to work with the public, especially with women and children whose lives have been turned upside down because of the war. I wouldn't mind if they were victims of crime or criminals themselves. I want to do something to make Manchester safer for everyone.'

Sergeant Duffy nodded. 'Indeed, Mrs Harrison, that's what we all want. Now, the interview is over and I'll ask you to wait outside while we decide whether or not you're successful.'

Helen got off the bus on Church Street and called into the tripe shop for three roll-mop herrings, then on to the bakery for a cob loaf and a scone. She thought she deserved a treat. It's not every day you get the chance to make people's lives better and she just knew that Jim would have been so proud of her, now that she had become a member of the Women's Auxiliary Police Corps.

Chapter 14

Helen felt transformed. She had passed her training with flying colours and at last she could wear the uniform of a WAPC. It was her in the mirror, but a more confident, stronger-looking version of herself. Her dark blue tunic and skirt, starched white shirt, black tie, lisle stockings, sturdy lace-up shoes and finally the cap, made it clear who and what she was. At least, the uniform said that, but inside she was still Helen who grew up in the corner shop, with a mother who didn't think she would amount to much. She felt like going back there to stand in front of her and ask, 'What do you think of me now?' But that would be foolish because her mother would always have a cutting remark to puncture her ambitions. And, right on cue, a wayward tangle of blonde curls fell from under her cap and spoiled the whole look.

There was a knock at the door. Frank! She'd forgotten all about him coming to mend the oven door.

She dithered. Should she change out of her uniform? Another knock. No, this was who she was now.

He shook his head at the sight of her and sighed. 'For God's sake, Helen, what have you done?'

'I told you I might join the police.' She tried hard not to be upset.

'I'll give you two weeks. No, make that one week,' and he walked past her into the kitchen.

'You don't understand, Frank, I want to do something worthwhile.'

He didn't answer, just started to root about in his tool bag, but she could feel the anger coming off him.

'Look, it's just like you and Jim joining the fire brigade.'

'No, it isn't, Helen. You're not cut out for dealing with the raw, disgusting mess on the streets of a city.' He turned away from her and set to work on the oven.

She left him there and went to take off her uniform, then she lay on the bed worrying if she'd done the wrong thing. She was to start her two weeks training the following day and she had been looking forward to it, but Frank's attitude had knocked her side-ways.

An hour later he called up to her. 'I've finished.'

She didn't answer. The front door closed – he had gone.

On their first morning as fully trained WAPCs, Helen

and Sissy, who had also passed her interview, reported to Sergeant Duffy in her office. The two of them lined up, as regimented as soldiers, while she inspected their uniforms. 'Don't ever let me see you less than perfectly turned out. No make-up, no rolling up skirts and, most of all, your cap must be placed at the front of your head not at the back. Now before you take up your duties, the chief superintendent has asked to see you.'

They were ushered into his office and lined up again. He made a brief speech about the changing force and how he hoped they would free up police constables to spend more time solving crime. He then presented them with the red and blue cap badge of the WAPC. 'Wear it with pride, ladies.'

Helen had been disappointed that she was made a clerk, but Sergeant Duffy had explained that there would also be opportunities to walk the beat with police constables, helping them with everyday policing. 'It's my belief that we need more women coppers on the streets and you will get the chance to be on the front line with the rest of us.' Sissy had been delighted to get her dream job as a telephone operator and confessed to Helen that she had no inclination to pound the beat.

After a week's clerking, Helen signed on for an extra shift at the weekend; she was desperate to be patrolling, and she would rather be at work than on her own at home. She arrived at the station and went straight to briefing room four. There were six officers there: three policemen; a WPC; Sergeant Duffy and Helen, the only WAPC. There had been a report that a group of children were sleeping rough having broken into one of the Victoria Arches opposite the cathedral. 'We've no idea how many are in there,' Sergeant Duffy told them. 'A lot of these youngsters are running wild, most of them are evacuees who didn't like the country life and some have run away from God knows what at home. We'll pick them up and bring them back here, find out who they are and see if we can get them back with their parents or put in children's homes. Any questions?'

An officer suggested, 'We could take the older ones to a rest centre?'

'Ach, let's see how many there are first, sure we don't want to swamp the centres. They're still busy with bombed-out families. Right, everyone, let's go.'

The series of arches that ran along the banks of the River Irwell close to Victoria Bridge were mostly used as lock-ups for storage; a few signs showed they were business premises too – a rag and bone merchant, a knife grinder...

A man in greasy overalls with a grimy face stood outside a welder's workshop and, as the police came towards him, he gave the slightest nod towards the arch next to his.

Sergeant Duffy ordered the two burly police constables to slide back the door and, as they did so, they shouted, 'Stay where you are!' The light flooded the dank, dark space, and Helen gasped at the sight. There must have been nearly twenty children there: grubby faces; wide, frightened eyes; dirty clothes. Some lying on the ground barely moved, others were getting to their feet. Two older boys tried to make a run for it, but they were no match for the constables.

Sergeant Duffy's voice reverberated round the brick arch. 'You're not in trouble. We're here to help you. First of all, we'll take you to the police station, where you'll get a hot meal. Then we'll take your names and addresses so we can tell your parents that you're safe.'

One of the older boys who had tried to run away shouted, 'I'm not goin' back to them! I can look after meself.'

The policeman nearest to him spoke sternly. 'If you can prove you're old enough, we'll let you go wherever you want.'

They walked the children to Bootle Street where the canteen had a hot meal ready for them. They looked half-starved, shovelling the stew and potatoes into their mouths and mopping up the gravy with doorstep slices of bread. There was tapioca pudding as well and, by the time they'd polished that off, they seemed less wild, placid almost. Sergeant Duffy assigned Helen to six of the girls ranging between six and fourteen. 'As well as names and addresses, try and get as much out of them as you can,' Duffy told her. 'Their story, if you like, why they're on the streets or if there's been any ill-treatment.'

Helen took out her notebook and pencil. The first girl, about fourteen, hair all matted, in a coat too small to button up, refused to give her name. 'I've done nowt wrong.'

'I'm not saying you have, but maybe your family are worried about you.'

The girl gave a snort. 'They wouldn't give a monkey's.'

Helen tried another tack. 'Why don't you just give me your first name then I can write it in my book.'

The girl rolled her eyes. 'Mary.'

'All right, Mary, so why are you not living with your parents?'

'No bloody room, is there? Wi' six kids in the house and not much t'eat.'

Helen had no answer to that. What was she meant to do? She should be helping the girl, but she hadn't a clue.

Then a girl, twelve maybe, was shouting at Mary, 'At least you've got somewhere to go. When we were bombed out, me mam left me with a neighbour and she took the baby and went to live with me auntie. I couldn't stand the woman she left me with, so I ran away.'

Helen clutched at the straw. 'Will you tell me your name and where your auntie lives?'

'I'm called Cynthia Green.' Her lip trembled. 'I'd go to me mam like a shot, but I don't know where me auntie lives.'

'But you must know what area she's from?'

Cynthia shook her head. 'I don't remember. Allus I know, is it's a long way.'

'There must be something you could tell us. Did your mam never say anything about where she lived?'

'Only thing me mam ever said was that me auntie lived in't same street where Gracie Fields were born.'

'Gracie Fields, the singer?'

Cynthia nodded. 'I think so.'

'Then your auntie and your mam must be in Rochdale. What's your auntie's name?'

'Betty Greaves.'

'Well, Cynthia, I'll see if there's any way we can find her.'

Next there was a girl who had run away from home because her mother's boyfriend threw her out; another hinted at abuse from an uncle. Both seemed relieved that they had told someone.

'We'll try to find you somewhere where you'll feel safe,' Helen told them.

She moved on to the remaining two girls. Helen had kept an eye on them as the others told their stories. Clearly sisters, the older one with her arm around a child of about six who looked so weary and showed no interest in what the other girls had to say. The child had her head on her sister's shoulder and never moved.

'And what about you?' Helen asked. 'Do you want to tell me your name?'

'Sylvia Hall and my sister's called Janet.'

'And what's your address, Sylvia?'

'I haven't got one any more.'

'Why's that?'

'It were bombed.'

'Can you remember what your address used to be?'

'Twenty-four Arundel Street.'

'And where are your parents?'

'I don't know. We... ran away.'

'From your parents?'

Sylvia shook her head. 'We were evacuated. It were all right at first, Mam wrote to us every week and she sent us presents for Christmas, but after that we got no more letters. Janet were frettin' – she cried every night to go home.'

Helen looked again at the little girl. She still hadn't moved.

'What did you do, Sylvia?'

'It were a secret, you see, we didn't eat our bread, we saved it up. And when we had enough to last us the journey, we set out for Manchester. We followed the railway line. After two days we were walkin' past a signal box near a station and the man inside came down to see what we was doin' there. I told him we were on't way to Manchester. He were kind to us, gave us summat to eat and got us on't next train. We travelled all the way to Victoria in the guard's van.'

Helen could scarcely believe her ears. 'And did you find the way to your house?'

'I told you, there weren't no house to find.'

'What?'

'It were gone, bombed like most of the street.'

'And your parents?'

'Weren't nobody to ask. We went back t'station, but Janet were too tired to walk any more and she were cryin'. I didn't know what to do, we'd no bread left. Then Cynthia come along.' She pointed to the girl Helen had just spoken to. 'She said there were a place we could sleep and she took us to the arches and shared her food wi' us. Then this morning you came and brought us here.'

Helen looked again at the young child; she still hadn't stirred. Something was wrong, she wouldn't have slept through all this. Helen kneeled down in front of the child and lifted her head. She was very hot. 'Janet, Janet, look at me, love.' Then she saw the red rash, raw as sandpaper, and recognised it instantly. She picked up the child in her arms and ran with her to the medical room.

The nurse had just finished tying a PC's arm in a sling when Helen arrived with Janet.

'And tell your sergeant you're excused battering down doors for at least a month.' Then she noticed the child. 'Lie her down on the bed,' she told Helen, 'and let's have a look.' She examined the rash – it wasn't just on her face, it had spread over her torso. She took her temperature and looked down her throat. 'Plain as the nose on your face – scarlet fever. It's rife in the city

– all those people crammed into air-raid shelters and rest centres. I'll call the hospital, she needs to be in an isolation ward.' It was then they noticed Sylvia in the doorway looking frightened. She must have followed her. 'And what about this one?' asked the nurse.

'This is Sylvia.' Helen took her hand and drew her into the room. 'She's Janet's big sister and she's been looking after her.'

'Right, Sylvia, listen to me,' said the nurse. 'Janet's poorly and I'm going to ring for an ambulance to take her to hospital and you can go with her. We'll need to tell your parents what's happened.'

Sylvia, who had been so brave, could take no more and began to cry. Helen gave the nurse a quick shake of her head. 'We're going to find her parents, aren't we, Sylvia?' At that moment Sergeant Duffy, having seen Helen leave the canteen with a child in her arms, had come to see what was going on. The combination of scarlet fever and a dozen other children in contact with Janet in a confined space changed everything. 'I'll contact the hospital now,' said the nurse. 'Those children you've found need to be isolated.'

'Come on, Harrison,' said Sergeant Duffy, 'we've a lot to organise. Let's get back to the canteen.'

Helen was worried. What had sounded like a simple operation to rescue children living rough had turned into a lot of work for a lot of people. 'Did I do the right thing?'

Sergeant Duffy stopped in her tracks. 'Of course you did. Here, give me your notebook.' She scanned Helen's notes. 'You've got some leads here that we can follow up. Well done. But better still, you spotted the scarlet fever and that little girl has a chance to recover. As for the other children, even if they don't have scarlet fever, you've bought us some time. They'll have a few days in hospital, where they'll be well fed, and by that time we might have tracked down their parents and that's better than sending them to children's homes where they might have infected everyone there. We've just a few days, Harrison, so I want you to start with those two little ones. See if you can find anything that might lead you to the parents. Don't do anything more than that, you're only an auxiliary, so you'll report back to me and I'll decide what happens then.'

It was logical to start with the address that Sylvia had given her and fortunately there were only two Arundel Streets listed in the Manchester street directory: one in Hulme, the other further out in Didsbury. Then she remembered that Hulme had been badly bombed at Christmas. She signed out at the station and caught the bus from Piccadilly. She asked the conductor about Arundel Street and he said, 'I'll give you a shout when we get to St George's Park, it's just on the other side of it.'

Once on the street, she kept an eye on the house numbers. At first there were houses with a few windows boarded up, then a few with damaged roofs covered with tarpaulin. Beyond those there was heavy damage: walls demolished; windows blown out; piles of masonry, slates, charred wood. She picked up the house numbers again and realised the rubble she had walked past amounted to five houses, one of them number 24, Sylvia and Janet's home. What must it have been like for them to have travelled so far to stand in front of the devastating sight? Surely, they must have cried. Did the neighbours see them? Sylvia never mentioned knocking on doors to ask where their parents were, maybe they were too frightened of being sent back. Someone must know what happened to their mam and dad. Then she remembered something, smiled and retraced her steps to the corner shop. She pushed open the door and the bell jangled a welcome – she was on home territory here.

Another bus ride and she joined the throng of working men in their blue and white mufflers walking the terraced streets to the hallowed ground with its high red-bricked walls and, above them, the steel structure of the stands. Across the blue corrugated roof, the white letters spelled out 'Manchester City Football Club'.

There were queues at every turnstile, but she felt sure that if she queued up, she would be treated like everyone else and would have to buy a ticket. There must be another way in, she thought, and eventually, on the opposite side of the ground, she spotted a door with the sign 'Players' Entrance'. It was open.

Inside, there was a brick corridor and a strong smell: a mix of damp earth, wintergreen, and the pungent stench of sweat. She hadn't gone far when there was a blast of raucous laughter as a door opened, and a man in the black strip of a referee appeared.

He looked startled. 'What you doin' down here? Players only in the dressing rooms.'

Helen was just as shocked to see him. 'I'm from the Manchester police. Is there someone I could speak to about a police matter?'

He didn't argue. 'Yes, all right, miss, I'll get one of the boot boys to take you to the office.'

By the time she got there, the match had kicked off, but when Helen explained the situation to the man in charge of the Tannoy system he agreed to make a public announcement at half-time. 'Come on then,' he said. 'You can watch the first half from the best seats.'

Helen had never been to a football match in her life and was amazed at the number of people crammed into the ground, most of them standing on the terraces. The noise was deafening: men shouting, cheering, and the awful clack-clack of the rattles in her ear. 'Should be a good game today,' said the Tannoy man. 'You'll be cheering for the boys in blue, I hope.' She kept her eye on the ball, the blues were racing up the field. She held her breath, the ball was in the air, they must score... in the stand everyone rose to their feet... Goal! And she cheered just as loud as any fan who had been coming here man and boy.

When the half-time whistle sounded, Helen listened to the announcement. Ten minutes later Mr Hall, father of Sylvia and Janet, arrived in the office. He was shocked to see a policewoman, but Helen quickly told him his girls were safe. Then she recounted their story of running away and finding their home had been bombed and their parents gone. 'We found them yesterday in Manchester and they've been taken to the children's hospital off Quay Street because we think Janet might have scarlet fever.'

Helen was surprised to see such an anguished look on his face. 'Don't worry, Mr Hall, I'm sure they'll be fine. They were just desperate to see you and their mother. There's visiting allowed on Sunday afternoons – you can see them then.'

He closed his eyes and shook his head. 'Their mam's gone. The house took a direct hit when I were workin' nights. I got home in the morning just as they were pullin' her out of the rubble. She were in hospital for two days, but there was nothing they could do for her. After that I went to live with my cousin in Longsight. Never went back to Arundel Street again.'

'And you didn't tell the girls?'

'No, I couldn't bear to tell them… best to leave them where they were… not knowing.'

'You didn't write either?'

'I were never much of a writer. Their mother was the one kept in touch. I wouldn't've known what to say.'

'Mr Hall, they're your children. You need to go and see them and tell them about their mother, then it's up to you whether you send them back to the people who were looking after them. Or maybe you could keep them with you?'

'I don't know.'

'What would your wife want you to do?'

He almost smiled. 'She'd want me to bring them back home if they were frettin'.' He seemed to reach a decision. 'Yes, I'll go and see them tomorrow afternoon. I'm thinkin' that when they're fit, they could stay with me at my cousin's till I find a place for us.'

The second half had already started when they parted, Helen to go back to the station and the girls' father to the football. 'Just one thing,' he said. 'How did you know I was here?'

'The woman in the corner shop where you used to live told me you never missed a blues home match.'

Chapter 15

Helen couldn't stop smiling on the way home. For once in her life she had done something to be proud of in reuniting Sylvia and Janet with their father. She couldn't wait for Monday to see what could be done with the other children – that's if they didn't send her back to clerking duties.

She hung her tunic and cap on the hook behind the door and took off her shoes. There wasn't much in the house for tea, so she emptied a tin of mackerel in a saucepan and lit the gas. She was just cutting some bread to toast when there was a knock at the door. She peeked through the parlour window and saw a man in a tweed coat wearing a brown pork pie hat stood with his back to her. He swung round and she juked backwards out of sight. Now he was banging loudly on the door and she had no choice but to open it.

'Ah, Mrs Harrison.' His foot was already over the

threshold. 'You're a hard woman to catch at home. I'll come in, if you don't mind. I'm sure you wouldn't want to discuss your business on the doorstep.'

She stood back – she could hardly refuse her landlord access to his own property. He came inside and cast his eyes around the sparsely furnished parlour. 'I've had a complaint from the neighbours, serious enough for me to come here on a Saturday night when I'd sooner be in the Nelson with a pint of best bitter in my hand. Now what I want to know is, who exactly is living here?'

'Just me.' She could only tell the truth, she'd done nothing wrong.

'So, you lied about the tenancy?'

'I don't know what you mean.'

'Is your name on the rent book?'

'No, but—'

'Then it's not a legal tenancy. When I showed you round the house you had a man with you and I understood him to be your husband. He's the one signed the agreement and now I've no idea who he is. I'll not mince my words, I've been told that various men have been seen "visiting" you.'

Helen was horrified. It was bad enough that Ada had wrongly accused her about men coming to her house, but now it seemed her lies could cost her her home. 'But he's…' she corrected herself. 'He was my husband.'

'And where is he?'

'He's dead.'

'Then you're a widow?'

'Yes, he died in the bombings at Christmas.'

'Well, I'm sorry to hear that.' He didn't look very sorry. 'But it makes no difference, you've still had men coming to the house.'

'My boss, my husband's friend—'

'And they bring you flowers?'

'That was... different.'

He shook his head. 'I don't want to know. The fact is, your husband's name is on the rent book and now that he's dead, you don't have the tenancy.'

'But you could just change it to my name. I'm working, I'm paying the rent.'

'I don't think so. I'm giving you notice, you'll need to get out by the end of next week.' He was smirking now as he looked around the room. 'And I don't expect it'll take you too long to pack up the few belongings you have.' She just wanted him to go, but he stood there, a strange look on his face. 'Of course, we could come to some sort of arrangement.' He reached out and ran his hand up and down her arm. 'You and I could go upstairs to inspect your bedroom.'

She was horrified. 'Get out! Get out! I'd rather sleep on the streets.'

'Well, you've got your wish. Out by Friday, Mrs Harrison, and that's an end to it.'

When he'd gone, Helen took the rent book from the drawer and studied it. There was Jim's name and signature and, next to that, the word 'tenant'. There was no mention of her at all, it was as though she didn't exist, but there in the book were the payments she had made, right to the end of the first column. It was so unfair. She screamed in frustration and fought back the tears. There was a time when she would have been overwhelmed by such a blow, but not now. She would just have to find somewhere else to live. She retrieved the *Manchester Evening News* from under the cushion of the fireside chair and turned to the columns of lodgings and houses to rent.

Sunday morning was dull and threatened rain and, by the time Helen had seen two lodging houses and a dilapidated house, she understood that everything had been snapped up by the council for those who had lost their homes in the recent bombings. There was one more house off Queen's Road, not far from Gwen's, that she would try, but when she got there it was all boarded up, and when she asked the next-door neighbour about it, she said it was gutted inside and needed a lot of work. It was no use, she'd have to start again tomorrow when she finished her shift.

Then the heavens opened. She was drenched within minutes and close to tears, but Gwen's house was just two streets away. 'Flippin' 'eck, Helen, have you been tramping the streets in this weather? Take off that wet coat. There's a brew on the side, if you want it.' Helen nodded. It was warm and steamy in the kitchen with the smell of meat in the oven and pots bubbling on the stove. A wooden maiden in front of the fire was festooned with damp clothes.

'I'd better mind my Ps and Qs with an officer of the law in the house.'

'Frank told you, did he?'

'Oh yes, he said you'd got the job, and I have to tell you he wasn't best pleased. "No job for a woman," he said.'

'But he's wrong, Gwen, they need more of us in the police. Imagine the women bombed out of their homes, evacuees on the streets, children abused.' Gwen gave her a look. 'No, really, people take advantage of them or they get into trouble. If something happened to you, you'd want to talk to a woman, wouldn't you?'

'I can see that, but do you like doing it?'

'I haven't done a lot yet, but I did reunite two little girls with their father after they were found sleeping under the arches by the Irwell.' Helen gave a wry smile. 'Mind you, I could end up being homeless myself if I don't find somewhere else to live.'

'Why, what's happened?' She handed Helen a cup of tea so strong you could stand a spoon up in it. They sat at the table and Helen explained about the house being in Jim's name. 'I didn't think to get it changed. Now I'm to quit by the end of the week. I've been trekking all over trying to find somewhere.'

'But why did he just come along now to get you out?'

Helen couldn't lie, but she was so embarrassed. 'It was that Ada next door. She told him I was living on my own and—' Helen could feel her face flush.

'And what, Helen?'

'She said I had men coming to the house.'

'What?' For a fleeting moment Gwen looked confused. 'You mean...'

'Yes, men visiting me in the house. You know what I'm saying.'

'But that's ridiculous! You can't let her get away with that. Did you tell the landlord she was lying?'

Helen looked down at her hands in her lap.

'Helen? You didn't, did you?'

'One night, my boss brought me home. He didn't come in – Pearl was in the car as well. Then a man I met through work; he came to my house...' Helen wiped her eyes. 'I wasn't even in, he left me flowers on the doorstep. And then there was Frank, wasn't there?'

'Frank?'

Helen suddenly had the uneasy feeling that Frank hadn't told her about his visits: the paraffin heater; the firemen's whip-round, fish and chips, helping her to buy furniture.

'Yes, when he brought me the widows' pension papers.'

'Oh right, he never said.' Gwen went on, 'Helen, this is awful. It just shows you how people can ruin a woman's reputation. What are you going to do?'

'I'm going to find somewhere else to live, but it won't be easy, there's not much out there.'

'You could stay here, if you like. It'd be a bit of a squeeze sharing with me and my sister, but we'll manage.'

'Thanks for the offer, Gwen, but I can't impose on you. I'll find somewhere, don't worry.'

'Why don't you go back to your mam's? It'll be different now you're working.'

'No, I couldn't live under the same roof as her again.'

'Well, the offer's here if you want it and you'll stay for your tea, won't you? You know what? When you've found somewhere else to live, we'll have a Saturday night out to celebrate. We haven't been dancing for ages, just the two of us.'

'But what about Frank, are you not out on Saturdays with him?'

'To tell you the truth, Helen, he never takes me anywhere. We end up in the pub every time and he's got nothin' to say to me. I don't know what's goin' on in his head, these days.'

Helen lay in bed that night thinking about her house. She didn't have much, but she loved what she had – especially her bed. If she went into lodgings, she would have to sell everything, probably back to that man in Collyhurst. She hadn't realised that just having her own furniture had made her feel more secure, a person in her own right, who chose, bought, and paid for every item. And her house too... She loved its sounds: the creaking of the stairs; the rumbling of the pipes; the way the damper of the fire drew the flames up the chimney on windy nights.

She had been content here. Jim was gone, but they had chosen this little house together and she could, if she closed her eyes, imagine him here looking out of the bedroom window over the park or hear his laugh again in the kitchen where he had kissed her that time when they came to look at the house.

She awoke in the early morning, cold and sad with the remnants of her dreams lingering – a bombed house where she clawed at the rubble searching for lost children and there was Jim, so handsome in his uniform, who took her in his arms and carried her away.

On the bus to work, she put aside her own problems and thought about the children she had interviewed. Hopefully, Sylvia and Janet would already be reunited with their father and when the girls were released from hospital they would be a family again. And she had an idea that might help her find Cynthia's mother in Rochdale. She worried too about the other children. They had seemed wilder somehow, and resentful that they had been found. There might be places in a children's home for them, but she suspected they might run away from there also.

Before she left work on Saturday, she had written a

note for Sergeant Duffy about finding the girls' father and, when she signed on, the duty sergeant told her to report to her immediately. She knew she'd been a bit overeager and had completely forgotten that she'd been told not to take any action. As she walked away there was a shout from the desk sergeant, 'Hey, get your cap on and make sure it's straight.'

She knocked on the door and there was a sharp 'Come!' in reply. Sergeant Duffy looked up as she came in, then back again to the report on her desk.

Helen stood to attention, looking straight ahead. A couple of minutes passed, then Sergeant Duffy looked up. 'What did I say about taking action?'

'That I wasn't to do it, Sarge.'

'What action did you take?'

'I went to the street where the girls lived and talked to a shopkeeper. Then I went to Maine Road to the football match.'

'And then what did you do?'

'I asked them to make an announcement at the ground.'

'And why would they do that for someone who had absolutely no authority?'

Helen said nothing.

'I take it you told them you were a police auxiliary?'

Helen whispered a reply.

'Speak up!'

'I didn't tell them I was an auxiliary.'

'You've been in the job for just over a month and you've the nerve to have public announcements made to a crowd of sixty thousand at a football match!'

'But I had to do it.' Helen's voice was strained. 'It was the only way I could find the girls' father.'

Sergeant Duffy shook her head. 'I don't know what to do with you, Harrison. Sure, you're a bright girl, but discipline is so important in the police.' She picked up the report again. 'And what's this you've written at the end? "I think I know how to find the mother of Cynthia Green in Rochdale." Will this lead to more subordination?'

'No, it won't, and it's a chance we could reunite mother and daughter.'

Sergeant Duffy leaned back in her chair and stared at her. Helen had no idea whether she was about to be sacked or sent back to her filing, never to be allowed on the beat again. 'All right then, convince me.'

It was a bright March day, with a chill wind and she was glad of her WAPC greatcoat over her uniform. She had been to Rochdale only once before when Jim took her to meet his sister and family to tell them they had got engaged. She could never have imagined then that she would be back eighteen months later, a widow and WAPC. She got off the train and headed to the town centre. It felt good to be out and doing something with a purpose. There was the open market and the splendid town hall and, close to that, the police station.

Outside, she paused a moment to check her tie, straighten her cap, and take a deep breath. The desk sergeant, a stout man with silver hair, looked up briefly as she came in, then looked again. 'Mornin', miss, what can I do for you?'

'I'm WAPC Harrison from the Manchester police, and I'm hoping you can help me. We've picked up a homeless young girl who's lost contact with her family. The only clue we've got is that her mother is in Rochdale staying with Betty Greaves, her aunt. We'd like to reunite them.'

'Well, that shouldn't be too difficult. Do you have the address?'

'Ah, no I haven't.' Helen caught his 'this is going to involve me in some work' look. She smiled. 'But I think I can find her if you or one of your officers could answer one question.'

He looked sceptical, but nodded. 'Go on then, pet, ask your question.'

'Do you know where Gracie Fields was born?'

He laughed. 'Our Gracie? Well, you've come to the right man. Walked every beat in this town over the last thirty years. I knew her mother, you know, nice family. Hang on a minute, I'll get someone to cover the desk and I'll take you there myself. It's not far.'

As they walked, he asked her about the WAPCs.

'Heard of them, of course, never met one before. What do you do then, find lost kids and take them back to their parents?'

Soon they were standing outside a row of shops on a main road. Helen was disappointed. 'Is this it?' she said.

'Not quite. You see, this shop used to be a chippie. Now look up.'

It was quite a grand-looking building above street level, but Helen was disappointed. 'Gracie Fields lived above a chip shop? I thought it would be a street of terraced houses where I could knock on a door and ask where Betty Greaves lived. On a road like this it could take ages to find her.'

'So now what?' asked the sergeant.

She was determined not to give up. There must be a way. 'Is there a butcher's on this road?'

'Why do you ask that?'

'Because Betty Greaves and her address would be registered with a local butcher so that she could get her meat ration.'

The sergeant nodded. 'Aye, lass, there's one just down the road.'

When Helen returned to Bootle Street, the desk sergeant greeted her. 'So, the wanderer returns; all right for some who can go on a jaunt.' But he had a twinkle in his eye.

'I'm to tell you to report to Sergeant Duffy on your return.'

For the second time that day Helen stood in front of her superior officer. 'Now then, Harrison, did you solve the mystery of the missing mother?'

'I did, Sarge.'

'Good work. You spoke to the mother and aunt?'

'Yes, they had no idea she was so unhappy with the neighbour, who was supposed to be looking after her, and they were so grateful that we'd found her.'

'Very good and, when we're sure she hasn't got scarlet fever, you can take her there. You might like to know that I telephoned Rochdale nick half an hour ago. I spoke to the sergeant you met, asked him what he thought of the WAPC officer I'd sent to find the mother.'

Helen held her breath – would she be in trouble again?

'He was impressed, said you did exactly what he would have done. He also liked the way you spoke to the mother and aunt and your professional manner towards him. What do you say about that?'

Helen blushed. 'I don't know what to say. I just did my best for the girl.'

'Aye, that's all well and good, but you must understand that I can't guarantee you'll get opportunities to handle cases like the missing children. And I warn you, Harrison, don't think you can go off pretending you're a detective. You're an auxiliary, a clerk, freeing up police officers, and don't forget it.'

Helen went from elation to deep disappointment in a few seconds. 'Yes, Sarge.'

'Look, I know you want to do more and if I can, I'll try to get you involved in some real police work. Maybe you could put your name down for an extra shift on Saturday night. That would certainly be an eye-opener for you.'

Helen hesitated. 'I'd like to do that only…'

'You've probably got family and things to do.'

'No, I'm on my own, but it's a bit difficult at the moment…'

'Is it anything I can help you with?'

Helen was reluctant to explain. 'Not really, it's just that I have to move house and I'm busy looking for somewhere.'

'Why are you moving?'

'It's a bit complicated. I didn't realise that there would be a problem with the tenancy when my husband died. Nobody told me I couldn't stay on in the house. Anyway, the landlord found out and he's evicting me. I've to be out by the end of the week.'

'He can't do that.'

'But he's done it and I have to go.'

'I take it you're up to date with the rent.'

'Yes, but he didn't care.' She didn't say anything about him propositioning her.

'That shouldn't be allowed. Sure, don't be worrying about it, I'll look into it. Come back to me at the end of the day.'

Helen couldn't concentrate on her work for thinking about the eviction. To begin with, she was hopeful that Sergeant Duffy might be able to change the landlord's mind, but by the time she went for her afternoon tea break, she was certain not even her formidable sergeant could help her.

'What's the matter with you?' Sissy greeted her. 'Lost a pound and found a penny.'

Helen explained the simple version. 'So, if Sarge can't do anything, I could be homeless by the end of the week.'

'Well, you're very welcome to stay with me until you find somewhere.'

'That's kind of you, Sissy.'

Helen returned to Sergeant Duffy's office before she went home. 'Come in, come in, Harrison.' She was beaming. 'I've good news for you. Seems your landlord had made a mistake and he's very sorry for the distress you suffered. He'll post a new rent book through the door with you named as the tenant. It'll be there for you when you get home.'

'But how—'

'The Failsworth police have had a word. You'll have no more trouble from him.'

She could hardly believe it, the weight on her

shoulders lifted in an instant. 'I don't know what to say, I'm so grateful.'

'Ach, think nothing of it, Harrison.' She winked. 'We look after our own.'

Chapter 16

Saturday night and the Plaza was packed. She and Gwen had queued up in the rain then paid their one and ninepence and had their hands stamped in case they wanted to go outside and get back in again. The last time she'd been here was with Jim just before their marriage. The moment she entered the ballroom the memories of that night flooded back. She had been so much in love and they had danced almost all night. She caught her breath and felt again the closeness of him: a slow waltz; his body against hers; the taste of him on her lips.

Gwen grabbed her arm. 'Come on, Helen, stop daydreaming. Let's get a lemonade and find a seat.'

They sat out a few dances, just listening to the music and looking at the couples moving around the floor. 'We'd better watch ourselves.' Gwen giggled. 'There's a lot of men in uniform tonight and you know what they're after.'

'We'll just say we're spoken for, that usually works.'

'Oh, I don't know, if there was a handsome sailor I might be tempted.'

'You wouldn't, would you?'

Gwen raised an eyebrow.

'But what about Frank?'

'Helen, when will you understand he's gone off me, I know he has. We don't go anywhere, and he hasn't said he loves me for months. Anyroad, forget about him, let's have a dance.'

There were plenty of women dancing together, while groups of men stood around watching. Every now and again one of them would pluck up the courage to ask a girl to dance, but as the evening wore on, fortified by the alcohol they'd sneaked in, they became bolder. Helen was quite happy to partner a man but, when the music changed, she thanked him, walked away and went back to the table. On one occasion she had noticed a very tall young airman watching her as she sat out a lively jive. Then later when she took a rest, he winked at her. She looked quickly away and was glad to see Gwen coming back to the table.

'You see that RAF lad over there, he keeps looking at me,' she told Gwen. 'Let's go to the Ladies.'

Helen stared at her reflection in the mirror and combed her blonde curls, powdered her nose and added some more of her tea-rose lipstick. Strange, that she looked just the same as she did that night with Jim,

THE GIRL FROM THE CORNER SHOP

but inside she had changed beyond recognition. In some ways she was stronger and she had her work and her home, but there was an empty space where once there had been love and joy and a deep satisfaction.

'Hey,' Gwen whispered, 'let's make a night of it.' And she pulled a bottle of Yates's Australian wine from her handbag and took a slug. 'Here,' she said, 'I think you need it more than me.'

Helen shook her head.

'Oh, go on. What's the worst that could happen?'

Back in the ballroom, they bought more lemonade, topped it up with the Yates's, and had a few more dances. Then Gwen went off to quickstep with a corporal and didn't come back straight away. It was embarrassing sitting alone. A man in civvies asked her to dance and she declined. She drank the rest of the lemonade and wine and thought about leaving.

'Hello, can I sit down?'

No need to look, she knew it was the airman. 'If you want.'

'I'm Teddy,' he said. 'What's your name?' His face was so eager. How old could he be, eighteen, nineteen maybe? A good-looking lad, well-spoken.

'Helen.'

He gave a nervous smile. 'I've been watching you,' he said. 'You look so lonely. Has your friend gone?'

Helen sighed. 'I don't think so, she's dancing with someone. She'll be back soon.'

'Can I buy you a drink?'

She shook her head. Why on earth had she agreed to go dancing? What was she expecting – that she'd suddenly feel happy again or at least forget the awful sadness? The music, laughter and constant chatter had no relevance to her. She closed her eyes and let the familiar isolation overwhelm her. The touch on her hand jolted her and she opened her eyes to see the concern in the lad's face, and coming towards her was Gwen and her corporal.

'Helen, it's so warm in here,' she said, her face flushed. 'We're just going outside to get some fresh air.' She giggled. 'I'm glad you've got some company. Don't worry, we won't be long.'

It was then that the young airman asked her to dance.

It helped that he was so tall. She rested her head against his shoulder, closed her eyes and let him guide her around the crowded dance floor. In the darkness, there was only her and the lad and the slowest of waltzes. The slightest movement of his hands and she felt his touch. He spoke softly of nothing and his breath on her ear made her shiver. Without warning, he stepped back from her. She opened her eyes and realised the music had stopped and people were clapping. 'Helen, are you all right?' Her head was spinning and she couldn't focus. He took her hand and led her back to the table. 'What's the matter?' he asked.

How could she explain that for the length of a slow

waltz the lead weight of grief had somehow been lifted? She simply forgot who she was in this young man's arms.

'You look so pale, you don't feel faint, do you?'

She stared at his hand still holding hers, and the startling thought that no one had touched her for so long made her want to cry.

'Maybe you need some fresh air,' he said. 'We could go outside for a while. What do you say?'

She jerked her hand away as though stung. 'No, no! I'm fine. Just leave me, please.'

'But—'

Her voice rose. 'Look, I'm all right,' and she pushed past him and fled to the Ladies. There she rinsed her wrists under the cold water and took a good look at herself in the mirror. What had she been thinking of, dancing with that lad and taking comfort in the way he held her? She felt deeply ashamed and, worse, she felt she had betrayed Jim.

Gwen was sitting at the table when she came back but there was no sign of the corporal or the airman. 'Well, I won't be doing that again in a hurry.' Gwen shook her head. 'I had a wrestling match with a man with wandering hands who thinks he's God's gift to women. How did you get on with the lad?'

'We just had a dance, that's all. I was thinking we should go.'

'Me too. Shall we call it a night and get some chips on the way home?'

Chapter 17

Helen was sick to death of paperwork. She had managed to get a couple of night shifts and really enjoyed being out on the beat, but she wanted more. So, when Sergeant Duffy came to ask her if she would be available to work the night shift on the Saturday she said yes right away.

'CID have got something going on, can't say what, but they want a strong presence in the city centre,' Sergeant Duffy explained. 'You'll walk the beat with me. It's a tough area, but it'll be good experience for you.'

Helen and Sergeant Duffy, wrapped up in their greatcoats, came out of Bootle Street headquarters into the cold night. The sky was cloudless and the half moon and stars could be seen through the smoke of thousands of chimneys.

They walked past the Free Trade Hall and on into St

Peter's Square where taxis waited at the rank outside the Midland Hotel to ferry home the wealthy citizens of Manchester.

'Sure, that's the life, isn't it?' said Sergeant Duffy. 'They'll have had a damn good dinner and plenty of liquor to wash it down. No rationing for that crowd.' They walked on into Oxford Street where the theatre-goers were pouring out of the Palace. By now Helen could see where they were headed and she felt uneasy to find herself in the vicinity of the Plaza ballroom. 'We're coming up now to an area where we have problems with a couple of dance halls and pubs. We're looking out for drunks, fights, sexual attacks, that kind of thing. We've tried to get the ballrooms not to give pass-outs, but it's impossible. So, we'll start here, round these backstreets. Mostly we just move the courting couples on but, if we suspect the girls are underage, we'll take their names and send them packing. If they claim they've been assaulted, that's a different matter altogether.'

They turned down the side of the Plaza on to a narrow, cobbled street. 'You'll need your torch to see what's going on.' They hadn't gone more than twenty yards when Helen caught a couple in a sweep of the beam. A sailor with his cap askew and a girl in a bright green dress hiding her face from the light.

'Police,' Sergeant Duffy shouted. 'Move along, you two, or I'll nick you for indecency.' The couple hurried away, doing up buttons as they went.

They walked on and Sergeant Duffy told her, 'Next couple we come across, you decide what to do with them.' But Helen was so shocked at what she had just seen, she couldn't trust herself to speak. It could have been her and the airman, if she hadn't come to her senses. No, she told herself: you didn't go with him, you sent him away!

Another sweep of the torch and there was a girl, so young, eyes wide with fright, a sudden cry. The man looked like late twenties.

'Stand where you are,' Helen shouted, but the man rushed past her, pushing her to the ground, and by the time she was on her feet again he had gone.

Sergeant Duffy had hold of the girl who was sobbing. 'There, there, love. You're safe now,' and she asked her to explain what he had done to her. The couple had only been outside a few minutes and they had been kissing. 'But he wanted more, touching me, you know? Then you shone the torch on us.' Sergeant Duffy turned to Helen.

'What next, Harrison?'

Helen asked the girl her name, age and address and wrote the details in her notebook. 'You don't look sixteen to me. How old are you really?'

The girl didn't look at her. 'I'm fourteen,' she said.

'Now tell me, are you on your own in town or did you come with someone else?' She had come to the Plaza with her friends and they were still inside. 'You shouldn't be in a dance hall at your age, so we'll go back there where you'll find your friends and all of you will go straight home. We have your details recorded, so we don't expect to see you around here again. You've had a lucky escape tonight. You might not be so lucky next time.'

When the girls were rounded up and sent on their way, Helen and Sergeant Duffy went back on the beat.

'You handled that well, Harrison, spotting she was a child.'

'But the man got away.'

'There was nothing you could do about that. The child is safe and sometimes that's the best we can do. It's like chipping away at concrete. Crime's grown since the war started, especially against women. I don't know what it is... Something in the air...' She shook her head. 'When you could be killed in an air raid at any time, some people go hell for leather to grab everything they can get, whether it be theft, grievous bodily harm, attacks on women – a whole catalogue of crime. Life's cheap these days.'

They walked further along Oxford Road towards the university and called into some pubs, checking with the landlords whether there were any suspicious customers. 'The black market is rife,' Sergeant Duffy told her. 'There are always spivs in pubs trying to sell stolen goods, like cigarettes. Sometimes the landlord will give you the nod that they're selling, but if it's someone they know they take their cut and turn a blind eye.'

It was one in the morning when they arrived in Canal Street. Helen had heard mention at the station of the area, a notorious red-light district, and she had seen some of the women brought in for soliciting. Now she was about to see it for herself. Some women were sitting on the canal wall.

'Hello, girls.' Sergeant Duffy greeted them like old friends. 'What's going on the night, then?'

'Just freezin' our arse off, waitin' for the punters.'

'This is Harrison, woman auxiliary, she's not been around these parts before.'

An older woman with a smoker's rasping voice called out, 'Well, she'd better watch out, with a figure like that she could be stealin' our custom,' and the girls gave a good-humoured laugh.

'Any dodgy characters around?' asked Sergeant Duffy.

'A couple, but they were just moochin'; didn't look like they had it in them.' More laughter.

'That one Marilyn went off with looked like he had a bob or two – nice overcoat. Not seen him before.'

'She's been gone a while,' said another of the women, 'hope she's on double time!'

'Well, girls, keep yourselves safe and we'll be back this way in about an hour. We're taking a break at Bridie's café, if you need us. In the meantime, don't work too hard.'

The windows of the café were steamed up and coming through the door Helen was amazed to see the place was packed at one in the morning. The woman behind the counter looked up, spotted Sergeant Duffy and shouted, 'I've told you before, no Ulster prods allowed in here!'

'Ach, away on with you, you Fenian culchie. I suppose you're still sellin' that rancid Irish stew.'

'Best Irish beef straight off the Holyhead boat.'

'Well if there's nothing else, give us two bowls and some of that soda bread.'

While they waited for a table, Helen observed the motley crew of customers: men in greasy boiler suits; a couple of nurses in their capes; gents in dinner suits; an old prostitute with grotesque make-up.

Sergeant Duffy followed her gaze. 'You'll find all human life washed up in a café in the wee hours of the morning. This is our factory floor, Harrison. Get used to it.'

'Are you ever afraid out at night walking these streets?' Helen asked.

'Not really, I do my job and most of the time I'm not afraid but, I have to say, there have been moments when I've feared for my life.' She shrugged. 'Keep your wits about you, Harrison, learn all you can and weigh up the risks. It's not our job to be martyrs.'

A table was vacated and no sooner had they sat down than Bridie brought them the stew. 'Did ye hear that aul traitor Lord Haw-Haw on the radio again, threatening us and namin' the streets they're goin' to bomb?'

'Ach, take no heed of that, Bridie, he'll not drop bombs on you. Sure, he knows this café's neutral territory, just like the rest of Ireland.'

The stew was good and Helen asked about the soda. 'I've never tasted bread like this before.'

'No yeast, you see, but plenty of bicarbonate of soda and buttermilk,' said Sergeant Duffy and she leaned across the table and whispered, 'She makes the best soda I've ever tasted, but don't tell her I said so.'

'I know you're Irish, but what was all that banter with Bridie?'

'Ah, now there's the conundrum. Strictly speaking, I'm from Northern Ireland, at least I have been since 1922, that's when the free state came into being and the six counties stayed as they were, that's to say, British. So, I'm British, not Irish, unlike your woman, Bridie.' She laughed. 'And now I've addled your brain at this time in the morning.'

'Why did you come to England?'

'Bless us, is this an interrogation?'

'I'm sorry, I shouldn't have asked.'

'It doesn't matter. I don't mind telling you. I worked for the RUC, the Royal Ulster Constabulary, as a telephone operator. I sometimes helped out – just being in the room really – when a woman was brought in for questioning or, more often, been attacked. I really wanted to be a police constable, but the job wasn't open to women. Then I heard there were a few policewomen in England so, with the bravado of youth, I came across the water.'

'And you joined the police.'

'Oh, it wasn't that easy, but I was a trained telephone operator and that got me a foot in the door. Then I met Police Woman Clara Walkden. She understood that women needed a different style of policing and more policewomen to sniff out what was really going on. Anyway, she saw something in me, and she made it her business to get me into uniform.'

She seemed lost in her memories and Helen watched in silence the hint of a smile on her lips. What she said next took Helen by surprise. 'You remind me of myself when I was younger. You know what I'm saying?'

Before Helen could answer, the café door flew open and one of the girls from Canal Street rushed in and shouted, 'Marilyn's been attacked! She's in a bad way.' Sergeant Duffy was first on her feet and Helen, hard on her heels, followed her out the door.

The girl was in an air-raid shelter off Whitworth Street. It was cold as a tomb, pitch dark and stinking of urine. A sweep of a torch and they found her. Helen felt the vomit rush to her throat at the sight of her. There was blood pouring from her neck, and spreading in a halo, staining her blonde hair, but it was her face, white as snow, that shocked Helen. She was so beautiful. Sergeant Duffy was on her knees trying to staunch the blood. Helen shone her torch on the girl and averted her eyes. 'Don't you dare throw up, Harrison! And keep that torch steady. She's alive, thank God, but she's losing so much blood. Now listen, Harrison, run to the police box, the one we passed outside the Briton's Protection pub, remember? Ask for an ambulance urgently, air-raid shelter at Whitworth Gardens, and a constable to assist us, then get back here quick as you can.'

In no time at all she was back and a few minutes later they heard the bell of the ambulance clanging towards them. 'You go with her, they'll take her to Manchester Royal Infirmary from here, stay with her to see if she can give us any information. I'll stay here to find out as much as I can from the women, the ones who haven't run away. Then I'll come to the hospital.'

Manchester Royal Infirmary was only minutes away and Helen prayed that Marilyn would hold on. The ambulance man was pressing a towel to the wound but still the blood dripped. At the hospital, the trolley was pushed straight through into a cubicle, where she was lifted on to the bed with the man still stemming the blood from her neck. Helen slipped into the cubicle behind him.

A nurse took over and a minute later a doctor arrived in his white coat, stethoscope round his neck. 'Keep the pressure on,' he told the man.

Helen sat on the chair in the corner and watched him.

As he took her pulse he said, 'Can you hear me?' No response. He shone a light into each eye. There was an almost imperceptible shake of his head.

He wasn't aware of Helen and she didn't dare speak when he was so intent on what he was doing. From the back he looked young to be a doctor. He gently turned Marilyn's head to one side and looked closely at the wound on her neck. She heard him sigh. 'She's gone,' he said to the man and that was when he noticed the police uniform. 'What are you doing in here?' he shouted. 'You're not allowed—' He stopped; looked puzzled. 'Helen?'

She was just as surprised as he was – the doctor was Laurence Fitzpatrick from the supper club.

At that moment there was the unmistakable sound of Sergeant Duffy outside in the corridor. 'Harrison, where are you?'

'In here,' called Helen, her eyes still on Laurence, but now Sergeant Duffy was in the cubicle.

'What's happening?' she asked.

Laurence addressed them both. 'Get out of here, both of you. A young woman has just died and we have to see to her.'

Sergeant Duffy was about to ask him something, but he said bluntly, 'Go, right now.'

Out on the street again, Sergeant Duffy explained, 'There's nothing more we can do. I've spoken to the girls on Canal Street and there were only two who saw the man with Marilyn, but they were sure he wasn't a regular punter. Of course, it was quite dark and all they could say was that he might have been wearing a tweed overcoat and a homburg, like plenty of other men, and he was tall, not a clue about his face, but one of them thought he sounded like "one a them actors in the pictures".'

'What do we do now?'

'Go back to the station. The incident will already have been passed on to CID. They'll interview the prostitutes again and there'll be a medical report. They'll probably want to talk to us as well, so make sure you have your notebook written up.'

They walked in silence for a while. Helen was going over everything she had seen from the moment they found Marilyn to her last breath. She never would have thought that a body could be so full of blood and the way it spurted... She shuddered.

'Is it the first time you've seen a dead body?' asked Sergeant Duffy.

Helen nodded.

'It's always a shock to the system, but this was a brutal murder. You have to push away the images and I know it's easier said than done, but you mustn't dwell on it. Now, what you need is strong, sweet tea. Come on, we'll walk back to headquarters.'

'Are there a lot of attacks on the women?' asked Helen.

'The prostitutes? They're always vulnerable and sometimes they're beaten up or robbed. That tonight was one of the worst incidents I've seen.'

'Why do these women end up on the street? Could they not get another job?'

Sergeant Duffy stopped and turned to her. 'My God, do you think they want to do this? These women are desperate and there's a pitiful story to be told by every one of them. I often think that, there but for the grace of God, it could be any one of us. It's our duty to protect them, Harrison, don't ever forget that.'

When they got back, Helen went to wash her face and hands in the ladies' lavatory, while she cried for a girl called Marilyn that she never knew and thought about Laurence Fitzpatrick who had tried to save her.

Chapter 18

It was a day that Helen had been dreading. She opened the bedroom curtains to let the sun stream in. Why couldn't it have rained? She wanted thunder and lightning, an ominous sky as dark as her mood. Looking over Brookdale Park the hawthorn was in bloom and the beds were full of marigolds. It would have been a glorious Sunday for Jim's birthday.

The bread was stale but she toasted it anyway, scraped the last of the margarine over it and covered it with scrambled eggs. Except it wasn't scrambled eggs it was dried egg powder mixed with water and it tasted like cardboard. She mooched around in her nightie then read an old copy of *Tit-Bits*. She should be washing her hair, her clothes, the lino... but she couldn't face any of it. In the end she went to her bedroom, put on Jim's cricket pullover, got back into bed and cried.

She must have fallen asleep because she awoke with

a start; someone was shouting her name through the letter box. She dragged herself out of bed and went downstairs. 'Who is it?' she shouted.

'It's me, let me in.'

She really shouldn't go to the door when she wasn't properly dressed.

'Come on, Helen.'

She gave a heavy sigh and opened it to see Frank standing there.

'Look at you, sleepyhead. It's a beautiful day and your carriage awaits.' He stepped to one side and waved his arm towards the road where a motorbike stood idling.

'What's going on? Why have you got a bike?'

'I borrowed it from a friend. I thought you might like to go for a spin.'

'Not today, Frank, I can't… Anyway, I'm not dressed.'

'I guessed as much when I saw the pullover. Or are you opening bat at Woodhouses today?'

'You know why I can't.'

'I know that you're sad, I know you've been crying. It'll be a hard day to get through, Helen, and I feel it too, but what would Jim say?'

'Jim can't say anything. He's dead.' The tears welled in her eyes.

He reached out as though he would touch her, then lowered his hand. 'Come on, Helen, you need to get out of the house for a while. You can cry all you want when you get back. Please, come for a ride.'

She hadn't seen him since he had left in a huff when he found out she'd joined the police, and she had to admit that she had missed him.

'I'll have to get ready.'

'Take your time, I'll sit outside on the bike.'

She had never been on a motorbike before and he showed her how to swing her leg over the bike, where to put her feet and, when he sat in front of her, he told her to put her arms round his waist. 'Hold on tight,' he shouted as he revved the engine, and they roared off. At first, Helen caught her breath at the speed they were travelling, while the roar of the engine was deafening and the wind rushed past her.

They went through Oldham and, beyond that, they were in open countryside where now and again they sped through little villages, always climbing higher and higher. Once they reached the top of the moors, Frank slowed the bike, pulled into the side of the road and turned off the engine.

It was cool up here and a stiff wind was blowing. There was nothing but rough moorland as far as the eye could see in any direction and the low-growing heather in bloom, painting the landscape purple. Trees were sparse and those that had gained a foothold hunkered down. Stunted.

'There's a bit of shelter just across the road there under that rocky outcrop.'

'You know this place?'

'Hmm, I used to come up here camping when I was a boy.'

Then she remembered. 'You and Jim.'

He nodded. 'I wanted to be here today. I wanted to show you.' His voice was low.

'All right,' she said. 'Show me.'

He took a haversack from the inside of the seat and threw it over his shoulder. 'Stick close to me. There's a lot of boggy ground up here and it can be dangerous if you don't know where to find the firmer paths.' They crossed the road. 'Over here the rocks are just below the surface and the land rises. It's not far.' They walked for about fifteen minutes over uneven ground. She slipped a few times and he reached out his hand to steady her or help her clamber over rocks. They saw no one, only a few scattered sheep, that looked up now and again and bleated. They circled the outcrop and beyond it was a sheltered hollow. They slithered down the slope where the wind had dropped and the sun was warm on their faces.

'This is it.' Frank was grinning and throwing his arms out wide as if to encompass the entire moors. 'There's the place.' He took her hand and led her to a grassy tussock flecked with cowslips and buttercups. She watched him as he took off his coat and spread it on the ground, his face like a boy wagging off school for the day. Of course, that was it – this was where he and Jim would have come when they were boys to be free from the back-to-back terraces, and the smoke from the mill chimneys.

Frank opened his haversack and pulled out doorstep sandwiches wrapped in newspaper. He handed her one, delved into the bag again and brought out two bottles of pale ale then levered the bottle tops off with his penknife.

They sat eating the butties and drinking the ale and Helen felt she was a million miles from anywhere. The silence settled around them... the noise and chatter and worries had been left behind in the city. There was no need to talk.

She closed her eyes and brought her darling, living and breathing Jim to mind: his smile, a wink, his sleeping face on the pillow next to hers. His strong arms and tender hands. Chasing her up the stairs, catching her in a real fireman's lift that made her howl with laughter. She saw all that and more in this quiet place.

The touch on her arm startled her, so intent was she to have Jim vividly in her head.

'It sweeps away the nonsense in life right down the drain, doesn't it?' said Frank. 'In the middle of nowhere you can think about what's important. When we were lads, Jim and me used to come up here a lot. Two on a push-bike, an old ex-army tent and whatever we could steal from Ma's pantry. This was our place. We'd pitch the tent, set traps for rabbits, and the best thing...' The hint of a smile played around his lips. 'We'd get a fire going. One summer's night we were camping here, asleep in the tent. I was dead to the world, but Jim shook me awake. "Get up, get up!" he shouted. I crawled out of the tent and caught the smell of burning. The ground was glowing red and crackling. We thought we'd stamped out the fire before we went to sleep, but the wind must have fanned the embers. The moor was tinder dry and the fire was spreading. I stood there mesmerised, but Jim had his wits about him. He was pulling the tent posts out of the ground and shouted for me to do the same. Together we yanked the canvas off the poles and spread it on the fire to cover it and we stamped and stamped on it. Then we moved beyond it where small fires had taken hold. We did the same thing again and again. At first it seemed that for every patch of burning ground we extinguished, other fires were springing up. I was frightened and I pleaded with Jim for us to run away, but he wouldn't give up. "Keep going," he shouted over and over and I couldn't leave him, could I? The canvas was almost gone, and our shoes the same, when we heard the fire engine bells. The wind had blown the fire over the ridge of the hollow and it began to spread down over an exposed part of the moor. Someone down there had alerted the brigade.'

Frank closed his eyes. Helen waited. He shook his head and looked at her. 'That were the first time he made me do the right thing, the first time he saved my life and it weren't to be the last. I don't remember us saying,

"Let's be firemen when we grow up." It was just the way we knew it would be; soon as we were old enough, we joined the brigade together. Jim could read a fire better than anyone I knew. He was fearless, but that didn't stop him from being cautious.' He paused. 'He were my best mate.' Frank bowed his head and Helen just caught the whisper. 'I still can't believe he's gone.'

She put her arm around him. 'I know, Frank, I know.' She was sure he was crying by the furtive wipe of his eyes and she ran her hand across his back to soothe him. The minutes passed and she thought of Frank and his grief, still as raw as her own after months of loss. He'd brought her here to the moors to share it with her and she was surprised that, in a strange way, it had brought her some release from her pain. People never mentioned her loss and she wouldn't ever bring it up. It was almost certain that Frank had been treated the same way.

'Frank, I'm glad you brought me here. I think you and me are in the same boat.'

He raised his head and looked at her. 'Are we?'

'Yes,' said Helen. 'No one ever speaks about Jim, except you and me. Who else says his name out loud? It's like he never existed, but you and I think of him every day. Don't you see, Frank? You're not alone.'

'You're right, no one mentions him at the station house; it's like they're embarrassed, but every time I climb into a fire engine I think of him there beside me, looking out for me, you know?' He looked at her as though an amazing thought had occurred to him. 'But you and me can talk about him, can't we, like today?'

'Of course we can; we'll talk about our good memories and I wouldn't even mind if they were sad sometimes.'

The ride back to Manchester was all downhill with the wind at their back and Helen felt invigorated by the whole excursion. Frank had been right, she did need to get out of the house and he was so kind to think of her.

She invited him in for a cup of tea when they got back.

'The kitchen looks different,' said Frank. 'Have you done something with it?'

'Oh, just curtains and cushion covers. I'm earning decent money so I'll do a bit more when I've time. The parlour's next, I think, seeing as there's not much in there. I'll paint it first.'

'I could help you with that. You'll need to emulsion the ceiling first. Me mate has stepladders, I could bring them round one weekend and give you a hand. I can't say when; you know what it's like when the bombing starts.'

'I understand that and I couldn't ask you to give up a day off. Gwen would have something to say about that.' She laughed. 'You know, she thinks you don't spend enough time together.'

'I'll do whatever I want with my free time. Same as

her when she wants to go out dancing and I'm dead beat. Her head's full of nonsense half the time.'

Helen tried to stick up for her friend. 'She just wants a bit of fun, she works hard too.'

'And you?' he said.

'Me?'

'I was surprised that you'd gone dancing with her.'

'I didn't really want to, I don't think I'll go again.'

'I'm glad to hear it. There's too many men in uniform trying to pick up girls. I wouldn't trust them as far as I could throw them.'

'That's a bit harsh.'

He turned on her. 'You don't know what these fellas are like. I worry about you and I know what Jim would say about it.'

It felt like a slap in the face, made worse because she still felt guilty for having taken some pleasure in the young airman's arms. 'You don't have to worry about me,' she said, a little sharply. 'I won't be going out dancing again.'

Chapter 19

Helen had spent the previous two days collating and filing reports of looting during the latest bombing raid. Most of them would probably go unsolved and that annoyed her, but what made her really angry was that people had taken advantage and stolen from shops or, worse still, from bombed-out homes.

'That looks interesting.' Helen looked up to see Sergeant Duffy smiling at her. 'What would you say to some real police work?'

'I'd say, yes please.'

'Good. Come into my office and I'll tell you about it.'

Sergeant Duffy asked her to sit down and Helen could see she was pleased about something. 'I've just had a very interesting call from CID,' she said. 'They've asked me to send you over to Newton Street nick. They think you might be able to help them, with a case.'

Helen couldn't believe it. 'CID, and they've asked for me?'

Sergeant Duffy was still smiling. 'They need a woman to help with an unusual investigation. It's a plain-clothes job.'

'What do you mean?'

'You'd pretend to be an ordinary member of the public in order to gather evidence and report back to the detective in charge.'

Helen was disappointed. 'But I couldn't do that. I wouldn't know how.'

'You're more than capable of doing this job. In fact, you're exactly what they need because it involves women who've been bereaved. This is a real chance for you to do something worthwhile.'

Helen's mind was racing. She'd do anything to help women like herself, but she knew nothing about collecting evidence. She wasn't trained to do that, and as for pretending...

'Look, at least hear what CID want you to do. If it might upset you, or maybe it's a bit too personal, just say no. I won't think any less of you.'

But Helen couldn't help feeling that Sergeant Duffy would be disappointed in her if she passed up this opportunity. 'All right,' she said. 'I'll go and talk to them.'

'Good, get yourself round to Newton Street nick right now. Ask for DC Kershaw.'

*

She hadn't seen nor heard of Ken Kershaw since he had returned the stolen garments to Fenner's Fashions. She was glad to hear that he was involved in this case and in fact she was pretty certain he'd asked for her specifically.

'Helen, nice to see you again.' He came striding towards her, hand outstretched. 'Glad you're going to help us. Come upstairs and I'll fill you in.'

She didn't like to say she had only come to hear what the case was about. Had Sergeant Duffy already told him she would do it?

The poky office was empty: four desks in a block; stacks of files everywhere. 'How are you doing at headquarters?' he asked.

'Well, I have even more filing than you, but I get to walk the beat sometimes. Sergeant Duffy said you might have something interesting for me to do, but I warn you I've no real experience.'

Ken cleared a chair of files and she sat down. 'Helen, you have more experience in this matter than anyone else in this building. First, let me reassure you that there are no obvious dangers involved, but it's a sensitive issue.' He sat back in his chair. 'We've been asked by a leading member of the church to investigate a so-called medium. His wife attended a seance without his knowledge, her brother had recently been killed in action, and her husband is demanding the medium be charged with fraud and taking money with menaces.'

'I didn't know seances were against the law.'

'They're not, but the clergy hate them.'

'I thought you wanted me to do something that would help bereaved women.'

'Exactly that. We want you to attend the next seance to observe what goes on. We're looking for proof of the medium causing distress or demanding money, and more importantly, whether any deception takes place.'

It wasn't quite what Helen had expected. 'So, I go to the seance and report back on what happened?'

'Yes, it's that simple.'

'Couldn't anyone do that?'

'No, it needs somebody in the same situation to really understand what these poor women are experiencing and whether they're being duped. You could help us decide whether it's harmless.'

She had never had much faith in the Church and the idea that the dead lived on somewhere beyond our understanding. She had even less time for charlatans who pretended to bring them back for a cosy chat. Taking advantage of a widow's grief was cruel and shouldn't be allowed.

'All right, I'll do it.'

'That's great, thanks, Helen. You just have to be yourself, see what's going on, and come back and tell us. Now the medium will be expecting the clergyman's wife – she had arranged to go back on Friday night – and we'd like you to take her place. You can say she couldn't come and you're her friend and recently widowed. Could you do Friday night?'

'Yes, I could.'

'Excellent! I'll pick you up at seven.'

In the days between agreeing to attend the seance and the Friday night, she worried about what to expect. What if the medium did have some sort of second sight and saw straight through her? What if she had to listen to the woman pretending Jim was in the room? That would be so upsetting. She even, in one of her more far-fetched scenarios, imagined that Jim would actually be there in the ether asking her what the hell she was doing there.

On the drive to Whalley Range, Ken went over again the sort of thing to look out for and the importance of 'keeping her cover'. She had understood it all the first time, and in her mind she went over her opinion. She didn't believe that the dead could talk to the living, that Jim would be waiting in this woman's house to pass on a thrupenny crumb of comfort to his grieving wife. If he'd had something to say, she would have heard it herself in her own house.

They arrived at a three-storey Victorian terrace with

a gate, garden and a glazed vestibule. It would seem seances paid handsomely.

'I'll be waiting just a bit further down the road when you come out. Good luck.'

She pressed the bell and waited. Why was her heart racing? She took a few deep breaths to calm herself. It wasn't the seance that made her nervous, it was the whole thing about plain-clothes, getting evidence, cloak and dagger. The door opened and there was a plump woman in a navy and pink printed dress. Her grey hair was shaped with permanent waves and her toothy smile looked friendly enough. 'Hello, I take it you're here for the meeting? What's your name?'

'Helen.'

She consulted a little diary. 'I've not got you booked in.'

'Oh, my friend Agnes couldn't come. I hope you don't mind, but I lost my husband recently and she thought it would be all right for me to come instead.' Helen was surprised at the ease with which the lies tripped off her tongue.

'Of course, it's all right, Helen. I'm Mabel. Come in, you're very welcome,' and she ushered Helen up the hallway, past a large barometer and a gilt mirror, into the parlour. There were four women already there. 'Chat among yourselves while we wait for one more lady,' she said and left them.

Helen said hello and tried to appear friendly while

saying very little as the others talked. She observed them closely. Joan, an elderly woman, explained that she'd been before. 'It were very interesting last time,' she said. 'My Albert passed with his heart two year ago and he said he were in fine fettle over the other side. Now I'm hoping he'll bring me sister Margaret over. It'll be great hearing from her again.'

A well-heeled woman, with a large cameo brooch on her lapel, seemed quite composed. 'I just want to know that my brother is happy at last, Lord knows he deserves it.' She turned to the woman next to her, who was already dabbing her eyes with a handkerchief, and asked who she hoped to hear from. 'My lad Ernie, he was at Dunkirk, drowned...' She offered nothing more.

But it was the youngest woman, a girl really, not much more than eighteen, that Helen felt so sorry for. Her face was pale and drawn, her eyes darting here and there like a frightened animal. Helen recognised herself in the girl as she had been in those days immediately after Jim's death, when her grief was raw and the shock had lodged inside her. God knows how she would react to a message from beyond the grave. The cameo woman tried to draw her into the conversation by asking her if she had only just been bereaved. The girl managed to nod and that alone set her weeping softly.

'And what about you, dear?' She smiled at Helen, drawing her into the conversation, and all eyes turned to her. 'Who are you hoping will come through this evening?' What to answer? What comfort could there be in a stranger making up some sentimental rubbish?

She said simply, 'I want to hear from my husband.'

The room seemed to have taken on an atmosphere of sadness and despair and she felt the weight of her own grief pressing upon her.

Nevertheless, the ice was broken and, as the minutes ticked by, they chatted as women do to pass the time. Helen listened to what was said and contributed a little, but was careful not to give away any of her story. The girl said nothing.

The medium returned and invited them to come into the dining room. The other lady they had waited for had not arrived. 'Sometimes that happens,' explained Mabel. 'Their courage fails them, poor souls.'

The room was lit by three table lamps, covered in chiffon to create a suffused glow. There was nothing on the round table other than a ruby-coloured chenille cloth. Helen sat with the window behind her and facing the medium. To her right was a large mahogany sideboard and to the left was a grand fireplace of black marble. The girl sat beside her and Helen could almost feel her shaking. Unlike the parlour, this room was distinctly cold.

When everyone was seated, Mabel explained, 'There is nothing to be frightened of, those spirits that will join us here tonight are just like us; they want to connect with those they love. We begin by creating the circle.

Please put your hands, palm down, on the table and spread them to touch the hands of the ladies next to you. Do not break the circle and please do not make any sudden noises, whatever happens. Clear your mind of everything except your loved one who has passed over.' Well, thought Helen, in for a penny in for a pound, and she brought to mind Jim's face that last night they were together at the working men's club.

The silence seemed to creep around them.

'Let us begin,' said Mabel and Helen shivered.

'Come, spirit. I sense you near. Is your loved one here? I'm ready and waiting to pass on your message. Speak to me.' Mabel cocked an ear as though listening, now she was nodding, then turning to Joan, the elderly woman. 'Ah, your husband is here again. You have such a strong connection to him.'

'How do, Albert?' The woman greeted him as though she'd run into him on Market Street.

Mabel smiled. 'Oh, he says he's got someone called Margaret with him? Do you know a Margaret?'

'Course I do. She's me sister. Hello, our kid, I don't half miss you. Are you all right?'

Mabel frowned and looked up, presumably at Margaret hovering somewhere above her shoulder, then she turned back to the living sister. 'She says, you're not to fritter away that money she left you in her will and you'd be better off using some of it to mend that crumbling chimney before it falls on your head, else you'll be keepin' her company before you know it.'

The woman was affronted. 'Well, you just tell her, the bloody chimney can wait. There was no point in her keepin' that money under the mattress. I'm goin' to enjoy it, for there's no pockets in shrouds.'

God, what a farce, thought Helen.

'Now, don't let's get involved in any arguments. That's not what we're here for,' said Mabel, sternly. 'Your husband says you're to calm down, or your nerves will get the better of you.'

Helen could tell she was seething, but the woman pursed her lips and said nothing. Helen had to stifle a smile at the thought of a dead husband giving orders to his wife from beyond the grave.

Mabel went quickly on to describe a softly spoken man in a pin-stripe suit and a bowler hat. 'That's John, my brother,' said the woman with the cameo. 'Can you tell him his wife has sold the house and moved to Cheadle. So, I won't have to see her ever again, thank goodness.' But it seemed that John was no more than a whisper that faded away.

The mother of the lad who died at Dunkirk was next to receive a message. 'I've a young man here, in uniform. His passing was quick and without pain,' said Mabel. 'Ah, I see, he drowned. Dunkirk, he tells me. Now he's saying, "I'm fine, Mam, don't worry. When you're in the kitchen cooking the potato 'ash, I'm there with you. Have you felt my hand on your shoulder?"'

The mother's face was in awe. 'Yes, yes, Ernie. I felt you there with me. I did. I did. Oh, love, it's so good to hear from you. Your dad has been so upset too. We miss you so much, son.' She wiped the tears from her eyes, and Helen saw they were glinting with wonder.

'Ernie, have you anything else you want to say to your mother?' asked Mabel and she did that listening face again. 'Right, Ernie. I'll tell her. He says, "We'll be together again someday and don't forget I love you, Mam, and tell Dad I said he's to look after you."'

The emotional atmosphere was now thick as broth and the girl was becoming more agitated.

'Ah, another young man. He's so desperate to talk to his wife.' For a moment Helen caught her breath. It couldn't be a message for her, could it? Mabel went on, 'Not long married, he tells me.' Mabel was flustered. 'I can't catch his name. Slow down, slow down,' she told him. 'Who do you want to speak to?' and slowly she turned to the girl and smiled. Helen breathed a sigh of relief.

'It's your husband, Violet.' For a moment Helen was startled. Mabel knew the girl's name? Then she remembered that she had been asked her name in the vestibule when she arrived: Mabel knew all their names.

But now Violet was crying out, 'Johnny, is it you?'

'Yes, it's Johnny. He's here, Violet, right next to you. He's smiling at you. He wants you to know you're more beautiful than ever. He says, "You mustn't be sad. Don't worry about me. You made me so happy and I'm so sorry about what happened."'

'But the baby?'

Helen saw Mabel's eyes widen ever so slightly at the mention of a baby. With barely a hesitation she called, 'Johnny, are you there? I can't hear you. Speak to him again, Violet, I'm sure he's still with us.'

'Johnny, we're going to have a baby.' She sounded desperate. 'I don't know how I'll manage without you.'

All Helen could think of was that it could've been her. How would she have managed?

But Mabel was back into her stride. 'He's here, I can see him! It's not often that happens. His love is so strong, Violet. Oh goodness me! He's kissing your cheek.'

Violet's hand shot to her face. 'I felt him! He's really here.'

'Listen, Violet, listen.' Mabel drew her back. 'Johnny says you and the baby will be fine, because he'll be watching over the both of you. He wants you to be brave and to know how much he loves you.'

For the first time, Helen saw the girl smile. The haunted expression had disappeared, to be replaced by joy and, yes, she was beautiful. Helen felt tears well in her eyes to see her transformed.

'I sense another spirit. A strong man in his prime. Helen, I think it might be your husband. I'm trying to catch what he's saying but he seems far off. Concentrate, Helen, and try to draw him to you. Focus on him.' And

Helen found herself silently calling his name. Wondering if he might have found his way to her.

'Ah,' Mabel sighed. 'He brings the smell of smoke with him. Can you smell it?' Helen gasped at her words. Why would she say something out of the blue like that? She breathed in, was there smoke? No, she couldn't catch it.

'I can smell it,' said the cameo lady.-

'So can I,' said the girl.

Helen shivered.

'Believe, just believe,' pleaded Mabel, and Helen tried so hard to bring him to her. 'I hear him now, Helen! "Be strong," he says. "I love you more than anything."' And she let out an anguished moan and fell forward on to the table.

Helen looked at her in disbelief. What was she to make of it all? The other women were struck dumb until a good minute later Mabel lifted her head and cried, 'The spirits have left us,' and a moment later she addressed them in a bright voice. 'Now, ladies, if you want to make a donation, I'll leave that up to you.' She took a fruit bowl from the sideboard and set it on the ruby chenille.

Helen put in half a crown, the other women gave notes while the girl had a handful of copper that could have come from a piggy bank. The women filed out, thanking Mabel and promising to return. Helen was the last to leave and at the door she turned to look back at the scene. 'Can you smell it now?' asked Mabel. Helen didn't answer, there might well have been a whiff of smoke in the air, but she couldn't be sure. 'He's proud of you, you know,' she said.

Ken was waiting for her in the car. 'Well, how did that go?'

Helen sighed and tried to release the tension in her body. 'It was a very strange experience. To tell you the truth, I'm not certain what went on in there. I need to think about it a bit more, so much happened in a short space of time. But don't worry, you'll have my report on Monday.'

'That's great,' said Ken. 'Just an outline of what happened and any sign of trickery, distress to the women, asking for money – that kind of thing.'

Helen didn't even try to sleep, instead she relived the event from the moment she entered the house to when she left. The waiting in the parlour for the sixth person to arrive gave the women a chance to speak about their dead relatives. She sifted the facts they revealed: a name, cause of death, a place. Were there enough clues there for the medium to fashion a reading? But she hadn't been in the parlour. Besides, she herself had been careful not to give anything away and said only that she was hoping to connect with her husband. Then there was the girl who didn't speak in the parlour at all. Could someone not in the room have heard the women's conversations? Was the door left open a crack? She didn't think so. There could have been a hole in the room somewhere, but she didn't see anything suspicious. Maybe it was hidden with a picture or... a barometer?

The dining room had been very cold, but the medium could have left the windows open all day to make it chilly. She recalled where everyone sat and wondered why there wasn't an empty chair either at the table or set to the side for the person who didn't turn up. Maybe there never was another woman on the list. And, come to think of it, the woman with the cameo brooch had kept the conversation going all the time they waited.

Once the seance began, the medium had been kind and most things she told the women were comforting.

Then it was her turn... and the whole whiff of smoke thing. Even though she didn't smell it at first, the suggestion was enough to evoke memories of Jim. Even now, as she thought of it, she could conjure up the smell in her mind. But that wasn't the same as actually smelling it.

She lay awake thinking of Jim, recalling how the smell would linger in their bedroom, especially at night when he came home after a late shift. He'd take her in his arms in their narrow bed and the smell of smoke in his hair would forever remind her that she was safe and loved.

*

Helen took her report on the seance round to Newton Street on Monday morning and gave it to Ken. He asked her to wait and she watched him as he read it: nodding; pulling a face as if in disbelief; smiling. 'This is really thorough, well done. It's not that simple, is it? I think you're right about an accomplice, most likely the well-dressed woman, who got the conversation going, while the medium was listening through some sort of unseen opening in the wall. So, what have we got? There was deception, but it could be hard to prove; there were some mysterious shenanigans going on, but in the end the outcome was all positive. The women left happy – they even left a donation.'

'So, is that it then?' asked Helen.

'Not quite, I need to speak to the DI. After that I'll go and see our clergyman and I want you to come with me. No doubt he'll have questions to ask you.'

'Do I have to go?'

'Of course.' He held up her report. 'This is all your work and, not only that, you experienced it first-hand.'

They arrived outside an imposing church with a steeple, in a good area of south Manchester. Next door to it was the manse. A woman answered the door and her face flushed crimson at the sight of Ken showing a warrant card and Helen behind him in uniform. 'My husband is in his study,' she said and led them down the hallway.

The minister stood up and came from behind his

desk as they entered into the room. He shook Ken's hand and gave a puzzled glance at Helen.

'This is my colleague, WAPC Harrison,' said Ken.

He barely looked at her. 'Sit down, sit down, please. I'm hoping you've got to the bottom of this wicked deception.'

'We've made a thorough investigation into the matter,' said Ken. 'Harrison, here, posed as a grieving widow and took part in the seance. I've brought her along today in case you have specific questions about what went on. She has also written a report that you might want to read.' He passed it across the desk, but the minister was staring at Helen.

'I understood from the chief constable that he would put his best men on the job.'

'With respect, sir, we needed to put a woman in there,' Ken explained. 'It was the only way to find out exactly what went on in order to determine whether a crime had been committed.'

The minister shook his head, picked up the report and scanned it. When he had finished, he said, 'Well, there you are. If this is what went on in that room, it's either the work of the devil or a shyster. Either way, it must be against the law to deceive grieving women by telling them lies and taking their money.'

'Excuse me, sir,' said Helen. 'Everything the medium said to the women was comforting and they all left the seance with their raw grief soothed – it was like ointment on a weeping wound. They were more content and accepting of their loved one's death than when they came in. Surely that's a good thing?'

He looked at her as though she was mad and turned to Ken. 'The medium was deceiving them and taking money under false pretences. I demand that—'

'How can you say that?' Helen challenged him. 'Isn't it exactly what you do as a minister? Don't you offer words of comfort? Don't you tell wives that their husbands are in heaven? Is it not the same thing?'

'Now look here, young lady, I'm a man of the church and it's my calling to give succour to the bereaved.'

Helen could feel the anger rising inside her and she fought to keep her composure. 'At my husband's funeral the minister told me, "He's in the arms of Jesus now." I didn't believe him, any more than I believed the woman at the seance, but I found her more comforting in her manner.'

The minister ignored her and turned to Ken. 'Is the outcome of this case to be determined by a slip of a girl?'

'No, sir, our detective inspector has reviewed the evidence and he has decided not to proceed.'

The minister stood up. 'I shall be writing to the chief constable!' he said. 'You can see yourself out, I'm sure.'

Back in the car, Ken burst out laughing. 'I can't believe you – arguing theology with a minister of the church – he looked like he was about to have a stroke!

And what did he call you, "a slip of a girl"? Well, you certainly got the better of him.'

Helen had no idea what theology was, but she knew she'd ruffled the feathers of an important man. 'Will I get into trouble? I won't lose my job, will I?'

'Course not, we've got far more important things to do than chase after someone who makes a few quid telling sad women what they want to hear. We've got an unsolved murder on our patch, not to mention the looting and a black market that's running rampant. That's what you call crime.' He looked across at her and smiled. '"A slip of a girl." I like that.'

By the end of the week, word of Helen standing up to a minister had got around, so too had the dismissive description 'a slip of a girl', only, by then, it had become a compliment.

Chapter 20

Helen woke with a start and looked round the room, certain that there had been a noise. There it was again – a sharp crack at the window. She rubbed her eyes and waited, expecting to hear it again. Instead, someone was calling her name outside in the yard. She jumped out of bed and drew back the curtains. There was Frank with a ladder in one hand and a box under his arm.

'What a sleepy-head! I've been knocking on your front door for ages.'

'Wait, I'll be down in a minute.'

She put on her dressing gown and ran downstairs in her bare feet to let him in.

'I hope you weren't planning a lazy Sunday. You and I have a big job on today.'

She clapped her hands. 'Is it the parlour? Are we going to paint it?'

'We certainly are.'

She knelt down to look in the box. There were tins of paint, brushes and rags. 'Oh, what colour is it?'

'Fire station red.'

She looked up at him, aghast.

He laughed and ruffled her hair. 'No, it isn't. The man in the shop said it was cream, but I couldn't guarantee it. Paint's hard to find, you know.'

She stood up and adjusted her dressing gown tighter. 'I'll get washed and dressed then.'

'Good idea – never paint in your nightclothes and bare feet.'

'Well, go on then.' She pushed him towards the parlour door. 'I won't be long.'

She boiled a kettle and washed at the sink then went in search of something to wear. Then she made them a brew and carried it into the parlour.

Frank was kneeling down, stirring a pot of paint with a stick, and he looked up as she came in.

'What's the matter?' she said.

'What are you wearing?'

'Oh, you mean the trousers? I'm going to be climbing ladders, aren't I?'

'Are they Jim's?'

'No, I bought them at a jumble sale, the shirt too.' She laughed. 'The turban is my own.'

He stared at her. 'You look so different dressed like that, I never would have thought...'

Helen wasn't sure what he wanted to say, but he

seemed embarrassed. She handed him his mug of tea and took her own. 'Where do we start?' she asked.

He gave her the smallest wall in the room and set up the ladders for her. 'I don't want you falling, so I'll use the chair. Have you painted before?'

She rolled her eyes at him. Did he think she was stupid? How hard could it be?

'Right then.' He set her pot of paint on the top of the ladder and handed her a brush. 'Try not to get it everywhere.'

She dipped the brush and held it up. The paint was running up her arm. 'No, no!' he shouted. 'Get rid of the drips on the side of the tin.'

'I know,' she said. This time she got as far as getting some paint on the wall, but she only used the brush one way.

'Helen, come down a moment.'

'Why, is this not right?'

'Just come down.'

He took her paint pot, got the right amount on the brush and handed it to her. 'Now face the wall,' and he went behind her and covered her hand with his. 'Up down, up down. Do you feel the rhythm?' She nodded. 'Now get more paint. That's right, no drips. Get the rhythm again. That's it, you've got it.'

She turned to him and winked. 'Nothing to it really.'

They painted through the morning, sometimes in companionable silence, other times they'd start a conversation and fall silent again. They talked about Jim and Frank apologised for being so grumpy last time they met. 'I shouldn't have said all that about you going out dancing. It were bang out of order. Why shouldn't you get out of the house to do ordinary things? It's not as if you were going to run off with some man.'

Helen chewed her lip, but didn't say anything.

'I won't lie to you though, I still don't agree with you joining the police. I worry about you, you know. You could get hurt.'

'Don't worry, I've had all the training. I know what I'm doing.'

'Helen, I work with highly trained people every day, but that doesn't stop them getting hurt sometimes.'

'But it's not like I'm a real policewoman. I do the filing and sometimes I man the switchboard and, if I'm lucky, I get to help women and children. Where's the danger in that?'

They stopped around dinner time. 'I've got some cheese and onion pie – but there's no onion in it, only potato.

'That'll do me. Don't suppose you've got any beer?'

'Just corporation pop. What did Gwen think about you helping me paint the parlour?'

'I didn't tell her.'

Helen suspected as much. 'Are things not quite right with you and Gwen?'

He puffed out his cheeks and sighed. 'I don't know. Sometimes I'd rather things were different.'

'But you wouldn't finish with her, would you?'

He flashed a look at her, eyes hardened, but he said nothing.

She felt like she was treading on private ground. 'I'm sure everything will work out between you. You've been together a long while.'

He shrugged his shoulders. 'Come on then, let's get back to work.'

They painted all afternoon and when it was finished, they stood in the middle of the room and marvelled at the transformation. 'It's so light and clean. I love it.' She smiled. 'Thanks, Frank. I could never have done this on my own.'

'Well, that's what mates are for.'

'I'm trying to save up some money to buy a sofa. Will you come with me again when I go looking?'

'Whatever you need, Helen, you've only to ask. Now, what would you say to a pale ale at that pub just along the road?'

'I'd say we've earned it. I'll just get changed, won't be a minute.'

'Never mind that, you look fine. Trousers suit you.'

They walked the hundred yards to the Horse Shoe and went into the snug. The babble of voices stopped immediately and all eyes turned upon them. Frank nodded to the room. 'All right?' and they went to the bar. The conversation resumed and they took their drinks to a little alcove in the corner.

'What went on there?' he asked.

'Did Gwen not tell you that the next-door neighbour accused me of having men at the house?'

'No, she didn't.' He was furious. 'If I'd known, I'd have gone straight to the woman's house to put her right! Oh, wait a minute, she meant me, didn't she?'

Helen nodded. 'I think she was spreading rumours. People around here think the worst of me, I know that. Then she told my landlord and he tried to evict me because there was only Jim's name on the tenancy.'

'I didn't know this; why didn't you tell me?' He jumped up. 'I'll sort them out!'

She grabbed his arm. 'Sit down, Frank, please.' He sat, still scowling. 'It's all been sorted out,' she told him. 'The police spoke to him about me and he's been nice as ninepence ever since, and as for Ada, she keeps out of my way. She knows she was in the wrong and I get the feeling that she won't cross me again. She's wary of the uniform.'

'You have to tell me when things go wrong, Helen. I'll protect you, you know that. I promised Jim, for God's sake!'

They left after one drink and Frank came back to collect his stuff.

'Wait here,' she said, and she ran upstairs, coming back with Jim's suit. 'Would you like to have this? He bought it for our wedding, but he hardly ever wore it. I'm not sure why I've kept it.'

'I don't know...'

'Well, just try the jacket on. Jim was the same build as you.'

The sight of him took her breath away. She tried to cover up her confusion by walking around him, smoothing out the shoulders and straightening the collar. 'What do you think?' she asked.

'It feels good.' She looked into his face and saw that he too was moved to be wearing his best mate's jacket and he tried to make light of it. 'Wonder if he left me any money in it.' He put his hand in the inside pocket and then he did it a second time. 'What's this?' he said. It was a crisp, white, folded five-pound note.

Helen gasped. 'Oh, my God, it's the money he won at the working men's club. How can that be? I searched the pockets. I thought someone had stolen it.'

He handed it to her. 'It was here all the time, Helen. Did you not know that some jackets have a double inside pocket, one for change and one for notes? That'll go a long way towards your sofa.'

All this time she had thought her mother had stolen the money. It had been the last straw in cutting off all ties with her.

'I'll have the suit, if that's all right,' he said.

'Yes, I want you to have it.'

He looked around the parlour and smiled. 'Look what we've done together.'

She nodded. 'You're a good friend, Frank.'

Chapter 21

'Bloody hell! This weather'll be the ruin of me. It's the end of May and every day has been cold and wet.' Fenner wagged his finger at Pearl. 'If we don't start shifting the summer stock soon, we could be out of business by the end of June, especially with these rumours about clothes rationing.'

'I know, I've been telling you for ages that we're in dire straits.'

Fenner yanked open the drawer of his desk, took out a Milk of Magnesia bottle, unscrewed it and gulped a mouthful.

'Harold, what have I told you? You can't go on like this, eating and drinking as much as you do. Not to mention the amount of money you're taking out of the business.'

'Don't you tell me what I should and shouldn't do – you're not my bloody wife! And as a kept woman, you cost me far more than a few bottles of whisky.'

She ignored his remarks. 'Anyway, you need to go to the doctor.'

'Will you shut up about that? You don't go to the doctor with indigestion!'

Pearl shrugged her shoulders and went back to their financial state. 'The two lads in the basement have had their call-up papers, so we won't replace them, and maybe we could lay off a couple of the packers. That might help.'

He tutted. 'I was thinking more about the office. You ladies don't seem to have much to do.'

Pearl could have screamed at him. He had no idea of the effort she had put in trying to keep them afloat. But maybe he had a point in Rita's case. She had never been a particularly good junior clerk, but since she came back to work after the bombing, she had been lazy and argumentative. 'Well, maybe we could lose Rita, she doesn't have many skills and her heart's not in the work. Her timekeeping isn't that good either. She's been late back after dinner a few times recently.'

'I could have put money on you saying that. You never wanted her back; you wanted that stuck-up goddaughter of yours to keep the job.'

'That's not—'

He held his hand up. 'I'll be the one to say who gets laid off in my company and I've decided that it'll be Dorothy.'

'Dorothy! You can't lay her off and keep Rita?

That girl hasn't a clue. I need Dorothy to help run this business.'

'Since when do you run this business?'

Too late she realised what she had said. 'I didn't mean that. I meant running the office, that's all.'

He glared at her. 'Well, there'll be one less of you sitting there supping tea by the end of the day.'

'Harold, please, she's got an elderly mother and she needs the money.'

'I'm not discussing it.' He stood up. 'Right, I'm off to do a bit of business. So, I'll leave it to you to tell her. Just make sure she's gone by the end of the day. I'll see you tonight.'

There was no arguing with him in that mood. She'd have to do as he ordered, but maybe she could talk him round; explain in detail that Dorothy did far more for the business than Rita ever did.

Back in the office, she sent Rita out to post some letters, then told Dorothy that Mr Fenner had asked her to deliver some bad news.

Dorothy was immediately wary. 'Have I done something wrong?'

'No, you haven't, but I have to tell you that you're to be laid off.'

The shock registered on Dorothy's face. 'It's to do with the accounts, isn't it? I'm not stupid, I know the business is in trouble. I thought I'd lose some hours, be made part time. I never expected...' She broke down in tears. 'What will I do? I've no savings at all and who's going to employ someone my age?'

Pearl could've cried too, but she was determined to reverse the decision. 'Look, he's very worried at the moment, but I'm sure I can talk him round. I'll speak to him and try to make him realise we won't manage without you.'

Dorothy's face hardened. 'I take it he's not sacking Rita.'

'Not at the moment. He wants to keep her for now, probably because she's cheaper than you, but I'll make him see that would be a false economy. You're the one we ought to keep.'

'You haven't a clue, have you?'

Pearl was surprised at Dorothy's harsh tone. 'What do you mean?'

'Well, he's not employing her for her filing skills, is he?'

'What are you talking about?'

'What do you think she's been up to when she comes back late from her dinner? And did you never notice he follows her in a few minutes later?'

Pearl tried to take it in. 'That afternoon when he sent her to deliver an urgent letter and she came back smelling of drink…'

Dorothy nodded. 'He'd followed her out, God knows where they went. Then last week when you were down in the basement doing a stock check, his office door was locked and Rita wasn't to be found.'

Pearl closed her eyes and when she opened them again, she asked, 'When did this start?'

'Almost as soon as she came back to work after the bombings.'

She felt for her chair and lowered herself into it. Her first thought had been disbelief, closely followed by a complete lack of surprise. He thought of nothing but himself. She knew there had been other times when he'd strayed from her. It was to be expected as a mistress. Yet he always came back to her; after all, he could have her anytime, and he knew she was grateful for the roof over her head, not to mention the job. She was never going to rock the boat.

But this was different. 'She's just a kid – eighteen, isn't she?'

'Old enough,' said Dorothy. 'She's not been the same since that bomb wrecked her house. It's made her harder somehow. I wouldn't trust—'

'Who wouldn't you trust, Dorothy?' Rita was standing in the doorway.

'None of your business,' and she went and sat at her desk.

'Come with me, Rita,' said Pearl. 'I want to speak to you.' The look on her face brooked no argument, but it didn't stop Rita rolling her eyes as she followed Pearl into the dressing room.

'What's to do?' asked Rita and Pearl felt like slapping the uppity look off her face.

'I'll tell you what's to do, you little slut! I know what you've been up to with Mr Fenner. What do you think you're doing? He'll use you and, when he gets bored, he'll toss you aside without a thought.'

'That's what you think. But he says he loves me and he's never been so happy. He calls me his little doll,' she giggled, 'and he loves playing with me.'

'That's disgusting!' The slap caught Rita across her cheek.

She let out a yelp. 'I'll tell him what you've done! He'll be so angry.'

'You're a disgrace, the man's old enough to be your father – grandfather even.'

'I don't care. He'll look after me, buy me things, I'll have everything I want.'

'You're a silly little girl, you won't last long.'

Rita laughed. 'I could last as long as you did.'

Pearl couldn't believe her ears. How could she know about her and Harold? They'd always been so careful.

'You're not so cocky now, are you?' said Rita. 'He told me all about you and him.'

Pearl started to protest. 'He wouldn't...' But she couldn't be sure.

'Wouldn't he? I know about your little house. Must be lovely to have a home of your own, nice clothes, a decent wage.' Her voice hardened. 'After the Blitz, when I was all those weeks lying on my back, I did a lot of thinking and I swore if I survived, I'd grab what I wanted, because you could be blown to smithereens at any time.'

'He's had flings before; they mean nothing.'

'Can you be sure? You make the best of yourself, I'll give you that, but he's after a younger model.' She touched the welt on her cheek. 'Slapping me won't do you much good either.' And she turned and walked away.

Pearl waited a few minutes to calm herself before going back to the office. Rita was nowhere to be seen. Dorothy was at her desk crying and she stood up when Pearl came in. She dabbed her eyes and asked, 'When do I have to leave?'

Pearl shook her head in despair. This was the worst thing she'd ever had to do in all the years she'd been at Fenner's. 'I'm so sorry, Dorothy, you have to leave today. I'll make up your wages and I'll write you a good reference, just in case. But I promise you, I'll do everything I can to get you back.'

On the way home Pearl called into the butcher's and was lucky enough to buy a lamb chop with her coupons and some potatoes from the greengrocer's. She wanted Harold to have a good meal before she talked to him about Dorothy. She did her make-up and hair and put on a low-necked turquoise blouse that he liked. On a week night, he would usually arrive around seven so she put the potatoes on and left the chop on the side to be cooked when he arrived. By eight o'clock she wondered where he was and, by nine o'clock, she feared that he wouldn't come at all. She went to bed at ten, but couldn't sleep and lay there praying that he'd gone straight home. The alternative frightened her.

She must have fallen asleep and awoke at the sound of him stumbling up the stairs. He flung open the door and switched on the light. She pretended to be asleep and sensed him leaning over her exuding a familiar smell of cheap perfume. He'd been with Rita.

What happened next made her scream. He grabbed her hair, yanking her head from the pillow, and slapped her full on the face. 'How do you like that, you bitch!'

She tried to pull away but he held fast to her hair. 'Let me go!' she cried.

He pushed her back onto the bed and she struggled to sit up. 'How dare you hit Rita like that.'

'She made me angry, insulted me. I couldn't believe you'd be chasing after an eighteen-year-old.'

'Why not? She makes me feel alive.'

'Can you not see she's a scheming little minx – she's only after your money.'

'You've got something in common then, haven't you?'

'How can you say that? We've been together for years.'

'Ha! Maybe that's the problem.'

Chapter 22

Helen had been working the Saturday morning shift covering for a poorly telephone operator and as she left the building she was looking forward to a lazy afternoon at home. There was nothing in the house to eat, but she'd call at the bakery for a meat pie and an Eccles cake if there were any left.

'Hello, Helen,' someone called behind her.

She turned to see Laurence Fitzpatrick coming towards her.

'What are you doing here?' she asked a little sharply.

'I could say I was just crossing the road and there you were.' He looked as though he was trying not to smile, but couldn't quite manage it.

She frowned. 'But that wouldn't be true, would it?'

'Alas, no. Truth is, I've been hanging round here for the best part of an hour. It's a wonder one of your colleagues didn't move me along for loitering.' The smile finally broke through and he put up his hands. 'I confess, I've been waiting for you.'

'I can't imagine why,' she said and set off walking.

He fell into step beside her. 'I want to apologise. I shouldn't have shouted at you that night in the infirmary.'

She stopped and looked at him. 'Of course you should have shouted at me. I was in the way, you had work to do and I had no business sitting there. I'm pretty sure you'd do the same again, if I was so stupid.'

He seemed to weigh her up. 'You're right, I would.'

'So why were you waiting for me?'

He looked away as though he was deciding whether or not to tell the truth, then he looked her in the eye. 'Honestly, I was curious. When I met you at the supper club, I couldn't reconcile the glamorous girl you seemed to be with your sad and serious temperament. Then you turned up in the hospital in the middle of the night and you're a policewoman. I just thought… I'd see if I could find you and apologise for shouting at you.'

She managed a smile. 'All right then, I accept your apology.'

He looked relieved. 'Have you had your lunch?'

'No, but—'

'There's a good café on the other side of Deansgate. Come on, I'll treat you.'

'I couldn't let you do that.'

'Tell you what, I'll toss you for it.' He took a half

crown from his jacket pocket. 'Heads you have lunch with me, tails I dine alone.'

The coin was spinning in the air before she could say anything. He caught it and slapped it on the back of his hand. There was mischief in his eyes and she couldn't resist looking as he removed his hand to reveal the King's head.

The café on Deansgate was grander than she had expected and most of the diners were businessmen. They sat at a window table and the waitress brought them the set lunch menu: Lancashire hotpot or meat and potato pie with bread and butter and a pot of tea for two, and for dessert steamed fruit roll and custard. When they had ordered, Helen said, 'How did you track me down? There's a lot of police stations.'

'I was lucky. The first place I went to was police headquarters and I spoke to the desk sergeant. I explained that I'm a doctor at MRI and I'd been a little abrupt with the policewoman who came into the hospital the night of the murder and I wanted to apologise to her. He saw straight through me. "Oh, yes," he said. "There were actually two women there that night and I'm guessing you mean the younger of the two." He went into the office and he must have checked some rota or something because when he came out he said, "If you're outside the building in about an hour you might see WAPC Harrison come out."'

The meal arrived and Laurence poured the tea.

'Don't suppose there's any sugar.' He looked round. 'I'll never get used to unsweetened tea. Always had three spoonfuls since I was a boy. My mother used to say too much sugar gives you worms.' He laughed. 'I was in the second year of medical school before I realised it was an old wives' tale.'

He kept up the conversation through the first course and Helen was content to listen. He had a way of spinning a yarn: lively and funny; laughter never far from his face. She learned his family came from Edinburgh.

'My father was a barrister, keen to get on in life with his young family, so he came south to Manchester. My mother never really settled here, she hated the dirty air, the smog and the rain, but she soldiered on. When my father retired, they went back to Edinburgh and my sister went with them. I stayed here because I was working at the infirmary and I like the city, even if it is dirty.'

Helen watched him closely as he spoke. His face was handsome in an odd sort of way: eyes as dark as chestnuts; thick hair with a touch of auburn; high cheekbones and a strong jaw. And when he smiled... could a man be called beautiful?

'What do you think, Helen?'

She hadn't been listening. 'I'm sorry...'

'I'm just saying it can be lonely sometimes when you work odd hours. You go to bed when everyone's getting up. They're out enjoying themselves and you're still at work. I find myself going to the pictures on my own and falling asleep, or I play cards in a club because I can't sleep. Then you eat on your own with no company. It'll be the same for you sometimes, I suppose.' He pointed at her wedding ring. 'Maybe, it's not so bad for you being married, you have somebody to talk to at home.'

She could have, should have, told him there and then about Jim, but she didn't want to go over the story yet again. It just made her so terribly sad and she'd grown tired of awkward condolences.

The waitress returned with the puddings. 'Now it's your turn,' he said.

'Oh, I don't have much of a story to tell. I haven't done much.'

'Of course you have – you've gone from the fashion business via a gentlemen's club to policewoman.'

'I'm not actually a policewoman, I'm only an auxiliary. I've spent most of my life in a corner shop. It's only since... only in the last few months that I've done something different.'

'And your husband? What does he do?'

'He's a fireman.' Not quite the right tense but what did it matter anyway, she was unlikely to see Laurence again.

But he seemed interested. 'It must be unusual to have a married couple both working in emergency services.'

'Maybe, I don't know.' She needed to switch the

conversation. 'And are you married?' She could have bitten her tongue off. What would he think of her?

But he only laughed. 'Thankfully, no. Maybe I'll think about it when the war's over. Anyway, I don't think any girl with an ounce of sense would marry me.'

She thought he was completely wrong. What girl wouldn't be interested in a handsome doctor?

'Now don't you contradict me like my mother!' and the smile left his face. 'I haven't the time for courting, there's too much work to do. Times like this past week during the heavy bombing when we were overwhelmed with desperately injured casualties. You try to patch them up but... all the time you worry about those left on trolleys or lying on the floor... that you can't get to...'

She wanted to reach across the table to touch him, but that was impossible and the words that came to mind were inadequate, but she spoke them anyway. 'You do your best, Laurence, it's not your fault.'

'I'm sorry. I don't know why I'm telling you all this.' He gave a wry smile. 'I invite you to lunch and pour out my problems. I bet you're thinking, what kind of fellow is he.'

'I'm thinking how awful it must be for you seeing all that suffering. It's bound to take its toll.'

He took a deep breath. 'I've never spoken those thoughts out loud before. Maybe it's because you're on the front line too. It couldn't have been easy for you to see what happened to Marilyn.'

'No, but I'll have to get used to it, won't I?'

'It's always hard, but when you're doing the job you don't think of it. It's only afterwards when you're on your own that you recall the whole picture and see the devastation.'

'Yes,' she said. 'That's it exactly.'

They came out into the afternoon sunshine and neither of them seemed in a hurry to part. 'What are you doing this afternoon?' he asked.

'I'm going home to sleep. I was on the early shift this morning. What about you?'

'I usually call in to a rest centre – you know, for people bombed out – when I have a half day. It's in the Whitworth Art Gallery,' he told her.

'An art gallery?'

'Yes, the rest centre is in the basement, believe it or not. It's not ideal. The people succumb to so many colds and infections. I give them medicine and some advice but, living in such close proximity, illnesses spread like wildfire.'

'I know, we found a crowd of children living in a damp railway arch. One of them had scarlet fever, so they all went into isolation. Fortunately, it hadn't spread, but they were so undernourished, they couldn't have fought off an infection.'

'You know, Helen, there are real problems in the rest centres with children getting into trouble, running wild, stealing, looting, most of it unreported. If you get a chance, maybe you could mention it to somebody at police headquarters.'

'All right, I'll tell my sergeant.'

'Good. Well, I'd better be getting on.'

'Yes, me too, thanks for lunch.'

'You're welcome.' He didn't move, just stood there looking about him.

'Goodbye then.' She turned to leave.

'Helen, wait.'

She looked into his eyes, saw the uncertainty. 'What is it, Laurence?'

'I'm glad I came to find you today. I enjoyed your company. Look, would you like to come to the rest centre with me?'

She was wary of getting involved. There was no point. 'No, I don't think so, I need to get home.'

'Yes, yes, of course you do. Well, maybe our paths will cross another time,' and he touched his forehead to bid her goodbye and walked away.

On the way home, she went over in her mind every moment of her lunch with Laurence. How normal it had seemed just to sit and talk with someone who didn't know she was a widow… Someone who didn't need to ask how she was or worry that she might burst into tears. Instead, she had learned something about his life and anxieties.

She came into the house to find a large brown envelope behind the door. Without taking her tunic off she went through to the kitchen and studied it: London postmark, quite thick, beautiful copperplate writing. She opened it carefully and emptied out the contents. The covering vellum letter was headed 'Fire Brigade – Widows' Pension Scheme' and with it was a pension book. She hadn't cried for Jim in a while, but there was no holding back now. She rocked back and forward, wiped her eyes and looked at the one line summing up Jim's life: his name, rank, date of birth, date of death. Was that it? His whole life reduced to a handful of words? Below that they informed her that, as the widow of James Harrison (Deceased), Death Benefits of one pound per week would be paid for as long as she remained a widow. She went to bed in Jim's cricket jumper and cried until she fell asleep.

Chapter 23

Helen was up early on the first of June. It was the Sunday of Whitsuntide and she had never in her life missed the Whit walks. Her mother always said that she had been wrapped in a shawl and carried as a baby in the parade; her mother being a Sunday school teacher and responsible for her class.

All over the city the children would be getting excited, in their specially bought Whit week outfits, visiting family members and kind neighbours who would slip a few pennies or, if they were very lucky, a sixpence into their pockets. How she wished she could have the snaps her mother had taken – one for every year of her childhood. She loved the pretty white dresses with ribbons, lace or little buttons cut like diamonds to catch the sun. Then there were her Kiltie buckled shoes and white ankle socks and a little straw hat held on with elastic under her chin.

She recalled the year when her mother couldn't do a thing with her hair and said she'd have to go without a hat. On that year's photograph, her hair looked like a halo around her head. Her mother hated it, but it was Helen's favourite photo because she was looking straight at the camera and laughing. Her childhood was happy enough, just her and her mother, and she had never wanted for anything. When did all that change? she wondered.

Looking back, she could remember when she was about eleven wanting to go out with girls from school, to the pictures or the park, but her mother wouldn't allow it. 'You don't know what kind of characters might be lurking in those places.' She didn't approve of the girls who knocked on the door to ask her out to play and soon no one came calling for her. She was thirteen and lonely when Gwen joined her class, having moved into the area. They became good pals and she gained a bit of freedom, even though the dire warnings of what could happen to easily-led young girls continued.

She had arranged to meet Gwen at the corner of Thorp Road and Oldham Road to watch the children from the churches in the area walk with their banners and ribbons. She spotted Gwen across the road and was pleased to see Frank was with her. It had been a few weeks since he came to paint the parlour and she had half expected him to call round to see her.

She ran across the road to meet them. Frank had his arm around Gwen's shoulder but his smile seemed strained. Gwen, on the other hand, looked radiant. 'We haven't seen you for ages,' she said.

'How's life in the police?' asked Frank.

'Oh, you know, working hard,' she said. 'I'm on the night shift at ten tonight. I should really be in bed.'

'Same here,' said Frank, 'but this one,' he nodded at Gwen, 'had me out dancing last night.'

There was something false about the way he spoke and she wondered if Gwen noticed it too, but she kept looking up at him and smiling. There was no hint of that coolness he'd expressed about their relationship when she last saw him.

The sudden sound of a drum in marching time further up the road put paid to conversation and she pushed those thoughts aside. The Whit walks had begun. Boy scouts led the way, followed by the first church with two burly men carrying a huge silk banner from which came ropes held by older children and behind them the little ones, some as young as three, with tiny baskets of flowers. The next church had a silver band in green uniforms with gold braid and everyone sang along to 'Onward, Christian Soldiers'. Another banner, more children, on and on they marched and the people who lined the road clapped and waved and shouted out to anyone they knew who was walking.

Seeing Frank talking to the man next to him, Helen

turned to Gwen. 'Lovely day for it,' she said and added with a whisper, 'You look like the cat that's got the cream.'

Gwen giggled. 'What do you mean?'

'Frank at the Whit walks, for a start, not to mention going out dancing.'

'Let's just say he's a bit more attentive, ever since I gave him a little taste of what he could expect when we were married,' and she giggled again.

'You haven't!' Helen was shocked.

'No, not quite, but he seems to like what he's getting so far – he's on a promise, as they say. Do you fancy being a bridesmaid?'

Helen laughed and hugged her. 'I'd love that!'

Helen ran up the stairs to the second floor of the station just in time to sign in when Tommy, the police messenger, came up behind her.

'Haven't seen you for a while,' she said.

'That's 'cause I'm always on the night shift. Me mam's not best pleased, she wanted me to stay at home tonight. She's convinced there'll be a raid; she says the Germans like to bomb when there's a holiday and we're all off our guard.'

'She might be right, and there's a full moon rising. You take care now and get in a shelter if the bombs are dropping.'

'See you later,' he said and off he went to the little staffroom to join the other messengers to wait for his first message.

Most of the regular telephone operators were women auxiliaries, but sometimes others, like Helen with different jobs, would be drafted in to make up the rota. As Sergeant Duffy had explained during training, 'A woman auxiliary needs to turn her hand to any role and that's how you've been trained.'

She was glad to see her friend, Sissy, was on duty and they sat next to each other on the high stools in front of the elaborate wooden switchboard that ran across the room. Each telephone operator had their own station on the board with sockets, connection wires and dials to pick up calls to connect with the emergency services, ARP posts and other police stations. Helen placed her headphones over her ears and adjusted her microphone. Almost immediately, a light on the board lit up and she answered her first call.

The first few hours were quiet with typical incoming calls for a Sunday night: a burglary in Chorlton; suspicious characters spotted near a warehouse at Red Bank; an inebriated woman unconscious outside Piccadilly station. Around two in the morning the telephonist supervisor sent Helen, Sissy and two other WAPCs on a break. Tommy and a few other messengers were still in the staffroom playing cards. 'So far so good,' Helen shouted across to him.

He laughed. 'There's time yet.'

Before the kettle had boiled, the air-raid sirens sounded and the supervisor was at the door. 'Back to the board. Quick as you can! There's bombers sighted over Cheshire.' She turned to the messengers. 'And you, lads – stand ready.'

Helen and Sissy rushed out of the staffroom to see the whole switchboard lit up. Headphones on, she plugged into a flashing light. Her training kicked in automatically – work quickly and accurately, writing down the details, confirm the report, put it in the tray. Within seconds it would be collected by a runner and in the hands of senior police officers moments later, when they would assess and deploy officers on the ground.

Before long the low droning sound of planes could be heard in the distance above the hubbub of the switch room. No one acknowledged it, intent as they were on processing calls in a quiet, efficient manner. The sound grew louder and louder, and now the ack-ack guns could be heard in response, but the noise of the planes never faltered and in minutes they were directly overhead. Seconds later there was an almighty explosion that shook the building. Helen was shaking as she took the next call. On the other end it sounded like chaos – shouting and screaming – then the calm voice of a policeman giving his police number and Peter Street police phone box as his location. He then informed her that the Theatre Royal had received a direct hit and he was checking for casualties.

It was clear that the city centre was being targeted and serious damage had been done to an area not five minutes' walk from where they were sitting. Around three o'clock there was a lull in the bombing and Tommy and another messenger returned to headquarters. They made themselves useful brewing cups of tea and the supervisor allowed a few operators at a time to go to the staffroom for a drink. When it was Helen's turn, she managed to have a quick word with Tommy. 'The Jerries got their bearings using the town hall,' he told her. 'Then dropped bombs all the way up Peter Street, like apples out of a basket. There's a lot of casualties and I'm hopin' I get out there again soon. There's a lot to do.'

'Well, don't take any chances, Tommy.' She left him then and had walked only half a dozen steps back towards the switchboard when there was a deafening noise and she felt a huge force lift her off her feet and throw her across the room. She must have passed out for a moment and when she opened her eyes it was pitch dark. Alarms were ringing and she sensed the chaos around her. She lay face down as debris rained down from the ceiling. Stunned for a moment, she struggled to breathe with the dust in the air, while the acrid smell of cordite caught in her throat. She struggled to her feet and stumbled back to the staffroom. The roof and the outside wall had gone. 'Tommy! Where are you?'

she cried. By the light of the moon she could just make out someone lying near the sink. She stumbled over the rubble. It was a messenger. She turned away from him and retched. He was dead, half his face had gone, but his blond hair told her that it wasn't Tommy.

She called his name again and this time there was a barely audible answer. A twisted steel ceiling joist lay across the room and somebody was underneath it. She was picking her way around it when there was a shout. 'Stop! Stop! This floor isn't safe.' It was the chief inspector. 'Turn around slowly and come towards me. It's too dangerous.'

'But somebody's trapped under here,' she shouted.

'Helen?' It was no more than a whisper.

'Yes, Tommy, it's me.' He was lying on his back in a pool of blood, a shard from the girder piercing his lower body. She knelt beside him, took his hand. 'I'm here, Tommy. I'll sit with you until help comes.'

She could hear the chief inspector shouting orders – something about a girl.

'I can't feel my legs,' he said.

'That's because there's some sort of joist lying across you. They're coming to move it.'

'Me mam'll be ever so angry. She never wanted me to sign up for a messenger. She'll stop me doin' it now.' He screwed up his face in pain. 'It hurts so much.'

'Listen to me, Tommy, I'm going to tell your mam how brave you are and what a good messenger you are.

You're doing your bit for the war and I'm sure she'll be proud of you.'

'I always liked going in your shop. I missed you when you left. You always gave me a penny chew when your mam weren't lookin', didn't you?'

'That's because you were my favourite.'

'I liked the Black Jacks best.' He shuddered. 'I'm cold.'

She took off her tunic and put it over him. 'There, that'll keep you warm. We'll get you out soon and they'll wrap you in a cosy blanket.'

'Has it gone dark? I can't see anything.'

'The bombs have knocked out the electric. Close your eyes, Tommy, and I'll stay with you while you sleep.'

His hand was like ice in hers... his breathing slowed... it stopped... and he was gone.

There was someone shouting her name and ordering her to come away, that it wasn't safe.

'I'm coming,' she called. 'I'm coming.'

After that, everything happened so fast. A first aider checked her for injuries and found the back of her legs cut by flying glass and an inch-long chunk embedded in her skull. 'We need to get you checked out at the hospital, but it'll be a while before there's an ambulance available, with all that's going on outside.'

'I'm not going to hospital, I'm going back to the switchboard.'

'No, you can't do that. You need to go to the first aid room; we'll try and clean you up, but I'm worried you might have concussion, you look a bit stunned to me.'

'I'm all right, don't fuss.' She went back to her position, not mentioning her double vision.

There were other flying glass injuries among the people on duty and every one of them stayed at their post and thought of the two messengers, young lads, lying dead on the floor in the staffroom.

It was after five in the morning when the all-clear sounded. By then Helen was exhausted, her head was splitting and she just wanted to sleep. But the first aider had arranged for those who needed treatment for their injuries to go in a police van to the infirmary and he insisted on putting her in the van, even though she protested.

The queue to be seen by the nurses stretched endlessly along the corridors. Most people were propped against a wall and some were lying on the floor. Around her were the walking wounded, but every now and again there would be shouts of 'Clear the way!' and the ambulance men would rush through them with someone on a trolley covered in blood. Helen slept a little and woke up stiff, and still the pain in her head was enough to make her cry. By the time she got to the door of casualty, bright sunlight was flooding the room. There were no empty cubicles and most of the injured people she had spent the night with were treated sitting in a chair.

The nurse who tended her looked younger than she was. Her apron was bloody and there was a smear on her cheek. A strand of mousey hair had come loose from her cap and she looked exhausted. She examined Helen's legs, bathed them and bandaged them. Then examined her scalp. She began picking small shards of glass from her hair and dropping them into a kidney dish, then she teased the other small pieces out of her skin, dabbing it with stinging iodine. Finally, she examined the bigger piece of glass embedded at the back of her head and touched it. Helen let out a scream at the sharp pain. 'Oh, I'm sorry,' she said. 'I'll have to get Sister.' She rushed off. Helen closed her eyes and tried to concentrate on the pain, now centred around the wound, willing it to subside and trying desperately not to cry out loud.

A touch on her shoulder and someone speaking her name. 'Helen.' She opened her eyes and there was Laurence. 'You're injured. What's happened to you?'

She turned her head and moved her hand over the glass shard.

'Yes, I see it.' He didn't touch it, but she was aware of him moving her hair, looking at it from every angle. 'Hmm, I think we can remove it. Can you stand up?'

'Yes,' she said and he took her arm and guided her towards a cubicle, stopping only to tell the young nurse that he would deal with this patient and asked her to fetch what he needed. She lay on the bed face down.

'Try to relax, Helen. I'll have to cut away some of your hair round the wound, I'm sorry. Then I'll give you an injection to numb the pain.'

His hands were gentle and slowly she could sense a movement in her scalp. And all the time he spoke soothingly to her. 'Everything's going well, don't worry. We'll soon have you sorted… nearly done.'

The pressure on her skull eased away.

'Now I'll put a few stitches in to close the wound.' She could sense the smile in his voice. 'Rest assured, my needlework is praised throughout the hospital.' When he finished, he asked her to lie still for a while. He needed to complete some paperwork and he would be back shortly.

She dozed off and didn't wake until he touched her again and said, 'Come on, Helen. I'll take you home now.'

She sat up, a little woozy, and stared at him. 'You can't take me home, you're working.'

'I've been working for twelve hours with only ten minutes off for a cup of tea and a sandwich. The worst of the night's casualties have all been seen to and I was just going to lie down for half an hour when I saw you.'

'I'm all right, I can make my own way home.'

He shook his head. 'No, you're not all right. I can see in your eyes that you're disorientated and, when that injection wears off, you need to be in bed, not walking the streets.'

He was right, she felt terrible, and together they went out into the new day.

She wanted him to leave her a few minutes' walk

away from her house. 'To clear my head,' she said, but he wouldn't hear of it.

'Will your husband be at home?'

'My husband?' In that split-second she had forgotten Laurence didn't know Jim was dead, but she quickly answered. 'No, when there are big raids like last night the firemen can be away for a couple of days. There's a rota and the men sleep at the station house, a few hours on and a few off until the buildings are safe.' She pointed to her house. 'This is me here.'

He went to get out of the car and she snapped at him, 'What are you doing?'

'I'm going to see you inside.'

'No, you're not. What would the neighbours think?'

'But I just want to make sure you can manage on your own.'

'I'll manage fine.' She knew what she had wanted to say, but it had come out all wrong. She was snappy and tired, the throbbing in her head had started again and all she wanted was her bed. 'I'm sorry, Laurence, I'm so grateful for what you've done for me, but I just need to sleep.'

'I know,' he said. 'But promise me you'll come back to the hospital if you don't feel right, and in a week you're to go to your doctor to get your stitches out.'

She smiled at the concern on his face. 'I promise,' she said.

Chapter 24

Never in a million years would she have imagined returning to that church. Now here she was, staring at the altar, thinking of Jim's funeral. She could almost see herself there wearing that little hat with a veil, and the borrowed widow's weeds. How long ago it seemed, but it was easy to feel again the fear that engulfed her that day.

After the bombing of police headquarters she had two days off, and when she returned to duty Sergeant Duffy spoke to her about Tommy's funeral. 'It's on Saturday morning and we always send representatives to the funerals of personnel killed in the course of duty. The chief superintendent will be there, as will the messenger supervisor. Tommy's mother has asked if you would be there too. Not only because you know the family, but because you were with him when he died and offered him such comfort.'

Helen couldn't answer, knowing she hadn't the strength to be at Tommy's funeral. The two days she had spent at home had drained her. She couldn't get Tommy and Peter, the other boy who died, out of her head. She had wept for them and their families and when she slept she dreamt she was sitting in a pool of blood, holding Tommy's hand as his life drained away. She was shaken too at the realisation that she had been only seconds away from death herself.

'It would mean such a lot to the family, Helen. Please say you'll do it.'

She thought of Jim and his funeral and all the people there. It was a terrible ordeal, but she had got through it. She should be brave, just like the lad was when he lay there talking about penny chews...

'All right, I'll go.'

It was only when she left Sergeant Duffy's office that it occurred to her that her mother might also be at the funeral.

The service was soulless and soon over, as though there was little to say about a boy of fourteen. Only the chief superintendent spoke of Tommy's bravery in becoming a Police Auxiliary Messenger, riding his bike delivering important messages at the height of the bombings. Helen had managed to hold back her tears, but when his sister went forward to place his messenger beret on the coffin, she could choke them back no longer.

The service over, she made her way out of the church and some people recognised her and nodded. But she didn't stop to talk. There was even a whisper. 'She was with the lad when he died, you know.' It was beginning to rain and she walked quickly away and out through the gate when someone stepped in front of her. 'Did you think I wouldn't recognise you, dressed up like that? I already knew you were in the police, from the dead lad's mother.'

'Hello, Mam. What do you want?'

'I want to speak to my daughter.'

'I've got nothing to say to you.'

'Really? I've been worried sick about you. You could've been dead, for all I knew.'

'Well I'm not dead, am I?'

'Don't get cheeky with me!'

By now the rain had come on heavy. 'I'm not standing here getting soaked,' said Helen and she crossed the street.

Her mother ran after her. 'I need to talk to you. It's important.' She caught her arm and pulled her into the doorway of a bakery. Now the rain was bouncing off the street and Helen resigned herself to her mother's ranting.

'For a start, you accused me of stealing money from your dead husband. And I'll have you know I'm no thief!'

Immediately Helen was on the back foot. There was nothing else for it but to own up. 'I made a mistake. I was confused.' She tried to explain. 'Jim had just died. I didn't know what I was saying. I found it later in another pocket of his jacket.'

'And you never thought to come and see me to apologise?'

'Look, Mam, I'd had enough of you always telling me what to do and making me feel small and stupid. I knew if I went back to the house, you'd bully me into staying. I wanted a clean break. I wanted to be on my own.'

'You could've let me know where you were.'

'So that you could turn up and demand I went back to the shop? Well, I'm telling you now, I'm never going back there. I was buried alive in that shop.' And to Helen's astonishment her mother began to cry.

'You don't understand what I've been through, since you left. It takes two to run the shop. I've struggled to keep it going and I'm not a well woman, you know.'

'There's nothing wrong with you, Mam.'

She tried another tack. 'And this is what you're doing now, is it?' She waved away the uniform as if to dismiss it. 'What kind of a job is that for a young woman? Mixing with criminals and scum.'

'I'll tell you what kind of job it is: one where I'm respected and where I get some satisfaction in what I do. And as for the people – the ones I work with – they're dedicated to keeping this city safe, to helping those who are suffering in this war – families bombed out of their homes, women and children who need protecting. We don't "mix" with criminals, we arrest them so decent people can sleep safe in their beds.'

'Well, that's quite a speech, isn't it? Pity you don't have the same care and thoughtfulness when it comes to your own mother. You do more for strangers than you do for me.'

Put like that, Helen couldn't deny the truth of it, but she was wary. In the past, her mother had often pulled the 'you don't care about me' card to get her own way and she wasn't going to fall for it any more. 'I'm not going to argue with you, Mam. I'm just going to say that I've made a new life for myself and at the moment I just want to concentrate on my job. I'm not saying I'm never going to see you again, but I need to live my own life.'

Her mother laughed. 'I've never heard such nonsense!'

That was the last straw. Helen walked out into the rain.

'Wait, at least tell me where you're living.' Helen didn't stop. 'But what if something happens to me?' She didn't look back.

She had felt drained and so sad at Tommy's funeral and now the bad-tempered conversation with her mother added annoyance to her mood. Although she had the rest of Saturday off, she couldn't face going home to an empty house so, when she reached Conran Street and saw a bus going into the city centre, she jumped on it. A wander round the shops might distract her for an hour, but what she really needed was something to take her mind off such a terrible morning.

Whitworth Art Gallery, on Oxford Road, was an imposing red sandstone building and she couldn't help wondering what the people from the bombed terraces thought about their temporary home.

She remembered reading in the *Manchester Evening News* that, following the Christmas Blitz, the council had made great strides in finding houses or lodgings for a lot of families, but months later the rest centres were still in use.

She hesitated under the grand semicircular portico. What if Laurence wasn't there? What would she say if they asked what she was doing there? At that moment the door flew open and first one boy and then a second rushed out. Within seconds they were rolling on the ground, the biggest boy landing a heavy punch. Helen ran after them and got hold of him by the scruff of the neck and pulled him to his feet. 'Get off me!' He started kicking.

'Stop it!' she shouted. He ignored her. 'If you don't give over, I'll take you to the police station.'

'I'd like to see you try!' He kicked her hard on her shin, slipped out of her grasp and ran across the grass and disappeared down the road.

'Is he always like that?' she asked the other boy.

'Nah, he's worse. You're lucky he didn't rob you as well.' He looked her up and down. 'You're not the peelers, are you?'

'Not really, I help the police. Are you staying in the rest centre?'

He rolled his eyes. 'Me mam says there's no rest for the wicked in there.'

'Will you show me where it is?'

He led the way across the large entrance hall towards some steps leading to the lower floor, but, before they reached it, there was a loud shout. 'Hello there!' Helen turned to see a well-dressed woman coming towards her, hand outstretched. 'Well this is a first – a visit from the constabulary, and a woman too. I'm Margaret Pilkington, director of the gallery.'

Helen shook her hand. 'I'm WAPC Harrison.'

'Good, good, now that you're here,' she went on, still with the loud voice she had used to greet her, 'I'll give you the tour and maybe we could discuss a few concerns that we have.' Helen could only follow her and listen.

'We packed up the exhibits soon as – sent them to Wales. I told the council the basement was available to house those poor people who would certainly be bombed out. We have space for two hundred, reached full capacity during the Christmas Blitz, over a hundred have since been rehoused. Thing is, we're left with, shall we say, the most challenging and vulnerable homeless. Ah, here we are.' They had reached the bottom of the steps and Helen had a clear view of mattresses covering the floor and the meagre belongings salvaged from the people's homes. 'I worry about the mothers, they once had a home to keep, family to feed, but now all they can do is sit around. And as for the children, well, they get into all sorts of mischief.'

They moved on into a kitchen and a sort of refectory. 'Ah, let me introduce you. This is Warden Walker. He's in charge of the everyday goings on. Ex-prison guard, so that's useful.' The sour-faced man barely acknowledged Helen before he started on what sounded like a well-rehearsed moan. 'They have it too easy: free food provided by the Co-op and paid for by the council while they wait for a house also paid for by the council. And as for the kids… Don't get me started.'

'Well, let's move on. There's someone else I want you to meet,' and Helen could have sworn there was a twinkle in her eye.

A knock on the door and a man's voice called, 'Come in.' It was a doctor's surgery and there was Laurence in his white coat, stethoscope in hand, listening to a little boy's chest. He looked up and his smile was enough to turn her day around. 'Right, Sam. Your chest is much better now, so you can play outside, but don't be out in the rain.' He ruffled the child's hair. 'Now off you go.'

He seemed really pleased to see her. 'Helen, you're here. That's great.'

'Are you two acquainted?'

'We certainly are,' said Laurence. 'I asked Helen to come and see if there was anything the police could do to make life easier for the people here.'

'Splendid, splendid! Well, maybe you could carry on from here, Laurence?' She was beaming. 'I look forward to hearing your thoughts, my dear.'

When she'd gone, Laurence asked, 'How's your head?'

'It's fine.'

'Good, what did your doctor say about the wound?'

'Oh, I haven't had time to go to the doctors.'

'Helen, I told you to get the stitches out.' He reached over and removed her cap. 'Sit down, I'll do it.'

'There's no need. I'll go to the doctor next week, I promise.'

'No need to promise. I'm doing it right now.'

He gently moved her hair away from the wound and held it back while he carefully snipped the stitches. When it was done, he let her hair fall and smoothed it into place. 'You're lucky the person who stitched you up knew what he was doing. There won't be much of a scar and nobody will see it under your hair.'

'Thank you,' she said, but her thoughts were still focused on the touch of his hands.

'So now what do you want to do?' he asked.

She didn't have a plan. She'd come on a whim to see him and somewhere in the back of her mind she thought she might ask the women if there was anything she could do to help.

'I suppose I could speak to some women; there were a dozen or so of them in the refectory.'

'That's a good idea. I don't think anyone bothers to ask what they think. Why don't you go and do that? I won't come; they'd probably not say as much if I was there. Come back to my office when you've finished.'

The women looked up as she came in; they didn't look very welcoming and all talk ceased. This wasn't going to be easy. 'Hello, I'm Helen, I work for the Women's Auxiliary Police Corps. Would it be all right for me to ask you about the rest centre?'

A young woman, nursing a sleeping baby, spoke up. 'Why would a policewoman want to ask questions about us? We've done nothing wrong.'

'Oh, that's not what I meant.' She took another tack. 'Look, do you have any problems, like people stealing from you, or disturbing the peace? Maybe I could...?'

The young woman finished Helen's sentence, '...get us a house to live in, instead of a basement?'

Helen shook her head. 'I'm sorry?'

An older woman spoke more kindly. 'If you could stop some of these young'uns running wild it might help.'

'We could do with a lot more disinfectant, there's only five toilets for the lot of us,' said another woman.

'And what about the wash house down the road? They say we can only use it in the afternoon, because we don't come from round here, so all the local women get in early and that gives them time to get their washing dry and we end up with damp clothes.'

Now they were thinking about how their lives could be easier, and they made some other suggestions that Helen wrote in her notebook. They weren't asking for much.

'You mentioned the children before. I saw a big lad with ginger hair outside beating up a child.'

There was an immediate reaction. Every one of them had something to say about the lad's behaviour and that of his brother. 'You don't know the half of it,' they said.

Helen was already thinking that a police constable could come and talk to the troublemakers. Put the fear of God into them. 'Look, I can't promise anything, but I'm going talk to my sergeant back at the police station – she might be able to help.'

Most of the women thanked her, a few looked sceptical, but at least she had listened to them and now she was determined to get something done.

She was on her way back to Laurence's office when the older woman caught her up. 'Can I have a word with you?'

'Of course.'

'Those brothers we told you about, the Howards.' She lowered her voice. 'They don't just beat up the other kids. They're thieves.'

'Really? Do they steal from people in here?'

'They're worse than that. Him and his brother are always boasting about robbing houses. It's their auntie gets them to do it, then she sells the stuff. Gives them a few shillings and when that runs out, she sends them out again. It's a disgrace, they should be in borstal.'

Helen was taken aback; she never expected to walk in here today to be told about burglaries. 'Thank you for telling me, I'll look into it. In the meantime, don't tell anyone you've spoken to me.'

The woman tapped her finger on the side of her nose. 'You can trust me.' And off she went.

'Well, how did that go?' Laurence asked.

'I thought they were going to eat me alive. They're not happy, are they? But they talked about a few things that would make their lives easier. By the way, can you get extra disinfectant? They're not happy about the toilets.'

Laurence laughed. 'You don't let the grass grow, do you? Sounds like a health hazard to me. I'll sort it. Anything else?'

'There's something I need to speak to my sergeant about.'

'Sounds intriguing.'

'It could be something or nothing. I'll let you know.'

'So, are you coming back again?'

'Of course I am.'

He looked so pleased. 'Come on then, I've finished here. I'll take you home.'

'No, I'm going to Bootle Street. My sergeant's on duty this afternoon so I'll call in and speak to her about the centre.'

'I'll take you there.'

'No, you won't, I'll get the bus. You shouldn't be wasting petrol giving me lifts.'

He put his hand in his trouser pocket and produced the half crown. 'Heads I take you home, tails you catch the bus.' The coin was already in the air. He caught it, slapped it on the back of his hand and laughed. 'Let's go, Harrison.'

It was such a short journey, but every moment spent with Laurence raised her spirits. She looked sideways at him as he focused on the road, chatting away nineteen to the dozen. Then he'd turn to her and smile. Maybe he liked being in her company too.

He pulled up outside police headquarters. 'The next time you come to the rest centre, I'll take you for a drink after.'

She should have said no, but he was almost a colleague now and definitely a friend.

The desk sergeant looked up as she came in. 'I thought you were off duty all day.'

'I just wanted to have a word with Sergeant Duffy. Is she still here?'

'Upstairs in the canteen.'

Sergeant Duffy was on her own, hand round a pint mug in one hand and a cigarette in the other. She didn't seem surprised to see Helen sit opposite her. 'Well?' she said.

'There couldn't have been a sadder funeral.' Helen swallowed the lump in her throat. 'He was only a lad. What kind of world are we living in?'

Sergeant Duffy took a long drag of her cigarette and picked a bit of tobacco off her tongue. 'Ach, nasty, brutish and short,' and she blew out a stream of smoke. 'So, what are you doing here? Your name's not on the rota.'

'I went to the rest centre in the Whitworth Art Gallery.'

Sergeant Duffy raised an eyebrow.

'I was invited by a friend... well, I hardly know him, really... Laurence Fitzpatrick, the doctor we met that night Marilyn died? He has a surgery there once a week.'

Still Sergeant Duffy said nothing.

'Some of the women talked to me about having to live in an overcrowded basement. I wondered how safe it was for them. Anyway, when I was leaving, a woman took me to one side...' and Helen explained about the brothers and their aunt robbing houses. 'I thought CID might be interested.'

Duffy flicked ash into the ashtray. 'Did you get any names?' Helen nodded. 'Right then, away you go and write down the details and put it on my desk.'

'There's something else,' said Helen. 'Some of the boys cause trouble, bullying the younger ones and disrespecting the adults. Would it be a good idea to send a police constable round there to give them a good talking-to?'

'I'm surprised you didn't do that yourself, while you were there.'

Helen was about to answer when she noticed the hint of a smile on Sergeant Duffy's face.

Chapter 25

Helen pulled back the curtains and raised the sash window on a beautiful morning. It was twenty-six Sundays since Jim had died and every one of them had been sad and lonely. Out of the blue, she recalled the seance and whispered, 'Hello, Jim, are you here, my darling?' There was no answer and certainly no smell of smoke in the air. But somehow, she had the feeling that the darkness in her life was receding a little.

She would get her chores out of the way: wash the bedding, mop the lino, tidy up; then the whole day would be hers. She had bought a second-hand Butterwick pattern for a dress and a good-sized remnant off the market a few weeks before, but she'd been so busy at work that she hadn't the concentration to do all that pinning and cutting. Maybe she could make a start on it today, then, in the afternoon, she could go for a walk in the park.

There was one egg left for breakfast – should she fry

it, boil it, scramble it? Choices were a luxury to savour. She had just put the kettle on when there was a knock at the door. She went through to the parlour and peeped out. It was Gwen.

As soon as she opened the door, Gwen rushed in. Helen had just enough time to notice her red eyes and uncombed hair, before she burst into tears.

Helen put her arm around her. 'Shush now, come into the kitchen and tell me what's happened.'

'I can't believe it. It's Frank.' Gwen wiped her eyes on her sleeve. 'I've lost him.'

Helen froze. Oh, dear God, had something happened to him? 'Gwen, calm down and tell me what's happened.'

'It's Frank, he's finished with me.' Helen let out a sigh of relief; Frank was safe and Gwen was trying to explain. 'We went to the pictures last night then a drink before last orders. The pub were packed and I'd barely had two sups when he said he had summat important to tell me. He didn't want to be courting me any more. He were sorry, he said, but he weren't the marrying kind.' She was sobbing again and could hardly get the words out. 'He wanted to do the right thing, so he were telling me straight. Then he said he'd walk me home.' Gwen's face was full of anger. 'I told him he could bugger off and I never wanted to see him again. Then he comes out with all the shit about how I'd find somebody else who'd make me happy. Can you believe he would treat me like that? Two years we've been together and I thought…' She shook her head.

'Did you have any idea he might do that?'

'Oh, he's been a bit down in the dumps for a while. But I couldn't blame him – it's a horrible job. You know that too, Helen, the things they have to deal with. Like I told you before, it got so he didn't want to go out much and he said less and less. To be honest, I think he hasn't been right since Jim died. Did he ever say anything to you about how he felt?'

Helen thought about the trip to Saddleworth Moor when he had cried. 'We've spoken about Jim, shared a few memories. He was devastated by his death.'

Gwen sighed. 'He never mentioned Jim to me. One time I said, "It must be hard for you, losing a mate," and when I asked him if he was all right, he didn't answer. I didn't know what to say after that. What should I have done, Helen?'

'I don't know. Men can be funny sometimes; they don't like to look weak.' She didn't let on that Frank had poured his heart out to her. 'Have you had any breakfast?'

Gwen shook her head.

'How would you fancy sharing a fried egg with plenty of bread and marge?'

They sat at the table and ate the breakfast and drank a whole pot of tea with Gwen trying to recall the moments when she should have realised he was falling out of love with her.

'I can't understand it,' said Helen. 'When I saw you at the Whit walks you looked so happy and you thought he was going to propose.'

'Ha! How stupid was I?' She looked away.

Helen waited, not wishing to pry, but she could guess.

Gwen shot a look at Helen and lowered her eyes. 'I'd never done it with a lad. You know what I mean? Too scared in case I'd end up with a bun in the oven and me da would kill me. But there's things you can do that won't end up with a baby. I wanted to please Frank and I thought it would tempt him to marry me. But it didn't work, so in the end…' She didn't meet her eye and she was crying again, great sobs that shook her, and Helen hugged her until she was calm.

She sniffed and wiped her eyes. 'You know what the worst of it is? I have this awful feeling that he's fallen in love with someone else.'

'Frank wouldn't do that to you, Gwen. It's more likely that he's got cold feet. Who knows, in a few months he could come back to you because he's missed you so much.'

'Do you think so?'

'I wouldn't be surprised and, if he doesn't, you're better off without him. You're a bonnie girl. You'll meet someone else and fall in love again.'

'I don't know if I could.' Gwen looked hesitant. 'Can I ask you something, Helen? You loved Jim so much, could you see yourself marrying again?'

Her words took Helen by surprise. 'No, I wouldn't marry again. I've already had my only love.' She shook the notion from her head. 'Come on, let's not get morbid. Do you fancy going out for a walk? It's a lovely day.'

The bedding didn't get washed, the lino wasn't mopped, nothing was tidied, instead they went on a long walk to Daisy Nook and sat on a bank by the canal. 'We'll get freckles in this sunshine,' said Helen.

Gwen laughed. 'We'll look like we've been to Blackpool.'

'It's so peaceful sitting here. Hard to believe that just down the road there are people who've been bombed out of their homes and all those people killed, some of them children. Did you hear that the police station where I work was bombed? Two young lads died.'

There was a shout from further up the canal. A man was waving to them at the door of a stone cottage. 'Come on, girls, do you want to have a go at this?'

'It's the lock-keeper,' said Helen. 'Look, there's a barge waiting to go through.'

They ran to meet him and he set them to work pushing what looked like a heavy beam to open the lock gates. The barge moved forward into the lock. They closed the gates behind it. 'Now this is the clever bit,' said the lock-keeper. 'You see how it's caught between the two closed gates?'

'How can the barge move on?' asked Gwen. 'The water on the other side is too low.'

'You'll see,' and he showed them how to use the paddles and they watched in amazement as the water level fell and with it the barge. Then they opened the final lock gates and, with Helen and Gwen waving from the canal side, the barge went on its way.

The lock-keeper's wife had been watching and came out with a tray. The four of them sat in the little garden drinking apple juice and eating seed cake. 'You're lucky to live here, it's so peaceful,' said Helen.

'Moved here when we got married, nigh on forty years ago.' She touched her husband's hand. 'Raised our children here.'

'Do they still live with you?' asked Helen.

'Our daughter's in the Wrens, somewhere on the south coast. John was in the RAF, rear gunner, he was shot down over the channel last June.'

'I'm so sorry,' said Helen.

The lock-keeper squeezed his wife's hand. 'It's been a long, hard year for us, but we're coming through it. It's like the canal, you see – we've been stuck in that middle lock, sinking and sinking but, in the end, we'll level out and carry on.'

When Helen came through the door of Bootle Street on Monday morning, she sensed a different atmosphere. The desk sergeant had no friendly smile, and in the canteen conversation was subdued, faces were grim. She spotted Sissy, staring out the window.

'What's to do? Has something happened?' she asked.

Sissy's eyes were red. 'There's been another murder. They found her early this morning in the shelter in St Ann's Square.'

'Oh, dear God, in a shelter just like Marilyn.'

'The caretaker told me a team of detectives have taken over the conference room and the chief superintendent has been there since seven this morning. Maybe we'll hear more later.'

The morning dragged by and Helen found it hard to concentrate on logging stolen ration books. She kept seeing Marilyn as she was in the hospital bed that night: clothes sodden with blood; eyes frozen wide in shock; her bloodless face drained of life. Her killer had not been found and now there was another dead woman.

Late in the afternoon, Sergeant Duffy addressed all the women police constables and auxiliaries. 'You will have heard about the murder of a young woman. She was found at six this morning by an ARP warden in the St Ann's shelter. I've spoken to CID and told them that, this time, the women of this force should be part of the investigation. I explained that women are sometimes wary or even afraid of policemen, but they'll often talk to another woman. I'm hoping that the powers that be will make use of our skills.'

By the following morning they knew her name: Norah Jennings. She was twenty-three years old.

The week went on and there was no sign of policewomen being asked to carry out enquiries. Sergeant Duffy walked around with a face like thunder and there were rumours that she had confronted the chief superintendent and threatened to resign if he didn't insist that CID must involve policewomen in the investigation. On the Saturday there was, at last, a request for the policewomen to join the hunt. 'About time too!' she ranted. 'But it's a pity they're not stepping up the night shifts.'

On Saturday afternoon, Helen was looking forward to seeing the women at the rest centre. She had persuaded the overseer at the wash house that the rest centre women should be allowed to use the facilities whenever they liked. Sergeant Duffy had sent one of the older constables to deal with the unruly children; 'He'll put the fear of God up them, don't you worry.' As for the tip-off about the burglar brothers, it was unlikely that CID had the time to chase it up, with another murder on their hands. Still, three out of four wasn't bad. And then there was Laurence... a cup of tea and a chat with him would be nice.

She knocked on his door to say hello, but there was no answer. She turned to walk away and there was Miss Pilkington coming down the stairs. 'I'm glad I've caught you, dear. Laurence asked me to tell you he's gone to Edinburgh to visit his mother. I believe she's unwell. He left early this morning.'

Helen was surprised at how disappointed she felt, now she'd have to wait another week to see him. She went to the refectory and was surprised to see that there were a lot more women this time. They were pleased to see her, and a woman in her thirties, who introduced herself as Brenda seemed to have taken the role of spokeswoman for the group. She thanked her for what she had done. 'The disinfectant, the wash house, oh, and that copper what came round didn't half sort out the kids. Do you think he'd come back and do the same to the husbands?'

It was good to see the women laughing and Helen was glad she'd been able to do something to help them.

But Brenda hadn't finished. 'I'm guessing you had a hand in shoppin' those Howard boys too. The police came and took them away for questioning. Haven't seen them since.'

So, CID had managed to follow up her lead. That was good news. 'If there's anything like that again, you must always report it.'

At that moment the door opened and a woman slipped in at the back. Helen glanced at her, then looked again. Could it be... surely not. Gone was the make-up, the immaculate hair and the fine clothes, but there was no mistaking her smile. It was Anna Maguire, her model friend from Fenner's.

Helen picked up her previous thought. 'I'm glad they got the boys, and the aunt too, I hope. I thought maybe the detectives would be too busy working on the murder case to go after them.'

Then they were all talking at once, voicing their fears. 'It's the second one in a few months.' 'We're not safe on the streets.' 'I'm frightened to go out.'

Helen tried to get a word in. 'Listen, please, listen.'

'Let her speak,' Brenda shouted.

'I know how you feel. I was frightened too. It's all right in the daytime, but at night in the blackout, you never know who's lurking. I can tell you that our detectives are working hard trying to catch this man, but until that happens, we women have to be very careful. I'll be honest with you, I don't think I'd go out in the dark on my own. So, my best advice to you all is to avoid going out at night unless there's two of you and make sure you stick together. We've got to look after each other.'

'But that's not fair, is it?' Brenda protested. 'We can't even go out when we want, because some bloody man out there hates women.'

'They'll catch him, I'm sure, but in the meantime, we have to be vigilant,' she told them and then a thought occurred to her. 'And if you've seen something that doesn't look right, I don't know what, tell the police. This man is going to slip up and when he does some woman will notice.'

A few women approached her afterwards asking for advice – lost ration books, getting a child into the nearest school – not crimes as such, but she was able to point them in the right direction. When they'd gone, she went in search of Anna and found her sitting outside in the sunshine. Her face was pasty, with a rash of spots on her chin and dark rings under her eyes.

'Well, just look at you in your smart uniform,' said Anna. 'Some of the girls here told me about the young policewoman who was helping them. I never dreamt it was you. I thought you were still at Fenner's.'

'No, that didn't last, the girl I was covering for came back to work. I didn't like what was going on there, anyway. But never mind me. What on earth are you doing here?'

'Same as the rest of them, bombed out. I was living in a lodging house – lost everything. And you know the kind of work I do, it isn't regular. I had nowhere to go, so I ended up here. It's a roof over my head and I get fed. I've been trying to get back on my feet, but look at the state of me, Helen. I heard from one of the girls I knew from the model agency, and she told me about a new gentlemen's club that's opening at the far end of Quay Street. They'll be taking on waitresses soon, but...' She shook her head.

'But what?'

'Who's going to take me on? I haven't had a bath or washed my hair properly since I got here. I've no make-up and look at this dress. I'm not exactly waitress material, am I?'

It wasn't hard to do the right thing. Anna had looked after her at Fenner's and now she had a chance to repay her. 'I'm not leaving you here,' she told her. 'You're coming home with me.'

Chapter 26

Since Jim died, Helen had learned to live with loneliness. Sometimes it would settle in like a dull ache for days on end. At work, there were the passing irrelevant conversations that eased it a little, but nights spent alone would aggravate it. Other times, it would flare up and consume her.

The week Anna stayed with her, it disappeared altogether. They had such fun getting her back to her glamorous self. A warm bath in front of the fire, her beautiful hair shining and Anna pronounced herself 'human again'. They went through Helen's wardrobe, decided on a dress and a few other essentials then added a pair of wedge-heeled shoes. 'I've some gravy browning you could use to colour your legs,' Helen suggested. Looking glamorous again, Anna had no problem getting the job, but Helen was disappointed to hear that she had been offered the chance to share lodgings close to the club with another waitress. Before Anna left, Helen went to the post office and drew out her savings.

'You'll need to buy some more clothes and you can pay the first week's lodgings.'

'Oh, Helen, you're such a good friend. I'll pay you back every penny.'

'No need, it's a gift.'

It was all the pension money she had saved, but she knew Jim wouldn't have minded.

The weeks slipped by. Anna had sent her a letter to say she had got used to the long hours and the money was good. She had heard nothing more from Gwen or Frank since their break-up. She wasn't surprised. Why would they think of her when they had their own worries? And then there was Laurence. He hadn't been back to the rest centre for nearly a month and she began to wonder whether he would ever come back at all.

One lovely July evening on her way home from work, she bought a copy of *The People's Friend* from the newsagent's and was looking forward to sitting out in the yard in the early evening sunshine to read the stories. She opened her front door and was immediately unsettled to see an official-looking brown envelope behind the door. She took it into the kitchen and sat in the armchair staring at it. The stamp was franked with the words 'Manchester Fire Brigade'. Why were they writing to her? She had no connection to them any more. She ripped it open. A white card, with a black border, and the words 'An Invitation' and beneath it 'Bravery Award Presentation'. They were giving Jim an award. What for, dying? Maybe it was something meant to please her – something to be proud of? She felt none of that, there was only sorrow and a wound split open again.

She went to bed early and, true to form whenever she was upset, she wore Jim's cricket sweater and cried herself to sleep. Then, in the early morning, she awoke with a start and sat up in bed. Something had disturbed her. She listened, but there was nothing. She lay back down and that's when she smelt it – a merest whiff of smoke.

The presentation was in the afternoon and, with five minutes to go, she was standing outside the imposing entrance of the fire station. When she had asked Sergeant Duffy for permission to attend, she hoped that it would be refused, but she was all for the idea. 'You must go, Harrison, it's a great honour for your husband and for you, so it is. You must be so proud of him, and don't bother coming back to finish your shift. I'll see you tomorrow.'

But she didn't need an award to be proud of Jim; she already knew how brave he was and so did all of his crew. The last time she had been to the station was the day he had died. There had been pandemonium then.

Frightened people had sought shelter in the building and she would never forget the exhausted firemen, their faces grim and grimy from the smoke. She sighed. Forgive me, Jim. I can't go back in there.

She walked quickly away, but someone was calling her. She hesitated… and there was Frank by her side, taking her arm. She pulled away from him. 'I can't do it. I can't!'

'It's all right, Helen. I'll be with you the whole time.'

She shook her head. 'No, no, I'm going home,' and she set off walking again. Frank ran in front of her and held both her arms tightly. 'Look at me, Helen. This isn't about you. It's about Jim and how he died. It's about those men in there who loved and respected him. You have to be there to accept their thanks and the thanks of the brigade and people of this city. He's being honoured, for God's sake, and I'm not going to let you spoil that!'

She couldn't answer. She was ashamed that she hadn't the courage to face them.

Now Frank's voice was soft and calming. 'You can trust me. I'll get you through it. Come on, now.' And she let herself be led into the building and along a corridor to stand in front of a closed door. She stepped back, her heart beating so fast, she thought she would faint.

'You know Jim would want you to do it,' Frank told her. 'Don't let him down.'

Closed eyes, deep breath and a nod. The door opened and she faced a row of people she didn't know, but she

THE GIRL FROM THE CORNER SHOP

recognised the mayor's regalia. There was the station officer who treated her so badly on the day Jim died and, standing behind those seated, the men from Jim's crew in their best uniforms. She imagined Jim alongside them and had to catch the sob in her throat, for he was never more handsome than in his full uniform.

Frank walked with her to one side where a chair facing everyone had been set out for her. He stood behind her and the proceedings began with the station officer's speech. So intent was she in holding back her tears that she heard only snatches of what was said. She became aware that the mayor was speaking when Frank touched her shoulder and spoke in her ear. 'Stand up, Helen, and take the citation from the mayor.'

They were all looking at her.

'Mrs Harrison? I'd like to present you with your husband's bravery award.'

She crossed the room and took the vellum scroll from the mayor. She might have gone back to her seat, but instead she looked from the scroll to the firemen and paused. 'This is an award for bravery,' she began, 'but I don't think it's right that you have to be dead to get one and I don't think Jim would want me to accept this. He would say you are all brave men.' Then she turned to the mayor and handed it back to him. 'I think you should be recognising the bravery of all the Manchester firemen for their efforts in saving lives and the city we love.'

Without another word, she went straight out the door. Frank caught up with her in the entrance hall. 'My God, Helen, where did that come from?'

'Leave me, Frank.'

'But I can't—'

'No, Frank, I want to be on my own.' She walked quickly away, her head down to hide the tears. She should have trusted her own judgement and refused to go into the fire station. It had sparked so many terrible memories of the day Jim died. Ten minutes' walk and she came to a busy junction, lifted her head and stifled a cry. In front of her was Piccadilly Gardens; there were no flower beds, only stagnant water in the sunken garden. Beyond it, on three sides were the burnt-out warehouses of the Christmas Blitz – blackened brick, roofless, with gaping windows. In all the months since Jim had died, she had never returned to this place; even today she had avoided it on her way to the fire station. This was the heart of her grief. She could have turned away then, but she felt compelled to absorb the horror of what had happened here. If she could face this...

The people on the pavements were going about their business; they'd grown used to it. She doubted that she would ever feel like that. On the left-hand side there was a narrow plot, where a building had been demolished. She stood in front of it and wondered if this was where Jim had fallen to his death. There had been talk of a narrow space between two buildings where the extended ladder had been... She stepped into the empty space. Is this where you fell, Jim? Then something caught her eye. She picked her way through the rubble and weeds to the far corner where, miraculously, a clump of wild violets had taken hold. She knelt down and ran her hand over their little heads. It was a coincidence, of course, but it was a comfort too.

She walked over to Stevenson's Square to catch the bus home, but with each step her thoughts darkened. The last thing she wanted was to go home; she had never felt so alone. Why did she send Frank away? He would have come home with her and they could have talked about Jim.

The queue was long, the bus was late and she found herself staring across the road at Fenner's Fashion Agency. She couldn't help wondering about Pearl. Had she really been involved in Fenner's plan to make her the mistress of his old crony, Charles Brownlow? The letter she had sent afterwards was plausible but, at that time, she was in no mood to forgive her.

Had she been too hasty in cutting her off? She could see now that, prior to that, Pearl had been so kind to her. When she was desperate, Pearl gave her a job. But not only that – she had always liked her.

The bus pulled up at the shelter but she stepped out of the queue and crossed the road. She stood a moment outside Fenner's. What if Pearl didn't want to speak to her? But if that was the case, she could just walk away.

She went through the heavy door and up the steps into the showroom. The mannequins were still there, but they were naked. She went to the open office door and there was Pearl, her head bent over a sales ledger. Rita was standing at the filing cabinet.

'Hello, Pearl,' said Helen.

She looked up, her eyes widened. 'Oh, Helen!' She was smiling. 'It's so good to see you.' Her face was suddenly serious. 'Is there something the matter? Are you all right? Is it your mother?'

'No, there's nothing wrong. I just wanted to see you.'

'And I've wanted to see you too. But look at you, what a surprise to see you in uniform. Are you a policewoman?'

'Not quite. I'm in the Women's Auxiliary Police Corps – we help the constables.'

Pearl was beaming. 'I'm guessing that detective had a hand in persuading you to join? Well, I have to say you look good in it, like those Andrews Sisters who sing in the films.'

Helen smiled. 'I suppose he did.'

Rita closed the filing cabinet drawer with a snap.

Helen turned to her, smiling. 'You must be Rita. I filled in for you when you were injured.'

'I know who you are,' she said and turned to Pearl. 'Is it all right if I leave a bit early? I'm meeting someone.'

Pearl pursed her lips. 'I suppose so, but be here on time tomorrow, not like today.'

Rita collected her belongings and, without another word, she was gone.

'What's up with her?' asked Helen.

'Plenty,' said Pearl. 'I'll tell you about it later. Now I'm going to lock up and you and me will go and get some tea. My treat.'

On the way, Pearl told Helen about the precarious state of Fenner's Fashions. How it had been going downhill for a while, and the clothes rationing made it a lot worse. 'You'll have noticed Dorothy wasn't in the office. Harold laid her off. He wanted to keep Rita because…' She sighed. 'Because he's been sleeping with her.'

'What? But she's only young.'

'Old enough, apparently, to take all she can from a stupid old fella.'

'And where does that leave you?'

'I'm still in my house, for the time being anyway. He still comes to see me, but I know Rita wants me out.'

'Surely, after all these years, he wouldn't put you out on the street.'

'He may have no choice if the business goes to the wall.'

They were early enough not to have to queue for a table at the Kardomah at the top of Market Street. Inside, it was so different and modern that Helen stopped to take it all in: the shiny red chairs and tiled tables; random black stencils painted on the walls; and on the far left a sweeping staircase leading to a mezzanine overlooking the floor below.

They opted to sit upstairs looking down on the diners. 'Helen, I just want to say one thing. I knew nothing about Harold trying to pair you up with Charlie Brownlow, please believe me. I would never have been a party to that. Yes, I've been Harold's mistress for twenty years, but I would never want to see any young woman take the same path.'

'I know that now, Pearl. I wasn't myself back then, I couldn't think straight. I'm sorry.'

'And I'm sorry too. I should have looked after you better. Maybe I should have left him then.'

'It's all water under the bridge now. I'm so glad I came to see you today.'

The waitress took their order – toad in the hole, with gravy. 'We've talked about me,' said Pearl, 'but what about you? You looked so sad when you came in the office.'

'I'm doing all right. The job is tough sometimes, but I'm so glad I joined the police. As for today, well, I've been upset. I went to the fire station this afternoon to receive Jim's bravery award.' She gave a rueful smile. 'I handed it back to them.'

'You didn't?'

'I did, I'm afraid.' She shook her head. 'I told them

every fireman should have one because they're all brave.'

'What did they say about that?'

'Don't know. I walked out.'

'What would Jim say?'

'He'd say, "Good on you!"'

They talked and talked, then ordered a pudding – Manchester tart – and a fresh pot of tea. 'Your mother came to see me, you know. She wanted your address, but I told her I didn't know it.'

'I saw her a few weeks ago. She asked me to come back home, said she was ill, but I don't know if that was true.'

'Would you consider going back?'

'Never,' said Helen. 'I sometimes wonder if she was always so mean-spirited.'

'She's always been a glass half empty person, but she wasn't hurtful when she was younger.'

'So, what happened to make her so bitter?'

Pearl thought for a moment. 'I shouldn't really tell you but, there's such a rift between you, it makes no odds. You know that your father died when you were three. That's true, but he left your mother two years before that to live with another woman. Elsie was sure he would come back to her, but he and the woman died together in a motorbike accident. It felt like she had lost him twice.'

'I never really thought about her life before me and

she told me very little about him. It's a sad story, isn't it? Why didn't she tell me? I might have understood her better.'

The café was filling up when they left. They stood outside and promised they would keep in touch. 'Send me a letter when you've got time and we'll arrange to meet again,' said Pearl, and she reached out and hugged her. 'I'm so pleased we're back in touch.' Her voice was full of emotion. 'We won't ever fall out again, will we?'

'No, we won't,' said Helen. 'I promise.'

She arrived home to find Frank sitting on the doorstep. He jumped up as soon as he saw her. 'Thank God, you're home, Helen, I've been worried sick about you.'

She unlocked the door and went inside and Frank followed her. 'Where have you been? It's nearly eight o'clock.'

'I've been out with a friend for my tea.'

'What friend?'

She was tempted to say it was none of his business, but he seemed upset enough without her adding to it. 'Pearl, my godmother, you met her at Jim's funeral.'

He seemed satisfied with that and sat down at the table. 'You're all right then?'

'Of course I am. Why wouldn't I be?'

He looked somewhat bewildered. 'Well, all that about not wanting Jim's award and telling those people they should have given us all one. That was a strange thing to say and then you just walked out.'

She busied herself pouring Vimto into two glasses and topping it up with water. 'I just said what I thought.'

She handed him the drink. He put it on the table and pulled a cardboard tube from inside his uniform. 'I think you need to have this.'

She knew right away that it was the bravery award and, for all her denial of it, she took it out and read it until the tears ran down her cheeks and she could see no more.

He went to her and took her in his arms. 'God, Helen, I hate to see you so sad and lost.'

All that strength she had found in front of those people, and the confidence Pearl had given her, melted away. But there was the familiar coarse material of his tunic against her cheek and she felt for a brass button beneath her hand. It could have been Jim soothing her with softly whispered words... She looked up at Frank and there was a gentleness in his face. She closed her eyes and caught her breath at the touch of his lips on hers. The kiss was sweet and she took comfort from it, but she had to draw back.

They stood facing each other. 'Helen, I—'

'No, don't say anything, Frank.'

'I... I have to say something. Hear me out, please.' He took a moment, seeming to collect his thoughts. 'When Jim died, I tried to help you. You were on your own and, at first, I thought I could be your friend. But the truth was, we were both lost without Jim. I realised that when we were on the moors.' Another pause, Helen waited. 'I felt so close to you, but there were only so many ways I could keep dropping in. Truth was, I wanted to be with you all the time. You know what I'm saying, don't you?' He went to touch her, but she stepped back.

'I love you, Helen.'

The shock of it stunned her and it was a moment before her mind could piece together this other side to his concern and friendship. How could she have been so naive, never realising his true feelings? And hard on the heels of that thought came the worst of it. She was the other woman. She was the cause of Gwen's broken heart.

'You finished with Gwen because you love me?'

'No, that's not right. I left Gwen because I didn't love her. I don't think I ever loved her, and if you say no to me, it won't make any difference, I won't go back to her.'

'Frank, you're my friend. You've done everything you could for me, but I don't love you.'

'I know you don't love me… you love Jim, but there's enough between us to hold us together. We could have a good life, like you had with Jim. You know I'll look after you and you won't be lonely any more. We could live here. It's a sound house and I could make it a lovely home. We'd have children, you'd like that, wouldn't you?'

Helen was amazed at how detailed his fantasy was.

'I know all this comes as a surprise to you and I don't expect you to give me an answer right away. I want you to think about the kind of life we could have together.'

'I don't know what to say, Frank.'

'Just think about it, that's all. I'm working night shifts this week, but I'll call round next Saturday night. Just to see if you're all right.'

Chapter 27

Sergeant Duffy stood in front of her policewomen – constables and auxiliaries – and briefed them on progress into the investigation of the murders of the two young women, Marilyn and Norah. 'There were clear similarities: both found in bomb shelters; they had their throats cut, but there was evidence that they had been partially strangled before that. The detective leading the investigation has finally...' she paused and rolled her eyes, 'decided that the deaths are connected and we're looking for one man. I'll remind you of what we know so far. There was a witness in Marilyn's case who said she went off with a man in a tweed overcoat and a homburg. She heard him speak and she thought he sounded like an actor in a film. There was also some uncertainty about hearing a car nearby in the vicinity of both murders. Marilyn was known to us as a prostitute and Norah was a waitress at the Grand Hotel who regularly worked until midnight. So, the only connection is that they were out late in the blackout, like a lot of other women, such as those working night shifts in the factories. I'll also mention both girls were blonde, but that's probably a coincidence.

'The good news is that the chief superintendent has at last come around to my way of thinking and authorised extra overtime for us to be patrolling the streets overnight. I've drawn up a rota for extra shifts. Your instructions are simple: get out there and talk to the women. Ask questions about unusual behaviour in men seen in any vicinity; women often have a sixth sense about these things. Make them aware that they have to keep themselves safe – advise them not to be alone if they can help it. Finally, report back anything that might relate to the murders, no matter how trivial.'

As they were leaving the room, Sergeant Duffy called Helen back. 'I've put you down for the same shifts as me. It's about time you stopped filing looting reports and got a bit more police work under your belt.'

Unlike some, who left the briefing grumbling about the night shifts, Helen couldn't wait to get out on patrol again, because every minute she spent with Sergeant Duffy, she would be learning about policing.

Two days later they were on the beat together. They left Bootle Street at ten o'clock and set off walking with the aim of reaching the Grand Hotel, where Norah Jennings had worked, around midnight.

'How was the award ceremony at the fire station?'

'Well, it didn't turn out the way anyone expected, least of all me.'

'What happened?'

Helen explained what she had done.

'My, my, you left them all sitting there?'

'Yes, I feel awful about it now, I don't know what came over me. I'm the last person who'd rock the boat.'

'Oh, I wouldn't say that. A slip of a girl telling a few home truths to a prominent clergyman sounds like "previous form" to me. But tell me, do you regret not having the award?'

'Actually, I do have it.'

'How so?'

'Jim's mate, he's a fireman too, was there and he picked it up and brought it round to my house. I suppose I was meant to have it.'

They walked up Peter Street, past the buildings damaged by the Whit holiday bombing, the Theatre Royal, Café Royal and the Gaiety, and on to the Midland Hotel. They went into the foyer and met with the night manager who seemed to know Sergeant Duffy well. She introduced Helen. 'This is WAPC Harrison.' He agreed to instruct the doormen and receptionists to speak to any woman intending to go out in the blackout, advising them to take a taxi.

Behind the hotel was Central Station and, in the arches underneath, a handful of women were soliciting.

Most of them were known to Sergeant Duffy. 'Sure, I know you have a living to make, girls, but don't take risks. Stay close to the others and please don't get into a car on your own.'

On to the Odeon cinema just as the final house emptied where they stood either side of the main door and called out, 'Don't walk home on your own, you've time enough to catch the last bus or tram. Be wary of strangers.'

By the time they got to the Grand it was almost midnight. They spoke to the receptionist who had been on duty the night Norah died. 'She was lovely and so pretty. Tall, like you.' She nodded to Helen. 'She wasn't one of those who would be hanging around looking for men.'

'Do you remember seeing her leave with anyone that night?'

She shook her head.

'Well, keep reminding your staff and female guests about not being in the blackout on their own. And if you see anything suspicious, ring Bootle Street station.'

One in the morning and the streets were deserted, but still they patrolled using their torches to light the way. They walked down to Hanging Ditch and just near the cathedral, Helen caught someone in the beam of her torch leaning next to a car. The man was startled; he turned and ran. Helen gave chase with Sergeant Duffy behind her. She managed to grab his coat, but he was too strong and the next moment she was being dragged over the cobbles. The coat slipped through her fingers and he was gone.

'Are you in one piece?' said Sergeant Duffy as she helped her up. She shone her torch on Helen. 'Grazed knees, stockings ripped to pieces, a cut on your cheek. Ach, you'll live.'

'I'm just annoyed I couldn't hold on to him. What was he up to?'

'Siphoning off petrol, I think. He'd only just started, look, there's his can and tube. He'll be long gone by now. Pick up the tools of his trade, it might keep him off the street for a few days. We'll wander back to the station now for a short break then we'll go out again.'

On Saturday afternoon, Helen returned to the rest centre. She hadn't been for two weeks while she was working night shifts, but she wanted to call in and see the women. She wondered too if Laurence would be there.

Brenda was sitting outside in the sunshine when she arrived at the Whitworth. 'Hello, how are you?' Helen asked and sat down beside her.

'I think we might have some good news soon. A few of us went to the town hall housing office earlier this week. I think they were a bit put out when we showed up but, fair dos, they brought us in to see one of the housing officers. We made sure they knew we were living in a basement and there were families and elderly people all mixed in together with no privacy at all.'

'And what did they say?'

'Turns out they've started work in our area repairing the bombed houses and renovating derelict properties that were boarded up long before the war. It'll be a few weeks, but at least we know the end's in sight.'

'That's great news; it'll lift people's spirits.'

'The atmosphere has completely changed now they've something to look forward to.'

'Anything else going on?'

'Yes, I'm glad to see you. I'm a bit worried about a girl who turned up last week. There's something odd about her.'

'In what way?'

'Well, she's on her own for a start. We've tried to talk to her, but you don't get much out of her. I think she's in a state of shock.'

'Because of the bombing?'

'Probably, but there's something else... She has a bag with her, but I don't think she opens it. She's not changed her clothes since she got here.'

'I could speak to her if you like.'

The girl was asleep on a camp bed at the far end of the basement. Helen stood back and studied her: about fourteen years old; grubby dress and cardigan; looked like she could do with a good wash. And there was the bag wrapped in her arms. Helen knelt down beside her and touched her shoulder.

She jumped up, her eyes wide with fear, and clutched the bag tighter.

'Hello, I'm Helen.' The girl said nothing, but looked quickly around her as though she was about to bolt for the door. 'Don't be frightened. What's your name?'

'Susan.' A whisper.

'Was your house bombed?'

A shake of the head.

'Where are your parents, Susan?'

She looked away.

'If you've any family or friends I could take you to them or I could ask them to come and get you. Would you like me to do that?' The girl looked like she was going to cry. 'Don't get upset, Susan, you're safe here.' Helen tried another tack. 'Maybe you could have a good wash, that would make you feel better.' She reached for the bag. 'Have you clean clothes there?'

The girl let out a shriek and clung to the bag as though it held her most precious possession.

'What's in the bag, Susan?'

She began to shake and slowly, from somewhere deep inside her, there came a strangled cry, softly at first then rising steadily until the piercing sound filled the basement and brought those within hearing distance gathering round to see what was happening.

Brenda was one of the first there. 'I'll hold her, you see if you can get the bag from her.'

Helen tried to prise open the girl's clawed hands, but she was strong. Then someone was at her side – a flash of a blade and the side of the bag split open. The putrid smell made her retch, but she pulled away the blanket inside and cried out. The baby was tiny, naked and dead. Helen jumped up and backed away from the horrible sight. 'Helen, Helen, it's all right.' And there was Laurence cradling the bag. 'Listen to me. I'll take the baby to my room. You and Brenda bring the girl, quick as you can.'

The girl offered no resistance, she wanted to be with the child, and once inside Laurence's office she sat meekly in a chair, never taking her eyes off it.

'Helen, you're responsible for the girl, so stay with her,' said Laurence. 'The baby is my concern.' He turned to Brenda. 'Will you please go to the telephone in the gallery office and ask for the police and ambulance to attend an incident at the Whitworth Gallery. Then wait at the door and bring them in here as soon as they arrive.'

The baby was still in the bag on Laurence's desk. Helen kept glancing over at it. 'She's probably concealed the pregnancy,' whispered Laurence. 'It could have been stillborn, or possibly it died shortly after birth. We won't know until the results of the post-mortem. Why don't you talk to her? Try and get her name and where she comes from. That might be helpful.'

Of course, she should be talking to her. The shock of seeing the dead baby had made her forget her training. No difficult questions, only name, address, age... She pulled up a chair next to her and took out her notebook. 'I know your name is Susan. Can you tell me your surname?'

Susan wiped her eyes. 'Matthews.'

'And how old are you?'

'Fifteen.'

'And where do you live?' She gave an address in Rusholme. 'Who do you live with?'

She began to cry again then sniffed loudly and said, 'Me mam and dad.'

'We're here to help you, Susan. Do you want to tell me anything else?'

She shook her head and fixed her eyes on the bag.

'Don't worry, I'll stay with you.'

The ambulance man was the first to arrive and Laurence explained the situation.

'Straight to the mortuary then, doctor?'

'Yes, I'll follow you there.'

But as soon as the man lifted the bag, Susan shot across the room. 'She's mine, you can't have her!'

He held it above her head and she tried to reach it, but Laurence stepped between the two of them and caught Susan's wrists. The ambulance man didn't waste a moment, he was out the door in seconds.

Now she was hysterical, screaming for her baby, but by then two constables had arrived and between them they carried her, thrashing and screaming, into the police car. She calmed down a little when Helen got in beside her and they drove at speed to Bootle Street.

Susan was taken to an interview room while Helen went with Sergeant Duffy to her office. 'So, tell me the story of Susan then we'll set things in motion.'

Helen gave an account of what happened, from being asked to check on a girl acting strangely to the discovery of the dead baby.

'What state is she in?'

'Frightened, desperate to keep hold of the baby, but it's been taken from her.'

'Do we know who she is?'

Helen read the details from her notebook.

'Good, good, we'll get the parents in right away. Now, Harrison, at this moment, you're the only person she knows so I want you to go to the interview room and stay with her until I arrive to question her. There's a police constable with her at the moment, but I want a woman in the room.'

Chapter 28

By the time the interview had finished Helen was exhausted, drained by the emotional strain of the previous three hours. Susan had been almost incoherent, crying out for her baby and begging to hold it again. Bit by bit Sergeant Duffy coaxed the truth from her. She had met a lad working at the fair in Platt Fields. He was kind to her, gave her a goldfish off the hoopla stall for nothing. She'd sneak out of her house late at night to be with him. She knew what they were doing was wrong, but she loved him. A week later the fair was gone and he never even said goodbye. It was a while before she realised what was happening to her. She got a bit fatter, but not enough for anyone to think she was expecting.

The baby came when her parents were out at work. She was frightened. Her da would kill her, she said, so she ran away and took the baby with her. When asked if it was dead when it was born, she said she thought it was, but she wasn't sure and she couldn't bear to part with it. In the end she was charged with concealing a birth, but further charges could be brought depending on the post-mortem.

All Helen wanted now was to get away from the station. She had struggled to keep her emotions in check during the interview. Now the dam had burst and she was overwhelmed with sadness. Outside, the rain was beating off the street, but she didn't take shelter, instead she set off running in a panic, tears mixing with rain on her cheeks, sobs thrown to the wind. She cried for the young girl giving birth alone, and for the dead baby, but there was more to it than that. She cried for Jim and herself as the anger raged inside her for her babies that might have been.

She didn't see the car pulling up alongside her, didn't hear her name being called, didn't see him get out of the car to catch hold of her.

'Helen, it's me – Laurence. Wait, please.'

Her eyes were blinded by the tears and the rain. She pushed him away, not wanting him to see her like this.

'Helen, for God's sake, let me help you.' He pulled her towards him and wrapped his arms around her. She hit out at him, her flailing arm catching him on the side of his head. But still he held her, until her rage was spent and she slumped against him.

'You're in a state, Helen, and we're both soaking wet. Look, I have the car here, we'll get in out of the rain.'

In the car she was shivering and desperately trying to stem her tears. Laurence gave her a handkerchief and she wiped her eyes. 'I'm sorry, I'm so upset about Susan and the baby.'

'I know you are, it was an awful shock for you to see the child like that but, you know, it's all right to cry. We'll sit here for a bit.'

'What are you doing here, anyway?' she asked.

'Waiting for you.'

'Have you been here all this time?'

'I was at the mortuary for about an hour. Then I came here. Your friendly desk sergeant told me you were still with the girl, so I thought I'd wait.'

'Why would you do that?'

'Because I was worried about you. You had a terrible shock finding the baby. It takes a while to get over something like that. You'll be a lot better once you're home. I'll give you a lift.'

'No! I can't face the empty house right now.'

'Why not? Won't your husband be there?'

She shook her head. 'I'll be on my own. I'll go to my godmother. She works in Stevenson's Square.'

'All right, I'll take you there.'

'Oh, wait! What time is it?'

'Half past six.'

She couldn't believe it. The showroom would be closed and she didn't want to go to Pearl's house in case Mr Fenner would be there. 'It's too late, I've missed her.'

'Helen, listen to me. If you want, I'll take you to my flat. It's not far from here. We'll have something to eat – you'll feel better for that – then when you're ready, I'll take you home.'

'I don't know...' It didn't seem right to go to a man's flat, what would he think of her?

'Please, Helen, just come for a while,' and there was something about his voice that made her realise how much he cared.

The house was a three-storey Victorian villa that had seen better days. She looked at it in awe. 'You live here?'

He smiled. 'Look up,' he said. 'See that tiny window in the roof? That's where I live.'

The flat was small and warm inside and she immediately felt at ease. There was a well-worn brocade sofa in front of the fireplace and on either side of that were bookcases crammed full. A sink and two gas rings on top of a small cupboard served as a kitchen. A closed door was most likely a bedroom.

'Make yourself at home while I cook us something.'

Helen wandered over to the bookcase and read some of the titles. 'Have you read all these books?'

'Quite a lot of them, when I was younger, but I don't have the time to read these days.'

She looked out the window at the back garden, far below her. 'It looks like an allotment, down there.'

'That's Jack's work, he's the old fellow who lives on the ground floor. He's got a great vegetable garden and he shares everything he grows with the other tenants. I'm cooking some of his vegetables for us now.'

'I like these film posters on the walls, where did you get them?'

'When I was a kid, I was fascinated by films and I got to know the projectionist quite well. He used to save the posters for me. Nowadays, I just ask at the box office for the films I like. You see that one over there, *Top Hat* with Fred Astaire, that's my favourite.'

'I would've thought you'd like that *King Kong* one best.'

'Oh, now...?' He pretended to consider. 'The artwork's very good, I'll give you that, but it's a sad film, isn't it? You can't beat an Astaire and Rogers for the wisecracks and the dancing, and anyway, I like a happy ending.'

She sat on the sofa and Laurence talked about films and music while he cooked. 'So what films do you like?' he asked.

'I loved *Gone With the Wind.*'

'So, you're a romantic as well. Right, food's nearly ready, can you get the cutlery from the drawer?'

The omelette was good, packed with vegetables that took away the taste of the powdered egg.

She hadn't realised how hungry she was, no wonder she had felt weak and weepy. 'The beetroot tastes really good, never would have thought to put that in an omelette.'

They washed up together then Laurence put the radio on low and they sat on the sofa. 'Do you feel better now?' he asked.

'Oh yes,' she sighed. 'I can't believe I got myself into such a state.'

'You'd have been fine in the end. You're stronger than you think.'

'I don't know, the sight of the baby was lodged in my head. I kept seeing it… that's why I couldn't face being on my own. What would I have done, if you hadn't been there?'

'Oh, I'm sure your husband would have taken care of you when he got home.'

Helen managed a smile. How complicated had she made things that day when she went for lunch with Laurence? Why hadn't she told him then that she was a widow? Because it was none of his business. If she had told him then it would've been like saying 'I'm available', but she wasn't available because she had no intentions of getting involved with any man at any time. Besides, she thought she would never see him again. But now she had got to know him as a friend, and he had been so kind to her, she could hardly turn round and tell him that she had lied – that she had no husband, she was a widow. What kind of message would that give him if she told him now?

'You know, Helen, I'm glad you're here. To tell you the truth, I didn't want to be alone either.'

He looked so sad. 'What's the matter, Laurence?'

'I've been away in Edinburgh looking after my mother; she'd been ill for a while. We buried her two days ago.'

'Oh, Laurence.' She touched his hand. 'I'm so sorry.'

'It was a mercy really, she was in a lot of pain, but it was so hard to say goodbye. You know your mother won't always be there...' His voice wavered. 'But then she's gone and everything crashes around you.' He turned away from her.

There were no words to ease the pain of losing someone you love, she knew that better than anyone. In those dark days after Jim's death, all she had wanted was someone to hold her, to stay with her so she wasn't alone. She moved closer and put her arm around him. He laid his head on her shoulder. She could sense his despair. The room grew dark. She had no idea how long they sat there. He was first to speak. 'I'm so glad you're here, Helen. You've calmed the grief and allowed me to think about her life and what a good mother she was, without getting overwhelmed. You'd have liked her. She was in the WRVS, you know. She believed in service in the community. I was telling her about you and your job.' There was a hint of a smile in his voice. 'She said she'd like to meet you some day.'

Helen was surprised that he had told his dying mother about her. Did he think more of her than she had realised?

'I suppose you need to go home now,' he said.

'I could stay a bit longer if you like.'

His face lit up. 'Will you? I could put on some gramophone records. Then later we could have supper, tea and jam butties.'

She felt so relaxed in the tiny flat, the horrors of the day had been set aside for now, and the company of Laurence had salved her loneliness. 'That would be nice,' she said.

He drew the blackout curtains and lit a small table lamp. They listened to the records and talked about all sorts of things. Inevitably, he returned again to his mother and childhood. It sounded idyllic and Laurence asked about her mother. 'We don't get on that well. She doesn't approve of my job and I don't see her very often.'

'And what about your father?'

'He died when I was three and I don't remember him at all. My mother rarely spoke about him and there were no photos of him in the house. Only lately, I found out that they had separated and that explained a lot.

He didn't ask about Jim – maybe, if he had done, she might have told him.

'Will you stay in the police after the war?' he asked.

'Sometimes I think I will, but on a day like today I wonder why I put myself through all that.'

'It's hard, I know. The bombings are the worst for me: the cruelty of it, the waste of life.'

'Why do we do it?'

'Because somebody has to and we're trained for it.'

She studied his face, so earnest and kind, and was struck by his common sense and decency.

'What is it?' he said.

'Nothing.'

'There is something, you're smiling.'

She teased him. 'Am I?' But she was smiling, because she'd been wondering why Laurence made her feel good about herself. The only other person who had done that was Jim. Why not tell him about Jim? He'd understand. 'Laurence, I—'

The sound of the raid alert cut across her words. 'Hell's bells,' he shouted. 'Come on, we've a shelter in the garden. I'll just grab some blankets.'

The Anderson shelter was like a little home from home. The far end had been wallpapered and she couldn't believe her eyes at an electric fire taking the chill off the damp underground. There were hurricane lamps too, hanging from the ceiling, and an old trunk in the middle, on top of which were games – ludo, snakes and ladders, dominoes and playing cards.

They were the last to arrive in the shelter and Laurence introduced her to the five other tenants. They seemed friendly enough but surprised to see her uniform. 'Eh up, Laurence,' said Jack the gardener, 'is she here to arrest you for the lamb chops the butcher slips you from under the counter every week?'

There were wooden benches with comfortable

cushions either side of the shelter. 'This is where I usually sit,' said Laurence. 'Sorry it's a bit of a squeeze,' and he put a blanket round her shoulders.

Hetty, Jack's wife, asked, 'Do you play cribbage, love?'

'I do,' said Helen.

Laurence reached for the cards, shuffled them like a magician and winked at her. 'Now watch yourself with this lot, they'll fleece you.'

They passed an hour in good humour and she watched him with his neighbours. They were older, but he had time for them all and they clearly had a soft spot for him. By the time the all-clear sounded – there would be no bombing tonight – she and Laurence left the shelter with the neighbours inviting her to come and see them again.

Back in the flat she said, 'It's getting late, I'd better go now if I'm to catch my bus.'

'Don't be daft, I said I'd take you home. Unless...' He bit his lip. 'Look, Helen, if you're going to be on your own tonight, you could stay here if you want.' He quickly added, 'Just for the company, of course. I'd sleep on the sofa. You'd be perfectly safe, I swear.'

From the moment Laurence had picked her up outside the police station she had not only felt safe, she had felt more alive than she had been since Jim died. The last place she wanted to be was in her own home. But staying in his flat, sleeping in his bed? She had only to say yes and they would have crossed a line.

'I'm sorry, I shouldn't have suggested that,' he said 'but I want you to know that I've been drawn to you from the first moment I saw you at the supper club. Then again at the infirmary when you were so pale and frightened watching over the dead girl. There is something inside you so sad and I want to take it away, Helen, but I don't know how.'

She could let this run its course, but…'Laurence, you've been very kind to me, but I can't stay. I have to go home.'

'I understand,' he said.

On the journey back neither of them said much. She was thinking about the hours they had spent together, how much she had enjoyed his company. She glanced across at him, a silhouette in the blackout, was he thinking about her too?

He parked the car outside her house and she felt him take her hand. 'Helen, about tonight, I hope you didn't think when I—'

'Laurence, you don't have to say anything. Thank you for turning an awful day into something lovely.'

'So, will I see you again at—' He didn't finish the sentence. He was looking past her, out of the car window. Someone was coming down the path with a torch. The car door was wrenched open, the light blinded them, and she was pulled from the car. She realised immediately that it was Frank and he was yelling.

'Where have you been, Helen? I've been sat on the doorstep two hours waiting for you.'

Oh God, with all the upset about the baby, she'd forgotten Frank was coming to see her after his late shift, expecting her answer to his proposal. By this time Laurence was out of the car, confronting him. 'Let her go!'

'Who the hell are you?'

'I'm a friend. I take it you're her husband.'

'Husband? No, mate, she has no husband, she's a widow.'

'Helen, is this true?' She could hear the shock in his voice.

It was bad enough that she had never contradicted him when he assumed she had a husband. She couldn't lie now. 'Yes.'

Frank was getting into his stride. 'Aye, and more than that, Jim were my best mate and me and Helen are getting married. So, I'm not best pleased to find her out late at night with a fancy man like you.'

'You're getting married?'

Her reply was feeble. 'I haven't said I would.'

Laurence stepped backwards. 'Why would you lie to me about your husband? I thought there was something special between us.' He shook his head as though clearing his mind. 'I got it all wrong.'

He walked away and she cried after him, 'Laurence, you're not wrong, there is something between us, I feel it too.'

He never looked back, just got in his car and drove off.

'Bloody hell, Helen, what are you up to? Out till midnight with some fella. What would Jim think?'

How dare he speak to her like that? And he had no right to be telling Laurence that she was going to marry him. She pushed past him to get to the door and opened it. Frank followed her, but she whipped round before he could step over the threshold and tried to close the door on him, but he pushed his way in.

'Now listen here,' he said. 'I don't know what's happened between you and that fella, and I don't want to know, but I'm prepared to let it go. I'll still marry you, Helen, and we'll have that life that you lost.'

She chose her words carefully. 'Frank, you've been a friend, looking after me since Jim died. You helped me through that terrible time. I've thought about your proposal and I've made a decision. I'm not going to marry you.'

'You're turning me down? Why would you do that?'

'Because I don't love you, Frank.'

'Maybe you don't now, but you will.'

'No, I won't, and I never want to be a fireman's wife again.'

'Helen, don't you think Jim would want you to be looked after?'

'For God's sake, Frank, stop living your life asking,

"What would Jim want?" He's dead! You have to move on and so do I!'

'I can't believe this. I finished with Gwen to be with you.'

'Don't you dare throw that in my face. You left her because you didn't love her. You've hardly bothered with her these last few months.'

His face was full of anger. 'If I walk out this door, you'll never see me again. How will you manage then?'

'I don't know, but I'll find a way.'

'Well good luck with that,' he shouted, and he stormed out, slamming the door behind him.

Chapter 29

For the first time since she joined the WAPC, Helen couldn't face going to work on Monday morning. She would rather bury herself under the bedclothes and wallow in self-pity. The awful scene on Saturday night played over and over in her mind. Was she stupid to have refused Frank? She could have been planning her wedding to a man who loved her. She did like him, he was handsome and, if the truth be told, she longed to have a man in her life again. Then there was Laurence. She hadn't known him very long, but that didn't matter, he was like no other man she knew and there was no doubt that she was attracted to him physically. Now she'd spoiled it all and she would never see him again. Why, oh why didn't she tell him about Jim right from the beginning?

There was no point in moping. She climbed out of bed and got ready for work, not because she wanted to, but because she would be doing something useful, even if it was only logging lost ration books. Not only that, she was worried about Susan.

It was dinnertime before she had the chance to speak to Sergeant Duffy. She knocked and put her head round the door. She was at her desk looking through statements. 'Goodness me, you look washed out. Is something the matter?'

'I've been worrying about Susan. Did they charge her?'

'Yes, under the Offences Against the Person Act for concealing a birth.'

'What'll happen to her?'

'She'll be taken to court, but I don't think she'll get a custodial sentence for that. She made a statement of her own volition and that'll stand her in good stead.'

'Thank goodness. Has she gone home?'

'Yes, but in the meantime they're waiting for the post-mortem. There's a possibility of infanticide.'

'Infanticide?'

'She may have killed the baby.'

Helen let out a cry. 'Oh God!' She couldn't hold back her tears or the awful image of the dead baby.

'Sit down, Helen.'

The idea that someone would kill a child was beyond her understanding. Had Susan done that? She could've just abandoned it on a doorstep where someone would find it. Then at least it would have lived. She wiped her tears. 'I'll be all right in a minute then I'll go back to work.'

'Helen, I don't think you're fit for work. You were in a state when you found the baby and all through Susan's interview you were struggling to cope. Then you come in today and you're crying again. Look, I know you haven't had much leave since you started work in the force. You're due time off. I think I'll send you home and you can take another day off on top of that.'

'But I'm all right.'

'No, you're not. Go home, that's an order.'

She left the station and wandered aimlessly. In St Ann's Square she was drawn by music coming from the church and went in to find a wedding in progress. The ceremony was almost over and she stayed to watch the army officer and his beautiful bride walk down the aisle leaving joy in their wake. She wasn't much for praying, but she silently asked God to keep him safe for his new wife.

She was still thinking of them as she crossed the square when she saw it, the bomb shelter, the one where Norah had been murdered. She walked quickly away. Marilyn, Norah, Susan – ruined lives, all of them – I'm not cut out for this job. Sergeant Duffy said she should go home, but that would make her worse. She just wanted to hide away somewhere to settle her nerves. There was only one place she could think of.

At the Deansgate Picture House she bought a ticket

and didn't even look at what picture was showing. Inside, the usherette led her to a seat. The dark soothed her a little and she closed her eyes, lost in thought. She must have stayed there for two hours, then slowly the chatter on screen and the outbursts of laughter around her registered in her brain. She opened her eyes and realised it was a George Formby film, though why women were running around in their underwear she had no idea. Next thing, he'd got his ukulele and was singing a lewd song. She couldn't bear such silly nonsense, but still she didn't want to go home.

Instead, she caught the Queen's Road tram to Gwen's house and as soon as she opened the door, Gwen dragged her inside. 'Oh, Helen, I can't believe you're here. Come upstairs, I need to talk to you.' It was clear to see she was agitated and had been crying.

'What is it? Has something happened?' Helen asked.

'Yes, and I don't know what to do – it's terrible.'

'Calm down, it can't be that bad.' Helen tried to soothe her. 'Do you want to tell me what's happened?'

'I'm pregnant, that's what's happened!' Now she was angry. 'It was that night after we met you at the Whit walks. He said it'd be all right. He, you know, took precautions. I thought we were going to get married. I wouldn't have done it otherwise. Then a week after that he finished with me and, remember I told you, I was sure he'd left me for someone else. He denied it, but I just know he's got another woman.'

Helen's blood ran cold. What if Gwen were to find out that she was the woman he was chasing? She tried to focus on Gwen. 'Have you told Frank you're pregnant?'

'No fear! I'm not telling him. Anyway, he won't come back to me.'

'You don't know that.'

'He said he loved me and he lied. I trusted him and look what he's done to me.'

Helen watched her weep. She wanted to tell her the truth – that Frank had left Gwen because he wanted to marry her – but that would make it even worse. 'Would you like me to talk to Frank?'

'No, I'm not running after him.'

'So, what will you do? Have the baby and keep it, or you could have it adopted?'

Gwen gave a mirthless laugh. 'I'm not having a kid with no father.'

'But—'

'I'm getting rid of it.'

'Oh no, Gwen, don't do that, please. Your mam and dad will help you. I'll help you.'

'Will you, Helen?'

'Yes, of course I will.'

There was a wild look in Gwen's eyes and she leaned over and grabbed Helen's hand. 'I've been talking to a girl at work; same thing happened to her and she got rid of it.'

Helen was appalled. 'Oh no, Gwen—'

'Don't say anything, Helen, just listen. You can go to one of these backstreet women and they'll do something awful to you and you could end up dead. But this girl knows a doctor in Longsight, a proper doctor, one who'll do a good job. She said it didn't take long, and she wagged work for two days after and stayed in bed.'

Helen could hardly bear it… another dead baby. It was a moment before she caught up with what Gwen was saying.

'—but it doesn't come cheap. Helen, I've nobody else to turn to. You've a good job and Jim's pension. I'd pay you back. Please help me, Helen.'

If Gwen had asked her for help for any other reason, she would willingly have lent her the money. But not to get rid of a baby. 'Oh Gwen, please don't do it. It's too dangerous but, more to the point you'd be killing your child.'

'I'll have it done on the cheap then. I'd rather die than have a baby!'

'I'm sure you don't mean that, you're just upset.'

'So, you won't lend me the money?'

'I couldn't live with myself if anything happened to you and I couldn't bear to think that I had paid for a baby to—'

Gwen burst into tears. 'But you're my friend, I thought you'd understand. Why won't you help me?'

She shook her head. 'I'm sorry, I won't do it for the

reasons I've told you and, not only that, it's against the law.'

'Oh, so here you are, the policewoman, telling me what I can't do. Who do you think you are, full of your own importance? You've played the grieving widow with me and Frank supporting you but now, when I ask for your help, you couldn't possibly do something for me when I'm in dire need!'

Helen couldn't believe her ears. 'You get pregnant, and I'm the one in the wrong, then you want me to give you money?'

'Get out of here.' Gwen ran at her and pushed her towards the door. 'Get out, you bitch!'

With every step she took away from Gwen's house, Helen railed against the insults she had hurled at her. She could never have lent her money for an abortion. Her stomach churned at the thought. Maybe she shouldn't have said anything about the law, but she worked for the police and she had sworn to uphold it. Then there were those awful, hurtful words; she was sure she never played the widow – she lived it.

She got as far as Rochdale Road then realised she was close to Frank's lodgings; she had been there once with Jim when he needed Frank to do an early shift. He might not be at home or he could refuse to speak to her at all after she had rejected him. Nevertheless, she had to try. The landlady answered the door, and told her no women were allowed in the lodgers' rooms, but she shouted up to him saying there was a woman wanting to speak to him. He looked surprised to see her.

'Hello, Frank.' Behind him she could see the landlady loitering in the hall. 'Could I have a word with you?'

He closed the door behind him and they walked as far as the gate. 'Well, I didn't expect to see you again,' he said.

Facing him now, she worried that he would get just as angry as Gwen had been when she had tried to give her advice. 'I wanted to speak to you about Gwen.'

He rolled his eyes. 'Tell her I'm not interested – it's over.'

'But that's just it, Frank, it's not over. She doesn't know I'm here, but I can't stand by and let you two ruin your lives.'

'What are you talking about?'

She took a deep breath. 'Gwen's pregnant.' He was about to shout, but she held up her hand. 'No, listen, she wants to get rid of it – your child, Frank, you can't let that happen.'

'It's got nothing to do with me. She can do what she likes with it!'

'How can you say that? Only a few weeks ago it looked like you were going to marry her.'

'No, I was going to marry you! So, don't tell me what to do with my life.' He turned and walked back to the house.

'But the baby, Frank?' She ran after him and caught

hold of his arm. 'You're a good man, a decent man. I can't believe you would let Gwen down like this.' He shrugged her off and went back inside, leaving her screaming at the closed door. 'What would Jim think of you!'

She walked all the way home, her mind in turmoil, and went straight to bed. She awoke in the early morning and decided to clean the house from top to bottom, scrubbing, polishing, washing and ironing, and all the while she pushed away the dark thoughts of babies and murdered girls.

When Helen returned to work after her leave, Sergeant Duffy had a quick word with her in the canteen. 'Good to see you back. Do you feel any better?'

'Yes, thanks.'

'Ready for the fray, then? We're on the lookout for five tons of black-market bacon said to be on the way to us from London.'

'Anything more about Norah's murder?'

'No, it's gone cold, but we'll keep on with the overnight patrols.'

'And what about Susan?'

'The post-mortem was inconclusive so the charge will be concealing a birth. She'll get six months' probation. That reminds me, the director of the Whitworth rest centre has asked if you could call in next Saturday.

Some of their residents are being moved into renovated housing over the next few weeks and she thought you might like to say goodbye to them.'

'That's great news. I'll try to get there.'

'You should. You know, the director spoke highly of you and that young doctor, not just what you did for Susan, but the support you gave the women there.'

Helen thought this might be a good opportunity to do more work in the community. 'Sarge, is there any chance I could get more time out on the beat and less in the office?'

'Aye, why not. We could do with more help out there, especially with this surge of black-market goods in the city. Leave it with me.'

She thought about the invitation to the rest centre on and off throughout the day. She really wanted to say goodbye to the women and to wish them well in their new homes after all the heartache and discomfort they had suffered. She wanted to see Laurence too, even if it was only to say goodbye. Their friendship shouldn't have ended as it did. After that terrible day with Susan, the evening she had spent in his flat had been lovely, and she knew they had got on well together. But remembering that awful scene outside her house made her shudder. She had misled him about Jim and she could still see the hurt in his eyes, as he turned his back on her that night.

341

By the time she got home she still hadn't decided what to do. If she went to the rest centre it would be very awkward, but then again it would be bad manners not to go. As it happened, on the Saturday morning Sergeant Duffy decided that she, too, would go to the rest centre. 'It does no harm to show your face,' she said, leaving Helen no alternative but to accompany her.

Margaret Pilkington, the director of the Whitworth Art Gallery, met them at the door and Helen introduced her to Sergeant Duffy. 'I'm so glad to see both of you here and I have to tell you, Sergeant, that Helen has worked hard helping the women with all sorts of problems. Now, I'll show you around if you like. 'Then she winked at Helen. 'Why don't you pop along and say hello to Dr Fitzpatrick?'

She took a deep breath and knocked on his door. 'Come in.' He was alone, sitting behind his desk. She had thought he would be angry at the sight of her, but it looked more like sadness in his eyes. 'Hello, Helen,' he said.

'Hello, Laurence, can I come in?'

He shrugged. She took that as a 'yes' and sat opposite him.

'How are you?' she asked. Another shrug. 'Laurence, I'm so sorry about what happened. I'd like to explain, will you let me do that?'

'I don't think there's much point. You're a widow and you're going to marry your husband's best friend. Congratulations on that.'

'But that's not how it is. He asked me to marry him and I said I'd think about it. I've given him my answer now – I gave it that very night. I'm not marrying him and he's made it clear he'll never see me again.'

'This has got nothing to do with me.'

'But it does, Laurence. The evening I spent in your flat was the first time I'd felt alive since my husband died. I enjoyed your company so much and I think you felt a connection between us – a spark – you said it yourself.'

He studied her face. 'I won't lie to you, Helen, I was attracted to you from the beginning and, when I got to know you better, I realised you were like no other woman I'd ever met. Sensitive and caring, and you seemed to understand me. At first, I thought it was because of our jobs and the horrors we had seen, but that night in my flat I knew it was more than that.'

He looked away but she had caught that brief look of anguish. She wanted to go to him and tell him she felt the same way but he turned to her, his face hardened.

'You lied to me, didn't you? And, for the life of me, I can't understand why a wife would deny her dead husband?'

His words were like a blow to her heart and she bowed her head in shame. He was right, she had denied

Jim, and she had never even thought of it like that. She couldn't stay a moment longer.

She got as far as the door when he stopped her.

'Answer me, Helen.'

She looked into his eyes; the anger had gone. He waited while she struggled to explain why she had done such a thing. 'I have no excuse and you can condemn me and reject me,' she said. 'But I will tell you, because I owe you that.' She paused to collect her thoughts. 'To be a widow is to be on the outside, not because people are cruel but because they don't know how to deal with your loss. Some people try to be sympathetic, but you can't keep absorbing people's pity – it wears you down. Others judge you, if you don't seem bereft enough. And to be a young widow is the worst of all.'

'Why is that?' he asked.

'That day when you took me to lunch, you automatically assumed I was married because of my wedding ring. In a way that protects me. Few men would make a pass at a widow. I know this is silly, but I always thought that if I told a man I was a widow, I would almost be saying that I was available. You assumed I was a fireman's wife and I didn't correct you. To be honest, I never thought I'd see you again.'

'But why didn't you just tell me afterwards when we met again?'

'Because... by then it would have been ludicrous to say. "Sorry I didn't tell you before, but I'm a widow."

Oh, Laurence, I got myself into a mess. And when I was in your flat and I could see how it was between us... If only I'd said something, but I couldn't bear to spoil the evening.' She sighed. 'And now, all I'm saying is – I am a widow, but I'm still a woman.'

She watched him mulling over her words, desperate for him to believe her. He nodded. 'Maybe we should start again, Helen?'

'Yes, Laurence, I'd like that.'

He stroked her cheek. 'One step at a time, eh?'

She nodded.

'How about next Saturday night? I'll pick you up.'

They left his surgery and there was Sergeant Duffy waiting for her.

'You remember Dr Fitzpatrick, Sarge.'

'Yes, I do. Good to meet you in happier circumstances.'

On the way back to the station, Sergeant Duffy said, 'I think he's sweet on you, isn't he? Do you like him?'

'Yes, I do. He's asked me out.'

'I'm pleased for you. You know, if you did want to marry again, as a WAPC you could still stay in the force. Whereas policewomen usually have to leave when they get married, but times are changing. I've heard of some being allowed to stay on. It wasn't like that in my day.'

'So, you never married?'

'No.' She sighed. 'It wasn't to be.'

'It doesn't seem fair, does it.'

'Ach, don't be feeling sorry for me.' There was a

twinkle in her eye. 'Just because I'm not married, doesn't mean I haven't got a man.'

Helen was a little shocked, but why shouldn't she have someone to love and still keep her job? 'I'm glad you have someone.'

'Maybe you and Laurence...'

'I'm just happy to have some company.'

Sergeant Duffy winked. 'Aye, company is good.'

Chapter 30

It was a proper date and she was so excited and nervous. Saturday night, and Laurence was taking her to a restaurant and afterwards they would catch the last house at the Odeon. He wanted her to see the latest Fred Astaire film. She had finished work at dinner time and called into Woolworth's on her way home to buy a new lipstick and some bath salts. The house was cold when she came in and she lit the paraffin heater in the kitchen to warm it up, then fetched the tin bath in from the yard. She boiled pans of hot water to fill it and when it reached a good six inches, she took off her clothes and slipped into the sweet-smelling water. She lay there a while and thought of Laurence, when he asked her out, and his lovely smile when she said yes. She washed her hair and rinsed it with a jug then climbed out of the bath, wrapping a towel around her head and another round her body. Upstairs, she laid her two best dresses on the bed and tried to decide which one to wear: the floral with a full skirt and a tailored bodice; or the pale-blue woollen one, with pearl buttons and lace on the cuffs?

Just before six o'clock, she was sitting at her dressing table mirror checking her make-up: a little foundation, a smidgen of rouge, the lovely new coral lipstick. Her hair had dried naturally, with her blonde curls resting on her shoulders, and the pale-blue dress was modest, but stylish enough. She stood up, hesitated, then opened her jewellery box and took out the delicate silver chain with its single drop pearl. She fastened it around her neck and straightened the pearl at the base of her throat, just as there was a knock on the door.

The butterflies made her a little breathless and she was sure her face was flushed when he came into the parlour. His overcoat was open and she noted his dark suit, white shirt and a red and black striped tie.

'These are for you,' he said and gave her a posy of violets.

'They're beautiful. Have I time to put them in water?'

'Of course.'

'Sit down, I won't be a minute.' She didn't have a vase, but a jam jar was just the right size. How odd that he had brought her violets, just like the little flower pressed in her book that she had picked from the plant found in the ruins of the building where Jim had died.

When she returned, he said, 'This is a lovely room.'

She had to smile. 'The sofa's my latest purchase. I had no furniture for a good few months after I moved in. Then little by little I bought some second-hand stuff and made cushions, rag rugs, anything to make it homely.'

'You were on your own then?'

'Yes, but I managed.'

The restaurant was just around the corner from the Portico Library. Laurence parked the car outside and took her arm as they went in. They were met at the door by a handsome, foreign-looking man in a white apron, not much older than Laurence. '*Bonsoir*, Laurence.' They shook hands.

'Good to see you, Philippe. This is Helen.'

He held out his hand and she took it, but to her surprise he raised it to his lips. 'Nice to meet you, Helen.' Then he turned to Laurence. '*Une belle femme.*' He smiled. 'Now, I have a lovely table for you, very romantic.'

When they were seated, she asked, 'Is he French?'

'Yes, his father came to Manchester after the last war and opened up this restaurant. I got to know the family when he was ill in hospital. Philippe runs it now.'

'What was he saying about me?'

Laurence laughed. 'He said you're a beautiful woman.'

'Oh!' She looked away.

'Don't be embarrassed, he was telling the truth. You are beautiful.'

She was glad that Philippe arrived just then with the menu. 'I will bring you wine too,' he said.

She studied the menu. 'I don't understand any of this.'

'Don't worry, we'll just have the cassoulet, it's like a stew with beans. It's what I usually have.'

Helen rarely drank wine and, when she did, it came from Yates's. This was different, a strange taste, but she didn't dislike it.

'Tell me about your house,' Laurence asked. 'Have you lived there long?'

'I moved there after Jim died. We had found the house together and we were supposed to move in on New Year's Day, but Jim died at Christmas in the Blitz. We lived at my mother's before that.'

'So, you moved out and went to live on your own?'

She nodded.

'That was brave.'

'No, it wasn't, it was foolhardy, but I was so full of grief. My mother was a hard woman to live with and I was so confused, I even thought she'd stolen money from Jim and that turned out to be wrong as well.'

He reached over and held her hand. 'I wish I'd known you then, I would have helped you.'

'Oh, I wouldn't have been that easy to help, but I managed to get a job at Fenner's Fashions and by the time I joined the police, the grief had eased a little.'

Philippe brought them steaming plates of cassoulet and chunks of crusty bread. 'This is delicious,' said Helen. 'Why does it taste so good?'

'The French have ways of making the simplest food special, maybe it's the herbs they use.'

'And what about you, Laurence? It's only a few weeks since your mother died.'

'Ah, you know, when I'm at work I'm concentrating all the time. It's not till I get home and I start thinking about her. Remembering little incidents when I was growing up, and the things she taught me, the advice she gave me. I hope I don't stop thinking of those ordinary things as time goes on.'

'You won't, I'm sure.'

They had crème caramel and finished the wine then Laurence asked for the bill.

'There is no bill tonight for my good friend and his lovely lady,' said Philippe and he turned to Helen. 'He is happier than I have seen him in a long time. You come back again soon,' and he kissed both Helen and Laurence on both cheeks. '*Au revoir, mon ami.*'

Outside, she was surprised that he took her in his arms and kissed her so long and tenderly that she wished it would last for ever. He ran his fingers through her hair and she sighed at his touch. 'Come on, Helen, it's time to go to the cinema.'

She'd forgotten all about the film. He took her hand

and led her to the car, but once inside he kissed her again. 'My darling Helen, I think I might be falling in love with you, but I won't rush you. We have all the time in the world.' She could hear the smile in his voice. 'This is only our first date, after all.' He started the engine and they drove to the cinema.

He was right, of course, one step at a time, but she had felt that quickening at his touch and it was hard to deny her desires. There would be other dates, but for now there was only the darkened picture house, with his arm around her shoulder and the chaste romance of Astaire and Rogers on the silver screen.

When they arrived back at her house, she invited him in and they sat on her sofa talking about everything and nothing. He was good company; made her laugh, made her think, and all the time she watched the expressions cross his beautiful face. She thought again about his words in the car, 'I think I might be falling in love with you'. It made her tingle.

'It's late,' he said. 'It's time you went to bed.'

'You don't have to go.'

'I know, but I should go,' and he took her in his arms and kissed her. She wanted him so much.

'You make me feel so content and hopeful, Laurence. I'm so glad I met you.'

'I feel just the same. Shall we meet again next Saturday?'

'Yes, and Sunday too?'

'We will.' A kiss on her cheek and he was gone.

She closed the door and leaned against it. He might be falling in love with her and it made her so happy, because she knew that she was already in love with him.

Chapter 31

Dear Helen,
I hope you are well. I need to talk to you. Please meet
me on Saturday afternoon in Kendal Milne's lingerie
department at two o'clock.
Yours,
Anna Maguire

PS Please don't come in your uniform – wear a nice
dress and make-up.

It was a warm afternoon when Helen left the station
and headed for Deansgate and Kendal Milne, the most
expensive department store in Manchester. She had been
intrigued by Anna's letter to meet her in the lingerie
department and the instructions not to wear her police
uniform. She had finished her shift at lunchtime and
would normally have gone home in her uniform, but

instead she went to the ladies' locker room to change into her best dress, and high-heel shoes. She unclipped her curls from behind her ears and brushed till they bounced. Finally, she put on her make-up as if she was going out for a night on the town.

The desk sergeant whistled as he watched her signing off duty. 'Please tell me this is the new WAPC uniform.'

'No chance, Sarge.'

'Aw well, thanks for brightening my day, Harrison.'

On the walk from the station to the store she had time to think again about Anna's strange letter. She was looking forward to seeing her again, but mostly she was just curious.

Helen came through the revolving doors of the store into a different world and she stopped a moment to take in the scene: the staff were well groomed and wore neat black dresses; the polished wooden and glass counters seemed to have plenty of stock, and the fragrance from the perfume counters filled the air. She walked past stylish hats, scarves that were probably silk, umbrellas, and so many handbags.

Beyond that, there was a wide staircase and next to it a list of departments. Lingerie was on the second floor and, as she climbed the stairs, she promised herself that she would return again to explore this wonderful... what was the word? Emporium, yes that was it, emporium.

Anna was waiting at the top of the stairs, dressed as though every stitch on her must have come from

Kendal's. 'Thanks for coming, Helen. First things first, this is for you,' and she handed her an envelope, inside which there were several pound notes. 'That's the money you lent me to get back on my feet.'

'Anna, it was a gift. I don't want it back.'

'Take it, Helen, please. I shudder to think where I'd be now, if you hadn't taken me in. I owe you so much, so don't argue.' Then she took Helen's arm. 'Now, we're going to wander round as though we're looking for some nice underwear. I might even buy some and, while we do that, I want to talk to you about the place where I'm working.'

'That's the bar where you're a waitress? But why are we here?'

Anna picked up a cream lace bra and seemed to study it. 'What do you notice about lingerie departments?'

'They have beautiful things.'

'That's true, but we're here because they're nearly always empty and men very rarely come in here. So, let's pretend we're buying.' They wandered around picking up items and replacing them while Anna explained. 'The club is not what it seems – think Fenner's supper club, but on a much bigger scale. It's a large building, three storeys, down near the canal on Quay Street. It must have been the headquarters of a cotton trading company, now it's fitted out as a bar and some other things.'

'Why are you telling me this?' asked Helen.

'There's something odd about it. It's a big operation

and there's a lot more than drinking going on. I'm just a waitress, but I'm sure there's illegal gambling and, certainly, there's some sort of brothel.'

Helen wondered whether Anna was telling her the whole story – she couldn't have afforded such high fashion on a waitress's wages.

Anna's expression was grim. 'I don't like the way they treat some of the girls, especially the younger ones.' A woman came towards them to look at a display of corsets; Anna moved away and Helen followed. She stopped at a rail of silk dressing gowns, picked one out, eau-de-Nil silk, and put it over her arm; no one was close now but she still lowered her voice.

'Then there's the men who own it. I don't mean Gerry, the manager, but the ones who suddenly appear and you think – they're up to no good. That's when there's – I can't describe it – the whole atmosphere around them is intimidating.' She grabbed Helen's arm. 'They frighten me.'

'Anna, do you want to report your suspicions? I could go with you to the police station and sit with you while you make a statement.'

Anna was horrified. 'Dear God, no! I can't be seen anywhere near a police station. That's what this cloak and dagger underwear shopping is all about. I can't have any connection with the police, but who would suspect my friend coming to have a drink with me in the bar where I work?'

'You want me to come to the club?'

'Just take a look at it. There won't be many punters in at this time of day, but you could meet a few of the girls.'

'I'm not sure,' said Helen. 'I'm only an auxiliary, you know.'

They went to the counter and Anna bought the silk dressing gown. It was expensive and quite a few clothing coupons were needed. The assistant wrapped it in tissue paper, put it in a Kendal Milne box and tied it with a cream ribbon. 'This is for you,' said Anna.

Helen was amazed. 'I can't take that, it cost a fortune and all those coupons you've spent!'

'Oh, don't worry, there's plenty more where that came from.'

Outside on Deansgate Anna turned to her. 'Come for a drink, Helen. Where's the harm in that?'

'All right. I'll have one drink, but I don't think I can do anything.'

They walked to the canal, past bombed buildings – some reduced to rubble, others without roofs. Anna stopped in front of an undamaged Victorian building with the words 'Calico Manufacturing Company' in gilt across the upper storey. A new brass plate had been screwed to the elegant front door and on it was written 'The Calico Club'.

The entrance hall was large with a marble floor, a chandelier hung from the ceiling and a curved mahogany staircase swept up to the next level. To the left, open double doors led to the bar, whereas the matching doors to the right were closed. She followed Anna into the left-hand room. Shafts of light from the high windows glinted on the stylish chrome interior. There was a stage, a small dance floor, tables and chairs and curved booths affording some privacy, and in the centre of the room were tables and chairs. Along one wall was a long bar, where a few men were drinking. Helen noted the customers were well-heeled and the bar well-stocked. The man behind the bar, dressed in a waistcoat, white shirt and a dickie bow, looked up from pulling a pint and called out to Anna. 'You're early today.'

'I've been out shopping with my friend, Helen; brought her in to have a drink and to see where I work.'

'Nice to see you, Helen, I'm Gerry. What'll you have to drink?'

'We'll have Scotch on the rocks,' said Anna.

'This is a lovely place,' said Helen.

'It certainly is,' said Gerry, 'and it's a good place to work too, isn't it, Anna?'

'Leave her alone, Gerry, she's not interested in working in a club. She's in the fashion business, a model. That's how we know each other. Come on, Helen, I'll introduce you to a few of the girls, bring your drink with you.'

The ladies' lavatory was down the corridor by the side of the bar. Inside, there were three girls: one putting on make-up, another brushing her blonde hair and one, who didn't look much older than sixteen, was in her underwear slipping into a low-cut black dress. They were friendly enough and Helen asked them how they liked working in the club. They weren't exactly enthusiastic – it's all right, it's a job, the money's not bad.

'Are you looking to work here?' asked the youngest girl.

'Do you think I should?'

'If you think you're tough enough.'

'What do you mean?' asked Helen.

'That's enough!' said the blonde, glaring at the young girl.

Back in the bar Helen and Anna sat in one of the curved booths and spoke in a whisper. 'What was that all about?' asked Helen.

'Some of the men are demanding, they drink too much and sometimes the girls are in the firing line. It's not right.'

'What about the management, can't they stop them?'

Anna shrugged. 'Gerry tries but there's not much he can do, especially if the man is a big spender. It's not just the girls, there's other things... I don't know what, but I'm sure it's not legal. I thought you might be able to do something.'

'I don't know,' said Helen. 'Maybe if you could find out more about what's going on.'

'All right, I'll try. We could meet again at Kendal's same time, next week?'

'Yes, and in the meantime, I'll speak to my sergeant, but be careful, don't take any risks.'

Helen left the bar and went out into the entrance hall, wondering what exactly she was getting herself into. She paused, looked up at the chandelier – surely this must be a respectable business. Then on a sudden impulse she walked across the marble floor to the double doors opposite. She was just about to open them, then stopped; someone was behind her. She turned. A tall dark-haired man in an immaculate hand-tailored suit, complete with waistcoat and gold pocket watch, stood watching her. His look was one of curiosity mixed with superiority.

'Oh, I think I'm a bit lost,' said Helen. 'This isn't the way out. It's there, isn't it?' and she went towards the entrance door.

'Just a minute.' He came towards her, taking in every detail of her appearance. 'I'm Henry Carter, the owner. I saw you in the bar with Anna, are you a friend of hers?' His voice was refined, his tone clipped, well-educated, no doubt.

She nodded. 'We used to work together...' She thought of Anna's introduction earlier. 'Modelling.'

'A model. Of course, I should have guessed. What's your name?'

'Helen.'

'Have you ever thought of working in a gentlemen's club, Helen? It's steady work and good money.'

'No, I don't think so.'

'Hmm, that's a pity. I'm looking for girls with a bit of class.' He opened the door and went down the steps with her. 'I'm off to London tomorrow, but if you change your mind, just let Gerry know and you can start right away.' As she walked away, she felt his eyes following her and she just knew that she would see him again.

Chapter 32

It was still early and for a brief moment she thought of going to see Gwen, but could she turn up on her doorstep when they had parted in such anger? She had thought about her so many times since then. The baby would be gone and in a way she felt bad that she hadn't given Gwen the money she had asked for, but she was certain she had done the right thing. Could she ever mend their friendship? There was only one way to find out.

The door was answered by Gwen's mother, all smiles. 'Come in, she's in her bedroom. Go on up.'

Through the half-open door, she could see her lying on the bed. 'Gwen, it's me, Helen.'

'Oh, Helen, you've come to see me?' There was a crack in her voice.

'Yes. I'm sorry, I should have come sooner. How are you?'

Gwen rolled over and sat up. 'I'm fine.'

Helen caught sight of her middle. 'Oh, are you…?'

Gwen gave a half smile. 'Yes, the baby's still here.'

Helen wanted to say she was so pleased about the child, but she wasn't sure how Gwen felt about it. 'You decided to keep it?'

Gwen patted the bed and Helen went and sat with her. 'I was at my wits' end, you know that, don't you?'

'Yes, but what made you change your mind?'

'I was so desperate that I went to the house where the woman lived, but I didn't go in, it looked filthy and I was scared. When I got home, I was in a state and Mam knew something was wrong. I couldn't keep it to myself any longer. Me and her just sat here in this room crying together. She said it didn't matter the child had no father, we'd bring it up together, her and me. Mam turned it right round for me and instead of…' She stopped, unable to say what could have happened, and wiped away her tears. 'Anyroad, I wanted the baby so much.'

Helen swallowed the lump in her throat. 'I'm so pleased for you, Gwen.'

'You know, I wasn't thinking straight when I asked you to lend me the money to pay that doctor? You were right about what you said and I should never have asked you. Thank God you didn't give it to me.'

There was a knock on the door and Gwen's mother appeared with two mugs of tea. 'Isn't she looking well, and what do you think about the baby?'

'I think it's great,' said Helen.

'I've already started knitting a matinee coat and bootees.'

When she'd gone, Gwen asked, 'Do you still see Frank?'

'No, I haven't heard from him in a while. I'm really busy at work.'

'You know I didn't tell him about the baby? I thought maybe I'd see him again, but he never contacted me. I think he's gone off with the other woman I told you about. It doesn't matter, I'm happy as I am.'

Helen didn't know what to say. She had told Frank about the baby and he wasn't interested, but the mention of the 'other woman' made her feel she had betrayed Gwen, even though she had never encouraged Frank to fall in love with her.

They parted again as good friends and agreed to keep in touch. On the way home she thought about the baby that was almost lost and how lucky Gwen was to have a family to look after her.

She got off the bus at Dean Lane and walked up Church Street to buy some groceries. The greengrocer had bags of soup mix and he assured her they contained plenty of barley and lentils as well as the usual cabbage, carrots and parsnips. At the butcher's there were a few ham shanks left, none of them with much meat, but the bone and marrow would give the soup a good flavour. At the bakery she bought a loaf and a slice of apple pie. She would make a big pan of broth to last her the weekend with the bread to dip in. The apple pie would be a treat with a cup of tea when she got home. Further along the street was a wool shop and she stopped to look in the window. She hadn't knitted anything since Jim's cricket sweater. On those awful days between his death and the funeral it was the only thing on which she could focus. After that she couldn't bear to knit again but now, looking at the lovely wool, she longed to touch it. The bell rang as she went inside and the woman behind the counter looked up from her knitting and smiled a welcome.

The broth was barely simmering on a low heat and she was just casting on the pale blue wool for her new cardigan when there was a scream next door and what she imagined was someone running about and shouting. She put down the knitting, uncertain what was going on, wondering if she should go next door to Ada's house to see what was happening. Seconds later, there was banging on her door and hysterical cries. She ran to the door and flung it open. Ada rushed past her into the house then turned and thrust the child into her arms. One look and Helen knew the child was unconscious.

'I only left her for a couple of minutes then I heard her making these strange breathing noises. She was lying on the floor gasping. I grabbed her and ran. Help her please!' The child was flopped like a rag doll, her face pale and her lips tinged blue. Helen laid her on the kitchen table, put one hand on her forehead and with the other she lifted her chin and quickly checked there was nothing blocking her airway. It was clear. Helen bent her head over the child, saw her chest rising, falling, and felt the flutter of her breath. The child opened her eyes and gave a loud cry.

She handed her back to Ada. 'I think she'll be all right now. Can you see her colour's come back? She might have had a fit. Has she been ill or out of sorts?'

'She's been grisly for a couple of days and she's had a temperature.'

'That'll be it, then. Now what you need to do is to go right away to the doctor, just to be sure.'

Ada, tears running down her face, hugged her little girl. 'Oh my God! I thought I'd lost her. Thank you, thank you so much. If you hadn't been here... How did you know what to do?'

'First aid – it was part of my training in the police.'

'I don't know what to say...'

'She'll be fine now,' said Helen, but still Ada stood there.

'Look, I'm sorry about the things I said about you.'

Helen waved her words away. 'Oh, don't bother about all that.'

'But I do.' She smoothed the child's hair, again and again, as she spoke. 'I wasn't fair on you from the moment you arrived, I know that. You just seemed to have so much freedom and I was hand-fast to the house and the child. But I owe you for what you did today and if there's anything I can do for you, anything.'

'That's all right, Ada. I'm just glad I was at home to help.'

Chapter 33

By the time Helen returned to work she had eaten all the broth, a lovely meat pie from Ada and had completed the back of her cardigan. She had also mulled over everything Anna had told her about the Calico Club and recalled what she had seen for herself, including the handsome Henry Carter who offered her a job.

It was late afternoon when Helen got the chance to speak to Sergeant Duffy about Anna's suspicions. She listened carefully and made notes and, when Helen had finished, she sat back in her chair and stared straight ahead. Helen waited and waited. Sergeant Duffy went back to her notes.

'Right then. We think there's illegal gambling, but this is a private club – a bunch of fellas with cards is not illegal. Then there's the brothel...' She shook her head. 'Maybe they're just hotel rooms. And unhappy girls in an intimidating atmosphere? Ach, there's women all over this city in jobs like that.'

Helen felt totally deflated. Sergeant Duffy was right, she'd heard things and joined up the dots, but there was no evidence at all. 'Sorry, Sarge, I got carried away.'

'Oh, hold on a wee minute, I'm not saying there isn't criminal activity. You've got a nose for this sort of thing, Harrison. Get something down on paper, about what you've seen and heard, just as you've told me. I'll send it over to CID, see what they think.'

On Wednesday Sergeant Duffy sent for her. 'I've had a phone call from CID; they want to talk to you about the Calico Club. Get yourself over to Newton Street, but don't get your hopes up, they're up to their eyes with two unsolved murders and a surge in black-market crime.'

It was a fair walk to Newton Street, long enough for doubts to set in. Who did she think she was, on her way to CID to tell them about… what? Her friend's suspicion that something odd was going on at a gentlemen's club? She could just imagine what they'd think. They left her waiting half an hour before they called her in.

'So, you're the girl who thinks there's an illegal gambling den off Quay Street?' Helen knew he was Detective Inspector Taylor by his name on the door and, by the look on his face, he was sceptical. She glanced across at DC Ken Kershaw, also in the room, and he gave her a nod as if to say, 'Go on, tell him.'

'Yes, sir, I had the information from a friend who works there and I've been on the premises.'

'But you didn't see any gambling, or evidence of a brothel?'

'No, sir, but I believe my friend is a reliable witness.'

He sucked on his moustache and turned to DC Kershaw. 'I wouldn't order a raid on the say-so of a prostitute and a WAPC. Could we not get a bone fide policewoman in there undercover?'

'I doubt it, sir. They'd have to look the part... if you get my drift. Whereas Harrison here...'

'I also have experience of working in a gentlemen's club,' said Helen.

DI Taylor shook his head. 'Really?'

DC Kershaw went on, 'Not only that, sir, she's already worked undercover on the seance and clergyman investigation.'

Now he was incredulous. 'This is the girl who stood up to that prominent clergyman?'

DC Kershaw nodded.

'Excuse me, sir, you might like to know that when I was at the club, the owner offered me a job.'

'Did he now?' The inspector seemed to change his tune. He sucked his moustache for a full minute. 'We could do with some positive publicity; the public think we sit here on our arses drinking tea. A headline in the *Manchester Evening News* and a few photos of criminals would work wonders for morale.' It was as though he had forgotten Helen was there. 'If we get her in there, who's going to handle her for the feedback of information?'

'I'd suggest a woman police sergeant—'

'God, not another one. In my day, women in the police did the filing and answered the phone!'

Things moved fast after that. It was agreed that Helen would meet Anna in Kendal's as planned and they would go back to the club to let the manager know that she would accept Mr Carter's kind offer of a job. Once she had started work, Helen would not return to a police station until the investigation had been completed. Every afternoon at four o'clock, Sergeant Duffy, in plain clothes, would be sitting in the last pew in the Hidden Gem church not five minutes' walk from the station, to enable Helen to report on her findings.

As soon as these arrangements were confirmed, Helen, under Sergeant Duffy's direction, immediately sent a letter to Laurence telling him that she couldn't meet him as promised on Saturday because she was being sent on a course in Cheshire to learn how to drive. She would write to him and let him know when she got back so they could arrange to meet up. She didn't want to deceive him, but Sergeant Duffy thought it would be safer, while she was undercover.

On her first evening in the club, she wore the cerise cocktail dress that Pearl had given her when she was waitressing at Fenner's supper club. It seemed so long ago. How naive she had been then. These past months in the police had stripped the innocence from her eyes. She had hated the revealing neckline back then, but now she saw it as just another uniform to help her do her job. She had also taken off her wedding ring.

Anna volunteered to show her the ropes. 'It'll be mostly waitressing to begin with. There's no money changing hands. They sign a slip – every member has a tab and they can add tips. You'll get those in your wages at the end of the week.'

'What about the other room across the hall?'

'That's a men-only area.'

'And upstairs?'

She lowered her voice. 'Some of the girls go upstairs with the men, you know what I mean? They earn more for that.'

It was around eleven when Henry Carter arrived at the club. 'I thought he said he was going to London,' said Helen.

'He was supposed to, but he had some other business, apparently.'

Shortly after, Gerry asked her to go to Mr Carter's office. 'Don't worry,' he said. 'He just wants to explain a few things to you.' He pointed to a door close to the side of the stage, with a brass plate engraved with the word 'Private'. She knocked on the door and heard his distinctive voice call her in.

He came from round the large desk and leaned back against it, his arms folded, with no more than a yard between them. There was a waft of some expensive masculine scent – she liked it.

'How are you doing out there?'

She smiled. 'All right, I think. There's a lot to learn.'

'Yes, I'll let you settle in, then I think I'll give you some extended duties.'

Her first thought was that he'd send her upstairs to the bedrooms. 'Mr Carter, I'll be blunt with you. I don't sleep with men.'

He threw back his head and laughed. 'What, never? That's a pity, but actually I have no wish to see you in that role. My idea is to do something I've seen in Mayfair: a striking woman in the entrance hall greeting the men as they arrive – a sort of hostess, if you will.'

'I don't think I'd be very good at that.' She was really thinking about the gaming room. If she could get in there—

'You would be perfect: a face to launch a thousand ships; tall and slender, with a strange sense of authority I've rarely seen in a woman.' He went back behind his desk. 'When I return, I'll show you what I want.' His voice was low and playful. 'But for now, go and sell some expensive liquor.'

Chapter 34

Helen slept late on Sunday. The club had been exceptionally busy and she didn't arrive home until nearly four in the morning. In the kitchen she filled the first of two large saucepans with water and set them on the gas so she could have a bath and wash her hair. Then she went out into the back yard to fetch the tin bath. She had just lifted it off the wall when she sensed a movement behind her and turned to see Frank, leaning against the coal-shed door.

'Hello, Helen.'

He looked tired and nervous, no sign of that anger when they last met, but she hoped he hadn't come back to ask her again to marry him. 'What do you want, Frank?'

He looked towards the yard door and back again to her, as if deciding whether to bolt or stay. She waited.

'Can I come in and speak to you? I'll not make a fuss.'

'Why would I let you into my house after the way you treated my friend Laurence that night when he brought me home?'

'I was in the wrong, but—'

'And what about Gwen? You finished with her, but not before you got her pregnant and, when I told you, you washed your hands of her.'

'I'm so sorry about everything, but I need to talk to you. Please. Helen, I've no one else.'

He looked so upset and she thought about that day on the moors when he cried at the loss of Jim. 'All right, come inside.' In the kitchen she opened the blackout curtains and turned off the gas under the saucepans. Her bath would have to wait. 'How long have you been standing out there?' she asked.

'I've been here since nine.'

'But it's nearly twelve. Why didn't you knock on the door?'

'I could see all the curtains were closed and I didn't want to wake you.'

'Well, I'm up now and you must be starving. I'll make us some breakfast.'

Frank watched her in silence and she said nothing either, even though it was awkward. But she would leave it to him to explain why he was here. They sat at the table and ate the tea and toast; a couple of times he seemed about to say something, then changed his mind. In the end she prompted him. 'Frank, do you want to speak to me, or not?' He nodded, she waited…

'I've been doing a lot of thinking about me and Jim. We were mates, all right, but it was more than that… When the bombs are falling you know you could be snuffed out like a candle but, when there's two of you looking out for each other, you know you've got a better chance of coming through the devastation. He had my back and I had his and I swear to God, Helen, I would have given my life to save him and he would have done the same for me.' He closed his eyes and when he spoke again it was in a whisper. 'I'd been watching Jim on the ladder but I turned away – believe me – it was only a second, but when I looked again, he was gone.'

'I know that, Frank, but it was an accident, you couldn't have saved him.'

'Maybe not, but I'll have to live with that.' He opened his eyes and looked at her. 'But then there was you.'

She was immediately wary of his words. 'Me?' she asked. Surely, he wasn't going to bring up all that nonsense about marrying her?

He went on. 'You know I promised Jim I'd look after you if the worst happened and that's what I tried to do. But somewhere along the line, it all got out of hand. I was terrified something awful would happen to you and that would be my fault too and I'd have let Jim down all over again.' His voice was rising. 'I kept coming to your house with all sorts of excuses to see you, to make sure you were safe, but it wasn't enough. That's why

I wanted to marry you, so I could take proper care of you.'

She held up her hand. 'Frank, don't say any more. I've told you I'm not marrying you.'

'No, no, listen. I know that and I...' He struggled to explain. 'In a way I do love you, Helen, but I'm not asking you to marry me. It wouldn't be right for either of us, I know that now, but I don't want to lose touch with you. You're still my best mate's wife, and I want you to know I'll be here whenever you need me.'

She sighed. 'All right, I won't fall out with you; Jim wouldn't have wanted that.'

'Thank you.'

She stood up. 'Well, I'll need to get on, I've a lot of cleaning to do.'

He didn't move. 'I need to talk to you about something else.'

She sat down again. 'What is it?'

'I can't get Gwen out of my mind. I let her down so badly; I'll never forgive myself.' He hesitated. 'Do you think I should go and see her? I mean, would she speak to me?'

Helen raised an eyebrow and it was a moment before she could speak. 'Why would you do that? You made it quite clear to her that you didn't want to be with her.'

'I know, I know, I was a fool. I thought I didn't want to get tied down, but now I want to do the right thing. The baby is lost, but we could still have children.'

She was tempted to tell him Gwen was still carrying the baby, but it wasn't for her to speak for Gwen. 'I don't know what she would say.'

'Could you not speak to her, ask her if she would meet me?'

A part of her thought she could do that – a go-between. On the other hand, it might not be a good idea to meddle in other people's lives. If Frank was serious, and he might well be, he was the one who should be making the running and Gwen should make up her own mind whether to believe him or not.

'If you truly love her, Frank, you'll find your own way to get her back.'

Chapter 35

A week passed and Helen had met Sergeant Duffy in the Hidden Gem every day before going to work at the Calico Club, but still she had no conclusive evidence of illegal activity, beyond Anna's certainty that the bedrooms were in constant use. Helen had tried to see beyond the suspected gaming room door, but a burly man was on duty outside when it was in use.

Sergeant Duffy was worried. 'CID won't want to wait much longer, Helen. They're talking about a raid and hope that they get lucky.'

'They need to wait. Anna says there's always something going on at the end of every month. She doesn't know what, but I'm going to try and find out. It's all connected with Henry Carter and his cronies from London. Have they dug up anything on him yet?'

'They've been in touch with Scotland Yard and they say there's no one of that name with a criminal record.'

'Maybe he's kept his nose clean. He's a smooth character, sounds like a gentleman – looks like a matinee idol in his Savile Row suits.'

'Watch yourself with him, Helen. Didn't he say he had a special job for you?'

'Yes, and I'm hoping it might give me the chance to find out what Henry Carter is really up to.'

Helen arrived at the club early but, instead of going in, she stood on the other side of the road and looked at the building. There was something odd about it. Inside, she knew there was the bar, the games' room, and four bedrooms upstairs. Add to that: office, toilets, storage behind the bar and that was the extent of the Calico Club. She crossed the road and walked down the narrow street at the side of the building and round to the back. There was a loading bay with large doors, heavily padlocked, and high enough for lorries to drive inside. And then it hit her. The back-end of the building was a warehouse.

She went inside and sat down at the bar where Gerry was replacing the empty optics.

'How was your first week then?' he said.

'I've enjoyed it and it'll be even better when I get my pay packet.'

'You'll be surprised at the tips you'll get; the men are generous.'

'It's a good bar, better stocked than most I've seen.'

Gerry hesitated. 'Mr Carter has his contacts.'

Yes, she thought, no shortage of cigarettes and spirits here.

'He said he might have a different job for me when he comes back.'

'He didn't mention it to me.'

'I thought it might have been in the other room across the way?'

'I don't think so, women aren't allowed in there.'

'What, not at all?'

'No.'

'Oh, that's intriguing.'

He turned his back and carried on with the optics. She'd get nothing out of him.

'Never mind,' she said. 'I'll go and get the warpaint on. See you later.'

In the ladies' toilet Helen laid out her make-up, such as it was. She never wore any when she was in uniform, but even so her stock had diminished. Maybe she could afford some more with her tips. She was about to apply her foundation when something in the mirror caught her eye and she turned to look at the door behind her. If she had noticed it at all in the week she had worked here, she would have assumed it was a broom cupboard and naturally it would be closed but, seeing it slightly open, she went to look inside. It was full of everything needed for a really good clean, and there was the cleaner's pinny hanging on the back of the door. She shook it and couldn't help but smile.

The following morning, she was waiting outside the club when a stout, middle-aged woman in an ancient overcoat and headscarf came down the street. Helen greeted her. 'Hello, are you the cleaner?' she asked.

'I am, cock, what can I do for you?'

'I'm one of the waitresses and I think I lost my watch here last night; the clasp wasn't that good, to be honest.'

'Oh dear, do you want to have a look around?'

'Oh, could I?'

The woman opened the door and they went in together. 'I've a set of keys to the rooms in my cupboard. Where do you want to look?'

'Oh, to be honest, I was here, there and everywhere.'

The woman took her pinny from behind the broom cupboard door and felt in the front pocket. She took out a bunch of keys and handed them to her. 'Take your time, love, see if you can find it. I'll be cleaning in the bar a good while.'

Helen couldn't believe her luck. For all the talk of locked rooms, the cleaning woman had all the keys to the castle. She went straight across the hall to the double doors and after a few tries she found the right key. The room was the same size as the bar, with maroon flocked wallpaper and maroon upholstered chairs arranged round various tables. Over the two largest tables there were black dust-covers. She raised one and smiled. There was the roulette wheel. The other revealed a blackjack cloth, and the various smaller tables had decks of cards, probably for poker and other games. She had seen the gaming tables with her own eyes, maybe now there could be a raid.

It had taken no more than a few minutes, leaving her plenty of time to look around upstairs. There were five doors in total. The first four rooms were similar and decorated in the style of some sort of French boudoir as imagined by a man. The bedclothes were dishevelled and there were full ashtrays, empty bottles and glasses lying about. The final door was set in a roughly plastered wall at the end of the corridor and the lock and key were much heavier. She knew at once it was the dividing wall between the front and back of the building. She turned the key, pulled open the heavy door and stepped out on to the top of a wooden stairway. Half a dozen skylights illuminated the vast open warehouse space below. She went quickly down and found stacked boxes of whisky, gin and cigarettes. Not a huge amount, but maybe there was more to come. She had seen enough.

She found the cleaner and returned the keys. 'It was upstairs, thank goodness. Don't tell the boss, will you? I get in enough trouble.'

'Don't worry, love. I'm glad you found it.'

*

That afternoon Helen sat with Sergeant Duffy in the Hidden Gem. 'I'm certain the four rooms upstairs are being used as a brothel. I've also seen the gaming room with roulette, blackjack, poker tables. There's no doubt that's what goes on in there every night.'

'I'll tell CID, chances are they'll raid it tonight or tomorrow.'

'No, they mustn't do that, not yet. There's something else, something bigger. The back end of the building is a warehouse; I've been in it – there are some boxes of spirits and cigarettes, but it's nearly empty. This club sells so much drink and cigarettes, I can't imagine where they get it all from. Do you think it could be tied up with all the black-market activity?'

'It could be. There have been rumours of London gangs in Manchester for months.'

'It's like they're building up to something in the club. Remember I told you Anna said every month there's something big goes on. She said the atmosphere changes and, you know, I can feel a tension in the air. Henry Carter and his men are Londoners and they're due back in Manchester any day now. I wouldn't be surprised if stolen goods were due to be shipped to the Calico Club warehouse.'

'The DI is desperate for some success, but I'm not sure they'll hang fire when the gambling would be easy meat.'

'But you have to convince them. If they wait, they

could crack a black-market syndicate and that'll be a far bigger catch than they ever imagined.'

'You're right, girl. I'll make them listen. Now keep your ear to the ground, stay in contact and, as soon as you get wind of anything, we'll pull you out and send in the constables.'

They stood to go and, to Helen's surprise, Sergeant Duffy hugged her. 'You're doing great work, Harrison, but keep your wits about you. These men are dangerous.'

That night there was a singer and pianist and the club was packed. They were run off their feet at the bar and several girls had been upstairs in the bedrooms. Helen was taking an order of drinks for a noisy table of four men when she felt an arm around her waist. 'It's Helen, isn't it? Do you remember me?' She turned and her heart stopped as she looked into the face of Charles Brownlow – the man who wanted to make her his mistress. For one awful moment she thought Fenner might be with him, but she didn't recognise anyone else. She brazened it out. 'Sorry, sir, I don't think so,' and she turned away.

She asked another waitress to take the drinks to their table. An hour later she was standing at the bar watching some of the customers dancing with girls when he sought her out. 'Did you think I'm that stupid that I wouldn't recognise you? I spotted you as soon as I came in. Your deportment, your striking features, you're even wearing the same dress, for God's sake.'

'I'm sorry, Mr Brownlow, I didn't mean to offend you. It's just that I'm a bit embarrassed, doing a job like this.'

'I'm not surprised, you could do so much better, if you'd let me help you.' And what he said next almost stopped her heart.

'I heard you'd left Fenner's and, maybe I'm mistaken, but I thought he said you were working for the police?'

She lowered her eyes, hiding the panic in her face. Then she felt his finger on her chin as he tilted her face upwards.

'You're not doing two jobs, are you?'

She looked him in the eye. 'Of course not. I did think about the police, but the wages were poor. Anyway, I'd rather be doing this and earning twice as much.'

He gave her a quizzical look, but she couldn't be sure whether it was because he didn't believe her or he was just weighing her up. Then he smiled. 'I'm sure you'll want to dance with an old friend.'

He held her close and let his hand slip lower and lower over her curves. Then he kissed her neck and whispered, 'I know it must be so hard for you, being a widow, and now you've ended up waitressing and no doubt have other duties.'

She ignored the innuendo. 'The thing is, I didn't tell my godmother Pearl or Mr Fenner that I'd ended up doing this. I don't think they'd approve, so, could I ask you not to mention it to anyone?'

'I'd need to think about that.' He danced her around the floor before he spoke again. 'I've heard that you girls sometimes go upstairs with the customers? Maybe we could do that?'

She was horrified at the thought and was tempted to slap his face, but she held her nerve. She had to get through these next few days before the raid without drawing attention to herself. 'I'm sorry, Mr Brownlow, I've been told that I'm not allowed to do that yet. I have to serve my time getting to know how the waitressing works first.'

'That's a pity,' he said. 'But maybe I could be first on the list when the time comes.'

Helen managed a smile.

Chapter 36

Pearl slipped away from her desk into the showroom and stood looking out over Stevenson's Square. There was Harold on the opposite pavement looking agitated. He had been waiting there for a good twenty minutes. She knew that, because she had made Rita file a fistful of invoices before she allowed her to go for her dinner. There she was now, running across the road, and Pearl winced to see her kiss him right there in public. But they had long since stopped being discreet. He was besotted with the hussy, buying her gifts and renting hotel rooms; she could see that from the business cheque book. Now, they were laughing together as they walked arm in arm to the taxi rank. She couldn't take much more of this.

An hour later Rita appeared at the office door, the cocky look gone from her face.

'I wasn't expecting you back for another two hours. Had a fall-out, have you?'

'Mr Fenner's taken ill.' She looked close to tears. 'I'm to tell you, you've to go and help him right away.'

Pearl was already reaching for her coat and scarf. 'Where is he?'

Rita looked terrified.

'Tell me where he is!'

'He's at your house.'

'What the hell is he doing in my—' And then she knew. 'He took you to my house? How long have you been going there? No, don't answer that, just get out of here and never come back!'

'But Mr Fenner said—'

'Just get out. Get out!'

On the bus to Ardwick, the rage grew inside her. I'll give him a piece of my mind, sick or not sick, the bastard. This can't go on; I'll have it out with him. I've a good mind to tell his wife. She's known about me for years, but she'll be furious to hear he's found himself yet another woman, not even a woman, a girl.

She put the key in the lock and opened the door. 'Harold, where are you?' No answer. She went through to the kitchen. Everything was just as she had left it. He must be upstairs. 'Harold!'

The bedroom curtains were drawn, but she could just see him lying naked on the bed, his back to her. 'For God's sake, Harold.' She switched on the light and walked round the bed. Her heart stopped at the sight of the blood on his face, his chest, and the bedclothes sodden with it. He was dead.

She stood where she was: didn't touch him; didn't cover him; didn't cry. Time passed. She shivered. Then she went out of the house to the telephone box on the corner and rang for an ambulance.

She waited in the kitchen for them to come and directed them upstairs. Not long after, a policeman arrived and she answered all his questions.

'No, I'm not his wife. No, this is not my house. No, I wasn't here when he died. My relationship with this man? I was his mistress.'

The policeman spoke to the ambulance men as they removed the body and he returned to tell her that it looked like a burst ulcer.

When they had gone, she put the bedding in the bath with some bleach and left them to steep. Then she went back to the office, sent everyone home early and locked up the premises. She said nothing about the death of their employer. She'd tell them tomorrow, when she had decided what to say.

Back home, she got a good fire going and ate the herrings she had bought for Harold's tea. Waste not want not, she told herself. Then she settled down to consider what she should do next. She'd make sure the business kept going to keep their staff in work. She thought maybe his son might take it on. She could ask

Dorothy to come back, now that she had sacked Rita. Then there was this house. Harold had said, right from the beginning, that he would leave it to her in his will. Tomorrow, she would check the death notices in the *Manchester Evening News* to find out where the funeral would be held; as his chief clerk, people would expect to see her there.

By the third day she was concerned that there still hadn't been an announcement, so she nipped out of the office to get the lunchtime edition, and there it was. She stood in the street and read it, 'Private family funeral, family flowers only.' That was strange. Harold was a well-known businessman in Manchester: he had hundreds of acquaintances; clients; friends from the supper club. And what about her, denied the chance to pay her respects?

She came back into the building to find half a dozen men wandering in and out of the rooms.

'Who are you? What are you doing here?'

A man in a pinstripe suit answered. 'We're from Smith and Hunt and this business has been declared bankrupt. All assets are being seized, including property and bank accounts.'

'There must be some mistake,' she told him. 'I'm the chief clerk and I'm sure the company is in the black.'

'You are probably not aware of other debts. Now you and all other employees must vacate the premises.'

They stood around outside as if in denial, reluctant

to move away in case there had been some mistake. She tried to suppress the panic rising in her chest. 'I'm sorry,' she told them. 'There's nothing we can do. Go home now and if I hear anything, I'll let you know.' She watched them go – bewildered faces, angry faces. Then she ran all the way to the bus stop, hoping against hope that she could get home before the bailiffs arrived. Too late, the locks had already been changed. Everything she owned was inside the house, leaving her only the clothes she stood up in and the thirty shillings in her purse.

A private funeral indeed! Aye, to spare the disgrace of a man dying in the arms of a young lover at his mistress's house, and a once thriving business run into the ground.

She would have to get a move on if she was to find somewhere to sleep. It was a cruel thought to stand in the cold and contemplate whether there was anyone who would give her a bed for the night, never mind until she found work. She thought of Helen. They had never been close, but at least they were on better terms now. She would go to Newton Heath and hope that her goddaughter would take pity on her.

She almost missed the house in the gathering gloom, walking straight past it, then realising she had gone too far. She knocked at the door. No answer. Knocked again. Maybe Helen was still at work.

'Hello there.' It was the woman from next door. Had

she been watching from her window? 'Are you looking for Mrs Harrison?'

'Ah, yes, she's probably still at work. I'll wait for her.'

'You'll have a long wait. She's gone already, on duty, night shift. Happen she won't be home till after three in the morning. Leastways, that's how it's been these last few weeks.'

Pearl's heart sank. Where could she go in this cold?

'What's your name? I'll tell her you called.'

'No, it doesn't matter.'

She set off walking and got as far as the chippy on the corner. Inside, she queued in the warm to buy a meat pie and ate it outside, sheltering behind a wall. She was deciding what to do next when a bus came towards her. She squinted to see the number then ran towards it. Maybe it was a mistake, but it was the only option she had.

The bell rang as she came into the shop. She had rehearsed what she would say, along the lines of, 'We've never got on, but I'm desperate and I hope—'

The sight before her stopped her in her tracks. The bustling shop she knew had gone and in its place were half-empty shelves and a floor that hadn't been mopped in weeks. There were no customers, just a girl sitting behind the counter smoking a cigarette and reading a comic.

'Where's Elsie?' she asked.

'You what?'

'Elsie, the owner.'

'Upstairs, of course. Who are you anyway?'

Pearl headed straight to the curtain at the back of the shop.

'Hey, where you going?' the girl shouted.

Pearl turned and walked back to her. 'I'm Elsie's cousin. Now, where are the shop keys?' The girl pointed at a set of keys hung on a nail.

She took them and told the girl, 'You'd better leave right now and don't bother coming back.' The girl protested, but Pearl would have none of it. When the door was locked, she went in search of Elsie and found her asleep in bed. She switched on the light and shook her. 'Wake up, Elsie, what's the matter with you?'

There was a moan and Elsie blinked at the light. 'Pearl, is that you?'

'It is.'

'What are you doing here?'

'I've come to see if you're all right.'

'I'm far from right, I'm proper poorly.' She certainly looked thinner and she could do with a bath and her hair washed.

'Elsie, I want you to get dressed and come down to the kitchen. I'll make you something to eat and you can tell me what's the matter.'

Chapter 37

A few days later, Helen arrived for work to find Anna waiting for her outside the club. 'What's to do?' she asked.

'Let's take a walk down the road before we have to start work,' and she linked Helen's arm. Away from the premises she explained, 'Carter telephoned Gerry just now. You know how he said you were to have a new job greeting the punters?' Helen nodded. 'Well, Gerry called me into the office and I had to speak to Carter on the phone. He said he wanted the two of us to go out and buy your new uniform and you're to wear it on Saturday. Black dress, high heels, all the underwear, and I'm to do your hair and make-up. What do you think about that?'

'Why is he making a big thing about me saying hello to men coming into the club?'

'If you ask me it's not about the men, it's about you, Helen. He's got you in his sights.'

'Well, with a bit of luck, I won't be here for much longer.'

'And that's what else I have to tell you.' Anna lowered her voice even though no one was near enough to hear. 'When I left the office, I pulled the handle close to the door, but I didn't close it. I listened to the rest of their conversation. Gerry said, "All right, same as before. I'll get everyone waiting in the warehouse from midnight Saturday and the lorries will get there sometime after that. I'll contact the buyers on Friday to make sure they're clear about collecting the stuff and that it's cash only."'

Helen's eyes widened. 'We've got them, Anna! The gambling, the brothel, the black-market goods.'

The next day, Thursday, Helen was in the Hidden Gem giving all the details to Sergeant Duffy.

'Thank goodness, I wasn't sure the chief constable would wait much longer. It's a big operation, they have the plans ready and now we've got the day and time.'

'It's nearly over, thank God.'

'Yes, it is, Harrison, but this is the most dangerous time. You think you're there and you focus on the ending, but that's when you can get careless. Keep your wits about you.'

The following day Helen and Anna were once again shopping in Kendal Milne. 'I can't believe there's a whole department just for cocktail dresses and accessories,' said Helen. 'This is going to take a while.'

'At least we can narrow it down to black.'

'But everything is so expensive.'

'Don't worry, Gerry gave me plenty of money and coupons.'

'I'm guessing they're stolen.'

'It doesn't matter.' Anna laughed. 'I'm hardly going to be arrested for having a few dodgy coupons on me when all of this is over.'

They went through the dresses first, discussing the designs. 'I think something slim-fitting like this,' said Anna, and she held it up. Helen nodded and Anna passed the dress to the assistant following behind them.

'What about this off-the-shoulder style?' said Helen.

'Very striking, madam,' and the assistant hung it over her arm.

A few others were added and they went to the fitting room. The assistant hovered, but Anna sent her to fetch the highest black court shoes they had.

Each dress seemed to suit Helen in different ways. 'That's why you should still be modelling,' Anna told her.

In the end they decided on a figure-hugging dress with a vent at the back and a neckline that hinted at her breasts, without giving anything away. The high heels were enough to give anyone a nosebleed, but Carter had been clear – she should be tall enough to look down on the short men and into the eyes of the tallest.

The underwear was beautiful: the softest silk against her skin, a brassiere padded to enhance her figure. No one would see it, of course, but wearing it made her feel so feminine.

Back on the ground floor, they bought make-up, perfume and pearl earrings, then swept out of the store laden with bags and boxes.

Once outside, Helen's excitement at spending so much money on beautiful things seemed to vanish.

'What's the matter?' Anna asked.

'I don't know. It was lovely to shop like that, without a care in the world, but it's suddenly hit me... what I'm about to do... and, to be honest, I'm frightened. Really frightened. I'm not even a proper policewoman, Anna, I'm a nobody. And everything that's going to happen depends on me.'

Anna put her arm around her shoulder. 'Hey, you've done everything right. Now it's up to the powers that be. They have to bring this whole thing to an end.'

'I don't know if I can do this any more.' Her voice rose in a panic. 'What if we didn't go back to the club? The raid could still go on.'

'No, Helen, we have to carry on as normal, otherwise Carter will smell a rat.' Anna gripped her arm. 'We went into this together and we'll see it through together.'

Anna was right, of course, but she couldn't help worrying. Then there was Charles Brownlow. She had a niggling feeling that he hadn't believed her when she told him she didn't join the police. What if he were to mention it to Carter? But why would he? He wasn't part of a London black-market gang, all he wanted was to bed her. Besides, if Charles had given the game away, Carter would have called off the whole operation and she'd probably have ended up in the canal. No, she couldn't walk away now, she had to brazen it out.

'You're right, Anna, we have to do it.'

'That's the spirit, we'll get these bastards. Come on now, let's have our lunch at Lyons' Corner House.' She laughed. 'We'll stuff our faces – Carter's paying!'

They came out of the restaurant into Albert Square and were about to go their separate ways – Anna to the club, Helen to meet with Sergeant Duffy – when she caught the sound of a newspaper vendor shouting the news. 'I can't believe it. They've caught him!' She bought a paper and read the headline:

'Suspect Arrested in Shelter Murders'

'Thank God they've got him. They'll be cock-a-hoop at the station.'

Helen couldn't wait to find out more and the first question she asked Sergeant Duffy was, 'How did they catch him?'

'After all the hours CID put in, and with not a single

lead to show for it, it came down to a bobby on the beat,' said Sergeant Duffy. 'He heard a scream coming from the shelter in Spring Gardens. He ran to investigate and found a man grappling with a woman. He had a knife in his tweed overcoat. Not from around here, he was a commercial traveller.'

'Let's hope the women will feel safer now that we've caught him,' said Helen.

'I hope so too, it's a good omen Right then, let's get on with the Calico Club,' she said. 'So, there's no change to what we know, is there? The goods will arrive at the warehouse in the early hours of Sunday morning. This'll be a big operation if we're to catch everyone in the net. You've done really well with this, Harrison.'

'It was Anna, really. She took all the risks giving me the lead and now we've got the date thanks to her eavesdropping on the telephone call. She could so easily have been caught.'

'I know, and we'll be careful to keep you, Anna and the other girls safe. Make sure you're all inside the club. You said you'd be in the entrance hall?'

'Yes, I'll be dressed in black.'

'That's good, I'll tell them to get you out immediately.'

It was time to part company, but both of them seemed reluctant to break the link between them. Eventually Helen said, 'I'll have to go now to get ready for my shift.'

Sergeant Duffy stood up. 'Helen, please don't take

any risks, keep your cover and act like any other young woman would under the circumstances. Good luck to you.'

When Helen arrived at the club it seemed busier than usual. Anna was waiting for her. 'Carter's here,' she whispered. 'It's starting already. He's in his office, getting everything sorted, I think. It's my guess the men have come to do a deal in advance for the goods and, by the bulkiness of their jackets, they're paying up front.'

'So, am I supposed to start now in the entrance hall? Should I go and change into the black dress?'

'No, he took everything from me, said he'd speak to you later about it and your duties.' She raised an eyebrow. 'Word is, it's going to be a hell of a night tomorrow.'

It was well after midnight when Gerry told Helen that the boss wanted to see her in his office. Her heart was thumping. What if he'd got wind of the raid? All the careful planning by CID would have been wasted; she'd be ridiculed. And worse, she still had an awful feeling that Carter could have found out that she worked for the police. Don't be stupid – if that was the case, she'd definitely be in the canal!

She knocked on the door and seconds later it opened and there he was. His dark suit, pristine white shirt, old school tie, all spoke of impeccable breeding. Could she have made a terrible mistake? And when he spoke…

'Ah, the lovely Helen, come in. You've been shopping, I hear.' The bags were by his desk. 'I'd like to see what my new hostess will look like tomorrow.' He handed her the bags.

Inwardly, she sighed with relief. He didn't know who she really was. She took the bags and managed a smile. 'I won't be long.'

'No, Helen, you put them on here.'

Was he serious? She wasn't going to do that. 'I'd rather—'

'Do it now, Helen.'

She had pretended to be a working girl, like all the others in the club. They did this and worse to make a living. He waited, expecting her to do as she was told. She met his eye and didn't move, seconds ticked by…

'No, I'm not going to do that.'

A smile hovered on his lips. 'Ah, Helen, you're a challenge, but I don't mind. The anticipation is sweet and I'll soon have you to myself.'

Chapter 38

Helen had a long lie-in on the Saturday morning. She had come home from the club at three and couldn't sleep, going over and over the plans for the raid and her part in it. Around six in the morning she fell into an unsettled sleep, flooded with half-remembered dreams. She was in the warehouse, but this time it was stacked with boxes piled high with spirits and cigarettes. Lost amid the maze and desperate to get away, she heard someone call her name. It couldn't be, could it? There was Jim, in his uniform, holding out his arms for her. Thank God, he wasn't dead! She tilted her head for him to kiss her and found herself looking into the face of Henry Carter. She recoiled in horror as she realised she was naked in his arms.

The knocking on the door took a while to rouse her. She sat up in bed and the full force of what she had to achieve in the course of this day hit her. More knocking.

There must be something wrong. Had the raid been called off? Was there a change of plan? She was out of bed and running to the door, expecting to see Sergeant Duffy standing there with some urgent news.

It was Ada with a bacon butty. 'I know you were in awful late last night. Thought I'd bring you this. I'll put the kettle on,' and without another word she marched through to the kitchen. Helen sank into the fireside chair and tried to focus. Ada thrust the butty into her hand. 'Best smoked-back, don't ask where it came from, you'd have to arrest me,' and then she was laughing. 'Now you're eating the evidence.'

She chatted on while she made the tea, and Helen concentrated on the delicious bacon, only half listening. But something caught her ear. 'What did you say, Ada?'

'The fella who came asking about you. I couldn't place him at first.'

'Stop, Ada, and go back to the beginning. A man came to your door to ask about me?'

'That's what I'm trying to tell you. He said he were an old friend of yours and he'd called round hoping to find you at home. He let it slip that he was going to offer you a job. Said he needed to see you right away and could I tell him where you worked.'

Helen's heart almost stopped. 'Oh, Ada, did you tell him I worked for the police?'

'Did I 'eck as like. I weren't born yesterday. I told him that you've already got a good job, but I couldn't remember what it was. I wouldn't trust him as far as I could throw him. Mark my words, he were after you 'cause you're a widow.'

'So, he doesn't know I'm working for the police?'

Ada shook her head. 'I give nothing away, me.'

'What did he look like, this man?'

'That's what I were tellin' you. I couldn't place him, but when I woke up this morning it came to me. He were the fella who brought you flowers that time. You know, the ones you put in the bin.' She was suddenly sheepish. 'I'm sorry, I seen you put them there and that night I nipped out and pinched them out of your dustbin.'

'Don't be sorry, Ada, I'm glad you got some pleasure out of them and, you're right, he was after me.' So, it was Charles checking up on her and Ada had the sense not to tell him she was in the police. 'Thank you, Ada, you're a life saver,' and she gave her a hug.

Helen arrived early for work and as she came into the entrance hall she noticed the chandelier was already lit, even though the club would not be open for another hour, and there in the centre of the hall was a pale wooden lectern and on it a leather signing-in book. She felt almost flattered because, like her new clothes, this was for her role as a hostess, greeting the members and guests. Gerry had ordered it, on Carter's instructions, and he had spent time explaining her duties; greeting customers and signing them in, issuing keys to the girls for guests wishing to use the bedrooms.

She went through into the bar and was surprised to find there were already half a dozen men there, though not the usual clientele. Anna was in the ladies' toilets waiting for her; none of the other girls had arrived.

'What's with the spivs in the bar?' asked Helen.

'They're here to unload the lorries. Gerry will send them to wait in the warehouse when the real customers start arriving.'

'What time do you think it'll all happen?'

'Don't know exactly, but well after midnight, I think. Either way it's going to be a long night. You might as well get dressed now and put on your make-up, then I'll do your hair – Carter's orders, swept up and sleek. I've got some sugar and water to tame the curls.'

Just before opening time Gerry gathered all the staff together in the bar and spoke to them. 'There'll be some special guests at the club tonight and Mr Carter wants you to make sure they have a good time. I'll let you know who they are.'

Anna leaned over and whispered in Helen's ear. 'They'll be his contacts waiting for the goods to arrive.'

'But where's Carter? He's always here before opening time.'

'I don't know.'

'Oh, Anna, what if he doesn't come?'

'He'll be here. Don't worry.'

Soon the club was filling up and Helen was so busy in the entrance hall dealing with customers, that she became absorbed in the new role Carter had given her. Then every so often she would be jolted out of the smiling hostess character by a stab of fear that made her stomach lurch. Within a few hours, the premises would be overrun by police officers and she would be at the heart of it. They would seize the black-market goods and lock everyone inside. It would be a long night sorting out the genuine customers from those responsible for the illegal gaming and the brothel upstairs, not to mention the London mob. But where was Carter? Had he gone to ground? If so, he'd get away scot-free and the thought of that made her blood boil!

There was nothing she could do but carry on. Then around ten o'clock he came through the door, straight to her desk and she gave him her best smile. 'Hello, sir, you're a bit late tonight.'

'I had dinner at the Midland first.' He stepped back and looked her up and down. 'You look wonderful, Helen. I'm sure you've been turning heads all evening.'

For a split second she was flattered by his compliment, but she pushed the feeling away. He was a crook and she was determined to see him arrested.

He went on. 'How would you like to have a drink with me later? Just the two of us, you know? I'd like to get to know you better.' He gave her a wink.

She pretended to be excited. 'Yes, I'd love that.' Little

did he know there would be no cosy drink, just a cold cell for him in Bootle Street nick.

He left the desk just as a group of young men arrived in the entrance hall to sign in. They were in good spirits, looking forward to playing poker in the gaming room. Just one more left to sign in and, with a welcome smile, she looked into his face.

'Hello, Helen.'

She gasped, but couldn't speak, for there in front of her was Laurence Fitzpatrick.

He looked bewildered. 'What are you doing here?'

She swallowed hard. What could she tell him? That she was masquerading as a hostess in an illegal brothel and gaming club to trap a black-market gang? 'I can't talk to you now, Laurence. I'll explain another time.'

He was shocked and angry. 'I'm not going anywhere till you tell me what's going on.'

She looked quickly around. Carter had disappeared into the bar but the doorman outside the gaming room was looking directly at her.

If Laurence caused a scene and broke her cover, the whole operation would be a disaster. How could she explain? At that moment one of the girls appeared at her side to return a bedroom key. Helen took it... now, if she could persuade Laurence... She winked at the doorman, then whispered in Laurence's ear, 'This is police work.

Don't make a fuss, just come with me and I'll tell you what's going on. Now, smile like you're happy to see me.'

She took his arm and led him upstairs, unlocked the door. His eyes widened – there was no mistaking the room's function. She had only a few minutes to convince him.

'You have to believe me, Laurence. I'm part of a police investigation into the black market, illegal gambling, prostitution and tonight there'll be a raid on the club. You mustn't give me away, please.'

He sat on the bed and put his head in his hands. She waited. He looked up and shook his head. 'Why didn't you just tell me what you were doing? I've been worried sick about you. After that first letter saying you'd gone on a course, I thought it would be a few days, a week, before I heard from you again, but there was nothing. I even went round to your house a few times after work but you were never there.'

'I know, I know, but I couldn't tell anyone, not even you. You must see that?'

He sighed. 'I can't believe this. You're in danger, aren't you.'

'Look, everything has been carefully planned. I'll be fine.'

'When will I see you again?'

'After the raid – tomorrow, I'll come to your flat.'

'And what do you want me to do now?'

'You should leave the premises.'

'But I could stay, just in case—'

'No, Laurence, just leave, otherwise you'll get caught in all the mayhem of a raid.'

He stood up. 'I don't like this at all, Helen,' and he took her arm. 'Come with me now. I'll take you home.'

She stepped back. 'No. I'm not going anywhere! I'll see this through, so help me God.'

Laurence stared at her, shook his head and left the room.

She waited a few minutes then followed him down. There was only the doorman outside the gaming room and she had no idea whether Laurence had taken her advice. She resumed her place at the lectern. The clock ticked towards midnight and Helen was on a knife edge. The lorries would be on their way by now and all she could do was wait, but there was comfort in knowing that, just like her, police officers were ready and waiting in their positions. Shortly after midnight, she was surprised to see Carter crossing the entrance hall carrying her coat. 'Come on then, let's go!' he shouted.

'Go where?' she asked.

'For that cosy drink I promised you. There's champagne on ice just waiting for us right now,' and he held out her coat.

Helen was thrown into confusion. 'I thought you meant in the bar after I finish work.'

'You don't think I'm socialising with the kind of people in there, do you?' he sneered. 'I'm taking you somewhere classy, the Midland Hotel. You look so wonderful I want to show you off.'

'But what about—' She stopped herself just in time.

'What?'

'Your special guests.'

'I don't care about them. I'd rather be with you. Come on now, chop-chop, my car's outside.'

She could have rejected him there and then, but it was clear that he had never intended to be in the club when the black-market goods arrived at the warehouse. He'd leave it all to Gerry and the men unloading the lorries. And once he got wind of the raid, as he surely would, he would disappear into the night. She had no choice; it was down to her to make sure that didn't happen. She had to go with him, but that was all right, because once in the hotel all she had to do was to excuse herself to powder her nose then go straight to the hotel reception and ask them to call the police. She gave him a sultry smile, he helped her on with her coat, and she took his arm. Very soon the club would be raided by dozens of police officers and arrests would be made, while she would be drinking champagne with the man who had planned it all. She just had to hold her nerve.

There was a half moon, low in the sky, when they left the club together. They crossed the road, he helped her into his sports car and closed the door. She took a few deep breaths to calm herself before he slipped in beside her. The engine roared into life and raced away from the Calico Club up Quay Street, across Deansgate, through Albert Square and up Peter Street. She had pounded the beat on all these streets. But never would she have imagined being in a sports car on her way to the Midland in the company of a London black-marketeer, with the intent to arrest him.

Chapter 39

Carter parked in front of the Midland, the best hotel in Manchester, and they walked together under the portico, past the commissionaires, and through the revolving doors. Helen had been there a few times before with Sergeant Duffy, but she stopped and looked around her as though she hadn't seen such luxury.

'I'll just get my key,' he said.

'You're staying here?'

'Yes, I always do; they look after me very well. I hope you don't mind but I've arranged to have drinks in my room.'

Her heart stopped. She'd be alone with him, with no chance to contact the station. Worse than that, it was clear he intended to seduce her. How could she have been so stupid?

'But you said we were going to a bar.'

'Oh, come on, Helen, don't be so coy. You and I both

know how this evening ends.' He put his arm around her waist.

Her stomach lurched. She had only seconds to decide. Then she remembered the police phone box outside central library across the road.

She pushed him away. 'Get off me! I'm not going to your room.'

He grabbed her by the arm. 'Sssh, don't make a scene.' He looked quickly around. 'People are staring at us. Come on, we'll go into the hotel bar; it's just over there. You can calm down.'

She deliberately raised her voice. 'I don't want to calm down! I'm leaving,' and she tried to pull her arm away.

At that moment there was a shout. 'What the hell's going on here?'

And there was Laurence, striding across the foyer towards them. He grabbed Carter by the scruff of his dinner jacket and pulled him away from her. Carter turned and threw a punch at him, but Laurence pushed him so hard he fell backwards.

'Who is he, Helen?' Laurence shouted.

'He's the owner of the Calico Club.'

But now, Carter was on his feet again, shouting at Laurence. 'Who the hell are you to interfere; this woman is with me!'

Two commissionaires, having heard all the shouting, rushed towards the men and tried to keep them apart.

'It's all right, Mr Carter, I'll sort this out,' said one of them, while the other was threatening Laurence with calling the police.

'Yes, yes,' yelled Helen. 'Quick, call the police!'

By now another man had joined them. He wore a badge on his lapel that identified him as the night manager and when he spoke it was with authority. 'I will not have a brawl and a screaming match in my hotel and, rather than call in the police, I suggest you follow me to my office to sort this out.'

'Helen, let's just leave,' said Laurence.

But she shook her head. 'I have to see this through.'

The night manager spoke quietly to the commission-aires as though giving instructions. Then he led the way to his office and once inside he asked Carter for his account of what had happened.

'It's quite simple. I asked this young woman, who is one of my employees, to have a drink with me and, before I know it, she's demanding money from me. Then this man arrives and assaults me.'

The night manager gave Helen a long, hard stare. She met his gaze. Then he turned his attention to Laurence. 'What have you to say about this?'

'I know Helen well. I followed her here to make sure she was safe in the company of this man. I saw him grab her arm; she was shouting for him to let her go. I tried to pull him away, but then he threw a punch at me, so I pushed him to the floor.'

'If you ask me, they're in cahoots,' said Carter. 'I've

heard of these women in hotels trying to get money out of businessmen by threatening to besmirch their good name.'

The night manager inclined his head in reply, then he turned to Helen. 'And now you, miss. May I ask your name?'

'Helen Harrison, sir.'

'Hmm, and what have you to say about all this?'

She took a deep breath. 'Henry Carter is the brains behind a London black-market syndicate based in the Calico Club—'

She was interrupted by a roar of laughter from Carter. 'Oh, for God's sake! What nonsense.'

Helen carried on, 'Tonight, thousands of pounds' worth of stolen black-market goods will be delivered to his club.'

Carter turned to the manager. 'This is ridiculous. I'm a respectable businessman and I'll have you know that I've spent a small fortune in this hotel.'

'I know that, Mr Carter, and we value your custom,' said the night manager, 'but I need to write a report for my superiors. I'm sure you understand that. Please go on, Miss Harrison.'

'What Mr Carter doesn't know, is that there will be a police raid on his premises tonight.'

Helen saw the fleeting look of shock on Carter's face.

'For God's sake, man,' he shouted, 'do I look like a spiv?'

'You certainly don't, sir, and I must admit it does seem far-fetched for a young woman to have knowledge of such things. What have you to say to that, miss?'

Helen looked Henry Carter in the eye. 'I'm a woman police auxiliary and I've been working as a hostess in your club for a few weeks. I know about the gambling, the brothel and stolen goods, sold on the black market.'

Now Carter was shouting. 'Can't you see she's lying! Who ever saw a policewoman looking like that? I'm not staying here a moment longer. I'm packing my bags and leaving this cesspit of a city right now.' He made for the door, but Laurence barred his way. Carter turned to the night manager. 'I'm telling you, she's lying. You can't possibly believe this slut of a girl over me.'

'I'm afraid I can, sir. You see, I recognised her right away in the foyer, even though she wasn't in uniform. She's been in the hotel a few times on police business.'

Helen watched Carter's eyes widen in fear, then suddenly he made a bolt for the door. Laurence, taken off guard, was pushed aside and Carter was out of the room, running across the foyer. Just then the revolving door stopped and two police constables came into the foyer, just in time to nab him. And there behind them was a smiling Sergeant Duffy.

She awoke to the sound of whistling and it was a moment before she remembered that Laurence had stayed with her and, by the mouth-watering smell of bacon cooking, he had found her Sunday morning breakfast treat. She lay there a moment thinking about the events of the previous evening. Everything moved so fast after Carter was apprehended. She and Laurence went back to the station where DC Ken Kershaw was coordinating the raid. There was just enough time for them to explain what had happened at the Midland, before word arrived that the raid had started. She stayed long enough to find out that Anna and the girls were safe and allowed to go free, while the black-marketeers had been identified and arrested. It had been a good night's work and, best of all, were Sergeant Duffy's words as she left, 'I'm so proud of you, girl, you're a damned good copper.'

She put on the silk dressing gown that Anna had bought her, and checked her face in the mirror. She looked a bit tired and pale, but inside she felt elated and so grateful that she had come through such a nerve-wracking experience.

Laurence was standing at the stove, still whistling, and she went to him and put her arms around his waist and pressed her cheek against his back. 'Thank you,' she said.

'What for?'

'For believing in me and having the nous to wait outside the club to watch what happened, when I had told you to go home. Thank God you followed us.' She laughed. 'I couldn't believe it when I saw you coming across the foyer like a knight in shining armour.'

He turned and kissed her. 'Oh, Helen, you were hardly a damsel in distress. Now, go on, sit down, breakfast's nearly ready.'

They shared the two slices of bacon and the one egg with plenty of fried bread. 'How are you this morning, did you sleep?' he asked.

'Like a log. How was the sofa?'

'A foot too short for my liking.'

They cleared the table and washed the dishes and Helen asked, 'What would you like to do today?'

'I don't mind, you choose. I'll be happy just to be with you,' and his lovely smile melted her heart.

'We could go out for a walk if you like, it's a lovely day.'

Brookdale Park was all a good park should be. In early September the rose beds were still in full bloom, the grass was neatly clipped and trees dappled the pathways. There were men, some in their whites, playing bowls and beyond them there was a bandstand surrounded by deckchairs where a brass band was tuning up. They sat together, holding hands and swinging them in time to the music: a lively mixture of patriotic and modern songs with a few well-known hymns included. Every now and again she would look towards him, studying his handsome profile and broad shoulders. Once, he turned towards her and caught her staring. He laughed then and said, 'What is it?' But she just smiled to have him close to her on such a lovely day.

Later they walked, hand in hand, on a secluded path under chestnut trees and down into a little ravine. She saw him look around, then he leaned against a tree and pulled her towards him. His kisses were slow and gentle, then he kissed her neck and the closeness of him sent her heart racing. She didn't know how long they stayed there, but it wasn't nearly enough.

'Helen, my darling, shall we go back to your house now?'

It wasn't far to walk, but Helen knew she was about to take a huge step in her relationship with Laurence. His kisses and his touch made her hungry for more and she sensed he felt the same.

The door closed behind them and Laurence held her close. 'Darling Helen, I love you so much' he said.

'And I love you, Laurence.' Then he kissed her with such passion that she longed for more.

'Shall we go to your bedroom?' he whispered.

Yes, yes,' her voice breathless.

He swept her into his arms and carried her up the stairs, but as he was about to lay her on the bed, she stiffened as if in panic.

'No, stop, please! I can't do this.' She struggled in his arms.

He set her on her feet and she backed away from the bed. 'It's all right, Helen,' but now she was weeping.

'What's the matter?' he asked. She could only shake her head. 'What is it, tell me?'

'I… I can't, I can't. I'm so sorry.' She ran out of the room and down the stairs.

He found her in the parlour, sobbing. 'Ssh, everything's all right,' and he took her in his arms again. 'It's my fault. It was too soon, we'll take our time. We've found each other, that's what matters. Don't cry, my love.'

'It was the bed, I couldn't…' she whispered. 'It's such a sad memory, I can't explain.'

Helen arrived early for her shift on Monday morning. It was good to be back in uniform and she was glad to find a stack of filing waiting for her. She half expected to be called to Sergeant Duffy's office to be questioned further, but no one sent for her. Then towards the end of the day, she was told by her superior to report to the chief constable's office. She'd only ever seen him once, getting into a police car. What could he want with her? Was she in trouble for not following orders to stay in the club? Would she be chastised for putting herself in danger? Maybe she wouldn't be allowed to walk the beat any more. She knocked, the door opened and there was Sergeant Duffy. 'Come in, Harrison.'

She marched into his office and stood to attention, eyes forward. 'Well now, WAPC Harrison, you've had quite an eventful few weeks, haven't you?' said the chief constable.

'Yes, sir.'

'Sergeant Duffy has brought me up to date with Saturday night's events – quite a story, I must say. I've brought you here to thank you formally for your commitment to this force. I can honestly say I have never come across a female officer who has proved herself so convincingly in such a short space of time. I commend you too for your bravery and your judgement. If you hadn't taken the initiative to go with Carter, we would never have apprehended him.'

'Thank you, sir.'

'He's been up before the magistrate this morning and he's been remanded to Strangeways. It'll be all over the papers tomorrow, and bear in mind that the *Manchester Guardian* covers the whole country. Thanks to you we've put Manchester policing on the map.' He stood for a moment, smiling. 'Now, I've been talking to Sergeant Duffy here, and I'm of a mind to offer you the rank of Woman Police Constable. What would you say to that?'

She was speechless. She had occasionally wondered what it would be like to be a WPC and she wasn't quite sure she wanted it. A glance at Sergeant Duffy, but there was no reading her face. 'I don't know, sir,' she said. 'Could I have some time to think about it?'

'Hmm, well I suppose so. Let Sergeant Duffy know tomorrow.' He shook her hand. 'Well done, Harrison, you're a credit to the Manchester police.'

She was walking back to the office when Sergeant Duffy caught up with her. 'He's right, you know, you are a credit to us. That's why I recommended you. When I think back to all you've done, I'm so proud of you.'

'Thank you, Sarge, but deciding whether or not to become a WPC is complicated for me.'

'Let's go to my office and talk about it.'

With her hands round a good brew, Helen explained. 'I like being a WAPC, not so much the office work, but being out on the beat and maybe I'd get more of that as a WPC, but I want other things too.'

'Sure, I can understand that, you're a young woman and there'll come a time when you might marry again and have a family.'

'I'd like to have children, but if I was to take promotion I'd worry that I'd be…' she hesitated, trying to find the right words, 'consumed by it and not want to stop.'

Sergeant Duffy nodded. 'You know I understand that, don't you?'

'Yes.'

'Can I ask whether Dr Fitzpatrick figures in these thoughts?'

THE GIRL FROM THE CORNER SHOP

Helen gave her a wry smile. 'I think he might do.'

'Helen, I really want you as one of my WPCs, you know that, don't you? But I'll understand if you decide for now that you want to stay as you are. Why don't you sleep on it, eh?'

'I will. Thanks, Sarge.'

When she arrived home that evening, there was a letter waiting for her and she recognised Pearl's handwriting at once. She would have been in touch with her before now, if it hadn't been for the Calico Club job. She ripped open the envelope and scanned the contents. She could hardly believe it; Pearl was living with Mam at the shop. How on earth did that happen? It was still light and it wasn't raining, so she set off, hoping nothing untoward had happened to either of them.

The shop bell rang as she came inside. The first thing she noticed was the smell of fresh paint, closely followed by a whole new layout in the shop. Pearl came through the chenille curtain and at the sight of Helen she let out a scream and ran to hug her. 'You're here, that's great!' and she went to the door and turned the sign to 'Closed'.

'What's going on?' asked Helen.

'Come into the back room and I'll tell you all about it.'

Pearl recounted her story: the circumstances of Fenner's death; the bankruptcy and closure of the business; the loss of her home. She wept a little, then wiped her eyes.

Helen was shocked. 'I can't believe Mr Fenner died. Oh, Pearl, I'm so sorry.'

'Don't be. The man's dead and I lived with him for so long, but the way it ended was cruel. I was out on my ear: no home, no job, and I lost friends I'd worked with for years. I went to your house when I had nowhere to go, but your neighbour told me you were working nights. So, what could I do? It was either Elsie or sleeping on the street. When I got here, I couldn't believe the state of the house and shop and since then I've been doing a bit every day trying to make it shipshape. Anyroad, I told her I would stay – she certainly needs me and to be honest I need her.'

'I take it she's upstairs.'

'Yes, she has a lie down before her tea.'

'But what's wrong with her?'

'The doctor said it was her nerves and he gave her a tonic. But if you ask me, she just hadn't the will to go on. She couldn't rouse herself to do anything.'

Helen was quiet for a moment. 'Do you think it's my fault, leaving her?'

Pearl shook her head. 'You had to go, you were buried alive in this shop. Elsie would have carried on telling you what to do for the rest of your life, but now, you are your own woman.'

'So, what's going to happen?'

'She wants me to stay, can you believe it? I told her we'd get this shop back on its feet and I'll do it, Helen, you know I will.'

There was the sound of movement above them followed by a shout. 'Who are you talking to?'

Helen felt a nervous flutter in her stomach at the sound of her mother's voice, but she swallowed hard and called up the stairs, 'It's me, Mam.'

Elsie was slow coming down and at first sight, Helen could see her mother had lost weight and her face was gaunt and pasty.

'What are you doing here?'

'I've come to see you. How are you?'

It was a moment before she answered. 'I told you before I wasn't well.'

'I know, but I'm here now, and it's good that Pearl's staying with you. She was telling me you're going to do up the shop together.'

'Ha! I'll believe it when I see it. This flighty piece,' and she waved a hand in the direction of Pearl, 'will be off chasing another man before we know it.'

Pearl gave as good as she got. 'I might just do that if you don't buck up your ideas, you miserable bugger. You'll stay for your tea, Helen? It's only tinned sprats, peas and potatoes, I'm afraid.'

Around the table, Pearl talked about her plans for the shop and the conversation moved on to Helen in the police.

'I hope you don't have to deal with criminals, like those black marketeers.'

'No, Mam, I'm just a clerk,' she smiled.

Helen left in time to walk home before the blackout and, on the way, she thought about her mother. She didn't welcome her with open arms, but when she was leaving she called out, 'Will you come again?'

And she answered, 'Of course I will, Mam, I'll see you soon.'

By the time she arrived home she had made another decision. She didn't want to be a fully fledged policewoman and she didn't think she would volunteer for any other undercover operation. In time, she might even be happy with clerking duties. And then there was Laurence…

She made herself something to eat then sat by the fire knitting the cardigan she had started several months before. There was a knock on the door. She opened it and there was Gwen and Frank, hand in hand. She was delighted to see them together. 'Come in, come in, it's lovely to see you,' and they went through to the kitchen.

'We have news,' said Gwen, wreathed in smiles.

'I thought you might have.'

She held up her hand and there was a lovely engagement ring with three little stones.

'I'm so pleased for you,' said Helen, and the way Frank looked at Gwen warmed her heart. 'I'm so happy for you both. When's the big day?'

'Next Saturday, four o'clock at the register office off Deansgate and you're invited, if you can make it.'

'I'll be there, don't you worry. Would it be all right if I brought someone with me?'

'Oh, who is it?'

Helen blushed. 'Someone I met through work.'

'A policeman?'

'No, he's a doctor.'

'Ooh,' said Gwen, 'I can't wait to meet him.'

Helen glanced at Frank. He was smiling at Gwen.

Helen cried at the wedding. Gwen looked radiant and Frank was so handsome in his uniform. It brought it all back to her – the bittersweet memory of her own wedding day. Afterwards, the dozen guests walked from the register office over to Quay Street to the Old Grapes for a drink. Laurence went to the bar while she went to hang up her coat.

'Hello, Helen, let me help you with that.' It was Frank. 'I wanted to thank you for everything you've done for me and Gwen. When Jim died, I thought I was taking care of you, but most of the time it was you looking after me. I still can't believe the way I treated Gwen but I promise you I'm going to make it up to her, especially when the baby comes.'

'I know you will, you'll be a wonderful dad.'

Then Laurence was at her side and Frank shook his

hand. 'I'm sorry we got off on the wrong foot, that night when you brought Helen home. I was out of order. Anyroad, no hard feelings, I hope.'

'Not at all, everything worked out all right for all of us.'

'I know you'll look after her.'

'I will,' said Laurence and he put his arm around her shoulder.

It was late when they left the pub, and as they walked to the car Helen said, 'Laurence, instead of you doing a round trip to take me home, why don't I just go home with you?'

'Are you sure?'

'Yes.'

'All right, I don't mind sleeping on the sofa.'

In his cosy flat, Laurence put on a gramophone record then poured them a nightcap. 'Single malt from the Highlands. Sip it slowly,' he said. He was leaning back on the sofa, his eyes closed, and she watched his handsome face. He had never mentioned the episode with the bed again, but he was so loving with his gentle kisses and chaste caresses. In the meantime, she had grown more and more in love with him. She leant over and kissed his cheek. He smiled and opened his eyes, then took her in his arms.

'Do you want to go to bed now?' he asked.

'Yes, Laurence.'

'All right, I'll just get a pillow and a blanket from the bedroom. Won't be a minute.'

She watched him go, then followed him. He turned around, the blanket in his arms. She took it from him, laid it aside and hugged him.

He gave her a quizzical look. 'What is it?'

She kissed him, he kissed her back. Her heart raced: here at last was the passion she had longed for.

'Helen, my darling, do you want to...?'

'Yes, I do,' and her breath quickened. 'Please...' They lay on the bed and Laurence kissed her again.

'I love you, Laurence,' she whispered.

'And I love you, my darling.' His hands, his lips, his body on hers...

In the early morning, they lay in each other's arms and talked about their future. 'You know I want to marry you,' he said.

'Yes, Laurence, but I remember you saying that, because of your job, you didn't want to get married until the war was over, and I'm happy to wait.'

'But that was long before I fell in love with you.'

'I would be happy just to live with you, she said.' But there was disappointment in his face.

'Would you really want that?' he asked.

She looked away. How could she explain it without hurting him? He turned her face towards him and wiped the tears from her cheeks.

'Helen, in the cold light of day, are you still sure you love me?'

'Yes, with all my heart.'

'Then tell me why you're crying.'

She paused to gather her thoughts, so much would depend on what she had to say. 'Jim died just before Christmas,' she began, 'and on New Year's Day I moved into my house alone. It was so hard at first, without him, but over the months I came to terms with his death. I never imagined I would fall in love again.' She stroked his cheek. 'And now I have you and I love you more than words can say, but...'

'But what?'

'It might seem strange, because I do want to be your wife, but I think it's fitting not to marry until the anniversary of Jim's death has passed. Would that be all right?'

Laurence smiled and wiped away the fresh tears. 'Oh, Helen, I understand you would want to do that. I should have realised.' He kissed her tenderly. 'Shall we get married on New Year's Day at the register office? In the meantime, if you want to come here at the weekend, we could be together. What do you think?'

'I think that would be wonderful.'

Chapter 40

Helen sat at her dressing table and fastened the pearl-drop necklace around her neck. She was glad of some quiet time with her thoughts and memories. The morning had been busy with Mam and Pearl arriving early to help her get ready. She had been pleased to see Mam looking so well and there was hardly any bickering between the two of them.

Mam had made breakfast for them and, after that, Pearl took charge with the same meticulous preparation as when she organised shows at Fenner's Fashions. First, she styled Helen's hair, smoothing out her blonde curls to frame her face, then applied her make-up so skilfully that she could have been a model on the cover of *Vogue*. Finally, she had helped her into her wedding outfit, a powder-blue costume with a pencil skirt and a jacket with a peplum. Helen knew it suited her so well because the assistant, her good friend Anna now working in Kendal Milne, helped her choose it.

She leaned towards the mirror. It was her face in front of her, but something in the way she held her head and the look in her eyes told her that she had come a long way from the corner shop. Mam had kept her close all the time she was growing up and, just when she thought she would escape with Jim to raise a family of her own, fate had other plans for her. Grief and despair had walked beside her this past year, but determination had been there too. She was naive, but she learned from every lesson, and once she joined the police, she found a way to make life worth living.

She went to the window and looked down over the park, recalling the day when she and Jim stood on this very spot and decided it would be their new home. Now, she was leaving it for good and tears pricked her eyes. Jim would have loved it here.

She was glad that Gwen and Frank were to take over the tenancy. He would make it a lovely house for his family. She would leave them the furniture – her eyes flitted to the bed – all of it. Laurence's cosy flat was all she wanted.

She sat on the bed a while with her memories of Jim. That last evening together they thought they had their whole lives in front of them: a house of their own and the promise of children. It wasn't to be, but she was so glad for the happy memories and grateful that he had left her that letter in his locker. She had read it so many times over the past year and taken comfort from it, but only today did she fully understand the depth of his love.

...make a life for yourself without me... in the quiet moments, you'll feel that love again... She closed her eyes and brought his smiling face to mind. 'Oh, Jim, you know I'll always love you,' she whispered.

Moments later, Pearl was calling to her. 'Helen, Laurence is here with the car. Time to leave for the register office.'

She came downstairs, to where her mother was waiting to give her the posy of violets. 'You look lovely, Helen,' she said. 'I'm proud of you.'

She went through to the parlour and there was Laurence, handsome and smiling, waiting for her.

'You take my breath away,' he said and he took her hand.

At the open door, she paused and breathed the air. She couldn't be sure, but she thought there might have been a trace of smoky fires in the wind.

Acknowledgements

I would like to thank the staff of the Greater Manchester Police Museum and Archives and the Greater Manchester Fire Service Museum. Their extensive knowledge of policing and fire fighting in WWII was invaluable, so too was their enthusiasm in bringing to life anecdotes and characters.

Thanks also to Jeff Easton, Helen Finbow, Beryl Jason for their contributions and, once again, I must mention Graham Phythian for his comprehensive book *Blitz Britain: Manchester and Salford*.

My heartfelt thanks to my agent, Judith Murdoch, also my editor Rosie de Courcy, Lauren Atherton and all the team at Head of Zeus. Above all, thanks to my family for their love and support.

About the author

Alrene Hughes grew up in Belfast and has lived in Manchester for most of her adult life. She worked for British Telecom and the BBC before training as an English teacher. After teaching for twenty years, she retired and now writes full-time.